Tender Offer

TANVIER PEART

frenchy
PRESS

The Frenchy Press

5325 Sheridan Drive, Suite 1196

Buffalo, New York 14221-9998

thefrenchypress.com

ISBNs: 979-8-9875061-4-1 (trade pbk.)

Library of Congress Control Number: 2025912130

First Edition: July 2025

Printed in the United States of America

1st Printing

Also by Tanvier Peart

Chance at Love Series

The Seven Month Itch (available as an audiobook)
Miles Apart
Tender Offer

Standalone

Ella Gets the D
Untitled Mafia Rom-Com (coming 2026)

Buffalo Steel Rugby Series

One Knight's Stand
Buffalo Rugby Romance Book 2 (coming 2026)

Author Note

Tender Offer is a romance novel with lots of hunching and steamy moments. If you don't want to read about tongue strokes in front of a pianist, bits pressed against the window, doing it in the office with an audience, and cake in cracks, this might not be your ministry.

There are vivid descriptions of sex and also strong language. This is the third book in the Chance at Love Series. You can read it as a standalone, though small parts overlap with *The Seven Month Itch* and *Miles Apart*. If you read those, you know Madison is nobody's favorite because she likes a married man. (It didn't go past a crush, but she's still hot in the .) We've only seen her at the surface, so I hope this story paints her in a different light. Preston lives in London and will use some words and phrases attributed to British English. There's mention of the Black mortality rate in the US, death during childbirth (off-page), and pregnancy. There are also *Dawson's Creek*, *The Menu*, and *The Dark Knight* spoilers. (Don't ask why. I don't know.)

As always, have fun and take care of yourself.

Spicy Chapter Disclaimer

Disclaimer: If you're my father, aunt, or another loved one who reads every book I write, I gave fair warning about this one. There's some freak behavior in here. If you don't want to read the spicy scenes, it would behoove you to stay away from the following chapters:

- Chapter 15 (Ravenous, a "play" experience)

- Chapter 16 (still in Ravenous)

- Chapter 34 (surprise workplace shenanigans)

- Chapter 35 (more workplace shenanigans but with an audience)

- Chapter 38 (oral transactions with...just skip this one)

- Chapter 39 (cake and booty)

- Chapter 45 ("I'm sorry" sex)

- Chapter 46 (more office hunching and "painting" with... don't read this one, either)

Ti amerò fino al giorno dopo per sempre.

I will love you until the day after forever.

THE PLAYLIST—PART I

#1 – "French Bossa Nova"—Ladji Mouflet (ft. Aupinard, Anais Cardot, Grace Dumdaw, and Chezile)

#2 – "I Get Lonely"—Janet Jackson

#3 – "Can We Talk—Tevin Campbell

#4 – "Anytime"—Brian McKnight

#5 – "Phresh Out the Runway"—Rihanna

#6 – "Ready for Love"—India Arie

#7 – "Anywhere"—112

#8 – "Breakin' My Heart (Pretty Brown Eyes)"—Mint Condition

#9 – "Wey U"—Chanté Moore

#10 – "Golden"—Kara Marni

THE PLAYLIST—PART II

#11 – "Ready or Not"—After 7

#12 – "Un-thinkable (I'm Ready)"—Alicia Keys

#13 – "I'm Kissing You"—Des'ree

#14 – "Love in Portofino"—Andrea Bocelli

#15 – "I Love You"—Faith Evans

#16 – "Bittersweet"—Lianne La Havas

#17 – "I'll Be Around"—The Spinners

#18 – "Missing You"—Case

#19 – "Lovesong"—Adele

#20 – "Epilogue"—Justin Hurwitz

Chapter 1

Madison

Fifteen Years Ago

Could this day get any worse?

The answer is a group of tourists stopping in the middle of the sidewalk to take pictures of a window display.

My silver sandals dig into my heels as I skid in a last-minute attempt not to pummel a grandmother in awe of a mannequin. I narrowly dodge the older woman with gunmetal curls and a disposable camera pressed to her cheek, but I collide with a bony shoulder.

"*Désolé!*" I shout to the tall brunette. Then I suck in a labored breath and speed walk into a swarm of people on Boulevard Haussmann who are moving at a snail's pace.

Of all the days.

The sun reaches over the buildings lining the street to wet my brow. I'm a mess of sweat and frustration.

A wrong-way ride on the Paris Métro put me four extra stops away from the Galeries Lafayette and a fashion show starting in three minutes. The Friday event speaks to my love languages: couture and free.

I have $600 of available credit, and it has to last the next two months. My part-time internship won't pay much, but it will give me some wiggle room to tour the area and afford the occasional meal I don't whip up in my tiny apartment kitchen. A croissant is a treat I can barely afford, not without worrying if it will blow my budget, but today it was a must for the metro ride. I had to make it here on time after skipping lunch.

Me and my hunger are arriving fashionably late.

A gap between a man draped in an untailored suit and a woman in a sundress appears in time for me to push through one of the many glass doors and into the historic department store. I stumble inside and gasp.

Wow.

The Galeries Lafayette could fit every Macy's Thanksgiving Day Parade attendee under its glass dome. Visiting New York City is still on my wish list, but I imagine nothing compares to a building this size. It's the love child of the Colosseum and the Marigny Opera House. I've never seen anything like it. The grandeur. The luxury.

With a tug to the strap of my powder-blue satchel, I step further into the temple dedicated to style and high-end living.

You need to move if you want to make it.

A swarm of shoppers pours out of elevators—surely it's a fire hazard. The sweeping staircase is another no-go unless I hike up my skirt and sprint to the fourth floor. How does Sarah Jessica Parker skip across Manhattan in Manolos and still look cute?

I'm in a Carrie outfit now, one of many affordable knock-offs I curated for this trip. Thrift store finds and visits to Wet Seal and

Charlotte Russe in Baton Rouge on weekends I could borrow the car went a long way. My blush tulle skirt channels *Sex and the City* for the affordable price of $9.99. What few designer pieces I do have are from clients who wanted to toss them in the trash. The *trash*.

One of these days, I'll have money to spend on labels and not live a life of hand-me-downs. Living in my sister Dominique's shadow was stuffy enough without having to wear the bland clothes she called "fashion." You'd be surprised at how many drugstore shelves you'd have to stock to afford Revlon and slip dresses.

I did it for years, and I'm not going back. For now, I'll fake it until I make it.

Mama taught me how to use a needle and thread at an early age, and that's come in handy as a stylist. I've worked hard over these last two years to make a name for myself. It's why events like this fashion show are important.

If only I wasn't so late.

I peek at my watch again and sigh. What's the point?

Rushing to one of the busiest shopping destinations on a Friday afternoon wasn't smart. But I didn't put on these Payless shoes for nothing.

Window shopping and sampling perfume that costs more than a semester of college threads the hours together. Three pass in a blur, lifting the sun from the center of the all-seeing dome through a kaleidoscope of colors. I still have a few hours until it's too dark to read street signs. My glasses are back in my apartment, and I forgot to pack my contacts.

I leave the Galeries Lafayette as I came: tired, a bit blind, and clinging to the hope that something will work out.

It's too late to join Tammi, my roommate for this trip, and the other study abroad students. A tour of Paris on a multicolored double-decker bus is not my idea of a fun Friday night, but it was a gamble to skip it for a twenty-minute fashion show. Clearly, the risk didn't pay off.

The walk back to my apartment's stocked refrigerator will sacrifice my feet. These heels were comfortable hours ago, but now they're running on fumes and half a prayer. That leaves spending money on a dinner that will cost a week's worth of meals.

Paris's ninth arrondissement is a medley of buildings spanning long, angled streets. It has a mix of department stores, museums, and banks. Not to mention Palais Garnier, the historic opera house. Nothing that regal was ever in the cards or my family's bank account growing up. Still, I remember reading about it in *The Phantom of the Opera*. I lived two hours from New Orleans and dreamed of attending a fancy opera in a custom gown with glittering diamonds coating my neck. That bubble burst, and so will the blisters prickling the bottoms of my feet if I don't find a place to sit soon.

Getting lost in the district's boulevards is surprisingly easy when you don't know where to go. My BlackBerry is laughing at me from where it lies next to my glasses on my nightstand. It's turned off to avoid roaming and data charges and is only for emergencies.

Heather once racked up a $500 bill during a spur-of-the-moment trip to Lisbon over spring break. Never once did she bat an eye about forgetting to sign up for an international plan.

Unlike me, my college roommate can afford it, as well as the summer yacht trip around the Mediterranean she's currently enjoying. Her father is too occupied with the demands of a Hollywood exec to care about his daughter ditching her year abroad to run off with a six-two model with perfect cheekbones and three middle names. Heather would still have more than half a year in France if she didn't blow off the trip, but her lack of interest is my ticket to calling Paris home until next spring.

We met during our freshman year at Bodie University. I was in a scramble to revamp my closet, which needed a resurrection, and she complained about her father subjecting her to a dorm. What style I did have on display caught her eye. One compliment turned into Heather telling a friend, who told a friend.

Before I knew it, I had a growing clientele of Bodie trust fund kids, who paid monthly styling fees for me to plan their outfits. It covers what's left of my tuition but not this study abroad trip in Paris—let alone a $500 cell phone oops for trying to find a place to eat.

My $35-a-month prepaid cell plan is nothing fancy, but it gets the job done. I keep it for clients and to call home, not that the latter is quick to answer. My parents refuse to part ways with the landline we've had since I was a kid. Their promise to be more available while I'm in France means Dominique is at the library twice a week to check her email. Daddy is always on the boat, and Mama is "too old to be learning that technology."

I stop in front of a restaurant on Rue Chaptal. The menu in the window does not suit my appetite or wallet. Mawmaw, rest her soul, is turning in her grave at the thought of me entertaining two pieces of lettuce as a meal.

"*Moun ka manjé ça?*" she'd say about those scraps passed off as a gourmet meal. My grandmother passed away six years ago, when I was sixteen, but she always kept us fed on rice dressing with leftovers. I miss her, but Mawmaw will have to understand tonight.

The farts in my stomach passed the point of embarrassment. Never mind that my toes are seconds from scraping the concrete like in a *Flintstones* episode. With all the miles I put on these cheap shoes, I need a break.

There has to be *something* still open that doesn't cost a small fortune and comes with a piece of bread. Frog legs are acceptable. They're a delicacy back home, next to gator and boudin. I'm losing hope with every restaurant I pass, but I did not come all this way to give up. On this district or on Paris.

The swap for me to take Heather's place wasn't easy. It was a race for me to get a passport and the proper visa, but I did it. Heather and I both pursuing business degrees meant I could keep the courses she selected in play. The school agreed, and off I went.

Mama had a fit about me leaving the country, but she didn't raise no fool. The host university here still calls me Heather, but I'll answer to Coco Chanel if necessary.

I'm here. Beyond the edges of the small city I've called home since leaving for college two years ago. I love my family, but I want more than the life waiting for me back in Breaux Bridge. None of them have ventured beyond the city limits in years, outside of the occasional visits to Lafayette and New Orleans.

I was always different, reaching beyond what was in front of me to touch possibilities. I want more—the glitz, the glamour, and everything that comes with it.

Coming to Paris is a new chapter in a story I've yet to write.

A break in the buildings appears. I peek into an open walkway with trees sheltering an aged path from the sun and see a modest cream property with sage shutters. All hope dissolves. It's not a quaint restaurant among rustic, wrought-iron buildings in the city's bustle. It's...a museum?

My overworked heels crunch against gravel on my way to the glass-paned double doors. The museum, which is focused on romantic life, houses antiques and paintings. I can't douse any of them in Tabasco sauce and eat them. Love is nice, but I want food. Still, I step inside in search of a place to sit and rest my feet.

"Like what you see?" a voice asks in French, breaking through the silence. It's low, a touch above a whisper, and very close.

My eyes lift from the portraits of women in gilded frames to the source, which is blessed with a perfect pair of lips. The bottom one has some weight to it and rests above a small patch of dark hair on his jaw. Warm honey skin peeks out from a crisp white shirt. A sequence of buttons draws my eyes up to a trimmed mustache, then to the sharp blade of a nose, and finally to cognac-colored eyes that are fixed on me.

The yellow parlor room is now two sizes too small, thanks to the presence of this runway model in the wild knocking the breath from my lungs. If he doesn't pout in front of a camera for a living, he should find an agent. His stare alone is stifling.

A brow raises in wait. I haven't answered him, and I get the sense he isn't in the habit of repeating himself.

My "No" lacks any outward sign that the man next to me, in a navy suit tailored to his form, has zero effect on me. He's not close enough to breach any personal boundaries but is thickening the air with his spiced cologne.

I steal another glance, this time at his near-black hair, which is thick and perfectly styled. There's a curl at the edges, teasing the texture of its natural form.

"Do you like what you see?" I say in a tone that would make Miranda Priestly proud. My breath steadies to keep my pulse from pounding like shoes in a dryer.

No one except statues should have erect nipples in an art museum, but thank God for padded bras.

Two dimples peek out at his nod. "Very much so," he says.

I redirect my attention to the antique table in front of me. Brass hardware. Tapered legs. It's a beautiful piece, like some I've seen in the antique mall on Bridge Street back home. Vintage furnishings don't turn me on. Gorgeous men do, and that's not the point of this trip.

"Did you need something?" Steel anchors my question, catching him off guard.

He considers me under a fan of black lashes. My sandals have three-inch heels but still put me half a foot below his gaze. Seconds pass, our eyes locked in a standoff.

Remember Lauren Conrad.

When life presents you with a choice between a fashion internship in Paris or renting a house with your raggedy, unbrushed ex, choose Paris every time.

My ex was far from a scrub, but I refuse to allow anyone or anything to distract me while I'm here. Present company included.

Men like the one next to me, who's silently calculating my measurements, are nothing new. The gold cuff links, the fitted suit, and a desire for a plaything on his arm—someone seen and not heard—come with the tax bracket.

I'm from the bayou, but I wasn't born yesterday.

"Have dinner with me." The fire in his eyes casts an amber glow as it sweeps over my collarbone and up to my lips. "Tonight."

Arrogant.

"I don't dine with strangers," I say, matter-of-fact.

The edge of a smile curls the corner of his mouth. "We should fix that." He extends a hand that comes with an expensive watch attached. "Preston."

Preston can't be more than a few years older than me, but he has an aura of importance and responsibility. There's a hunger in his stare, a hunger that has to do with more than just food.

I am no one's conquest, but I can do dinner. My credit card will send a handwritten thank-you letter.

I place my hand in his, reveling in the softness of his touch and the circle his thumb rubs across my skin. Preston is the kind of man to make you sing '90s love songs in a dark corner after he breaks your heart, a heart he promised to cherish. He's gorgeous, obviously loaded, and maintains the most unnerving eye contact.

My promise to not lose sight of why I'm in Paris takes new form. I look him in the eyes and lie to his face.

"Heather."

Chapter 2

Preston

Now

I'm rarely on the receiving end of rejection. For one, I don't take no for an answer in business. I get what I want or find another way for the odds to work in my favor. That's what makes the woman across from me struggling to let me down gently so damn entertaining. Because when the fuck does this happen?

Tonight, apparently.

I steady my expression to keep from cracking a smile. Justice is fighting for her life the way her hands keep fidgeting over the white tablecloth. Her trepid brown eyes dart everywhere but to me. They finally land on the night sky twinkling over the frosted valley.

This holiday is full of surprises.

Vail, Colorado, is an experience. It's no Maldives, but it comes with the advantage of anonymity and being a continent away from the life waiting for me back in London. Time is a luxury even I struggle to afford. I don't give it freely for anyone to waste, but I can't help seeing her one more time.

Round tables and rattan chairs with patrons enjoying the finest dining in the valley fill the once-empty ballroom. Large crystal chandeliers hover from high ceilings, set low for an ambiance that's absent from this table.

Choosing a spot near the floor-to-ceiling windows was intentional. I read body language, and Justice shifting in her black dress tells me she's nervous. Normally I don't give a shit who withers in my presence, but I've developed a soft spot for her in the days since we met. I want to take the edge off the conversation we're about to have. One that will end with her severing whatever was building between us.

Justice is a breath of fresh air. She's awkward and a touch anxious but sexy as hell.

Her lighthearted giggles drew me from the stables the first time we met two days ago. She's here with her best friend for this week's singles' retreat at the resort. I've steered clear for privacy but filled in for one of the horseback riding instructors. With my schedule, I seldom get to enjoy riding anymore. An opportunity presented itself to shed my suit for flannel and an Appaloosa, so I took it.

The need to fuck had me circling Justice and her infectious grin. But the more time we spent on our horses in the snow, the more I got to know her. Every quirk matches her beauty, woven in rich chestnut. Stunning women aren't rare for me, but her easygoing personality kept my attention.

To Justice, I'm Preston. A guy who spends time outdoors. I'm in a tailored charcoal suit tonight, and it doesn't matter. Finding out I was rich didn't change her perception of me.

My phone buzzes in my pocket in rapid succession. Stephanie knows to forward me items that require my immediate attention. Two weeks is all I have for this holiday, and the persistent hum of pending messages is threatening to cut it short.

"Preston, I need to tell you something," Justice says, meeting my eyes from under coiled black curls.

Ah, yes. The rejection.

"That you and your ex are no longer estranged?" I still the sarcasm tempting my tone when a frown knits her brows.

The shock of my discovery threatens to siphon the blood from Justice's face. She lets out a breath at the smile dusting my mouth. She feels guilty, but she shouldn't.

I'm neither upset nor surprised that she's reconciling with her ex, who is also here for the week. On paper, they're still married—once headed for divorce until life rerouted their paths to collide after seven months of no contact.

How the hell do you compete with fate? The simple answer is you don't.

I'll admit Justice captivated me, but it's clear she's still hung up on her husband. She admitted as much and wouldn't be tripping over her words right now otherwise.

"Were you spying on me?" Her cheeks flush on a gulp. She's a doe caught in headlights, questioning if I'm someone who follows women for sport.

I smirk. "Relax, Justice. I'm not a stalker." I like to watch, just not the way she thinks.

Did I review security footage of her at yesterday's salsa lesson, cozied up to her ex once she'd let her guard down? I did. I own the damn resort. An emergency business meeting arose, which took me away from the hotel. I peeked at the video of her on the dance floor to make sure she was okay after I broke our date.

It's safe to say she was.

My departure created the space for Terrence to go after her. Can't say I blame him. She's unlike many of the women I encounter. Her presence draws you in. I can be myself without expectations, which is why I'm clinging to whatever time we have left together. It feels good not to carry the Donnelley Brand for once.

We owe each other nothing. Two days and a kiss are no match for her fifteen years with her former ex. It's the same amount of time since I've seen Heather.

Heather.

I haven't uttered that name since she walked out of my life. Remembering is a fucking knife to my gut.

My phone buzzes again, a reminder that the space I've carved out for myself will expire sooner than expected. I assure Justice that I'm not a serial killer and sit through the story of how she and Terrence reconciled. I never considered myself a masochist, but I have no explanation for why I'm still here, mingling with rejection, when I could be elsewhere. Preferably fucking. I haven't had sex on this holiday, and I am not crossing the ocean with blue balls.

"When you find your soulmate, it's hard to let go," she says. An apology plays across the faint smile she forces through a frown.

A sharp pain lodges itself at the fragmented memories pressing against my ribs. Cinnamon brown hair and heart-shaped lips transport me back to the only relationship strong enough to tilt life on its side. To a time when I stood in the sun, trying to catch flecks of gray glinting in the hazel eyes that still haunt me.

I never meant to hurt you.

Fifteen years, and I can still see Heather clear as day.

Regret and yearning are present at the table, a reminder of how exposed I am outside of the Donnelley Brand and its CEO demands. I've kept myself busy while on holiday so my mind wouldn't wander back to when I was just me. Beyond my status, when ordinary was extraordinary.

Justice doesn't realize that the mirror she's holding up forces me to contend with scars still tethered to the edges of my mind. No matter how hard I try to forget, I can't let go.

"Honestly, I envy your situation," I say to Justice, who's staring at me like I have two heads.

"I thought you said you don't do long-term relationships?"

I don't do feelings anymore, either, but I'm still at this dinner, which would typically never touch the shadow of my calendar. They're uncorked—the feelings—forcing me to assess the man I am today and the one decision I made that cost me everything.

"I'm not opposed to anything long-term," I admit, "but part of the reason I'm hesitant is I was once in love with someone who got away."

In my forty-one years, no one has compared to Heather—not even Justice. I've fucked my way across continents to try and fill the empty space she created once she left. I was twenty-six and never realized what I had until she walked out of my life.

"I was so young, just coming into the business. I didn't know what I had," I say, the scent of late-night eclairs on the balcony wafting in the distance. "I would marry her today if I ever found her."

The arrogant little shit I was had an inflated ego. I was impenetrable. No one could shake me until a woman in a French museum with a masterpiece of curves turned my world upside down.

Diving headfirst into pussy and the career my father molded for me have yet to make whole what's missing. I should've fought harder to keep her instead of pushing her away. Every resource is now at my fingertips, but I let too much time pass. Heather isn't her actual name, but what we shared was real.

Pressure squeezes the hard granite formed over my heart. Tonight is the first time I've told anyone what I've held in silence.

Finché c'è vita c'è speranza. As long as there is life, there is hope.

Nonna always challenges me to open up. "We're not meant to carry our burdens alone, *zuccareddu.*" Easier said than done.

But tonight, it feels right to release the weight.

Justice is still a stranger, but my gut says to trust her. I was ready for rejection, but I'll leave with a gift I haven't felt in fifteen years. Hope.

Dinner is pleasant, light conversation over a four-course meal. Lamb chop fondue and onion soup decorate the table next to votive candles and red roses. Justice wastes no time digging into each plate. I don't discuss my wealth, but her jokes about "eatin' good" pull a grin every time. The way she puts away the twin lobster tails, truffle fries, and creamed spinach she orders should be a topic of study.

She's humming around a bite of chocolate cake when something near the entrance to the ballroom reaches for her attention. I follow her line of sight through a sip of bourbon and freeze. The swallow I'm holding burns in my throat at the illusion only feet away.

A man who I assume to be Terrence takes measured steps to the bar, wearing a dark button-down and jeans. He's tall and has a muscular build, blocking the view of the woman by his side. It's hard to make her out, but what few glimpses I get prickle my skin.

French manicured feet in black heels keep pace across the ballroom carpet. I start at the toned pecan legs and move up the profile to find flared hips in a knee-length black dress and a thick ass that switches with careful precision. Her face is still hidden, the result of a half-foot height difference. Thick, wavy hair flows down her back, and my heart pistons at its cinnamon hue.

It can't be.

"Hey. Is everything okay?"

"Yeah, I'm fine." I swallow the wire caught in my throat and plaster on a smile. "I take it that was Terrence and the woman he's about to let down." Her presence tugs for me to bear witness with a familiarity that shouldn't be there.

"It is. Her name is Madison. They dated for a few months in college. She broke up with him, believe it or not."

The surrounding chatter of diners and Justice fades under the blood pounding in my ears. My mind races to keep up with the impossible reality that my eyes aren't deceiving me.

The magnetic pull.

The body I licked and held sacred.

Sweet notes of magnolia stroking the memory of the last time we made love.

Madison is Heather.

"...she's been pining after him all these years in a not-so-subtle way."

Has she now?

Hearing that the woman who's invaded my dreams for over a decade is hung up on another man lands like a punch. She was unforgettable, and I'll be damned if she acts like I wasn't.

Everything clicks into place. Heather—or Madison—only mentioned this ex once. Not even by name, which was clearly a running theme, given she withheld her own. He meant nothing then and only serves as a distraction now.

I smirk into my tumbler. It's a small gesture that mimics a genuine smile to mask the predatory urge to reclaim her.

The instinct to chase overwhelms the shock of seeing her again after all this time. Here, of all places. My pulse skitters at the vow I made fifteen years ago—to never let her go should life ever bring us back together.

My evening with Justice wraps up. I walk her back to her room and wish her well before heading to security. Now that Madison is here, I won't make it easy for her to leave a second time.

Chapter 3
Madison

I'm joining a convent when I get home. A house of nuns far away with good weather and quality panty hose. The only choice is to leave love on the altar and commit to the single life for eternity.

My back hits my hotel room door. Everything is how I left it. Drapes peeled back for a view of the winter valley. A single wineglass rinsed in the sink. The bed with the faux fur duvet I left to get ready with an excitement I later ditched at the bar.

Alone. Again.

Dating is a fruitless disappointment, a minefield of headaches and wasted outfits. Whether I'm back in New York or on location at a fashion shoot, it's all the same. The pool of options is infested with boys who refuse to grow up or guys who prefer women half my age.

Two-day shipping on "the ideal man" isn't an option. Trust me, I checked. I've Bumbled and tumbled until I almost put myself out of my misery. Is it too much to ask for an emotionally available partner with all his front teeth who won't pick up a ride-share customer in the middle of a date?

I've had enough of men and sanding layers of dust off my vagina with toys every other night. My vibrators are tired. *I'm* tired.

A bottle of wine, a dry spell from mediocre sex, and *The Last Holiday* on repeat led to a computer search for the cure to the mess my love life has become. Christmas alone didn't sit well with my family, but I needed the break, and I deserved a taste of paradise. When I stumbled across a seven-day singles' retreat in Vail, Colorado, from my suite in Aruba, I figured, why not? My luck with finding a decent bachelor is somewhere in Hell, anyway.

Sharing my life with someone was the furthest thing from my priorities until I looked up and realized the years were whipping by at lightning speed. I never wanted to settle down in my twenties, and I put off serious relationships to build my styling business. Now, at thirty-seven, I'm ready. If only the prospects were better. At this rate, I'll be ninety and still swiping left.

Running into Terrence at a singles' retreat was a sign, or so I thought. I didn't know he'd be here when I booked this trip on a whim, and I all but launched myself at him during the opening mixer on the first night. A white collared shirt under a navy sweater doesn't scream turn-on, but a year of no sex and a now-available ex will do it.

He stood alone, drawing eyes around the crowded ballroom. Women were powerless against his caramel perfection, his straight brows furrowed over black-rimmed glasses, his wide nose. His thick lips stretched into a smile at my approach.

Terrence has been that guy since college. The years have been good to him, sharpening the square jaw now covered in a trimmed goatee. He still has a crop of black curls he keeps styled above a taper fade and looks more attractive than the day we met at Staci's house party our sophomore year.

I never had a one-night stand until him. He wasn't my first, but he was the first to soften the heart I didn't want to give away. His passion matched the inferno of his body, but his care made me feel safe. One hookup turned into several. Before we knew it, we were in the two-month relationship I ended before my trip to Paris. It wasn't his reputation for playing the field that made me hesitant to try long distance. It was his desire to be a family man one day, and I refused to sacrifice my dreams to live in any man's future.

I didn't believe in coincidence, but I became a convert when Terrence popped up at this retreat, fine and fair game and without a wedding ring. Sifting through a lifetime supply of emotionally un-available men will have you hoping the ex who treated you right will see you as more than just someone from his past who he occasionally runs into because of work.

He was safe, familiar. He never hurt me. If there was a chance for us to have another go, I'd take it. Love would eventually come with time.

Harboring a forbidden crush on a married man was never a goal. It sounds bad, I know. I'm not in the habit of chasing after any man—married or otherwise. The crush just...happened. It was clearly a one-sided connection that I allowed to grow through his kindness and my self-assurance I deserve more.

Was it wrong? I'll admit it was.

I didn't set out to harbor feelings for an old flame, but it's hard not to think about one of the only stable relationships in my life after so many awful attempts. The crush evaporated…until whispers of his separation surfaced.

Somewhere along the way, I stopped caring in order to mask my own pain. I'm not proud to admit it, but flirting was a game I mastered. Simple teasing and friendly banter hit the mark whenever my path would cross with Terrence's throughout the years—him training celebrities and me styling them. He never caught on, but Justice did. I knew it stung, but I didn't care.

Women like his wife are put on a pedestal. Men trip over themselves to move the world for their comfort. I wasn't the quiet cheerleader who belonged in a Disney special like Justice or the homecoming queen like my sister, praised for settling down into a life of tradition. I couldn't compete, and I found myself resenting how quickly men offered forever to the type of woman I'd never be.

Nice guys might finish last, but good girls are always the prize.

Karma has a way of catching up with you. She sat my ass down tonight and forced me to look at who I've become.

The stiletto heel I attempt to hop out of catches on the carpet. I stumble, slamming my knee into the bedroom doorway.

"Shit."

Pain reaches up the hem of my black off-the-shoulder minidress, which did me no favors tonight.

Any hope I had for a healthy relationship came crashing down eight minutes ago. Terrence walked me to my room and all but told me to have a good life. I'm still processing the embarrassment.

Everything was perfect.

My hair that took two hours to straighten.

My makeup that requires an advanced degree in contouring.

These titties propped up to perfection.

All of it wasted on a man I should've purged from my system years ago.

She is my heartbeat.

Of course he still loves her.

Slate tiles in a palette of brown and gray come to life at the flick of the bathroom light switch.

Prominent cheekbones, naturally thick arched brows, and a slightly downturned nose stare back at me through a gold-framed mirror. They reflect generations of Dubois women fortified in melanated shades and Creole flavor. It's still a struggle to see beyond the beauty marks and face the blemishes that run skin-deep.

"What are you doing?" My sigh floats through my resentment of how pitiful I've become.

Terrence didn't need to tell me he was reconciling with Justice. Chance might have brought us to the same place, but destiny reunited them.

I had to break a world record with how many times this man rejected me this week. Terrence made no attempt to even text "Hello," let alone pursue me. Tonight was the first time he reached out in the seven days we've been at this retreat. Deep down, I knew it wasn't to profess his undying affection, but I told my intuition to take a back seat.

I want to be loved by someone who won't break my heart. The problem with love is that you can't force yourself into a heart that still belongs to someone else.

I know you're going to find someone who makes you come alive the way Justice does for me.

I did once, and it almost broke me.

The tear I let fall isn't for Terrence but in mourning over what I'll never feel again. What I haven't felt since the man whose name I refuse to utter eviscerated my heart fifteen years ago.

I still wear the burns of a thunderous glare seared into eyes once soft and affectionate. The merciless lines of his face that traced the contours of his shock and anger.

The choice to stuff away any memory of that moment in Paris is a fail-safe. To remember the beauty of what we shared resurrects shards still piercing my heart. No one else has come close to hurting me, and I won't keep opening myself up to more pain.

There's no excuse for what I've done with Terrence or for who I've become. Tomorrow, I'm turning the page.

And looking up a convent.

Chapter 4

Madison

The melody to "Ain't No Mountain High Enough" stirs me out of a dreamless sleep. I reach across the duvet that's swaddling me in warmth to search for the source of the upbeat anthem echoing across the room.

Vail is a special kind of cold, one New York never prepared me for. My cute winter outfits didn't stand a chance, which is why I kept my butt inside. January is Januarying here.

I swipe the phone off the nightstand and draw in a deep breath to prepare for Tammi handing me my ass. "Hel—"

"How'd your little dinner date go, Ms. *My Best Friend's Wedding?*"

A groan seeps into a yawn when I look at the screen. "This couldn't wait? It's six a.m., Tam."

She clicks her tongue. "First service doesn't start until nine here. I have time." Her voice holds no shame about our two-hour time difference. "So, how did it go?"

A laugh slips out when I replay Terrence's apology. He didn't want to hurt me, but I knew where last night was headed once we bypassed the restaurant for the bar.

He was back with Justice, and I was left figuring out why I put myself in this situation to begin with.

"I didn't chase anyone in a bread van," I say and lie back to inspect the beige ceiling.

"At least you'd have something to snack on while trying to break up their marriage," Tammi snaps.

"Where's your grace, First Lady?" I soothe the burn over my chest at the shot fired from Detroit. Cheaters are awful in my book, but here I am acting like a pick-me girl with no home training.

"You get what you get before my coffee. The first lady hat doesn't go on for another forty minutes," she says. The hardness in her tone softens. "Seriously. You okay?"

"You were right."

"Of course I was." She chuckles at my snort. "How'd it go?"

I tap the screen for speakerphone. "We met for drinks at the bar instead of dinner. Terrence said we needed to talk. Then he apologized and told me he loves his wife." I shrug. "You called it. I should've listened."

Tammi warned me not to go after him. He only asked me out to tell me he still loves his estranged wife. Deep down, I knew it was coming. All of our run-ins were my desperate attempt to bring us together. Terrence showed me more than once I was never a priority.

"Maddie."

"Don't."

"He's meant for his wife. Let go."

I huff out a laugh. "Oh, I got that loud and clear."

Nothing is a blow to the ego like your crush telling you he only kissed you because he saw the woman he actually wants with someone else. What we shared in the back of the theater during movie night felt like the start of a new chapter. Instead, it was the end of a saga. I'm not the star of this love story. I never was.

Tammi is silent. She hasn't pulled a single punch since we shared an apartment during our study abroad trip to Paris. She was only there for the summer, but we've kept in touch over the years. Aside from Kojo, she's my only friend. Someone who doesn't use people to climb social ladders and never hesitates to call me out from a place of love.

"You're someone's choice, not an option." Her voice cuts through the silence. There's no edge or playfulness in her tone. It's gentle but loud and clear.

The feelings I harbored aren't a secret. Tammi might be a pastor's wife, but she has *Love & Hip Hop* tendencies. She knows I'd never cross any physical lines while Terrence is still with Justice. I do have *some* morals. But my crush was still a source of tension in our friendship, to the point where she stopped talking to me for half a year.

Tammi was always quick to remind me of the harm it caused. She deals with vultures trying to prey on her marriage while praying with her husband. Smokey and Tyrese couldn't appear in the same room without you assuming they're twins. It's no surprise that Calvary Macedonia keeps half of Detroit in its seats with Smokey's megawatt smile, bald head, and sleepy eyes.

I had to talk Tammi off the ledge a time or two from "knocking a Jezebel's wig loose." Her husband only has eyes for his wife, and he sets boundaries with their congregation. That doesn't stop the occasional person from shooting their shot.

Smokey and Tam grew up in Detroit together. He got caught up in street life and joined the military after tragedy hit his doorstep. They were always close but never dated. Years passed, but the love they had for each other didn't. When Smokey moved back, he made his intentions known.

He's handsome in his own right, but he met his match with my friend. I know she tempts the devil with her full curves in radiant chocolate brown. Her thick natural hair is the envy of everyone in the presence of her crown, myself included. At thirty-eight, she doesn't look a day over twenty-five and is Ryan Destiny fine. Smokey can't keep off her, which is why they've had five kids in the seven years they've been married. I wouldn't come up for air, either.

"I'm giving up men," I say, staring at the shadows on the wall. "It's time to reset, away from exes and dating. No more retreats, apps, or forcing love."

"It's not a bad idea," Tammi says. "Cut off all communication with exes and flings for a fresh start."

"The only fling here is me tossed to the side." I blow out a breath that's more tired than frustrated. "I'm done searching for my someone."

Terrence has all the qualities of a partner. No one has matched him since Preston. The latter is in a league of his own, tucked away out of sight and in the furthest corner of my mind.

Preston is a song you commit to memory, a melody you hum without thinking. Remnants of his scent still coat the air on any given day. What happened between us was a spiritual experience—two souls tying together. Erasing him from my psyche took years of practice, and even still I've yet to master it.

"You'll find each other when it's time. Remember, you're the choice, not an option."

"I'm the choice," I repeat.

"Doll Baby, lemme part them cheeks. We got nine minutes," a raspy bass croons on the other end of the line.

"Smokey Mayfield Wright! Madison is on the phone." Tammi can pretend she's upset all she wants. The hitch in her voice says otherwise, and I don't blame her for whatever Bible game they're about to play.

"My bad. What's good, Maddie?"

"Hey, Smokey."

"I need to get at my wife before this service for, uh, prayer," he says, convincing absolutely no one. The man is sprung on Tammi, and I love that for my friend.

"Let me go and get ready," she laughs. "Text me when you make it back home. Love you, girl."

"Love you too," I say. "Bye, Smokey!"

"Be easy!" The good pastor tells Tammi to put on her Sunday hat before the call drops. Those two are wild.

One day.

I call in my breakfast order to room service for the sixth time this week. A slice of brioche with fresh jam and honey in one of the restaurants would be faster, but that's not happening. I limited my trips outside the room since running into Justice and her best friend. Justice would cry if she stepped on an ant, but Emma glares like a protective sister every time she sees me. It's the same look Dominique gave my middle school bully before she got two months of detention for introducing her hands to the conversation.

My mouth is spicy, but I'm no fighter.

I'm showered, dressed in a knit sweater and vegan leggings, and packed when the doorbell rings. The chime is faint but loud enough for me to hear in the bathroom. After the finishing touches on my makeup, I do a final sweep for anything I forgot to put in my suitcase. New York is my final destination this afternoon, and I'm leaving with more clarity.

The single life was never a problem. Fear of losing myself in a man was.

The doorbell chimes again.

"Coming!" I grab cash for a tip out of my purse and scurry to the door.

Polished Italian shoes catch my eye. Their brandy color complements the syrup-brown suit over toned thighs. I follow the herringbone pattern up pleated slacks to a matching vest over a taut chest—the gold chain of a pocket watch clings to a button above a noticeable bulge.

A navy tie hides behind a dome-covered plate in soft hands. No doubt it's my food, but why is this three-piece suit hand-delivering my meal? Maybe Sundays are wash days for the traditional black-and-white uniforms? I know custom threads when I see them.

The familiar scent of musk with subtle notes of nutmeg reawakens the memory of French toast sizzling in a cast iron skillet. Me with my hair tossed up in a scrunchie, his cologne on the dress shirt that brushes against my thighs.

My heart hiccups to find its rhythm amid this déjà vu.

The broad chest.

The razor-sharp jaw decorated in five-o'clock shadow.

I'm too stunned to speak the words caught in my throat. He shouldn't be here. He's—

My breath is sharp. I crane my neck and scale up lips I've tasted to reach a cognac gaze that travels over my face with cautious examination. My feet sink further into the carpet.

Fifteen years, and he still takes my breath away.

The base of his throat works on a hard swallow. Sadness clouds his eyes in the aftermath of the last time we stood face-to-face. Words we can't retract splinter our skin.

Instinct kicks in when he clears his throat. Standing in Preston's presence is one thing; the sound of his voice will be my undoing.

My face burns in remembrance of how effortlessly he discarded me. I've allowed enough people to toss me aside. It stops today.

No dating or exes.

I snatch the domed plate from his hands and slam the door in his face. I don't trust what I'll do if he calls out to me. The temptation to slap him and the desire to crush my mouth to his battle it out as I run back to the bedroom. There's nowhere to hide. The floor I'm on is too high up for me to go out the window. I'd sooner wear off-brand face cream before anyone would catch me scaling the side of the building.

What the hell is he doing here?

Who let him out of the house looking that fine?

Life isn't just unfair, it's playing in my face. It's like God took every one of Preston's features I fell in love with, made them finer with each year, and dropped him off in the hallway.

He's seconds from glamouring away my dick drought. I'm searching for an exit strategy that doesn't require me to go through the front door. If I wasn't already contemplating therapy, seeing him would have me on the couch in no time.

Preston is here. In Vail.

Another knock rattles the wooden barrier between past and present.

"Can we talk?" His voice is a low, smooth timbre.

I tell myself it's okay to ignore my desire to open the door and the echo of his longing. I can grab my things and walk out without a second look. I'm fifteen years late to repay him with the sting of rejection.

"Please, Puff."

Every reason why I should pretend Preston isn't standing in front of my hotel room dissolves at the pet name he called me during the months we shared in Paris.

Before everything fell apart.

Chapter 5

Preston

Pain dances across my nose from the door she slammed in my face. I inhale and straighten my suit jacket.

This is a first.

People usually trip over themselves to kiss my ass. The attempts to earn my attention get old, but they come with the territory. There's always someone waiting to pitch a business proposal that is neither original nor feasible. My name alone opens doors...except this one, apparently. I anticipated Heather's reaction but didn't move quick enough.

Madison, not Heather.

Time sped up the steps it took to reach her door and slowed when it opened. Her presence froze me in place, imploring me to reacquaint myself with the soft lines of her body, a body I exhausted for hours at a time.

The indent of the full waist I held.

Round hips and shapely thighs.

Toned legs that still hold definition.

The fresh scent of magnolia that once drifted through the open French doors of the balcony still coats her skin. The blissful hazel eyes that once held a world of excitement are now cold. Distant.

Guilt wedges itself deep. Being this close to Madison lulls me back to a euphoria—when life was simple and status didn't matter.

I've missed Heather, but I won't lose Madison.

"Puff," I sigh. The nickname is now foreign, much like the actual name of the woman I've loved, a name I only learned yesterday.

Madison's love of puff pastries threatened shortages in every bakery within walking distance of my penthouse. Her sweet tooth is next level. The name "Puff" stuck after teasing her about the eclair she stuffed into her school bag and the mille-feuille we'd eat for dessert on the weekends.

I knock again. "Come to the door. We need to talk."

Silence drowns the sound of my heartbeat. A thousand and one scenarios raced through my mind on the way to her room. What I would do. What she would say. It took a pep talk just to make it down the hall and work up the courage to knock.

Business hardened my exterior over the years, gave me the necessary calluses to lead with logic, not emotion. I don't get nervous, but I haven't got a fucking clue how to start a conversation that's fifteen years late.

"Puff. I'm not leaving until you open up." Call it possessiveness or stupidity. I can't will myself to leave her doorstep.

Sweat dots my hand as I form another fist to knock again. I've closed multimillion dollar deals with less hassle.

The door swings open to a face that looks ready to rip it off its hinges. Below my eye level is a woman who's contemplating how to get away with murder. For a long moment, she stares up at me with narrowed brows and a dangerous scowl.

My pulse charges at the ache to touch her. Flames ignite from the edges of her glare. The pull to close the short distance between us demands action.

I open my mouth to speak, but it's quickly closed by a slap I didn't see coming, one that connects with my jaw.

Damn. Does she box?

"I deserve that." She almost lifted me out of my shoes. "Ma—" The door slams in my face again.

I'm a prideful man but am not above begging.

The door swings open again, and I hop out of the way. Madison's once-bare feet are now in black riding boots. A knee-length peacoat covers endless curves in a storm that passes me with her luggage in tow.

"Puff."

"Don't call me that! You lost the right to."

I lengthen my stride to follow her down the empty corridor and into the lift before the doors close. Madison shifts to the back of the car to make space for a couple with two children. One is in a pushchair that faces the metal doors holding Madison's distorted reflection. The other is a toddler in corduroy, wiggling in a man's arms and staring straight at me.

Slobber coats the tiny fist attached to her mouth. Her chubby face scrunches in a fury I diffuse with a wink that earns me a toothless grin.

If only I had the same effect on the woman who refuses to acknowledge my presence.

I step out of the lift once it reaches the foyer and nod my goodbye to the family. Madison brushes past me with a high chin, her magnolia scent taunting my nostrils.

The Ravine isn't a property I frequent, but it has simple luxuries that make for the perfect holiday in the valley. Windows extend up to exposed beams on the ceiling, revealing a mountain backdrop. Each of our resorts has its own unique flavor. This one reflects a taste of the outdoors with the warmth of luxury in a palette of taupe, gray, and cream.

Being unplugged and thousands of miles away from London elicits a peace I haven't felt since I met the woman who's weaving through guests shuffling across wide plank flooring. Madison reaches Reagan, a front desk attendee, who accepts her room key with a smile that dissolves when she sees me. My headshake is subtle enough for her to continue checkout. Only a few people here know I own the Donnelley Brand. I'd like to keep it that way.

"How was everything?" Reagan asks Madison.

"Beautiful. I enjoyed the amenities," she responds.

Satisfaction purses my mouth at Madison's praise for my resort. I pride myself on curating a memorable experience for my guests.

Reagan types away on the computer. "We're glad to hear that, Ms. Monroe." Her eyes shift to mine, then drop back to the screen. "We have you on the one o'clock shuttle back to Denver. Feel free to dine in one of our restaurants or partake in a spa service until then. You'll receive a text twenty minutes before the sprinter arrives."

"Is there anything leaving sooner? I'd rather not stick around if possible." Madison directs her comment to me over her shoulder.

The urgency in her voice draws Reagan's brows together. Her brown eyes trace over Madison's features, no doubt assessing why someone who enjoyed their stay would want to leave early.

I school my expression and tuck my hands into my pockets. My distance from Madison won't arouse suspicion that I'm the source of her discontent. I'm off to the side, but I'm still close enough to remind her I'm not going anywhere.

No one knew about my plan to show up at her door with the breakfast she ordered—or that I followed her downstairs to stop her from walking out of my life for a second time.

It's a battle to keep my shit together around her. It has been since that day in the museum, when she drew me into her orbit.

"One moment, please." Reagan searches for a solution she won't find. Singles' retreat activities ended last night. Guests are checking out today, putting our small fleet of sprinters to use.

"I'm sorry. All other shuttles are full," Reagan says. "Is there anything else I can help you with?"

"No. Thank you," Madison mumbles, angling herself away from me. I gave her space to sort out her itinerary, but I have no intention of leaving. Not until we talk.

An idea forms. Luck might just be on my side today.

With a nod goodbye, Madison heads off to the seating area across from three fireplaces. It's a cozy spot with bookcases but nothing else to entertain her for the next five hours. She resigns herself to an oversized chair near the mantel. The sooner she breaks free from the resort and my presence, the less she'll look like I ran over her cat and hit reverse.

But like I said, I'm not leaving her side until we talk.

"Reagan, are there any vehicles available to take off the premises?" I ask, my eyes never leaving Madison.

"There's a town car near maintenance," she says. "I'll have one of the staff bring it out front."

"Not necessary. I'll retrieve it myself, thank you. Please inform Ms. Monroe that you secured a personal escort to the airport, courtesy of the hotel."

"Yes, Mr. Donnelley." Reagan hesitates. "Should I call someone to take her?"

My smile widens. "I'll handle it. And let's keep this between us, okay?"

Chapter 6

Madison

I must have pissed off someone in the afterlife if fate is resuscitating another ex on this trip. Not just any ex. *The* ex.

My thoughts race in a million directions at the blurred lines between memory and reality. I never forgot a single detail about Preston, and I will never unsee his hard, determined face when I opened the door.

He rendered me speechless, standing in his full glory, demanding my breath and all my words. I played out this scenario in my head thousands of times. What I would say to the man who discarded me like an out-of-season sweater faster than he could say "I love you." Yet when I had the chance to unload years of hurt and frustration, I froze.

Hearing "Puff" after all this time damn near knocked me through the basement. It's the nickname he'd whisper in my ear in his embrace. I relished in the way he held me, with so much love and affection. The embers are still there, stoking a growing fire behind his stare. It was a struggle to fight against the spell that drew me to him and the tears I refused to let fall, but I did it. The slap wasn't intentional, but I won't say it didn't feel good after the way he kicked me out of his life.

The travel magazine I'm haphazardly scanning while pretending I'm okay crinkles on a page flip. Nothing has calmed my nerves; my knee is still bouncing in an erratic rhythm. How can I relax when the phantasm who's tormented me for the last fifteen years is only feet away?

Preston leans against the concierge counter, too casual for someone who's just waltzed into my life and tossed it on its head. Reagan beams up at him with wide eyes and a smile stretching across her round face. Her long, blonde ponytail shakes as she nods enthusiastically at whatever he's saying. She's grinning at every refined tooth in his mouth.

The man is still as fine as the day we met. Here I am, battling the occasional gray hair between my thighs, and he's swaggering around like Mariano Di Vaio's melanated older brother. It's not fair.

Reagan picks up the phone as Preston rises to his full height. Our eyes connect before he's down the hall, taking with him the woodsy musk assaulting my nose from yards away. The athletic ass I've bit and gripped without shame teases me from a growing distance.

Time to get out of here.

This retreat is testing the remnants of my sanity. I'd walk to the airport if Denver wasn't three hours away by car. These boots would barely survive a stroll around the resort, much less a trek through the snow-covered valley. If my pride doesn't take me out, the temperature will.

I sigh at an incoming text and reach for my suitcase. My rideshare, per the app, won't arrive for another three hours. So much for Plan B.

Exactly how I'll kill the time remains a mystery. Food is an option since I left mine in the room.

Speaking of breakfast, how did Preston get my order?

Jazz filters through the lobby in soft waves. A trio entertains a gathering crowd near the entrance with their piano, saxophone, and bass. The gentle melody reawakens the holiday spirit that's reflected in the garlands and wreaths still adorning the resort.

It's a deceptive beauty, like the man who once lulled me with promises he broke along with my heart.

"Excuse me, Ms. Monroe?" From behind the wooden desk, Reagan motions for me with her hand. "Good news. We have a car to take you to the airport."

"That's wonderful!" I say, too excited to leave this resort and never look back.

"It's our pleasure. It should arrive shortly, if you want to make your way to the entrance."

"Thank you, Reagan. I appreciate it."

I walk with a renewed pep in my step to the heated area between the foyer and the entrance. A black town car pulls up the circular driveway after a sprinter drives off. No one else is outside or waiting for a ride. I pull my peacoat closed and head into a numbing wind.

The trunk opens before the driver's side door does.

A man in a hooded lumberjack shirt under a padded black vest steps out. His back is to me, a model of perfect posture and an even more perfect ass. A yellow beanie extends to the nape of his neck.

No men, remember?

It's harmless to appreciate natural beauty. Mountains. Glittering snow. A glorious butt wrapped in denim.

I smile at my rescuer, who's saving me from my own personal episode of *The Twilight Zone*.

It's short-lived, because he turns around, exposing his profile and that damn kissable jaw that's coated in five-o'clock shadow.

"Not happening."

"Come on, Puff," Preston says to my back as he rushes around the car.

"Why are you here?" It wouldn't surprise me if Reagan comped his stay and filled his tank with gas. Preston is both charming and a bastard.

"I'll answer everything in the car." I dodge his attempt to grab my arm. "Madison!"

I still at the sound of my name. It's the first time he's said it and not "Heather." I became "Puff" and dreamed of how "Madison" would sound spilling from his lips.

Preston's breath traces the air. His voice is low. "Let me take you. Please." He reaches for me again. "We owe it to who we were to talk, even if it's only to say goodbye."

Goodbye.

I'm catapulted back to the day everything changed. Our last goodbye ended in heartbreak and my humiliation. I begged Preston to listen, to give the love we grew a chance. Now he expects us to talk fifteen years later?

"Go to Hell," I say through chattering teeth. My desire for any discussion died with the part of me who believed in love's ability to conquer all.

I pull my arm out of the comfort of his grasp. I'll stare at a wall for five hours before I get into a car with him.

A grin plays across his lips, triggering his dimples and activating my annoyance. He's too fine for his own good.

"Funny. I didn't take you for a quitter." A glint of humor crinkles his eyes at the same words I offered him in a challenge years ago.

Bastard.

Chapter 7

Madison

Fifteen Years Ago

"**A**re you going to stare at the building all day or go in?"

For someone so arrogant, he sure is scared to cross the street.

Preston tosses me a glare before studying our dinner destination. "There's a perfectly good restaurant three streets over that won't give us food poisoning," he says with a sigh.

"You said I could pick where we eat. I choose this."

"*This* hardly counts as a place to eat." He frowns at the facade of stone and glass framed in steel.

"Funny, I didn't take you for a quitter." My snort morphs into a laugh when he reaches for me. His fingers graze a belt loop on my boyfriend jeans, but he isn't fast enough. I dash across Rue de Compiègne and squeal when I'm lifted into the air. Arms wrap around me, pinning my back to a suited chest. The hold isn't vulgar but still entices curious glances from people questioning what is wrong with us.

"I don't quit." Preston's tone is stern but doesn't match the smile coating his mouth. He pecks me on the forehead and steadies my wedge-wrapped feet on the curb. "You made me chase you for another dinner date. I'm always up for a challenge, love."

It's true, he had to work for date number two. Technically, the first date was out of my need to save money, but that's semantics.

Preston surprised me that night. It's clear he comes from money, but unlike the rich people I know, he doesn't flaunt it. He was the perfect gentleman. Kind, attentive, and interested in more than my body. After our meal, his driver took us to my apartment, where we said goodnight. He never pushed to come upstairs. Instead, he sent me on my way with a kiss to my cheek and waited until I turned on the light in my bedroom before leaving.

That was months ago—two, to be exact. We've emailed here and there, but Preston being away on business makes it impossible for our schedules to sync. Not that I waited around. He works long hours, and he isn't rushing whatever this is. I refuse to spend my time waiting around to hear from him. He puts work first, so why shouldn't I?

My internship hasn't started yet, but I swore to myself this wouldn't be more than a fling. Yet a friendship is forming, the connection between us building by the day.

I didn't play too hard to get, but I showed Preston he'd have to work for my time. Tonight's date comes four days after our last. He said he missed me and didn't want another long stretch to pass before we saw each other.

"Don't chicken out," I tease.

"That's to be determined." His thumbs brush the small of my back. Silence holds his stare.

"What?" I search for what he isn't saying.

"Nothing." He pecks my lips. "Come on, Heather."

We've only shared pieces of ourselves thus far, cautious glimpses of who we are below the surface. Preston is conservative with the details about his life and career. The cards he keeps close to his chest tip just enough to reveal that he works for his family's real estate business in London, which explains his lack of a French accent. It's clear he comes from money. The fashion brands adorning his body speak for themselves.

Pretending to be Heather keeps boundaries in place. Without them, space opens for feelings and the inevitable mess that comes with relationships. I changed a few details, but the lie flows easily. My friends at Bodie, if you can call them that, assume I'm the type to blow through money the way they do, without a care. To them, I'm Madison Monroe, a debutante from southern wealth who knows fashion, not someone who grew up near Bayou Teche surrounded by swamps and cypress trees.

I like Preston, but I can't afford to show him more than the pieces of myself I do. Wine, dine, and sex is all I'll entertain until it's time to leave Paris. We've yet to do the last, which keeps intimacy off the table for now. So, I place my hand in his and allow him to lead us through the door of McDonald's.

It's not the most impressive choice in a city with world-renowned restaurants, but I wanted a taste of home. Tammi thought I lost my mind pushing for a date under the golden arches, but why not? I'm curious how American fast-food chains fare abroad.

The interior is surprisingly clean, to the point I do a double take to make sure we're in the right place. Ivory tiled floors fill the front room, which showcases classic American staples in the newly installed café. We peruse macaroons and assorted pastries before doubling back to order dinner.

The horror on Preston's face when we receive our food deserves a photo next to the employee of the month. Our fries—*frites* as they call them here—touch the paper sheet on our tray, and he inspects his burger in its cardboard container.

"First time?" I giggle and sink my teeth into my cheeseburger.

A groan escapes me. I get so lost in flashbacks of praying the ice cream machine worked the few times we went to our local McDonald's that I almost miss Preston scarfing down the last few bites of his Royal Cheese. Littered trash and crumpled napkins are the only evidence of the once-pristine tray.

Someone's hungry.

"Not the worst, right?" I bite my lip to hide a smirk.

He tosses the last of his fries into his mouth and nods. "We'll find out tomorrow," he snickers. "This is my first meal of the day."

"*Preston.*"

He lifts his hands. "I know. Time escaped me. I head out again soon."

"You just got back," I say around a frown and a sip of my milkshake.

His sigh is as heavy as the dark circles that line his eyes. He's too young to be this stressed. "Trust me, I know."

Preston agreed to take things slow, with no expectations. But moments like this—when he's vulnerable over fast food—seep beyond any barrier we've kept in place.

Our fingers interlace when he reaches for my hand, the touch spreading through my skin like warm honey. A warning bell chimes; we're getting too close.

"When do you leave?"

"Later tonight," he says.

It shouldn't bother me that I won't see him for another couple of weeks, but it does.

"Shouldn't you be packing or something?"

Two dimples appear through a smile. "I wanted to see you. I always want to see you."

Chapter 8

Preston

Now

Driving Madison to the airport seemed like a good idea until I took the car off the property. Dual citizenship grants me an American license, which humbles me the moment I put the car in drive. It's been years since I've been behind the wheel, much less on the right-hand side of the road. A few trips around the maintenance building and a YouTube video later, I was ready to go.

That hasn't stopped my nerves from hovering above the floor next to my nuts.

I don't get anxious, but I've been scratching the same spot on my cheek since I drove the four-door sedan up to the entrance of The Ravine. I've dreamed of the day I'd see Madison again. Now that it's here, I'm doing a shit job of keeping it together.

The steering wheel groans under my grip. I expel a long breath, careful not to swerve us off the road as I steal another glance at her. I'm under no delusions she's in the car for anything more than a swift exit out of Colorado. I'm merely a means to an end. A despised chauffeur offering passage in scratchy bucket seats with subpar heating.

Madison hasn't looked my way in the two hours and eight minutes we've been on the road. The heat emanating from her body threatens to fog every window.

Her attention is outside, somewhere beyond the snowcapped pines that speed past the guardrail. The glare reflecting in the glass holds every feature I want to relearn by heart.

Long lashes sweep across her cheekbones when she faces forward. The wavy strands that once graced my pillow pull my eyes off the road. William would laugh in my face if he could see me right now. My brother calls me unforgiving in the boardroom, and he's seen firsthand how ruthless I get. Negotiating and capital allocation require a level of tenacity passed through our DNA. He doesn't know about Madison and would question why I'm so rattled.

Until her, no one *could* rattle me.

The slopes of her curves drew me to her in the museum. But it was the fire crackling under her beauty smoothed in pecan, the fire that had her seconds from cussing me out, that had me hooked. My attraction is undeniable, but lust gave way to intrigue. It was in her heart where I found peace and my counterpart in her intellect.

How do I start a conversation fifteen years too late?

"I'm sorry, Puff."

The road bends through dead air, the scent of aged leather and cigarettes mixed with magnolia. Sunlight casts itself over a mountain range. London winters get cold, but not below freezing like this.

Heat sputters through the vents to paint the edges of the frosted windows.

"I don't know what twisted game you think you're playing, but I am not the one." The force of Madison's words presses into my chest. "I won't let you hurt me again. I won't let anyone," she says, so low I almost miss it. Her chin trembles as she lifts it in spite. There's nowhere to stop and hold her, not that she'd let me. But I'd endure every scream and bruise if it meant erasing the anguish on her face.

She bites her lip and looks out the window. "Why now? After all this time."

A world of apologies won't fit in the time we have left before we reach the airport. It takes superhuman strength not to reach for her hand. "I needed time away, and I chose the property that was farthest from my life. No one would search for me here."

Madison whips around, shock and confusion urging her brow to her hairline. "You want me to believe you didn't orchestrate this?" She scoffs. "*Property*." The word is sharp across her tongue. "You own The Ravine?"

I nod.

She shakes her head and rolls her eyes. "Real estate." Every glimpse I gave Madison of my career plays out in her gaze. "I take it you own more than one hotel?"

"Six in this country," I say.

"Here I thought you were a realtor or something. Guess we both kept secrets."

It was clear early on that Madison wanted me for me. It wasn't my intention to withhold who I was, but we fell into each other's lives faster than either of us expected, and we proceeded with caution in different ways. I see that now. But I couldn't see it before, and it drove her away. Hindsight is a rearview mirror of regret, and you can't make things right once time runs out.

"I never had the chance to explain. I should've—"

"We're not doing this," she snaps, unable to meet my eyes. "It wouldn't have mattered what I said. You were crystal clear that night. Let it rest, Preston."

"I searched for you," I say, my confession thick with emotion. "Letting you go ate me alive. I saw you everywhere—in every bakery window I passed, in every sunset."

I should've done more. Hired a private investigator or flew to the States to look for her myself. Back then, the internet wasn't what it is today. Any attempt to locate the woman I loved became an impossible search, especially since she was living under a different identity.

My father will never admit the wedge he created when I tried to find her. I don't need him to, because I lived it. Silence was his only response when I begged him for help. The university wouldn't release her information. Even with all the money I had, I couldn't pay for the answers I needed.

"I gave up in my thirties," I admit. "Business left me no time, and I assumed you'd moved on. My life became in service to the company that's been the Donnelley crown jewel since my great-grandfather founded it."

All those lengthy business trips to every part of the world but the US weren't a coincidence. Sixty-hour workweeks exhausted me, along with the remnants of confidence I had that we'd eventually reunite. Once thirty-five hit, I assumed the role of CEO, and that came with more responsibilities to shoulder.

Women and sleepless nights numbed the loss, but only for so long. You never forget your first love.

The exit for the airport appears. I pull the car up to the curb.

"Madison."

"Preston, please. Pop the trunk." The door opens, and her boots are on concrete before I get the chance to ask her to stay.

I hit the button for the boot and twist out from the front seat. Madison hauls her luggage out of the boot and steps onto the pavement, headed toward the entrance.

"Wait." I reach for her. Adrenaline shoots through my veins, quickening my pulse to a beat that might land me in the hospital. I don't miss the flicker in her eyes, the hint of longing in her gaze that she extinguishes with a blink.

Time withers in a blur of travelers and the hazard lights of idling cars. The thought that she will be the one to walk out of my life this time has my hands stretching out to cup her face. I close my eyes and bow my head to trade the memory of her scent for the possibility of a new beginning.

With one final look, she peels herself away from me. Her hands clutch the collar of her open peacoat as she steps back to put distance between us. "We had our chance. Let's leave it where it belongs: in the past." She falls in step with a small crowd and disappears into the airport.

I stand on the curb until security yells at me to move. Finding the piece of my heart I lost is a gift I won't take for granted.

"See you soon, Puff."

Chapter 9
Madison

My boots skid across polished floors. On a scale of a light jog and qualifying for the Summer Olympics, I power walked away from Preston to keep from summoning wandering eyes or airport security. It's a battle to suck in these jagged breaths.

He was so close I thought he'd kiss me. And, like a damn fool, I would've let him.

The tic in his jaw and his eyes blazing down to mine lifted every hair on the back of my neck. He made no attempt to hide the fact that he wants me, and if I wasn't so strong, I'd have folded like a pretzel in the middle of the sidewalk.

Through a shudder, my breasts tingled against the fabric of my blouse. The mint in his breath mixed with the cold air skated across my cheeks and down to my lips. His gaze implored me to stay, and his mouth inched closer to seal itself with mine.

Every memory of the months we shared thawed until the reminder of how he left me shouted with flashing lights.

Preston might think our reunion means we owe it to each other to see where things go, but I know better. This isn't some rom-com where a bouncy musical number plays while we kiss to the applause of random strangers who believe in happily ever afters. This is real life. The sequel is rarely better than the original, and I won't chance finding out if that's true for us.

I make my way to a customer service agent and resist the urge to steal another peek at the man from my past who made an unwanted cameo in my present. Bad things happen when you don't heed the signs. Preston's presence raises too many questions.

"Of course he owns the hotel," I mumble to myself as I search my purse for my wallet.

"I'm sorry, miss?" The agent studies me with a look that asks why I'm talking to myself.

"Hi," I say with a half smile and approach the counter. "My flight to New York leaves in a few hours. I'd like to get on an earlier one if possible."

If Preston is still outside, there's no stopping him or his charm from suffocating this entire airport. He's already suffocating as it is. Those model qualities he inherited aged like wine.

You wouldn't.

Lingering around this airport might get me two federal cases: one for indecent exposure, and the other for murder.

"We have a flight to JFK in forty—"

"Yes!" I mistakenly toss her my library card along with my driver's license. *Keep your mind on his sins and not the sanctuary between his legs.* "I'll take it, thank you."

"Aht! Play where it's safe, Regine!" Kojo's *Living Single* nickname hits me as he swats my hand away with metal chopsticks I now regret buying.

It's rare for him to get mad, which would make his hostile glare funny if my knuckles weren't on fire.

"Dramatic much? It's one bite. Please?" I chuckle at his glower and ease back to my side of the sofa with a wound in tow.

"Unless we're swapping bodily fluids, you know better than to play on my plate. I told you to order your own, and did you listen? Consider this your consequence."

Kojo moves in slow motion, taking his time in lifting the food he refuses to share to his mouth. His tongue peeks out right before his lips wrap around cooked dough. The sharp blades of his hazelnut cheekbones dance in recessed lighting with each exaggerated chew.

He knows he looks good in all his Kofi Siriboe glory. No one is immune to his aura. I, too, would fall victim to that buttery smile if I didn't consider him my brother...or a prick in cashmere at the moment.

He has one more time to fondle his fried chicken and waffles dumpling before I kick him out.

The tease left Atlanta in advance of fashion week. In a few weeks, New York will come to life with couture and innovation. My friend will be a part of that magic with a show for Rustin, his fashion label. After a set design walk-through, he swung by my place with takeout from my favorite Taiwanese spot in the East Village.

I guess I'll play nice since Kojo brought me dumplings and hired me as a stylist for his show. He doesn't need one, but we've been working together since life connected our paths in France years ago.

"Weren't you supposed to get in later tonight?" Kojo toes off the black house slippers I keep for his visits and tucks his feet under himself.

"Changed flights," I confess to the perfectly waxed brow that's now lifted at me. "Did I interrupt one of your dates?" The flavors of my pork and chive dumplings skip across my taste buds.

He shakes his head. "You have me for three more hours. How was your trip?"

I shrug off the inquiry and reach for my wine on the mirrored tray that rests atop the velvet ottoman.

My apartment is a haven of peace in shades of emerald. I fell in love with it years ago and pulled all my money together to afford the five-thousand-a-month rent. A one-bedroom unit is more than enough for me. It gets tight when my niece stays here instead of her dorm where she belongs, but I can't picture myself living anywhere else.

I have wall-to-wall views of Hell's Kitchen, an in-unit washer and dryer, and a parking space I never use. The building underwent a major renovation, and now it has all the amenities I need to save on unnecessary memberships, like the gym.

Every picture frame and decorative accent in my home tells the story of where I've been. I've come a long way since Breaux Bridge.

"I believe I asked you a question."

"It was fine," I say, my focus still on the Bordeaux in front of me.

Kojo frowns. "What aren't you telling me, Regine? I told you to leave the snow alone. Y'all have winter here. Running over there like Elsa thinking the cold wouldn't bother you was a choice."

"The snow was fine. I stayed indoors," I say.

"Lemme guess, the pool of single people had piss in it?"

Kojo will always find a reason to laugh, even at my expense. He questioned why I'd fly to the middle of the country to meet men when I could swipe right here in Manhattan. He doesn't get it, not that I'd expect him to. Kojo only cares about the legs he's between. Nothing long-term or serious. I've had casual hookups, but I want more than a warm body on a cold night.

I want pursuit. Devotion.

"My ex was there." The words somersault and don't stick their landing. I gulp the rest of my wine in one go and ignore Kojo's shocked look.

It takes a second for what I said to register. Then Kojo's jaw drops to the vintage rug I found at a sample sale. "Who was it? Don't skimp on the good parts!"

I contemplate telling him about Terrence but think twice. He's not the ex who taunts me in my dreams, and I don't need Kojo's questionable influence encouraging me to reconsider a problematic crush.

Kojo doesn't condone cheating, but he's found himself in a few complicated situations, love triangles included. His advice would be to proposition Terrence and Justice to open up their marriage and let me slide in. If Tammi is the angel on my shoulder, Kojo is the devil dressed in high fashion.

There's also the tiny problem that he's friends with Emma.

He'd have a hard time explaining to Justice's best friend why he encouraged me to pursue her husband. The thought alone would implode any semblance of a relationship between them. Emma isn't as close to Kojo as I am, but she's still someone he considers a good friend. The lingerie company she works for is providing pieces for his fashion show. She already wants my head on a spike for how I treated Justice, and I won't let my mess bleed onto him.

"Now is not the time for internal monologues, Regine." Kojo snaps his fingers to get my attention. "Back to your ex. It better not be Barnabus and his scandalous ass."

"Bradley," I snort.

"Whoever." He waves a hand before reaching for his drink. "The ex."

"It's Preston."

"*Preston*? Please tell me he's not a boat-shoe-wearing elder who takes his teeth out and needs his butt wiped. You know I don't mind an age gap, but I draw the line at Dick Van Dyke."

"Kojo!" I howl at the plea in his eyes. Like he doesn't fawn over Jeff Goldblum. "Preston is in his early forties."

"Oh, thank God," he says through a long sigh. "I thought your business was struggling and you needed life insurance."

"Never that."

He recrosses his legs and sits back, more relaxed now that he knows I'm not dating anyone sixty years my senior. His eyes close. "Paint the picture for me."

"Over six feet tall. Dark hair. Warm honey skin. In shape but not bulky. Dimples."

"Ooh. Elis had dimples." Kojo licks his lips. "Who does he look like?"

A nightmare wrapped in a fantasy.

I sigh. "Mariano Di Vaio but with melanin. His mother was Black Sicilian."

Preston was a newborn when she died. Black women have the highest maternal mortality rate in the country, an unnecessary fate too many mothers experience, including his. Doctors mistook her discomfort as common pregnancy symptoms, but it turned out to be sepsis. Antonia Parisi took her last breath hours after giving birth. She died alone, her pleas for anyone to listen to her falling on deaf ears.

That's the only story I know about Preston's childhood. He never spoke about his father—only his maternal grandmother and a brother who was in school.

"He sounds fine."

"He is," I confess.

"So what's the problem?"

I grab the empty takeout containers on my way to the kitchen. "It's a long story."

"I have time before I go between Demi's legs for dessert." His hip check is a signal to move so he can do the dishes.

My kitchen isn't the smallest, but it doesn't fit multiple people in it at once. I slide over to one of the brass barstools, my feet lazily swinging in slouch socks. I enjoy dressing up to go out. But once

I'm in, I'm all about comfortable loungewear. The oversized flannel shirt I'm wearing is quite comfy, thank you very much.

"So?" Kojo places the glass he washed on the drying rack.

"So. You already helped me mend a broken heart from him once. I'd rather not go down that path again."

His face twists. "When did I do that?"

"Fifteen years ago," I say. "In Paris."

The steady flow from the kitchen faucet is the only sound in the room. Memories surge, taking me back to the night I ran away from a man who tore me down with his words and a look I'll never forget. It was the same night I met Kojo, who was putting on a makeshift fashion show in front of the venue I rushed out of like Cinderella minutes before midnight.

His face held the same look then as it does now. Drawn brows. Pursed lips. Eyes sweeping over me for injuries. He wipes his hands on his black chinos and reaches me in two steps for a hug.

Kojo and I spent most of that evening walking, the threads of our friendship reaching out to bind us together. I never mentioned Preston's name, but I told him everything. In hindsight, disclosing so much of myself to a complete stranger in the middle of the night in a foreign country was wild. But that's me and Kojo. We're platonic kindreds who fit together effortlessly. Little did I know, he also attended Bodie and was in France for an internship he'd gotten through a fashion connection.

He was my rock those last few months in a foreign city. He helped mend me back to life in ways I'll never be able to repay. I've cried myself to sleep too many times reliving the love Preston and I had before it crashed and burned. I'm not doing it again.

"What do you need from me?" Kojo brushes my hair from my cheek and presses a kiss to it.

"I'll be okay. Seeing him again threw me for a loop, you know? He just showed up to my room with the breakfast I ordered like it was nothing."

"How was he there with that basic toast and jam you call a meal?" We chuckle.

"Leave my food alone since you won't share yours." I push him away with a laugh that stretches into a sigh. "On the way to the airport—"

"You shared a ride?" Kojo presses a hand to his chest and gasps. I meet his gaze and burst out laughing.

None of this is funny, but how can I keep a straight face when he's staring like Durand Bernarr in front of a camera?

I wipe tears out of my eyes. "It was the only way to get home. He got a car and drove me to the airport himself."

"Aww—oop!" Kojo catches the compliment he was about to give and tosses it over his shoulder. "Nothing wrong with a ride, and a free one at that. How did he end up at the same hotel? Was he there for the retreat?"

"No," I say. "It's the wildest thing. He owns the resort and just so happened to be there on vacation. This man *owns* several hotels here and abroad. Why are you looking at me like that?"

Kojo scurries over to his coat, which is draped on a living room chair. "What's his last name?"

"Donnelley." Why does it matter?

He's back at my side with his face glued to his phone. Identical brows plummet, and a finger zips across the screen.

"What are you doing?"

"The hotel I'm staying at is a Donnelley Brand."

"*Okay*. He has money. So what?"

Wealthy men never impressed me. Their hearts are usually stone, and they treat anyone they deem beneath them like shit. That's one of the things that attracted me to Preston. He was different...until he proved to be the same as the rest.

"Regine!"

"What?!" I jump at his shout. He scared the shit out of me.

There's only one other time I've seen Kojo look like this, somewhere between excitement and death. We were in the same room as André Leon Talley—may he rest in peace—and I had to catch this fool after he touched the hem of his garment. Kojo is Preston's height. Silk is slippery, and we almost ended up on the floor.

Now his eyes lift with a world of questions.

"Is this him?"

"Yes," I say to the photo of Preston in a tux at some event. Fabric does look good on him.

"He doesn't just own a few hotels. The Donnelley Brand is worth billions. You've been with a billionaire and didn't know?! *Girl!*"

"What?" I snatch the phone. Sure enough, there's an article that reports his family to be worth over three billion.

No wonder he was so tight-lipped. A billion is a lot of zeroes, and he has three! Well, his family does.

This can't be the same man who inhaled McDonald's burgers and watched '90s movies with me when his schedule allowed. I never thought I'd meet a billionaire, but it turns out I loved one.

I need another drink.

Chapter 10

Preston

"**I**s there anything else I can get you, Mr. Donnelley?" a silky voice calls from the doorway.

"That will be all, thank you." I don't bother glancing up from my screen.

Heels click across weathered oak, signaling Stephanie's departure. She's a phenomenal executive assistant...when she's not sending subliminal messages involving my dick.

"Please tell me you tried it," William says from the door that should be closed. My idiot brother leans back with his lip between his teeth. "What a woman."

Stephanie is brilliant, overqualified for her position, if you ask me. She graduated top of her class with an MBA and isn't hard on the eyes. She's peng, as we say here, but her slim figure and large bust are what have my brother in a chokehold. I've always gravitated more toward wide hips and thighs.

The ample curves I've anchored to the bed with steady thrusts pulls my attention back to the computer. A smile ghosts the seams of her full, red-stained lips. Her stare is practiced, like it's second nature to pose for photographers, rivaling the best supermodels. Cinnamon brown hair flows over her shoulder in thick waves above the silhouette of voluptuous breasts. The dress that caresses her body has my erection straining against my trousers.

I've been hard all morning, searching for every glimpse into Madison's life I can find between a lineup of meetings. It's become a ritual in the weeks since I drove her to the airport. Time is rarely on my side, and that's made any attempt to get to New York a failed effort. But following her digital footprint requires no passport.

I have so many tabs open, it's a miracle my laptop still functions. Photos of her online, her social media, and the files my private investigator sent consume the screen. Three weeks is nowhere near enough time to catch up on the years I've missed. I need to know everything about her.

Madison found her footing as a stylist. It's been her dream since we met, and she's living it on her terms. I grin at her success, which is cataloged through these photos. She did it.

"Bruv, are you listening? You're missing out."

This again.

I massage the bridge of my nose to wish my brother away. "Give it a rest, William."

"She's proper peng," he says about Stephanie.

"Need I remind you of the no-fraternization policy?" My warning provokes the smirk he inherited from our father.

Between the two of them and our grandfather, generations have violated that policy without consequence. Our family name demands power, and that unlocks consenting legs.

I've fucked plenty in my office, but never an employee. Sex in the workplace gets messy, especially if there's an uneven power dynamic, which is always the case when a Donnelley is involved.

"The holiday was supposed to remove the stick from your ass. You've been a mope since you got back."

"I don't let sex dictate my life. That's the difference between you and me," I counter.

I was William twenty years ago. An entitled little shit with a degree, access to a trust fund, and the rest of my youth to fuck my way through. I never remembered names or faces and sidestepped commitments. Until I laid eyes on a woman who changed the beat of my heart.

Madison altered something in me. At twenty-six, with the promise of more power at my fingertips, I saw a different path with the woman who reveled in high fashion but enjoyed strolls around our neighborhood before sunset. She might've pretended to be someone else, but there was no faking the lighthearted laughs that filled our living room and the blinding smile I'd get when I put work away to focus on us.

The future we were creating rivaled any title or recognition I'd gain by stepping into my father's shoes.

When Madison left, she took with her my ability to care. I leaned into the bachelor life and fucked any woman in my path. I never made a public spectacle of my private life, never officially dated anyone out in the open. My brother and father lauded my conquests without realizing I was dead inside, missing the piece of my heart I allowed to break.

Once I became CEO, I reduced all sexual activities to a few women who'd maintain my privacy and not expect emotional attachment.

William crosses my office to stand next to the window that spans the length of the wall. This high up, I have a view of Westminster and the flat across the street I keep for convenience. It's clear out, with a mix of frost and light winds. Another cold day in London.

"Tell me you at least enjoyed Ravenous while you were there." My brother stuffs his hands into his gunmetal suit pockets and sighs. The accusing glance he casts is full of the disappointment he inherited from our father.

His pear-shaped jaw and steel blue eyes are the only physical markers of their shared genetics. William is his mother's child, and I'm mine.

My father married Briar less than a year after my mother died. They had William two years later. His sandy blond hair and teardrop face make him the spitting image of the woman who's loved our father faithfully despite his own disinterest in upholding his marriage vows.

Outside of the Donnelley name, the thick brows, and the semi-thin lips, I'm nothing like William or our father. I lack the proper English accent thanks to years of boarding school, and I wear my mother's features with pride. From the pictures Nonna showed me, she was a knockout. Thick hair framed the graceful lines of her face. My honey hue is a mix of my mother's caramel and Nonna's mahogany shades. Our wide cheekbones hold the same smile.

I was only hours old when she died. Every story Nonna shares implants memories I couldn't experience. But her spirit is alive in the culture my grandmother instills, from generations of Black Sicilians who've called the island home and asserted their place.

"Preston. I haven't seen you in weeks. What's gotten into you?"

I scrub a hand over my face. "It was exceptional," I say about Ravenous. There's no enthusiasm behind my tone, but it's not a lie.

Ravenous is my after-dark project. It won't be available at every Donnelley property, but it provides select guests a taste of pleasure away from prying eyes. It's not a full-fledged sex club, but it offers elements of exploration and voyeurism.

The Vail pop-up was exquisite. I chose our Colorado property because of the unsuspecting location. It was a last-minute decision, but we pulled it off with great success. Who knew my holiday would coincide with a singles' retreat or be the place where I found Madison?

The shows and demonstrations were everything I hoped for, a top-tier experience for our first go at a pop-up playspace. Guest concealed their identities behind masks and cloaks, which made it easy for me to slip in on the nights I went. I like to watch, and I enjoyed a few shows, including a personal performance with a dancer and her toys.

"That's what I'm talking about!" William's mouth twitches. "How was the action?"

I didn't sleep with anyone, a fact that disappoints him. My flight from London to Colorado was a different story. The flight attendant assigned to my family's jet kept my glass full and the head of my dick at the back of her throat.

"Don't you have work to do?"

"Oh, sod off." William dismisses me with a hand. "Like you've been productive, the way I caught you daydreaming. What's got your attention, anyway?"

"Nothing."

My corner office is far from small. The engineered gray oak flooring, black walls, and recessed ambient lighting reflect a transition from my over-the-top predecessor to a modern aesthetic. The seating areas around the room border my desk, which is stationed front and center. The sleek wood trimmed in gold is long enough to serve as a conference table for meetings, but it does a shit job of keeping my nosy brother at bay.

He rounds the corner before I have a chance to close the window with a hundred open tabs.

"Who. Is. That?"

William goes completely still. He shamelessly gapes at a photo of Madison resting on a lounger in a bikini. Her face is to the sky, her eyes closed, the sun kissing her smile.

"Madison," I say to her image.

William's whistle is low. "No wonder you've been glued to your computer. I'd be beating the—"

"Knock it off! Don't be a fucking ass." What gray hair I have is because of this prick. I love my brother, but he needs to learn when to shut the fuck up.

He lifts his hands and takes a cautious step back. "Apologies. I meant no disrespect." He tips his chin to the screen. "She's a looker."

"What now?" I sigh at whatever is about to come out of his mouth.

He hesitates with a bite to his lip. "You've always had a thing for '90s women. She looks like the one in that movie you made me watch, with the Terminator."

"*Eraser*."

He snaps his fingers. "That's the one. Looks just like her."

After primary school, I was off to a boarding school in Connecticut, two and a half hours from New York. My father agreed to let me stay in the States through secondary school under the condition that I attend an Ivy League university and dedicate six years to learning the business in France.

Maia Campbell.

Tatyana Ali.

Lisa Bonet.

I soaked up every Black American '90s sitcom and fell in love. It's one of the reasons Justice caught my eye at the singles' retreat. You can't tell me she isn't related to Tia and Tamera.

Does Madison favor Vanessa Williams from back in the day? Yeah, I'll give William that. But she's more than a replica; she's one of a kind.

"We met fifteen years ago, in Paris," I say to William, who plops himself into a chair in front of my desk.

His brows do their best to fight gravity. "And you saw her on holiday? Did you two keep in touch? I'm not following."

I tell Stephanie to hold my calls and fill him in. He was still in uni when I was in France. I kept my relationship with Madison away from outside influence. Everything was perfect until secrets we couldn't overcome surfaced.

"That's heavy, Pres. What's the move?"

I scrub a hand over the goatee I've let grow. "Get her back."

William cackles. "What are you waiting for?"

"I lost her once, and I'm not rushing anything. You'll see once I return."

I fly to Malaysia in two days. Then to Indonesia before a small stint in California to check on a project there. There's no time to go to New York. So, I'll do the next best thing, even if it might get me slapped.

Chapter 11

Madison

"Promise me no glitter. I mean it." I roll my eyes at the laughter from the other end of the phone.

"Auntie, I'm a whole adult now."

"And you're not too grown for me to go across that butt," I say, acting every bit like my mama. "Promise me you'll behave while I'm gone."

"I always do," Jewel promises. The lie of the century.

College kids being hungover, sleeping in late, and dealing with the aftermath of their questionable behavior aren't new. Jewel isn't my child, but she keeps my nerves in a cyclone with her activities. They don't involve a keg or partying, but they'll still land her in jail and me six feet under if my sister finds out.

"Where are you going?" I hold my breath and pray it's the library.

"There's an action near your place tomorrow," she says. "I'll water your plants and get the mail. If we're not arrested, some of us are going to Albany to demand leadership prioritize investments in climate protections in the executive budget."

"Jewel Avery!" I whisper-shout from my window seat. "Don't make me revoke your access to my apartment. I thought this was a sign-making get-together. No arrests!"

Is she trying to get her mother to hop on a plane and knock me out? I wouldn't hear the end of it, how I corrupted her daughter and led her down a path of anarchy and criminal conviction. Instead of a life full of "secular living and Jack Daniels," as she calls it, my oldest niece chose civil disobedience in the name of climate justice.

Jewel is no longer the chubby baby whose socks would cut off her circulation. She's a woman coming into her own. Her third year at Brooklyn University has been full of rallies and calls to action. The economics degree she's pursuing comes with a concentration in environmental justice. Jewel studies the socioeconomic disparities caused by the climate crisis and the need for a just transition framework.

She's a powerhouse at twenty, joining other climate activists across the five boroughs to fight for critical funding for the communities hit hardest by climate-related threats. She rallies here in the city and goes to the state capitol in Albany to advocate for divestment from the fossil fuel industry and support for a green economy.

It's not uncommon for Jewel to protest in front of polluters' buildings. Her targets are billionaires and financial institutions with track records of harmful investments that contribute to pollution, widespread floods, and wildfires.

She better stay on the public sidewalk and not end up in handcuffs.

"No arrests, I promise." Jewel's smirk is loud and clear.

"Good. Your mother wouldn't let me hear the end of it."

"You should call her."

"I will soon," I say to her gentle plea. Jewel is wise beyond her years, but the tension between me and her mother predates her existence.

For Dominique, Jewel choosing a school in New York was the final straw. My sister will never admit it, but she feels betrayed by her daughter. Jewel left. I did too. So, we navigate through our landmines of resentment and unspoken words whenever I happen to go back to Breaux Bridge. I wish we were closer, but I let too much time pass to fix what needs to be fixed.

"I have class in five. *Mo linm twa.*" I smile at Jewel's Creole and end the call.

No matter my schedule, I promised Dominique I'd look out for her. That includes keeping the language passed down through our family alive. It's rare for anyone to speak it these days, but we do our best to uphold Mawmaw's tradition.

I smile to no one but myself. The kids will be alright.

Jewel threatens a few heart attacks, but she's admirable. She has her mama's fire in her big brown eyes and matching curls. Dominique believes I turned Jewel against the small-town life that's waiting for her back home.

But how could I when my sister named her daughter after the first Black woman in the US to earn a PhD in political science?

Even when we were younger, Dominique went on and on about Dr. Jewel Prestage and her work to improve civic education in Louisiana schools. She was my sister's inspiration until life changed her trajectory. Married to her high school sweetheart right after graduation. Pregnant with Jewel, the first of four kids, six months later. A life of diapers between part-time work at her husband's family restaurant.

As Mawmaw used to say, make plans and watch God laugh. She was big on life callings. Jewel's takes her to protests. Dominique's is to make her house a home. Mine is currently en route to London for the next fashion week.

I rush a text to Kojo as the announcements hit the intercom.

See you in a couple of days!!

No doubt he's tangled up in a bedsheet. Expecting Kojo to answer before noon requires a miracle.

He stayed out to celebrate his fashion show here in the city, which became two more after-parties and a threesome. I know because he texted, "Three's company in this piece!" with a cat and eggplant emoji. When it comes to pleasure, my friend doesn't discriminate.

I'm heading to London early. One, I need a head start on scouting the area for a new client and to tackle a long to-do list before our wardrobe assessment. Two, I didn't want to dampen Kojo's after-party since Emma was in attendance. We'll figure out how to navigate each other's space with our mutual friend. For now, distance is the best answer. Another mess for another day.

When I open the internet app on my phone, cognac eyes I've tried to forget since I saw them up close stare back at me. They're calculated with the same power that pinned me to the carpet the day he showed up at my hotel room.

Fifteen years wasn't long enough to forget Preston.

My vagina throbbed an SOS at my name on his tongue. At this point, hypnosis is all that's left to erase him from my psyche.

Discovering he's a whole billionaire had me back down the rabbit hole. Kojo checked my temperature six times for memory loss. I knew my ex came from wealth, but I never connected the dots to the top one percent. I wore Kmart panties around that man.

Internet access was on a CD back in the day. There was no way free AOL hours would have revealed Preston's billion-dollar family. He said he was an apprentice when we were together, not a CEO. I assumed he was one of those trust fund kids who inherited some fancy position with a matching title.

Apparently, Preston has transformed the Donnelley Brand since his father stepped down. More properties are sprouting up underneath the banner, which doesn't explain why he came to Colorado, of all places. He's been on the other side of the world since we bumped into each other. His company's headquarters is in London, which is the only excuse I have for stalking his whereabouts.

I want to hate him—to keep him in my past—but it's impossible. Every article about him unlocks a new puzzle piece.

Pretending he doesn't exist is not an option when I'll be in his backyard. It's reason enough to keep my head on a swivel and prevent another run-in during my time in England. I'm betting on him staying away from the fashion scene. He's James Bond in a suit, but he avoids the spotlight.

With my phone in airplane mode and a vow to stop acting like I have an internship with the CIA, the plane reaches cruising altitude.

Leave Preston alone.

No more searches.

No more scratching curiosities.

London is for fashion week, and for my business. No men, and definitely no Preston.

Chapter 12

Madison

Fifteen Years Ago

"I think you're making a mistake."

"This view of the Eiffel Tower says otherwise." I bring the porcelain teacup to my lips for a cautious sip of Earl Grey tea. The citrus aroma blends with rising steam to scent the morning air. Drinking tea out on the balcony has become my favorite pastime.

"You're moving too fast," Tammi says.

"And you're wasting my minutes." I chuckle at her teeth kissing on the other end of the phone. "I told you the circumstances. I had a choice to make."

Heather failed to mention that the nine-month study abroad trip I inherited only came with three months of housing. She opted out of the dorms and never got around to booking a rental for the school year. Imagine my shock when the building owner told me I had forty-eight hours to vacate the premises. Another tenant had rented the unit for the remainder of the year, leaving me assed out in every sense of the word.

My so-called friend shrugged off my eviction with an "oops!" and that was that. The host university had no available rooms, and my savings account dared me to find the thousands of dollars I'd need to keep a roof over my head. Not to mention, the paid internship fell through, courtesy of Heather, who eventually stopped responding to my emails.

Preston flew back from a business trip to move me into his penthouse. "No" wasn't an answer. Neither was me leaving early. That was two weeks ago. Did I expect to be shacking up with a man who was only supposed to be a fling? No, but Tammi never misses the chance to scold me about it.

"Okay, Julia Roberts," she says. "Keep pretending to be *Pretty Woman* with a man you barely know. Preston could be out eating people whole while you're playing house."

Tea shoots through my nose at a cackle too undignified for this district. Between the luxury shops and the five-star hotels, she might be onto something.

"*What's your dream?*" Tammi mocks. I double over in laughter.

"Tam," I plead.

"Lemme guess. You're perched up in a fancy white hotel robe with your toes out and your hair down. Is Edward negotiating mergers?"

I shift in the lounger to tuck my bare feet under the thickest cotton to ever grace my skin.

"Hmm?"

"The robe isn't white. It's navy," I mumble.

The line goes quiet until we both bust out laughing.

"How are you not waking the dead with that donkey laugh?" I wipe the tears from my face.

"Bitch, everyone is asleep." Tammi snorts like what I said is offensive and not the truth.

"Excuse me, Ms. PK? What was that? Pastor Johnson didn't catch what you said."

"*Bitchhh*," she whispers.

If Tammi's dad is anything like mine, she has him wrapped around her finger—pulpit and all.

Tammi went back to her college before Labor Day. We had fun as roommates, and we email to stay in touch. She's one of the realest people I know, even if she jumps to conclusions all the way from Detroit.

My laughter fades through a sigh painted in frosted air. "You act like I had my bags packed and waiting by the door. Preston is in and out. We're—" What are we? "We aren't looking for anything serious."

Come spring, my time in Paris ends. I'll go home, and Preston will continue with whatever business has him working long hours between cities. Tammi can save her speech. Our chemistry is off the charts, but I know his type.

"Clearly not." Tammi's neck roll swivels through our six-hour time difference. "You're in his penthouse right now."

"With my own bedroom and private bath," I clarify.

"He still doesn't know your name! He's probably flying back and forth to his wife and kids—or his mistresses scattered across every major capital."

I grab my tea and head inside to an empty living area with fancy molding and Buckingham Palace floors. Every room comes with views of the district.

"Tam, I promise I'm okay. I like Preston, but I'm not some naïve girl who thinks meeting a handsome man—"

"Who might have a hidden family—"

"He doesn't." I laugh and sit on the sofa. Like clockwork, room service delivers fresh fruit with a pastry every morning. Today's is *pain au chocolat*. I hold the phone in the crook of my neck and dig in. "His family business keeps him on a plane, not a wife and kids."

"And where is he now?" Detective Johnson interrogates.

"London, I think."

"See!" she says, like she solved a game of Clue.

"No!" I mock her *aha!* tone. "We talk on the phone, and we email."

"Every day?"

"Just about," I say around a bite of flaky dough. "There are times he works late, but he always makes a point to check in. Stop looking for a scandal that isn't there, Tam. He's kind and considerate. Being with him is easy, but we have an expiration date. Simple as that."

"Maddie. I don't want to see you get hurt. Just...take care of yourself, okay? Getting so close so quickly could be a recipe for disaster, especially if you're not up-front about who you are." Tammi gentles her voice. We've only been friends for as long as I've known Preston, but we tell each other everything.

"I hear you," I say. "Put your books away and get some sleep."

She yawns. "Don't have to tell me twice. Same time in two weeks?"

"It's a date."

Tammi and I kicked off our junior year with jobs. She's interning at a financial services company to build her résumé. My part-time gig is less sexy. I tutor French students in English at the host university. The money is decent, and the hours are flexible. I don't have to rely on my credit card, and I earn spare change to buy international calling cards.

Preston offers to pay for whatever I need. Money is no object to him, but to me, it's freedom. I refuse to put myself in a situation where I have to rely on a man to take care of me. Staying in his penthouse already crosses that line.

Tam's words sit with me for the rest of the day. Am I in over my head? I've never lived with a man before. So far, it's good. There's no pressure to do anything I don't want to do—not that I see him all the time. We haven't had sex yet, which is an anomaly. We can't keep our hands or mouths off each other, but it never escalates to more.

Preston is affectionate with forehead kisses and hugs. We go out on dinner dates or strolls whenever he's here, and he still makes his presence known while he's away, sending the sweetest handwritten cards with his flowers.

Maybe Tammi is right. Maybe Preston has someone else who satisfies that physical part of him. I don't want to believe it, but if he pays for this penthouse, he can afford a harem.

We talk about our lives to a certain extent. Part of the reason I hold back is because he does. I can't be homeless *and* sprung.

I told myself not to jump into another relationship, and I won't with someone who lives overseas—even if he takes my breath away with a single look.

When our time together ends, I'll walk away.

No hard feelings.

No regrets.

Chapter 13
Madison

Now

Styling is an art I don't take lightly. It requires a certain finesse to assess trends, experiment with looks, and cement a personal brand. Fashion shows. Photo shoots. Red carpets. My résumé is photographed moments of time in unforgettable fabrics.

I've come a long way since I was a poor college student who chased after rich kids to touch up their closets. Celebrities and other high-profile clients now absorb my time, but I don't discriminate. If you can afford my fee, which includes travel and accommodations, I'm yours.

Wearing hard wigs that double as helmets.

Stepping out in clothes two sizes too big.

I translate personal brand through fashion. I am a source of answers. Right now, I've got nothing.

Designer labels extend from the polished floor of the temperature-controlled closet to the ceiling, which anchors not one but two crystal chandeliers. Everything is neatly in place, organized by season.

Why am I here?

When Bellamy reached out about my services, she made it sound like she needed help with her wardrobe. I won't turn down any work while I'm here, but I did a double take when I first walked into her London apartment and spotted a piece from last season's fashion week. It's casually hanging next to dresses from notable fashion houses.

Either she needs constant reassurance, or she tripped and hit her head on the heated tiles warming my toes. My lip sinks between my teeth as I catalog the forest of high-end clothes.

Vanilla mixed with spice wafts into this makeshift mini boutique. Bellamy stands in the entrance, a belted figure of slender hips tapered into long, straight legs. Her black body con dress settles against her narrow waist and jutting breasts.

I wouldn't call you a liar if you told me she just strutted off the runway. Her face is delicate, carved from high cheekbones and a prominent jawline. There are no blemishes. Only pouty lips and chestnut eyes that drag up my form for the second time today. Aside from the black patent leather heels I left in her foyer, I'm still in the same outfit she saw me in earlier: a chocolate brown crew neck top and vegan leather skirt.

Her gaze snags on mine, and a manicured brow lifts. I don't know what she's searching for, but I clear my throat. I'm attractive, but I'm not the damn Mona Lisa.

"Apologies," she says with a hint of an English accent. "Do you have everything you need?"

"Yes." I reach for my tablet on top of the chaise and scroll through her digital folder. "I have your style preferences. A look through your wardrobe helps with that. We did your color analysis, and I have your body measurements for the best silhouettes to complement your figure. We're in a good place for a styling session."

I'm so caught up logging my notes that I miss Bellamy unzip her dress. Black fabric pools over gold heels. It matches the lace thong resting on skin that has never fought cellulite a day in its life. Blood-red nails dig into the hip she juts out, activating the muscles of her toned thighs under a halo of light.

"Why wait?" A challenge brews in her tone, which she lowers along with her lashes. I assume she's eyeing the tablet clutched to my chest until the heat from her stare incinerates the glass and plastic. "You have a beautiful shape," she says to my breasts, concealed in the comfort of a padded bra.

"Thank you?" How else do I answer that?

"They look natural." Her jaw tightens. "How fortunate for you, to not need enhancements like the rest of us. I got mine redone a few years ago." Her fingertips trace the rings around her rosebud nipples, which are pointed at me like double barrels of a gun.

"That's nice." Does she expect me to praise her surgeon?

Aside from her own wardrobe, there are no clothes here for Bellamy to try on. So why is she showing her literal ass?

"We'll have fun." She tosses a smirk over her shoulder and spins, careful to step over her dress still on the floor. Her sashay is practiced choreography as she fastens a silk robe to her body. "I need new suits, evening gowns, and lingerie. When will you have them ready?"

"A few weeks. We can schedule a fitting," I say.

Bellamy's grin spreads. "Let's see what you got."

Chapter 14

Madison

"Please tell me you ate her pussy."

"Kojo!" I glance at the couple three seats away from us. The way the older woman smirks around her teacup proves she heard my loud-ass friend.

Motormouth leans against the low-backed booth with a dreamy grin. He's wearing a black dress shirt and pants. The diamond studs under his dreads, which are pulled back into a bun, wink in the light of the sconces on the back wall.

He separates a bite of ice cream and brings it to his mouth. "Don't knock it until you try it." The spoon breaches the pink flesh in slow motion. He swirls the ice cream in his mouth for good measure.

Freak.

"Unlike you, I don't sleep with clients." I sip my espresso.

"At least I'm not dropping dust from my thighs when I walk. It probably looks like the catacombs down there. Just dead and full of webs."

We fall over laughing.

Tears stream down my cheeks. "I hate you."

"Lies." He fans himself with a napkin. "Do your clients usually strip like that in front of you?"

"No. You know how it gets backstage or on set. Nudity isn't a big deal for me. It's the way she did it." I shake my head, replaying the look in Bellamy's eyes. They were cold. Calculated. "Her energy was predatory. I felt like she was sizing me up the entire consultation."

Kojo shrugs. "Maybe she was."

After Bellamy dropped her dress, I took a few notes and got the hell out. I appreciate beauty in all forms, but something didn't sit right. It's what was behind her eyes—a darkness tempting me to overlook it—that made me grateful for Kojo's call about lunch.

We're at this bistro in Notting Hill. It's a cute spot with coffered ceilings and stenciled wood floors. The all-day brunch and the fact that it's a stone's throw from the two-bedroom apartment we rented for the week made it a win-win.

"The next time Kendall Jenner wants to put on a show, call me." My laugh cuts off at his *you think I'm joking?* stare. "Anyways"—he rolls his neck—"since you're on a no-men diet, what are we doing for Valentine's Day?"

I frown. "Valentine's Day?"

"Yes, Valentine's Day," he mocks. "I want to be outside with my friend, and I have just the thing."

My sigh says I'm already over whatever he's about to pull out from his clutch.

"Now, before you try to act like the spirit of Cicely Tyson and stay indoors, take this." He slides over a black lacquered card.

"Ravenous?" I read the gold letters.

"The place to release your desires," Kojo says like one of those holograms in a sci-fi movie where everybody dies from a bad decision.

"Count me *out*," I chuckle. I'm not trying to catch a cramp or get caught up in some orgy. Pass.

"Come on, Maddie Baddie. It's safe."

I lift a brow. "Are you sure you didn't find this on the street?"

"No, prude." He laughs. "A friend who has a show this week passed it along. It's an exclusive event; they have one in London each year. No names. No faces. Consent waivers. The whole nine. I see you biting your lip. Let curiosity take care of that kitty cat. Come and watch, or cum from watching. Up to you."

"I don't know, Kojo," I say through a long breath. "I've never done anything like this."

"It's one night."

I *am* tired of my toys and fingers...

Dating and casual sex are in time-out. I'm serious about that. But is looking at the menu *that* bad if you don't order anything? There'd be no regrets—about empty carbs or men.

An echo of the past forces itself on our table. It was a similar café. The upholstery was navy instead of gray, and I was across from a man who showered me with sweet nothings. My heart skips at the pleasure that consumed me that night and each one after. Until he took my heart and broke it.

"Let me think about it," I say to cut off another thought about Preston.

They've been nonstop since I touched down days ago in London. It's an upstream swim against a tsunami to keep from wondering what he's doing, who he's seeing. A billionaire bachelor doesn't stay at home to reminisce about his ex.

Why do you care?

I don't. I'm simply curious.

"Let's swing by the store before we head back," I tell Kojo. "I want to cook tonight."

Valentine's Day this year is a special form of punishment. The holiday is usually hit-or-miss, between boxes of chocolate and super-sized stuffed animals. You're either a sucker for the gimmicks or you despise the commercial displays of affection and rain on everyone else's parade.

Celebrating has never been a big deal to me. I live out of my suitcase this time of year anyway, shuffling between clients and fashion shows in different cities. Any relationship, or lack thereof, doesn't dictate how I spend the day. I go out with friends, a romantic interest, or by myself.

I don't need a man to define my worth. I do just fine by myself, but I can admit I get lonely. Journaling while singing India Arie's "Ready for Love" has yet to manifest my match. I want to share my life with someone who isn't my best friend, niece, or the cat at the animal shelter I came dangerously close to taking home.

I already have one lonely pussy to care for. I don't need another.

Valentine's Day in London has given me no problems until now. Because you know what's worse than pretending you're okay with being in the same city as an ex you swear never crosses your mind? Pretending it doesn't stir the tiny part of you that's yearning to see him again. The part that still remembers the love we once shared, the love that's become a rubric for every man who will never measure up to what we had.

There was heartbreak, but there was also affection. Reverence.

Every forehead kiss, loving glance, and adoration he wrapped around "I love you" found a home in the heart I tried to conceal. I'll never forget, and that scares me.

The more I fought to forget Preston's beautiful face today, the more I saw it. He was everywhere. The server at brunch. A man walking his dog. I wasn't safe in the apartment Kojo and I are renting.

Wouldn't you know our host subscribes to a business magazine with Preston on the cover?

A trip to the spa to pamper my stress away didn't help, either. Neither did the mini shopping trip.

Any attempt to erase him is a lost cause, which is why I'm in my closet, choosing an outfit for tonight. He's still overseas. I double-check before sliding into a backless minidress and heading into the night. Kojo already had me sign my life away in waivers and rush an STI panel in case my "curious ass wants to feel a leather tongue."

Ravenous is a last-ditch effort. Maybe it's the distraction I need.

Chapter 15

Preston

Black sedans round the corner and stop at the designated entrance. Eldridge Court is our flagship hotel, and it's full of surprises. The car park is only accessible through a gated entrance. So is the destination for tonight's debauchery.

Guests exit their vehicles wearing the hooded black cloaks and masquerade masks we provided for the evening. Anonymity is the standard for all members who participate in our activities. Aristocrats, entertainers, and persons deemed the upper crust of society require an additional layer of privacy beyond our standard NDA. They enjoy the thrill of fulfilling their fantasies through hidden identities.

I switch cameras to the small crowd heading into the private lift that leads to a section of the hotel that's inaccessible to the public. My great-grandfather would turn in the family mausoleum if he knew about Ravenous. My father looks the other way—not that his opinion matters. His infidelities alone would draw twice as much press. He and the other board members will never step foot inside our primary location or any one of our pop-ups.

There's a knock at the door. William pops his head around it, his cloak already in place above his all-black suit. "Almost done?"

Unlike the offices in our Westminster building, my study in Eldridge Court is a model of tradition. Custom walnut paneling runs from the ceiling down to the bookcases. My father sat at this executive desk, as did his father, and his father before that.

I hate this room, but it's my office. Eldridge Court is a bitch to get to because of roadwork and endless congestion. If it were up to me, I'd let this place collect dust with the rest of the books and family heirlooms.

"Yeah." I check my watch and flip back to the underground car park feed. Madison's driver alerted me that he was pulling into the procession of town cars. As part of the experience, all attendees have the option of utilizing our car service to take them to and from the event. I personally organized Madison and her friend's evening, down to the masks.

A car rolls to a stop. The feed from the security camera isn't the sharpest, but the sliver of thigh that peeks out from underneath the cloak steals my breath. I have vivid memories of those thighs wrapped around my waist.

Black satin conceals the valley of her body from the world, but I relearned every dip and soft line when she stepped back into my life. The lace Venetian mask I chose rests above defined cheekbones to hide most of her face. The intricate crystal details will make it easier to spot her among the crowd. Only sixty people are in attendance tonight, a decision I made to keep the event intimate and any competition minimal.

I have no claim to Madison, but once she takes me back, she's mine.

"Bruv, are you gonna stare at screens all night or go get her?" William asks with a dejected sigh.

I grab my mask, join him in the private lift in our office suite, and head downstairs.

The slow whine of the cello blends with the violins in a haunting melody. The jazz band, outfitted in classic dinner jackets and black evening dresses, plays in the corner of the reception space. Each musician wears a mask. So do the wait staff weaving through the cloaked figures in the corridor.

Walls the color of black pearl reflect dim lighting off scattered gold frames. We have red rooms and areas with strobe lights, but we pride ourselves on not being a total cliché.

William takes off toward the east wing. He pulled a hamstring at the last event and had to ice his nuts for a week after swinging from the ceiling. His gold and black jester mask is fitting, considering the pending antics of a walking jokester. It also guarantees I won't catch him bare-ass scuba diving into someone's pussy. *Again*. There are certain things siblings shouldn't see, and his dick is at the top of the list.

I travel deeper into Ravenous. The ballroom holds a demonstration every hour on the hour. Guests can learn and mingle in a safe space before exploring other parts of the club. The stations bordering the ballroom are sectioned off with seating and satin fabric panels between daybeds. There's no sex allowed in the main areas and limited alcohol consumption at the only bar.

Outside of the ballroom, almost anything goes so long as there's consent. Monitors stroll throughout areas to ensure the safety and agency of our guests. We outfitted hotel rooms into BDSM spaces and assigned monitors who know how to navigate boundaries.

I swallow hard at the discomfort that hardens my chest at the thought of Madison locked away in a private room. Sleeping with her tonight isn't my intention. I want to see her, be in her presence without pissing her off and chasing her away.

"Fuck," I mumble before I turn on my heel and rush to the other side of the club.

Black walls blend with crimson. The music shifts from classic jazz to a sultry instrumental. William calls it lift-fucking music, which is fitting since we have an installation just for that.

Video panels simulate traveling up and down in a lift. Those looking for the thrill of getting caught "stop" on the occasional floors. The security camera inside the stationary unit provides the option to cast the feed on a screen to voyeurs outside the installation.

Cages housing masked nude dancers pleasuring themselves with toys appear when the corridor opens. The units are narrow but tall enough to stretch out—literally. Smoke billows beneath the door of a closed conference room. Guests gather around a fogged glass window to watch cloaked participants going at it on top of a large conference table. Others are against the wall, masks peeled back to expose their mouths to pleasure and body parts.

I huff under my breath and speed by the show, which stars my brother and two women. One woman is on her knees, sucking him off. The other is balancing herself on top of a water dispenser while he drives the long nose of his gold mask into her pussy. That's why he packed two masks for tonight.

I turn down the corridor that's accessible to guests. The other end is under construction for an installation opening soon.

Makeshift doll boxes showcasing guests on display glimmer on the groups that form around the illuminated units.

Trios. Couples.

Solo performers.

Every eye in the open room is on skin that's beaded with sweat. All except one hooded figure who's standing in front of an empty box.

My steps are cautious as I approach Madison. She's staring at her reflection, and her breath catches once I'm behind her. Silk rises and falls as our eyes lock and her lips part.

Soft moans and the music pouring from the speaker system are no match for the uneven rhythm of my breath.

To be this close without her recoiling fills me with a hope I haven't earned. I want her.

Madison slowly turns to face me. I'm not ready for the gaze she casts. It's a steady longing, searching over the black horns curling above my head. Black tend bronze feathers extend from my hairline to my cheeks, with a bronzed plate of spikes lining my eyes. No one knows it's me behind the mask, but Madison stares, determined to solve the mystery.

"I wish you were someone else. Someone I shouldn't want," she says, sadness lining her tone. Long lashes drop at a sigh that flares my nostrils.

I'm not a jealous man. I have a good heart, and I own a mirror. I know I look good, but if Madison is insinuating longing for Terrence in any way, I'll lose my shit. I can't ask her. If I do, she'll recognize my voice.

She quells my desire to commit an international crime when her dark eyes slide back to mine. The simple touch of her hand pressed to my chest heats my skin, awakening a desire I haven't felt in years.

"You look like him," she whispers. "Your eyes." Her finger brushes over my mouth, and I gently take it between my teeth. My dick pulses at her moan. "Your lips. Pre—" She catches herself, and I release a quiet breath.

She wants me.

Madison scans the room. "This place is about fantasies, right? You can't be him, but maybe for tonight I can imagine you are."

The invitation drips down to the base of my toes. I reach for her hand and guide us toward a room only I can access.

Chapter 16

Madison

I'm deep in an abyss of ass and satin, fighting hallucinations.

Do you know how far gone you have to be to fantasize about your ex at a sex club instead of the man in front of you who's ready to lick you from crack to crease?

I couldn't control the gasp that escaped when I envisioned my billionaire former lover underneath the intricate minotaur mask. Even with feathers covering most of his features, he looked familiar. I froze under his observant gaze, which seemed to last an eternity, one I lived in another life. The black-clad figure staring down in silence prickled my skin and forced me to contend with the broad length of his chest and shoulders.

I never summoned Preston here, but that didn't stop him from stalking my thoughts and haunting my desires.

If I can't escape him, Mr. Tall, Fit, and Fine will have to do.

The masked stranger pulls me with a protective hand. The muscles rippling under his cloak rattle my thighs as I move to keep up with his long stride. These damn stilettos are no match for his Viking legs.

We weave through small groups frozen in place by the scenes before them. My jaw hasn't come off the floor, and neither will the woman in a makeshift doll box. She's strapped to a sex swing wearing nothing but heels and nipple clamps. A cloaked figure stands between her legs at shoulder height, swabbing her insides with a vibrator. The box has to be soundproof, the way her head tips back and her chest heaves.

The ecstasy coating the air is intoxicating. I've never seen anything like Ravenous, and I question where my curiosities would take me if I released my inhibitions.

Public sex is somewhere on my bucket list, tucked away from judgment. I don't have the guts to do anything completely obvious, but it's an itch I'd like to scratch.

Light shifts from red to soft gold against black walls. I make a mental note to ask one of the people wearing a monitor band for the time. Ravenous has a no-phones policy, and Kojo and I promised to meet back at the bar by one a.m.

We walked the entire floor together before he kissed my forehead and disappeared into a private room with a woman and a man. I didn't expect to do anything but watch strangers tonight, but life had different plans.

My company for the night stops in front of a door down the end of another hall. We're alone, the edges of the jazz band a faint melody. I should feel nervous, cautious about walking off with a complete stranger, but I'm not, and I don't know why. He's an unknown force but strangely...familiar.

He types a code into a keypad to deactivate the lock. I gasp for the second time tonight once we cross the threshold.

Candles light the room like fireflies. A pianist strokes the keys of a grand piano next to oversized windows draped in dark velvet. The silhouette of the masked musician dances across flames reflected on oak floors.

It's a spacious suite with a large ottoman across from the musician conjuring a dark tune. Vases of pink peonies surround a seating area with two Chesterfield sofas and a coffee table. They're my favorite flower. I received them weekly in Paris from—

My eyes flutter shut at the kiss on the back of my neck. A breath fans across my skin to raise every hair. Soft lips move to my collarbone as my loose waves are swept across my shoulder.

Every press of his mouth sings through my veins. I settle back to enjoy the feel of the hard body against me. He sways us to the music and lowers his head for a deep inhale of my neck. He's yet to speak, but the deep moan that ripples through his throat tempts my knees to buckle.

Gentle fingers free the ties of my cloak. The breath he exhales is slow at my sequin dress, which outlines my curves and kisses the tops of my thighs. I might be on a break from dating, but one thing I'm not shy about is my body. I'm not just a snack; I'm the entire menu.

I didn't know what to expect walking into a private room with a stranger, but a pianist, a crackling fire, and my favorite flowers were not it. The gesture is intimate. Intentional.

I reach for his mask to prove my mind isn't playing tricks on me with these reminders of Preston. He hisses and steps back. His headshake is firm, but his kiss on the back of my hand is soft. Eager lips part, and his tongue licks the pulse point in my wrist. That's all it takes for the dam to break and our mouths to collide.

I compare every man to Preston, even Terrence. Blame it on my delusions, my imagination, or my denial. But there is no doubt he has a twin walking the earth. He's right here in front of me, forcing reality to bow to my memories of this same touch in Paris.

"Preston," I pant between breaths.

He sucks my bottom lip into his mouth and glides his tongue across the surface. His hands cradle my face, and I'm seconds from levitating from the high. The way he kisses is hungry, like he's been waiting for me all night.

I slide my hands under the straps of my dress and revel in his erratic breath. The tease of my nipples between my fingers is his summons.

"Touch me," I say at his hesitation, my consent a whisper through a dark tune.

The breath is knocked out of my lungs at how fast he pulls me to his chest and lifts me off the ground. The erection tenting his cloak is aggressive as he leans forward to suck a bud into his mouth.

He massages my breast with his tongue, gliding it across my areola in a wet trail. I shudder at the graze of his teeth and surrender to the suction as he laps at my hard peak. The cool air of the room mixed with his warm breath has me crawling up the slab of muscle that is his body. His grip tightens to keep me still.

Only one man has ever made me come through nipple stimulation. Preston might as well be here, the way I'm chanting his name.

My head thrashes from side to side, my knees quivering. I roll my hips at the orgasm charging up my body and scream loud enough to incite a wellness check.

Aftershocks ripple through me in waves. It's then I remember we're not alone. My eyes widen at the pianist, who's still playing like I didn't just hump this caped crusader who had my titty in his mouth. Lust overrode my senses and any fucks I might have given about someone else in the room.

The man—whose name I still don't know—sets me on my feet and picks up my dress.

"No. Please," I say at his attempt to secure it in place.

His stare shifts from me to the source of the music over my shoulder. His eyes are full of affection when they return to me, and it makes mine well with tears. It's been years since anyone displayed this much care for my needs—fifteen, to be exact. I miss it, and I don't want it to end.

I peek over at the pianist. His eyes are on me, his fingers rolling over the keys with ease. Knowing someone is watching vibrates my body with arousal. I've fantasized about it but never acted on it.

The lace of my Venetian mask burns my skin. I'm a stranger here, with the freedom of anonymity to explore limits I'd never try outside of Ravenous's walls. Curiosity shifts to confidence when I face the man whose arms I'm still in. He's waiting patiently.

"Taste me while he watches."

The masked man's stare is so intense I swallow and look away. He draws me back with a thumb under my chin and kisses me with a softness that makes me melt. Our dance is a slow glide to the ottoman across from the piano. I lie down, and he drops to his knees between legs I spread to welcome his size.

With his focus on me, he removes his cloak, folds it, and puts it under my head. A hand trails up my left leg. He kisses my ankle below the strap of my heel and guides his thumbs up my thighs. His ragged breath on my bare pussy inches from his face excites my back to arch.

I close my eyes at his inhale and jump at the first swipe of his tongue. Open-mouthed kisses up my lips become sweeping strokes with a flick to my clit.

"Oh my—" I choke on a moan when he takes my swollen pearl into his mouth. My body arches off the ottoman like I've been possessed.

His tongue is relentless, diving deeper into my heat. I match his tempo and submit to the explosive pleasure surging between us. Preston's body double is completely lost in the moment, eyes closed and mouth anchored between my legs.

I steal a glance at the pianist, who's staring down at me. The flames in his eyes sear a pathway from my parted lips down to my bouncing breasts.

Movement near the door summons me to a woman in all black. The sheer material of her sleeveless dress teases her voluptuous breasts and the neatly trimmed mound between her thighs. She's not wearing a cloak, but she does have a mask that covers her eyes. It's not until her hands fold over her chest and a hip juts out that it clicks.

It's Bellamy.

Her glare closes the distance, her focus shifting from me to the man between my legs before it settles back on its target. Me.

Is she mad?

What is she doing here?

Every question torpedoes from my body as the two fingers inside me curl into my G-spot. I buck forward and lock eyes with the minotaur who's pumping into me while my essence coats his chin. His eyes flash, and I cry out, lifting onto my elbows, unable to give a damn who sees me gyrating against his face.

"I'm coming." My legs vibrate, and my jaw goes slack as tears cloud my vision.

With a final swipe and an ungodly slurp, I scream. My breasts crush against the hardness of his chest when he pulls me to him. Each breath lacks control but settles when he kisses my face.

I suck on the tongue he offers, tasting my mess. We're so caught up in each other, we don't notice we're alone in the room.

Chapter 17

Preston

"We have coffee and scones in our office—the one we pay a shit ton of money for across the street." William turns up his nose at the pillowy treat he pokes with his fork.

This café is far from hideous. It actually supplies some of our office snacks, unbeknownst to him. He could at least add preserves or clotted cream to the damn thing if he's going to complain.

I sit back and wipe my mouth with a napkin. "It will do you some good to stretch your legs."

He smirks. "They stretch just fine over good pus—"

"I'll take this week's projections." If my brother wasn't phenomenal at his job, he and his ignorant dick would be out of one.

William slides the tablet we use for our weekly meetings across the wooden table. We're expanding our brand to Southeast Asia, thanks to the man across from me who's whining about scones. My brother is wild in his free time, but he's one of the reasons the Donnelley Brand has been so successful since I took over. As COO, William oversees the implementation of our strategic plans and daily operations through our general managers, among other tasks.

He's my right hand, someone I trust with my life. We give each other shit but hold ourselves accountable.

"Have we filled all of the open positions in Laos?" I roll my eyes when he scowls after taking a sip of coffee.

"I fly out on Monday," he says, his hand raking through blond waves. "KD should be there to go over budgets since we missed each other last week."

I look up from the tablet with a stare to remind him not to fuck around. "Stay out of trouble. That goes for the both of you," I say about our CFO, who primarily works out of our Paris office.

William flashes a devious smirk. "You're one to talk. If I recall, your New Year's trip before you ran off to wherever-the-fuck Colorado was more than business."

I volley back my own. "Do as I say, not as I do."

The end of last year had me by the balls. Between wrapping up projects, last-minute site demands, and the board, I was up to my ears in stress. Nonna put her foot down and told me I needed a break. She's half my size and twice my age but still cracks her kitchen towel like a whip.

I spent Christmas with her in Sicily, then swung over to Paris before heading to the States. Pussy has always been a stress reliever. I was face-deep in it and only came up for air when breathing was necessary.

My knee bounces when I remember the rush of nestling myself in the valley of Madison's thighs at Ravenous. She was a feast I consumed like a starved man until the pressure from her legs almost sent me into the afterlife with her orgasm. I had one of my own after I escorted her back to her friend at the bar. It's a miracle I still have a penis the way I pulled my dick over the last two nights. My trousers are tightening now at phantom images of her parted mouth glistening in the candlelight.

"Look at you over there love drunk." William's bark of laughter breaks me out of the fantasy. The prick doubles over in his gray suit, silently convulsing at my expense.

A waitress stops at our table to fill up our waters. "He's fine," I say in response to her cautious looks at my brother, whose head is now rattling the table.

She hesitates but nods before rushing off.

"You're such a child." I toss my napkin at his head, and he uses it to dab his eyes.

"No"—he wipes a stray tear—"you're completely smitten. Admit it, bruv."

I lift a shoulder. "Never denied it."

"Alright." William checks his watch and stands. "I'll leave you to it. Some of us have business to conduct." He reaches in his pocket to pull out money but stops at my headshake. "Let me guess, you bought out the café for your meeting?"

I cut my eyes at him, and his lips spread into a grin.

He laughs. "Tell my future sister-in-law I said hi. Can't wait to meet her."

Meetings take up the next two hours on the second floor of the café that's become my satellite office. The lower level is open to patrons, but the top floor will stay closed until I'm done. It's a bit of a hassle coordinating security, which is why William and I conduct business at the office or approved locations.

I'm finishing up a call when Madison's voice floats up from the bottom of the wooden staircase. The café itself is small, but there's enough chatter below to suggest the wait staff are in the middle of a lunchtime rush. I make a mental note to leave through the private entrance.

The sound of heels moving up the steps accelerates my pulse. I adjust my red and blue tie and run my fingers through my hair for the twelfth time. You'd think I was closing my first deal with how I'm acting.

Madison examines the white subway tile walls adorned with hanging plants and vintage photos. This floor is narrower than downstairs, with only six or so tables with metal chairs. I pulled two together for my laptop and paperwork.

Her back is to me, granting me a full view of that thick ass stuffed into a knee-length skirt. It's been years since I made those cheeks clap, and I miss the beat.

It takes her a minute to notice that the floor extends back to where I am. Her lips part when she peeks over a shoulder.

I stand, button my suit coat, and make my way to her. She hasn't moved from her spot next to the stairs, and I haven't taken my eyes off of her. With our height difference, I'm at the perfect vantage point to watch her cheeks heat and her deep breaths stretch her shirt beneath her jacket.

A flashback of me licking and rolling her light brown nipples between my teeth sends blood straight to my dick. The bulge growing behind my zip earns her full attention.

Her tongue drags over her lower lip. "What are you doing here?" The question is for my erection.

"Forgot my measurements?" I keep my tone low and force down a smile.

"I'm meeting someone." Her brows kiss. "A prospective client."

"In need of a stylist," I finish for her and motion to my tables.

"Doubtful." Her glare sharpens on my custom-fit navy suit.

I grin. "Never said I didn't have a tailor." I motion again to the tables. "Please."

She mumbles, "You don't need me," in a strut that does nothing to deflate my erection.

The gentleman who makes my suits is a retired Italian designer in his sixties, and he's worth every euro. But Madison is still wrong. I need her, more than she knows.

I unbutton my suit coat and mentally prepare for a battle that will be bigger than any boardroom showdown to date. Having my assistant schedule a consultation under her name was a gamble. Madison made it clear she wants nothing to do with me. The fact that she's still sitting here would make me question it...if her thoughts weren't already showing her hand.

Every line on my face is under investigation as she searches for an answer that's staring back at her. I'm the man from Ravenous, the one who sent her over the edge with his tongue.

The whispered chant of my name on her lips skated across my body, shattering every assumption that a second chance isn't in the cards. Madison wants me. The proof was in her calling out for me and creaming my face.

She blinks through hooded eyes. "Sorry."

"No worries, Puff." She shifts in her seat at the nickname. *Good girl.* I straighten, widening my legs so our knees touch.

Madison puckers her lips and tilts her chin. "If this is some kind of game, your security won't make it upstairs fast enough before I throw you out the window. Time is money, and I don't like mine wasted."

Masochism might be an unlocked kink the way my dick is petrified against my leg. No one in their right mind would talk to me how Madison just did. She doesn't give a shit about my title or net worth. It's one of the things I love about her.

"I assure you, I'm not here to play any games, Ms. Monroe," I say. "I don't have a stylist, and I'd like to hire you."

"Doesn't look like you need one." Her accusing gaze hardens the delicate edges of her face.

I grin. "You think I look good?"

"Preston." She pinches the bridge of her nose. "I cannot afford for you to play with my business." Her scowl drops in a plea. "If you're not serious—"

"I'm not here to play with your head or your heart." I take her hand. To my surprise, she lets me.

I don't speak out of fear she'll snap out of the trance that's charging the air between us. Being this close to her again stimulates my mind and body.

Contemplation softens her features as she fights to resist the force that's pulling us back together. To finish what we started, heal what we left undone.

With her eyes on mine and a long breath, she surprises me.

"We do this on my terms. I'm here for the rest of the week, and I can squeeze in a wardrobe analysis." Her eyes narrow. "*If* our professional agreement works, I'll consider keeping you on as a client. You'll pay an hourly fee for my services. Flights and accommodations for any special events are on you."

"No."

"No?" Madison's eyebrow raises.

I commend her for her business prowess, but I wouldn't be where I am today if I didn't go after what I wanted.

I roll my bottom lip between my thumb and index finger. Madison tries to maintain her curtness, but I earn a living reading people. Right now, her tone is terse, but the desire pooling behind her dilated pupils and shuttering the breath she fights to steady says otherwise.

"I'd like to hire you for a closer collaboration." I shift my knees away in preparation for any blows to my shins. "Three months. You here in London, with me."

Her eyes grow two sizes. "Are you out of your mind? I can't leave my life behind!"

"Not leave, relocate. Temporarily."

She scoffs and stares out the window.

"I imagine your clients aren't all in New York," I continue, my focus steady on her profile. "You'll still travel as needed."

"And where will I stay? Your place?" she deadpans.

I swallow a smirk. "Might I remind you, I own several properties. You'd have access to the finest amenities."

Silence settles in the middle of the table. I'll make some concessions, but I have no intention of letting her waltz out of my life. Not without a fight.

Madison processes what a temporary stay would mean. Triumph floods through me when she draws in a deep breath and sighs.

"I have responsibilities in New York. I don't want to be away that long."

"You're free to come and go as you please," I say.

After a long pause, she traps me in a stare that lets me know I shouldn't push more than I already have. "Three months. You pay for my stay and a base salary of seventy-five thousand. Any needs or special events outside of standard work hours activates an hourly rate of two hundred and fifty pounds. I leave when I want to, and I won't stay beyond our three-month agreement. Do we have a deal?"

Madison's response is sharp, her tone final. I would've agreed to sign away the deeds to all my homes the moment she said yes.

"We have a deal, Ms. Monroe." I smile and extend a hand, which she shakes. I lean closer. "Just so we're clear, your rates are too low. Let's triple your fees. I'm in a different league, and so are you."

I press a kiss to the tremor in her jaw. "I look forward to our arrangement, Puff."

Whether Madison knows it or not, she gave me a priceless gift: her time.

Chapter 18

15 years ago

Date: September 16, 2009, 6:02 am

From: thatsmystyle@email.me

To: PresD@tdb.com

Subject: My knickers

Could you reach out to Jeeves about the laundry service? He refuses to believe I'm staying with you.

Also, stop eating my eclairs when you swoop in.

Your Disgruntled Roommate

Date: September 16, 2009, 6:08 am

From: PresD@tdb.com

To: thatsmystyle@email.me

Subject: Who is Jeeves?

Jean-Pierre might be amenable to your requests if you stop calling him Jeeves. Where did you come up with such a name?

If you didn't hoard pastries like a cult member waiting for doomsday, I'd have nothing to steal.

P

Date: September 16, 2009, 6:15 am

From: thatsmystyle@email.me

To: PresD@tdb.com

Subject: Ask Jeeves...duh!

Your fancy hotel butler manages the suite. Jeeves is the cartoon butler from Ask Jeeves. He answers questions. You tell me to ask your butler whenever I need help.

Ask Jeeves.

If you assist with laundering my knickers, I'll overlook your theft.

Your Still Disgruntled Roommate

Date: September 16, 2009, 6:23 am

From: PresD@tdb.com

To: thatsmystyle@email.me

Subject: ....

I bet you're laughing at that attempt at a joke, huh? Fun fact: You're in Paris. No one says "knickers."

Hard to steal what's in our kitchen. Tell you what, I'll replace your coveted eclairs with English pastries.

P

Date: September 16, 2009, 6:30 am

From: thatsmystyle@email.me

To: PresD@tdb.com

Subject: Where's your English humor?

I had one giggle, for your information. Don't the English say "knickers"? Pardon me for trying to fit in with my new roomie.

Your Pantyless and Still Disgruntled Roommate

Date: September 16, 2009, 6:23 am

From: PresD@tdb.com

To: thatsmystyle@email.me

Subject: Let me know when you find it

In case you didn't notice, love, I lack both the proper English accent and their humor. Blame it on boarding school.

I'll send a message to Jean-Pierre. Your panties are safe with me, Puff.

Enjoy your day,

P

Chapter 19

Madison

Now

"A quarter million dollars for three months of work? *Girl!*"

"Shh!" I smack Kojo on the thigh and pray no one heard him shout my business.

A blush creeps up the V in my blouse at the people next to us talking in hushed whispers. They appear around our age, possibly younger, with crossed legs, lip filler, and matching glowers.

I sit taller and do my best to ignore the volleyed gossip in French, but I fail. Speaking Creole growing up, plus my time in Paris, makes their business my business. I focus on the empty runway until my patience dissolves, along with my last fuck to give.

"I can assure you I'm not gargling dicks behind the palace," I say in French, my tone flat but high with irritation. "Even if I were, sex work is work, no?"

The duo turns as white as our chairs, their stenciled brows reaching the auburn hairlines of their matching ponytails.

"Focus on the business that pays you, not mine." I smirk at security, who's coming over to escort them to their proper seats. They argue with the Jason Statham lookalike but wilt when he extends his hand and ushers them to leave. They storm off in a huff, doused in the stench of too much perfume.

"Enjoy the show from outside!" Kojo wiggles his fingers over his shoulder with a wink. Tonight's shade is served in indigo and Nsu Bura fabric. "That's what they get for talking shit. Now—back to your man tripling your fees."

"Preston is not my man." I stretch out my feet in patent leather heels. My calves will be the strongest on the earth. A small sacrifice for tonight's ensemble.

Kojo and I are at one of the kick-off events for London fashion week. We're in our versions of pantsuits with white dress shirts to commemorate the menswear collection that's minutes from gracing the stage. He hasn't stopped laughing since he heard about my new client sabotaging my morning.

The irony of Preston popping up in my life once again while taking up space in my mind like a public storage unit... I haven't stopped thinking about him, including on Valentine's Day, when I summoned him with every moan.

I'm still grappling with my decision to work as his stylist. What does it say about my boundaries or common sense that I not only said yes but agreed to three months in London? Every muscle in my mouth balled up to say no, but I couldn't do it.

Preston found a crack in my armor. It's spread since our first encounter after a fifteen-year hiatus, denting excuses in place to shield from the disappointment that seems to follow every decision I make about a man.

Leaving and never looking back would have been the easiest choice, but that wouldn't satisfy the lifetime of questions I have. So, I agreed, and I hope I don't regret it.

"See your forbidden lover in the crowd?" Kojo flashes his perfect white teeth.

I roll my eyes. "What kind of friend are you, encouraging me to get with a man who already broke my heart?"

"The kind who knows people can change. That was almost two decades ago. You're far from twenty, and I bet the circumstances would be different this time. This man already showed up at your door with breakfast, chauffeured you to the airport, and offered to pay you three times your styling fee just to keep you here." He huffs. "If you find out he likes dick, please send him my way."

I cackle.

Kojo is bisexual and proud, with a Rolodex of partners that's as long as it is impressive. He damn near got me with the lick of his lips. We came close to sleeping together years ago, but we like each other too much to ruin our friendship.

"Regine, a man does not go to such lengths just to spend time with you, especially if he already had you."

I arch a brow at his audacity. "*Pfft*. I've had men sprung for less."

"Be that as it may," Kojo chuckles, "Preston is ultrarich with access to the best—which you are. His time is money. If he's investing it in you, it's likely for more than sex. He can get that anywhere. Didn't you say he acted out of character when you first called it quits?"

My silence is Kojo's invitation to keep scraping at the scar I've tried to heal.

"Madison," he says, to get my attention, "you've been looking for love for so long. What if it found you after all these years? You already agreed to take him on as a client."

"I don't mix business with pleasure," I say with a pointed look. Kojo has zero shame, and he'd bust it wide open for a bigger discount.

"Don't judge me. Anyways." He sucks his teeth. "My point is, don't close yourself off to an opportunity that's waiting for you. You entertain men who are either unattainable or should be on the curb with a dusty couch. And before you lie to my face, need I remind you about Earl? *Earl!*"

"Shh!" I snap.

Earl wasn't my finest moment. We shared a weekend after we met at a bar. In my defense, it was a gastropub with an international selection of fine wines. One glass turned into a few dates, and soon I was picking up the check and cleaning up his toenail clippings around my apartment.

But that's not all.

He called himself in love and broke his lease to move in with me. Only one of us got that memo, and it took me threatening to take his behind to *The People's Court* before he finally left. Earl needed a mama more than a relationship, with his laundry demands and constant need for lunch money. I knew he wasn't the one when we first met, but I prioritized decent sex over seeing enough writing on the wall to fill the Louvre.

I'll give Kojo Earl, and the many others I knew deep down weren't a match. But liking unattainable men is a stretch.

Need a reminder about Terrence?

The guilt from that one still stings. Did I know he'd never leave Justice? Yes. Did I try to earn his attention? Also yes. He's the only other partner who treated me like I matter. Seeing Terrence out whenever our work schedules would cross gave me something to look forward to when I needed a recharge from the dating world.

"This is exactly why I'm giving up relationships," I mutter. I'm messed up in more ways than one, and I'm putting myself in time-out.

"Whatever you say, Regine." Kojo smirks.

"I'm dead serious. I need a break."

Preston is a business transaction. I do my job, and in three months, I'm out of here.

Chapter 20
Preston

Passing clouds lift over the buildings across the street, teasing the first streaks of sunlight since this meeting started. It's the only thing keeping me in my chair and not reaching across the conference table to put hands on the man who's daring me to defy gravity.

"It's settled. We continue with the Maldives project as planned." Steel blue eyes scour the room for objections. His mouth coils to bare the edges of white veneers. A brow raises to signal my move.

Victor Donnelley railroading board meetings is nothing new. Neither is the father-son duel he insists on carrying out to prove that, even in retirement, he's still the chairperson and the largest shareholder of the Donnelley Brand.

It's a testament to his strength that no one has tried their hand at knocking some humility into him. I'm not a violent man, but I wouldn't blame anyone who took a swing. He's ruffled a lot of feathers over his years on the board. My grandfather is the only one who stood up to my father and put him in his place. Their relationship—if you could call it one—did not reflect the love a parent has for their child. They were competitive. Ruthless.

Hugh Kidwell, my father's longtime ally, looks beyond the table of annoyed board members, too timid to speak. If opposites attract, these two are soulmates.

Where my father favors David James Gandy, Hugh was Jason Alexander in a past life, down to his five-foot-five frame and balding hairline. They've been business partners since I was a kid, and they've always had the same dynamic:

My father says jump.

Hugh asks how high.

"We have a responsibility to reduce our footprint," I say to command the attention back in the room. Six active board members and not one backbone. The only voting member of this body who doesn't kiss my father's ass without a fight is my brother.

William slouches in his executive chair, grinning at his phone, no doubt because of a woman. Always enjoying a life of "peace and pussy." Certain burdens were never his to carry in the first place, like running the Donnelley Brand.

His eyes snap to me when I clear my throat.

"As I was saying"—I stand and button my navy blazer—"it's a minimal investment to ensure our site doesn't destroy local ecosystems."

While our properties are boutique in scale, coral reefs suffer from new development. It costs nothing to not be a prick, a lesson my father could never afford.

I grab the clicker to activate the screen on the back wall. Heads swivel in a streak of gray hair and suits to the projections my finance team created. Sustainable initiatives go a long way when done with intention. I've fought for this company to be the best, to help urge the industry to prioritize equity over exploitation.

"We have an opportunity to move in a new direction," I say, taking in each head nod. "If there aren't any questions, I'd like to call a vote."

One thing my father taught me is to never back down from a fight. He's never fought fair, so I square my shoulders and wait with arms crossed over my chest.

I've never been afraid of Victor Donnelley—or any man.

"Very nice presentation, Preston. Thoughtful, but not compelling enough. I cast my votes in the negative." Condescension spills from the frown lines in his smirk. My father glances at Hugh, who nods at the table. The old prick can't even look me in the eye.

I press my lips shut at his cowardice. We've held board meetings in this room since the Donnelley Brand purchased the building under my father's reign. Every meeting is the same: Victor Donnelley voices his desires, and the board folds. Only three members vote in the negative, but we don't have enough voting shares to overrule him.

With the power of two votes at my father's fingertips, the final blow comes from Hugh's son.

Michael isn't a prick like his father, but he's eager for validation. Hugh was intentional in securing his son's board placement. Not his daughter, who he encouraged to stay in Paris. She's the damn CFO without a seat at the table.

I don't waste a breath asking Michael if his head is out of his father's ass today. His awkward tugs at his collar are a giveaway it's not. He nods like a bobblehead, reaches for his water glass, and downs it in one go.

William scoffs at the display and rocks in his seat.

"I believe that does it," my father says. His timbre is a gavel that signals the end of the meeting.

He stands and shakes hands with his minions. After the CEO reins passed to me, he grew his shares to maintain his influence as insurance. He knew I'd lead differently, and now he makes it impossible to step outside the bounds he created to maintain our family legacy.

"Nice attempt, son." He pats my back like he's not the reason for my defeat. "Today wasn't your day."

If it weren't for the smug look on my father's face, I'd give him credit for sounding like a caring parent. He's tried to be one here and there over the years, but he soured our relationship with the same bitterness he and my grandfather once held for each other.

"Let me not keep you," I say. "It's Hendon today, or is it Beckenham?"

"Gotta be Canonbury," William calls from the other end of the table. A tight smile masks his disdain for our father disrespecting his mother. The indiscretions are no secret. He's kept long-standing mistresses across London since he remarried, and he rotates weekly visits.

At sixty-three, Victor Donnelley is a handsome man who feels no shame pulling ladies in with his silver fox appeal or cheating on his wife. I told Briar to leave him decades ago. She's still holding out hope that he'll slow down and commit to only her now that he's retired. It's been eight years. It hasn't happened yet.

My father waits for the remaining board members to trickle out the door before he responds. A muscle tightens his jaw, ruffling the age lines around his mouth. You'll never see him sweat, but there are a few tells when you get under his skin.

"Where I go does not concern you or your brother." He kisses his teeth.

Tell.

"If you worried more about this company and less about playing Captain Planet, maybe you'd do more than waste our time with your eco-friendly bullshit." His nostrils flare.

Tell.

I temper my response to his sharp retort and chuckle when he puts his hands on his hips.

Tell.

It shouldn't satisfy me to make my father this rattled, but unlike him, I'm not a liar or a cheat.

I stuff a hand into my pocket and graze the silk lining, holding an old charm I keep for good luck. "Better get on, then" is all I say.

He looks between me and William, who's now at my side. With a huff, he rips his overcoat from his chair in a dramatic fashion.

"Prick," William mutters. "The board will get its head out of its ass one day."

"Agreed." I nod. All good things take time. I look at my watch and head back to the conference table to pack up my laptop. "I'm on my way out. I have a date tonight."

"Where?"

I smile. "My wardrobe."

Chapter 21

Madison

I know a date when I see one.

Who in their right mind has a small table for two with restaurant-quality linens in their closet? Billionaire or not, Preston is not slick. He's fine—and wearing the hell out of that fleece jogger and hoodie combo—but he's not slick.

The rust-colored fabric is the perfect contrast against his warm honey skin. It was a surprise when he opened his penthouse door. I wasn't expecting the casual look or the music with soft lighting. Preston swore it's his way of unwinding after a long day.

With the *Waiting to Exhale* soundtrack.

Chanté Moore's "Wey U" filters through his walk-in closet, the location for our business meeting that isn't a date.

A man in an all-black outfit wheels in a silver cart with two matching domes. The closet is so big, it takes him a minute to navigate around the island and round ottoman.

Preston raises his hands when I cut my eyes to him. "Not a date. I figured dinner and business can coexist."

"Dinner and business," I mock.

His shoulder lifts. "It's pretty common. Have you eaten?"

My stomach answers with a long gargle. "I could eat."

He wets the lower lip that's been taunting me since he caught me staring. "Sounds like it." I roll my eyes at his deep chuckle.

The man, who I assume is a server, places a dome in front of me. "Sirloin tip roast with honey-roasted carrots and parsnips," he says.

"Thank you" comes out in a moan at the buttery flavors wafting from the plate. My toes curl in the cotton slippers Preston gave me when I arrived.

He thinks of everything.

Including the candle the server sets between us and lights.

"Not a date?" I deadpan.

Preston's mouth spreads into a dimpled smile. "Came with the meal."

I can't look at him or take what he says seriously. Between the candlelight shining on every line of his beautiful face and the woodsy musk permeating from the clothes in his closet, my kitty is purring.

"Is there anything stronger than water?" I tug at the collar of my sleeveless turtleneck. The server's eyes slide to Preston for the okay, and the man leaves at his nod.

Alcohol is nonnegotiable. I'll show my ass and every hole tonight if Preston runs his fingers through those dark curls again. He knows he's fine and isn't playing fair.

The closet is a gorgeous display of carpentry. Strips of lights travel across the top of walnut cabinets that showcase suit jackets, dress shirts, and pants perfectly organized by season and color.

"I remembered," Preston says, pulling me in with the gentleness in his voice, "how you'd organize our wardrobe at the start of each month."

A lump forms in my throat. The organizing trick is a simple tool to rotate clothes and maximize your closet. I've given the recommendation to clients countless times, and it never once made the butterflies in my stomach take flight. This gesture is more than an efficient way to hang fabrics. It's a declaration, standing proudly while daring me not to overlook its significance. He kept a piece of us after all these years. A reminder of a time when his custom suits and my Wet Seal outfits blended so effortlessly.

Preston is at least a foot away on the other side of the table on this non-date, but it feels like he's deep in the recesses of my thoughts, soothing questions I spent years agonizing over.

Did our memory live on through the hurt and anger?

Do I still cross his mind during the songs we slow danced to in his living room?

I clear my throat and fight through the sting of tears. "It's a good system to maintain," I declare, sawing into my steak, which melts like butter. "Makes things easier to find." I nod at the juiciness of the sirloin and force down images of Preston chasing me around our bedroom after he caught me moving his suits.

The server returns with two glasses of red wine. I gulp half of mine, unable to wash down the years of repressed emotions firing through my rib cage. Everything tastes bitter now. The rich Bordeaux we stocked in Paris, conveniently here on the table. This beautiful dinner.

It's fitting, because that's what I've become. Bitter.

I hate myself for wanting to be loved even a fraction of what Dominique and Justice enjoy. Worst of all, I hate myself for still holding pieces of Preston, turning them over in my hand and sniffing the memories when I need the high.

It's pitiful to hold on, especially with how things ended.

How could I ever love a woman like you?

The sting from the words he tossed out before turning to walk out of my life emerges from the ashes. I planned to tell him everything that night. My real name. Why I pretended to be someone else. How desperately I wanted to make what we had work.

"There's no going back." My voice carries over the table in a troubled whisper.

Preston watches me with a tenderness that's anchored in remorse. "I would apologize every day for the rest of my life if it were enough." He sighs and bows his head. "I lost everything good when I let you go."

"But you did let me go. How could you love a woman like me?" I parrot back to him with a newfound strength. This conversation is fifteen years too late. "You tossed me away without a second glance. What did you think would happen now? We'd fall back into old habits with your nostalgic wine and wardrobe confessions? I made mistakes, but I didn't deserve how you treated me. Not after what we shared. You hurt me."

A dam bursts in an explosion of flash powder and lighter fluid. I want a fight with the man who was so cruel to me that night. I couldn't save myself then, but I can now before I'm in too deep.

"I can't erase the past, but I take responsibility for what I said. I regret that day, and each one after." The sheen of Preston's tears catches in the candlelight. "I am sorry."

"Don't." My voice cracks, along with another piece of my armor. I wanted a battle, but I'm caught off guard by his surrender.

He's bracing for my fury. His attentiveness and lack of will to strike back are disarming. It lifts a weight still shackled to my past from the center of my chest.

I'm sorry.

I've wanted those words—yearned for them—to know I was enough. I always was, but hearing him say it is a balm for the pain I've carried for too long.

"You deserved to know who I was, not who I pretended to be," I say in a shaky confession. "I should've told you sooner, but I never expected for us..." *To fall in love the way we did.*

A summer fling was the ceiling we set. Life had other plans. It rerouted our initial attraction into a friendship that became the foundation for a love that burned bright until it exploded. I'm not sure we'll ever heal, but I'll own up to the part I played in our demise.

"That never should've mattered, Puff," he says, reaching into my heart and soothing it with my nickname. "I allowed my emotions and external influences to cloud my judgment. It's no excuse, but I own it."

I never met anyone as repulsed by my presence as his father was. He sold his son a lie, that the woman he fell in love with was an opportunist who was lying to get his money. The sting didn't come from the assumption. It came because Preston believed the lie so easily.

The darkness in his eyes that night matched his father's glare. I've never been so humiliated in my life—and in public, no less. Enough time has passed for us to forgive each other, but where do we go from here?

"I have to go." The same fight-or-flight instinct kicks in, forcing me to stand. I toss my napkin onto the table. It was a mistake to come here. I exposed more than I intended to show.

Preston reaches for me with a slight tremble in his hand. When it covers my wrist, the contact sends my pulse into a fury. Sadness tugs his thick brows together and deepens a frown on the face I once thought I'd spend a lifetime loving.

"Please don't leave...out of my life for good." Pain laces his plea. His stare tells me everything he feels. Sorrow for the time we lost. Hope for the future we could have.

My mind and heart clash in hard blows. My heart tells me he's my person, the reason any relationship or attempt at love ends before it starts. My mind reminds me of the aches and scrapes that came from getting too close. Six months was all it took to experience a love I'd never felt before, a love that almost destroyed me.

"We owed it to each other to say goodbye. There was always a point when we'd have to let go," I say, standing my ground and restraining the quiet part of me that screams in curse words to give this a chance. Any more of his groveling, and I'll cave. "You paid me to do a job, and I intend to finish it. Given our history and my policy not to date clients, I think it's best to keep our interactions professional."

Preston's face softens. His brows unfurl with a dejected sigh. "I'll see you out." He gestures for me to go in front of him.

The walk back to the front door is silent. Kismet only happens in holiday romance movies, not in real life. A billionaire and a secret identity makes for a hell of a story, but who am I kidding? That's not how this works. I was never the Hallmark girl. Lifetime, maybe.

Tonight, we put everything on the table for the closure we needed. I did the right thing, so why does it still feel like a mistake?

The door transforms into a solid chest when Preston spins me around. I stifle a gasp and suppress a shudder at the brush of his thumb on my chin and the gold flecks catching fire in his eyes.

A younger Preston might've ended things abruptly, but the mature version isn't giving up so easily. Gone is the man who shed tears at the thought of me walking out of his life. In his place is the one who doesn't lose, who takes what he wants at any cost.

The hairs of his goatee tickle my skin as he whispers into the shell of my ear, "I'm not letting you go this time. I can't."

Whatever fight-or-flight instinct I had bends the knee to the slow sweep of his tongue and the gravity of his stare.

I feel around for the anger that stretched and spiraled in the closet. It's no longer here, just like the handle that somehow disappeared from the door my back is pinned against.

That's the problem with a soul tie. It traps you if you aren't careful.

Preston leans around me to grab the door handle, which is inches from my hand. The scent of his cologne and the soft cotton of his hoodie brush against my face. "See you soon, Puff."

I'm out and down the hall to the elevator, speed walking in house slippers, my heels and coat be damned. Thank God I had half a sense and kept my phone and keys in my cargo pockets. Whatever I left can stay there another day. Possibly forever.

There's no doubt in my mind that Preston will come for me with everything he's got. My defenses aren't ready, but they will be.

Chapter 22

Fifteen Years Ago

Date: September 21, 2009, 10:53pm
From: PresD@tdb.com
To: thatsmystyle@email.me
Subject: Miss you
It's getting harder to be away from you.
P

Date: September 21, 2009, 11:12pm
From: thatsmystyle@email.me
To: PresD@tdb.com
Subject: Re: Miss you
So don't be. Miss you too.
Puff

Date: September 21, 2009, 11:15pm
From: PresD@tdb.com

To: thatsmystyle@email.me

Subject: Re: Miss you

Careful. I might not let you go.

See you soon,

P

Chapter 23

Madison

Now

I'm in a damn Hugh Grant movie.

In *Two Weeks Notice*, George Wade was an annoying billionaire who couldn't wipe his own ass without asking for help. Preston must've seen it, because he has one more text before I snatch his nuts through the phone.

The man owns a Monopoly board of luxury hotels but can't choose a tie?

He's been texting nonstop since I left London the morning after my hundred-meter dash from his penthouse. You would've thought I was on the run the way I packed my suitcase and exiled myself from London.

I needed time and space between us, so I hopped on the first flight to Los Angeles ahead of a red-carpet fitting. Kojo is here on business and hasn't stopped laughing in my face about Preston "running me out of England."

Technically, he didn't *run* me out; I flew.

I'll go back at some point. For now, I'm staying half a world away from his charm and that mouth.

I'm not letting you go this time.

He hasn't made it easy for me to ignore him, but I don't take his calls.

...which brings me back to Hugh Grant.

My phone chirps with another text. I bite down a smile at the message preview and cross the street. This fool is not asking me about pajamas.

Preston

Went with green. Does my stylist approve?

I swipe to the attached photo of Preston on his couch. He's in green buffalo check flannel, his feet crossed at the ankles. I never had a foot fetish, but I understand why people lick toes that look like his.

Preston has beautiful feet. Long. Slight veins. Manicured.

I shift around a group of suits and type my response.

You're joking. Pajamas?

Preston

Do I ever joke?

Go find a hobby.

Our texts shouldn't amuse me this much, but they do. Preston messages me about random fashion advice he doesn't need, and I call him out on it. He knows he's being annoying asking about scarves and pocket squares, but he doesn't care.

Like Hugh Grant in *Two Weeks Notice*.

An image loads, a book in his lap.

Preston

Found one. Back to my question.

I'm not answering after you texted me about socks at six this morning.

To his credit, he's been mindful of the eight-hour time difference, but he still bugs me with random questions and forces an answer. I emailed him a full styling guide based on his wardrobe, which should last him until I'm back in London. I'd find his attempts cute if they didn't start at the crack of dawn.

Preston

Did you forget we're both early risers, Puff? I had a meeting this afternoon that required the proper attire.

They can't see your socks under the table, Preston.

Preston

Testy. Are you always this mean to your clients? I love stroking your buttons.

"Ooh!" A sneer slithers through my growl.

Our back-and-forth reminds me of our daily emails in Paris while he was away. There was a thrill at rushing to the computer to read our thread. His dry sarcasm and my snappy responses rooted our short-lived relationship in a friendship I've yet to experience again.

I leave my needy ex of a client on read and wait for the crosswalk light. Los Angeles is a different kind of busy. The traffic on the street and the people on the sidewalk make my neighborhood in Hell's Kitchen look like a quiet suburb.

Kojo keeps us away from the tourist spots in LA, but I'm half a block from sweating the crotch out of my underwear. Nearby parking was nonexistent, which meant a four-block trek in five-inch heels. I should've ordered a car, but someone insisted I rent one for the days we want to play *Baywatch* on the beach.

How am I the one with a driver's license? I don't need it in New York, but I'm always putting it to use so Kojo can play passenger princess.

At least the weather is perfect for this wrap dress. A sixty-four-degree day in late February is spring to me. No coat necessary.

I double-check the address as I approach a brick building with steel-framed windows. Kojo swears by this place every time he's on the West Coast. Through the glass, servers bustle around seated patrons forking bites between conversations. The place is packed for ten forty-five.

I smile at the hostess and scan the lacquered black tables for my friend. Kojo said he was meeting someone here. I didn't want to impose, but he insisted I come by after my call with a client in Vegas.

His grin reaches me from next to a painted brass column across a white marble bar. He's in a color-block shirt that complements his hazelnut skin, which is glowing thanks to his dedicated skincare routine.

I match his smile, but it drops when I see the person at his side. The one who's ready to do me bodily harm. The one who I forgot lives in the area.

Emma.

Had I known Kojo planned to meet with her, I would've faked an illness—anything to get out of attending. It was only a matter of time before he pushed us together, extrovert that he is. We all work in the fashion industry in some capacity. Emma doesn't know I styled her company's pieces for Kojo's fashion show when we were in New York earlier this month, which could make this awkward encounter deadly.

I'd hoped our paths wouldn't cross until enough time had passed that the singles' retreat became water under the bridge. My wishful thinking is not only delusional, but dangerous.

Death and retribution fill Emma's calculated stare. Sweat from my palms seeps into my dress, which is now clinging to me from my trek from Timbuktu.

Will she attempt murder in broad daylight?

A crease forms between Kojo's brows. I open my mouth to speak but snap it shut as Emma impales me with her glower.

"Madison." My name grinds between her teeth.

Kojo looks between us. "You two know each other?"

How do I tell my best friend—one of my only friends—that I've been a complete bitch to Emma's best friend because of years of hurt and jealousy? My behavior almost cost me my friendship with Tammi. I can't lose Kojo.

My stomach drops at his heavy sigh. His shoulders fall, and a frown filters between the tense lines of his face.

"This was a bad idea. I should go," I say, one step closer to the door. "We'll work something else out. I-I have to go."

I don't wait around for the stain of Kojo's disappointment to set. Outside, quick gasps of air silence the car horns until one speeds around me.

Shit.

I choke back the sob charging up my throat like bile and look both ways before running to the other side of the crosswalk.

Don't cry in public.

My phone rings in my purse. "Hey." I fish out my black shades to conceal my face and sniffle. "What's up?"

Tammi is quiet. "Are you okay? I was finishing a school run and felt the urge to call you."

My breath hitches through a forced laugh. "Your timing is impeccable."

"What happened?"

"Oh, you know. Karma. Kojo invited me to brunch with one of his friends. When I got there, it was Emma, Justice's best friend." Tammi's sigh matches mine. "I don't want to be the reason his friendship or his business deal goes south."

"Maddie."

I sniffle again. "What if he doesn't speak to me because of what I did?" The words catch on a knot in my throat.

"You didn't do what you're accusing yourself of doing."

"But I wanted to! You stopped speaking to me because I wanted someone else's husband. I don't blame you; I deserve it. I-I just can't shake—"

"The guilt?" Tammi's voice is a whisper.

I clung to any justification for feeling the way I felt about Terrence. I was hurt, and I told myself there was no harm in flirting with him, regardless of his marital status. It was a game to me half the time, one that he didn't notice. He was so caught up in Justice that he never looked my way.

That dismissal fueled my hatred. So did the men left in the dating pool. I'm a damn good catch, but I only attract moochers, cheaters, and deadbeats.

"Do you regret the harm you caused Justice?"

"You know I do, Tam," I say.

"Forgive yourself for harboring bitterness for so long and move forward. When the time is right, try to make amends."

I snort. "If only it were that simple."

"Who says it can't be? Look, did you show your ass and act all types of thirsty over a married man? Yes, you did. Grace is real, because I would've beat the dust off your—"

"Tammi!" I laugh, knowing she's picturing someone in her congregation. "Breathe."

Her smile reaches the phone. "My point is that you have grace and mercy, the grace to do better and the mercy that no one has snatched your edges. I love you, Maddie. You don't have to be the villain in someone's story in order to be loved. Let it come to you—*unattached*—in its own time. Actions have consequences, good and bad.

Emma has every right to feel some kind of way about you. Let time do the healing."

"What if she doesn't forgive me? I don't want to put Kojo in a situation where he has to choose between us."

"Forgive yourself and do better. You and Kojo are thick as thieves. Give him time to process. Y'all will be okay."

My feet are crying by the time I reach my rental car. I unlock the Lexus and rest my head against soft black leather.

"Let me let you go. I'm meeting Smokey," Tammi says. "Love you."

"Love you too. Tam?"

"Hmm?"

"I'm telling the church you're out here trying to fight."

"Kiss my ass," she snickers.

I cackle when the line goes dead. Then I drive back to my hotel.

My phone pings from the corner of my hotel room. It's past ten, and I have neither a life nor a booty call lined up. Who's texting me at this hour?

Kojo sent one right after my call with Tammi, asking to grab dinner and talk, which we did. He was more hurt that I kept my feelings from him, and he told me to give Emma space. We'll have to figure out how to coexist since I'm helping him with the styling aspect of his business.

For now, I'll count it as a win. My head is still on my shoulders, and Emma and Kojo's relationship is still intact.

As for my flirting with a married man, Kojo brushed that off with the flick of a hand. He flirts with anything with a pulse, but he encouraged me to pipe down with Emma's best friend and her husband. That is one pep talk I didn't need. I left all interest in Terrence at the singles' retreat and haven't looked back.

Mawmaw always told us God don't like ugly. I'm far from it physically, but my actions haven't reflected my home training. Tammi told me to forgive myself, but how can I?

Guilt swallows me whole at the most unexpected times. Some days, I feel the urge to craft an apology letter for my bitch behavior. Other days are milder and don't include a pen and paper but a vow to do better.

Forgiveness isn't that simple. There's always a price to pay, and I can't shake the feeling that mine will be high given the way I've acted.

My phone chimes again.

"Who the heck is it?" I ask myself and the cast of *The Fresh Prince of Bel-Air* on TV.

It's not Kojo. I left him to come back to my hotel. He should be bouncing between the legs of the lovers he has scattered across Los Angeles. Every visit is like a scavenger hunt for him, one that includes multiple players and no map.

My night might lack orgasms, but it did include wine by candlelight and cake in the tub. It's not a sex marathon, but it comes with '90s reruns.

Unlike my friend, my legs are closed for the evening. I'm staying on the Redondo Beach peninsula, about forty-five minutes from LA, far away from traffic and overpriced neighborhoods. I get enough concrete living in Manhattan. I want sand.

My room isn't a suite, but it's spacious, with a private patio and a view of the marina. The cream and blue hues are an extension of the small waves that drift in from the South Bay. It's one of my favorite places to stay when I'm in LA.

Flipping through premium cable isn't my go-to on a Thursday night, but I'm off dating for the foreseeable future. The only thing I'm modeling tonight is comfort and a gold eye mask under my lids.

I rip off the comforter when my phone starts ringing. I stomp the short distance from my pillowtop bed to my makeup bag, which is cushioning the nuisance. Kojo better be in the ER and not sending me clips of his choose-a-hole journey.

Another scenario quickens my steps. "Not Daddy," I murmur, crossing the teal carpet in a hurry. Mama called last week to tell me the doctor advised him to lay off bowfishing after agitating his back in the shop.

Buck Monroe is hardheaded and hard of hearing. He and his mechanic friends are always into something whenever the garage isn't open. My daddy loves to pretend he's twenty-eight and not fifty-eight. My parents had me when they were twenty-one, knee-deep in diapers and pull-ups in the early years of their marriage. Mama flings weights with gym buddies half her age. Daddy rides ATVs and skydives, of all things.

I promised to swing by soon. My annual visit only lasts a few days before I'm back to a life of fashion and travel.

"Shit." I scramble to pick up my phone and answer without looking. "Daddy? You okay?"

"That's new," a low voice says with a soft chuckle. The mellow bass vibrates through the line with an energy that seems out of place for how early it is on the other side of the pond.

"Preston." I release a breath and press a palm to the side of my silk scarf. "I thought you were my daddy."

"I can be."

The hairs on my neck raise from the velvet baritone. I fold my arms over my cami, as if he can see my nipples standing at attention.

Hold yourself together. We don't tingle over a voice!

I sigh. "I'll hang up if you're calling about shoestring colors or suspender patterns. It's been a long day, and I've reached my limit for your games."

The line goes quiet.

"What happened, Puff?"

"Not your concern."

"If it concerns you, it concerns me. What happened?"

An anchored sailboat sways next to the dock. Moonlight skims across its white body and bounces over quiet ripples.

"Puff?"

Feelings aren't a topic I discuss freely. Tammi and Kojo have to pry them out of me. To say I don't like being vulnerable is an understatement. I'd rather endure a public mammogram than face judgment.

Tammi caught me today when I was on an emotional sprint. It was a fluke. I was too busy running for my life in my least comfortable heels in case Emma's claws matched her mouth.

I don't throw my problems at my friends. They have enough to deal with without my mess.

"Puff?"

"On second thought, shoelaces and suspenders sound better," I mumble. "Don't you have a hotel empire to run?"

"Ah, a subject change. Must be awful."

"Preston."

"I called you because I can't stop thinking about you. I figured I'd try my luck and forget these damn texts."

His declaration hangs firm. Final. Preston filters his personality through sarcasm, but he never minces words.

A smile pokes my lips as I imagine his stoic expression. He's probably behind his desk in a crisp suit. "You telling me you picked out your own socks?"

"I have since my nanny stopped dressing me," he says, as if personal staff is an ordinary expense. "What's bothering you?"

I bite the inside of my cheek and stare at the geometric carpet. In what universe do I talk about my love life with my ex? Not just any ex, *the* ex, the one I randomly bumped into, who texts all the time and hosts candlelight dinners in his closet.

The remnants in my wineglass disappear with a single gulp. I sink back into the queen bed. "You really want to know?"

"There must be an echo on the line—you're repeating a question I've now asked twice," he says with posh sarcasm.

"Smart-ass."

He mirrors my smile in his tone. "Full of compliments, aren't you? Don't dodge me, Puff."

The breath I release is long, but it soothes the tightness in my chest. "Have you ever made a mistake you regret? One you don't want to define you for the rest of your life?"

"Yes."

"How did you get over it?"

Leather groans as he shifts his weight in his chair. "I haven't. I never will," he says with the same finality as the declaration he uttered days ago. *I'm not letting you go this time.* "The worst regret of my life haunts me every fucking day. We're human, Madison. We make mistakes we'd trade the world to take back. But we get the chance to do better if we're lucky."

"That's actually good advice," I say, tracing the pattern in the comforter's stitching. Silence is a heavy mist. "Well—"

"Don't," he warns. "Don't shut me out."

Goosebumps sprinkle across my forearms as I remember all the ways he had me.

Facedown.

On my side.

In the air.

Touching my toes.

The sex was immaculate, but the intimacy extended beyond eternity.

I reach deep to snatch the scraps of my restraint, though my inner heaux is ready to edge temptation.

This can't happen. *We* can't happen.

"Preston," I sigh. "We've been down this road before. It's a dead end."

"Not like this. Let's use our time together to get to know each other again," he says. "The real us."

I ready a rebuttal but pause at Tammi's reminder. Her call to forgive and stop courting bitterness.

"Let's be friends," he says, like it's the obvious choice. Maybe it is.

When the time is right, try to make amends.

"Okay."

"Good. Now I can stop texting random shit just to talk to you." I snort at his lame attempts. He gets an A in persistence. "I have a day's worth of meetings to get through, to run my empire, as you say. Thank you for taking my call, Puff. I miss talking to you."

So do I, I don't confess.

"As for whatever's got you down, I'm eight hours into your future. I promise it's bright."

"Good luck today."

"Sleep tight, Puff."

Chapter 24

Preston

"**K**ey performance indicators suggest our average daily rate is steady with flexible pricing options. Revenue per available room projections are high, as are occupancy rate trends." The screen switches to more graphs and charts. "We're outperforming last year's Q1 across properties."

A smile finds its way through the iron curtain I wear in the boardroom. I don't make a habit of showing anything more than contentment or disappointment. Too much emotion gets used against you, even at the hands of my own father.

William slaps the table, his face split into a grin. He sweeps over the results of a year's worth of work showcased in bold black letters with a nod.

"We fucking did it," he says. "The board would be foolish not to support your vision based on these projections."

"*Our* vision," I correct.

My eyes skate over the presentation before landing on the source of our future victories. KD studies me under long lashes. Her focused stare would scare off the strongest men, who'd crumble under the weight of her brilliance. The firm lines in her set jaw release her stone mask enough for a half smile to peek through.

"Thank you," I say.

She traces the necklace I gave her for her birthday ages ago. "Thank you" comes in a smooth, even tone.

Since becoming CEO, I've fought to get her a position on the board. Me and William's shares are no match for the misogyny upheld by decades of tradition. Women have never had a place on the Donnelley board, and that includes the first woman CFO, whose own fucking father gave his son the shares reserved for her.

Hugh still holds a grudge that I chose his daughter as CFO and not Michael. KD and I have been friends since we were kids, but she earned her position and proves it time and time again—despite her father's lack of support.

Her armor is tested under the weight of her father's shadow. It's something we have in common, but for different reasons. People who've attempted to diminish my work ethic because of the melanin in my skin have found themselves on the receiving end of my ire. KD has fought for visibility and acceptance within a male-dominated industry. She's hardened over the years, keeping mostly to Paris and only using her nickname, which has become a permanent moniker. She has a beautiful mind for mathematics and a scorned heart from the people who should love her the most. It's why I'm protective of her...not that she can't hold her own.

"This calls for a celebration." William rubs his hands together, catching the light of the chandelier in his gold cuff links. "Destin in an hour?"

"I'm down," I say, packing up the paper version of our presentation.

"I'm open," KD says. Heels clack across aged wood on her way to turn off the flatscreen hanging between two vintage mirrors.

I gave her full range to decorate the Paris office. The once-stuffy replica of the CEO suite in Eldridge Court now has life via weathered gold molding and French baroque ceilings. There are enough crystal chandeliers around the office for a fashion event, one KD and her team could host with their wardrobe alone.

Except for Madison, I've never seen anyone so runway ready. The slit in the middle of KD's thigh stretches up her form-fitting dress when she reaches down to grab her oversized handbag that doubles as a briefcase. She's a beautiful woman with a toned figure that's six feet without heels.

Her eyes lift to mine, brighter now that the workday is finally over. "Ready?"

"Would you like to order, or wait for your party to arrive?" the waiter asks in French.

"No need," KD says. She rattles off her dinner order and mine. "William off chasing tourists again?" She straightens the white napkin in her lap.

"Maybe an ambulance. He has a thing for paramedics." I return her smirk and settle into the booth's unforgiving leather.

My brother and I fly out to Paris monthly to review financials with KD. Like clockwork, he suggests a dinner he never attends. I thought he was trying to push me and KD together at first, but he runs after the first woman he sees the minute he leaves the office.

"You look good, Preston." Her eyes linger on my navy and orange plaid single-breast waistcoat over a white shirt. "Is this new?"

"Trying something different." I widen my legs to adjust myself under the table. The fit of these trousers is a vise on my nuts.

She sips her water. "Color looks good on you. What sparked the change from a wardrobe full of gray?"

It takes the strength of my grandmother not to scowl at the plate set in front of me. My brother is truly an ass for choosing a restaurant that serves bubbles.

"Tofu and oyster foam," the waiter says with a proud nod.

At least one of us is safe from eating this infant-size science experiment. Whatever's on this plate can stay there.

"Try it. You'll like it." KD points her knife at the foam sliding off what looks like a glob of mozzarella cheese. She cuts a delicate bite and savors it like it's the best thing she ate today.

No wonder Ralph Fiennes killed everybody in *The Menu*. I've contemplated murder myself at business lunches and dinners that ran too long with crumbs for fine dining. I enjoy a well-prepared meal, but I draw the line at unseasoned samples that barely fill my thoughts, let alone my stomach.

"Preston." KD all but laughs in my face. Her eyes crinkle at the giggle she's holding in.

"Sod off," I huff, taking a bite that will seal my fate with a toilet.

She rolls her eyes. "This is a five-star restaurant."

"That's one star for each sprout on this fucking plate." I lift the tofu. "Apologies, four."

I startle at the bark of KD's laughter. Her head tips back, angling her forehead to the ceiling. The snort that escapes her tempts me to check her temperature for a fever.

"Preston, you are something else." She dabs at her eyes with a content sigh. "I missed you last month."

All playfulness leaves the table. The air thickens, smothering what was once a lighthearted exchange between close friends.

I crossed the line with KD, breaching a boundary we have yet to reestablish. Our sex is casual, without expectations. William put two and two together when I stopped in Paris after Christmas. I never travel alone to meet KD—I've had no reason to, outside of our monthly meetings. He never picked up on the fact we've been fucking on and off for over two decades. We only have sex when the mood strikes, and we never let it cloud our work.

KD checks all the boxes. She's a knockout, a tenacious business-woman, and she has a drive that exceeds mine. Our fathers pushed for everything but an arranged marriage. They wanted to unite London's most prominent families. I have love for KD, but I am not *in* love with her. My affection never grew to anything deeper, not that I tried. The spark just isn't there.

Only one woman claimed my heart and kept it with her.

My phone chimes with the melody I saved for Madison. I'm six hours ahead since she went back to New York, and I find myself smiling the same way I did when I read her emails fifteen years ago.

Madison

I got in trouble when I was little for telling my grandmother in church I was tired of eating coochie.

My laughter spills out in a half cackle, half cry. The force collapses my chest over the table. Had I not pushed aside the tofu foam, I would be wearing it on my face.

Please explain before they cart me off for laughing too loud inside this restaurant. Remind me to tell you about the food.

KD clears her throat.

"Apologies. One sec," I say.

Madison

Couche couche (sounds like koosh koosh) is a Cajun staple. Mawmaw cooked it all the time. It's a fried cornmeal mush she'd make with bacon fat and sugar. I struggled with certain words when I was little and called it coochie.

I crack up again. We've been sharing random facts about ourselves, and this is the wildest one to date.

Stares from nearby patrons burn my cheeks. But none are as intense as the woman across from me, who's ready to scorch my ass with the fury set into her glower.

KD looks from me to the phone in my hand. "New friend?" Her curt voice delivers its first lashing.

"Rekindled love," I volley back.

Her brows smooth under the press of her manicured nail. "Love." The word trickles through her lips before they press into a stubborn slit. "Since when do you care about love?"

"I never stopped with her."

If I hadn't known KD since we were little, I'd miss the pained look she quickly chambers. It's not my intention to hurt her any more than it is to pretend sex between us would lead to forever. We both agreed, no feelings. Other women never bothered her before.

"I see," she says, slowly counting back to the four days we spent under each other. I left for the States right after, and I suspect one of us developed feelings. "How quickly things change. Should we be picking out china while you're here?"

I lift my scotch for a sip. "We're not there yet. Far from it."

"So it's not serious?"

"We reunited unexpectedly during my holiday. We're friends for now, but I'm fighting for more."

Something flashes in KD's eyes, but she quickly extinguishes it. There's never been a reason for her to be jealous. We've both been with other people, which shouldn't make Madison an issue.

"Ready for a nightcap? I'll grab the check," she says.

I spoke too soon.

"I have someone in my life."

She waves me off with a scoff. "You said yourself, you two are friends. Friends fuck, Preston. You've never been monogamous with any woman you've dated."

"Except for her, but you know that."

She and my father are the only people who know about my time in Paris. KD saw me at the height of love, and when I fell apart in the aftermath.

"It's her," I reiterate.

Her slight gasp is audible among the clatter of plates and chatter from nearby tables. My head cants to the side in search of a reasonable explanation for why my friend is looking at me like a scorned lover.

She forces a smile that doesn't reach her eyes. "Good luck with the long distance."

"She's moving to London on Monday, for three months. To be my stylist," I say.

KD's fingers squeeze her glass. Her gaze swipes over me in disapproval of the outfit she praised only minutes ago. "How wonderful." Her eyes snap to mine. "She has great taste."

After dinner, I walk her back to her place a few blocks away. The food was awful, but at least we rerouted our conversation away from my personal life after I told her to let it be.

I reach my next destination and sit at a small table in the corner. Then I take a selfie and text it to Madison.

I still have a double cheeseburger at the McDonald's you took me to whenever I'm in Paris.

She hearts the photo of me damn near gnawing off my fingers after that scarce and undercooked dinner.

Madison

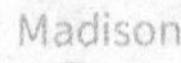

Eating among the commoners looks good
on you.

We text for over an hour before she's off to style a photo shoot. I loathe this form of communication, but I would be lying if I said I'm not enjoying our exchange.

This time around, I'm showing Madison all of me.

Chapter 25
Madison

"I cannot believe you didn't pack me in your carry-on. Look at that view!"

I pan my phone around Westminster from the open living area. Tammi's eyes grow two sizes at the floor-to-ceiling windows and the panoramic backdrop with Westminster Abbey and Big Ben in the distance. This high up, I'm on top of the world. A giant would have to scale the building to reach me, and he wouldn't need to duck inside. The height alone in this apartment is wild.

"This is sick."

Tammi kisses her teeth. "Sick is Smokey Jr., sneezing with an uncovered mouth and snot hanging like an ornament. This is luxury."

It hasn't hit me that I'm in London for three months. My common sense is still in customs at JFK, waiting to get over jet lag and tell me I'm making a mistake. I don't give clients this much of my time, but I folded at Preston's proposal.

Wonder why.

I got cold feet over the weekend. A month ago, I was cursing his existence when it collided with mine at full force. Now, we text all the time. It was a plot twist I never saw coming, one that frayed my resolution to never speak to him again.

Preston is more than an attractive face with a mouthwatering body to match. Underneath his charm is a calming presence, pulling me to him. Scabs from the hurt I've carried fall away with each message we send.

Did I make the wrong choice coming here?

Tammi sits on the other end of the video call, a world away. After Kojo told me to wave my ass at Buckingham Palace like a Union Jack flag, I called her for advice. She was my last line of defense who did the opposite of encourage me to keep my butt at home.

After a lecture longer than a Sunday sermon about why I waited so long to tell her about Preston, I spilled it all—Ravenous included. Tammi asked every question under the sun, for "praying purposes," while I stared at two empty suitcases.

I expected her to hold a grudge on my behalf. To my surprise, she challenged me to focus on who Preston is today, not who he was fifteen years ago.

His father is a different story. If I never see him again, it would be too soon.

So here I am. A five-hour time difference away from my life, in a penthouse that costs more than a small village, second-guessing for the sixth time whether or not I should be on this continent.

Jewel got so annoyed with my constant texting, she told me she'd respond next month. After I "got myself together" and stopped stressing. Her words.

"Want to talk about it?" Black curls press to Tammi's chocolate brown cheeks under an ivory winter hat.

"You've said enough." I roll my eyes and continue with the virtual house tour.

"See him with fresh eyes and an open heart" is what she told me after I chickened out. Every excuse I threw popped me in the forehead when Tammi tossed it back in my face. The fact that Preston is spouse-free won her over. So did his obvious attempts to squeeze himself back into my life. She thought the closet dinner was adorable, which had me staring at my phone sideways.

"We all change, Madison. Sometimes for the better," she made sure to mention.

While that's true, I'm here for a job, not for love.

I repeated that mantra on the ride to the airport, on the plane, and en route to my temporary home. Preston had his assistant coordinate my travel, which included Jesse, his driver, to escort me back to the very building where I put my slippers in sport mode. (It took Tammi twenty minutes to stop cackling when I told her about my Tom Cruise sprint down the hallway. She was one giggle away from me hanging up.)

When Preston said I'd be somewhere close, I didn't think he meant the other penthouse on the same floor.

I follow a yellow brick road of honey-colored hardwood from the living area past the kitchen. There are two bedrooms and two bathrooms. Beyond a door is a large room that floats in the sky.

"And your silly self wanted to stay home. Look at this!" Tammi's scream is so loud I pull the phone away from my face to rescue my eardrums. All of London hears her hollering. "Stop being a lazy host and show me around," she huffs with wide eyes and a big mouth that's on the verge of drooling.

The entire wall is glass, with drapes that are two Shaqs high. A king-size bed faces the city. There are overhead lights, simple nightstands on either side, and a reading chair in the corner.

I gasp.

"What is it?"

Tammi repeats the question until I pan the camera to an open closet of shelves and hanging rods filled with clothing and accessories. They're all my favorite brands.

Light reflects off the curated inventory like a diamond. Dresses, skirts, pants, and tops are all carefully placed on satin hangers.

"I only brought two suitcases with me," I say.

There's a folded card on a shelf with my name in cursive.

"Read it!" Tammi's round face holds the biggest grin. She tips her travel coffee mug at the camera, motioning for me to get on with it.

I flip the view back to me and raise a brow. "Did you take Ellis to school while you're in my business?"

It's 8:20 a.m. back home. Tammi already made three school stops and daycare drop-offs. The look she gives me tells me not to question her.

"I'm in the grocery store parking lot with a laundry list of things to do—laundry included. This is the first moment of silence I've had all day. The only gift waiting for me at home is the chance to pee without a child clawing at the door. Open. The. Damn. Card."

"Alright," I say. It's pointless to argue with a tired mother.

"Flip the camera back so I can see."

Puff,

I took the liberty of securing a wardrobe to ensure your comfort here in London. Thank you again for coming. It means more than you know.

Yours,

Preston

"Should we send for the rest of your things, or will you buy everything new once you marry this man?" My attempt at a glare activates Tammi's belly laugh. Her cheeks tint red as her breath skates across the screen.

Detroit winters will never be my testimony.

I flip the camera on the way out of the bedroom. "No one is getting married. Where is your spirited lecture about chastity belts and joining a convent? Dating is a bad idea right now."

"First, I'm not Catholic, and I'm pretty sure nobody is walking this earth in an iron diaper," Tammi says. "Second, I agreed with you taking a break from dating before I knew Preston was pursuing you. If he was coming like the others, keep him on read. The man is rolling out the red carpet and a literal penthouse. Why not consider something more if it feels right?"

"Because I make the wrong choices!" I gape at her like Tracee Ellis Ross to prove the point she's missing.

"Make it make sense for me."

I slide onto a barstool at the white marble island across from the kitchen with the grace of a jet-lagged traveler who's questioning her life decisions. Handleless taupe cabinets glow in undercabinet lighting above a textured gray backsplash.

"This"—I motion around luxury I'll never afford in this life or the next—"is unreal. I'm in London for *three months* for a man I loved fifteen years ago who reappeared out of thin air. How do I know I'm not making a mistake being here? I've been burned too many times to wear another scar."

I rub my self-inflicted headache and startle at Tammi's grin. It reminds me of the *Smile* movies. I'd question possession if she wasn't blinking.

"Please stop looking at me like that," I groan.

"Do you hear yourself, Ms. I Don't Like to Share My Feelings? Don't cut your eyes at me. Do you know what I think?"

"I'm sure you'll tell me." I pick at a cuticle, which reminds me to find a new nail place here.

"I think you're scared. I also think you've self-sabotaged to protect yourself from getting hurt again. The men you date always fall short of your expectations, the same way Terrence distracted you from what you *haven't* admitted. Preston is your standard. You're afraid having him in your life again will lead to the same outcome."

My heart thuds against my ribs. I open my mouth to argue, but nothing comes out.

"Love can feel like a roll of the dice, but true love is divinely connected," she adds. "Life has seasons, and your paths are crossing again. Hold firm to your boundaries, but don't block yourself from what might be the love you've been waiting for."

"I'm here for a job," I say out loud, to prove to myself and Tammi that I have zero intention of rekindling anything with Preston.

Tammi's tired sigh is heavy. "You have to stop loving him before you can fall in love again," she deadpans. "Lie to yourself until you're blue. You haven't been hopping from man to man for this self-imposed time-out. I supported it because I support you, but it's been a year, Maddie. Take a break from dating if you want, but you're not fooling anyone. Do me a favor and enjoy your time in London. Hell, live for me! Someday, you'll admit why you're there. Until then, date or don't. You know what you want, and you need to get out of your own way."

"It's not that easy, Tam. He's a billionaire with—"

"Aht, aht! Those are excuses to feed your self-sabotage," she snaps. "I'm not freezing my ass off in a parking lot to hear that. This man is showing you his intentions. It's up to you to take it for what it is or keep things professional. Talk to him about how you feel and go from there. All this back-and-forth is about to piss me off. He flew you out and put you up in a penthouse, and you want to boohoo about it."

"Okay, okay! Message received."

We end the call after her *hmph* and my promise to see where these next three months lead. I'll admit I'm excited, but I'm also scared. I only have a few business acquaintances here. No friends or family.

Things with Preston have been better than expected. But without our texts, what happens once the thrill wears off?

Chapter 26

Madison

Fifteen Years Ago

"This is absolutely ridiculous, you realize? How in the fuck did I die of exhaustion? I took a nap!"

Preston strokes his chin, which is covered in stubble, and stares at his computer. His jaw works as he reads the next prompt. Glimmers of light from the screen reflect in cognac eyes that are desperate to prevent another fatality. He rolls his bottom lip between his teeth and taps the keyboard, making his choice.

A wooden raft holding his wagon floats down the river, and he navigates it with keystrokes. It shifts right, then left, before crashing into a rock. Preston's face drains of color as a black box appears on the screen, sealing his party's fate in white letters.

"They killed Sarah and my oxen?!" he yells at the screen.

"Don't forget the hundred and seventeen bullets you lost." I bite the inside of my cheek to keep from laughing in his face, but I fail when his glare burns a hole through my neck.

My hand doesn't reach my mouth in time to stop a loud cackle. It drowns out the game's patriotic tune that's blaring through the desktop speakers.

Preston could pose for the cover of a magazine right now. No one would ever expect his tousled hair and hooded stare are from playing *The Oregon Trail*. I meant for the game to be a way to relax. He came home in a sour mood, and it's been my mission to lift his spirits in the best way I know how: my favorite '90s games.

As you might've guessed, it backfired. I'm in tears, and he's one river away from throwing his computer over the balcony.

He cuts his eyes at me. "You're laughing pretty hard for someone who died of the shits."

"At least I didn't go out from exhaustion."

"I took a nap!"

"Don't get your knickers in a twist," I mock in an awful English accent and take off in the sprint of my life when he jumps up from the chair.

I squeal at the grip on the back of my cotton robe and pull it off right as I dip out of the home office. The hallway is a blur of crown molding. It fills with the echoes of my laughter and the heavy footfall of our high-speed chase.

Open pocket doors next to the dining room provide a short-lived reprieve. Soon, Preston skids inside wearing plaid slippers and a predatory scowl. My thighs tense. His eyes never leave mine as he takes mirrored steps from across the table. I fake left and pull out a chair behind me, which hits the parquet floor in a thud.

I make it two steps into the living room before I'm in the air, curled to his chest like I'm weightless. His veiny forearms are on full display.

He leans forward and lowers his voice. "Got you." His musk mixes with his minty breath.

Those two words quiver my spine. "Yes, you do," I whisper back, my lips inches from his.

If I wasn't in Preston's arms, I'd question the days that stretched to weeks to separate us. I'd wonder if there is someone else.

But all doubt fades with the soft caress of his gaze and a kiss that sends the pit of my stomach into a free fall. He walks us back to his room, where we make love for the first time.

Wispy clouds drift across the night sky, prodding a cool breeze to float through the parted balcony doors. We dampened the sheets in Preston's bed with sweat but kept them intact.

Preston's lashes flutter against his skin. He's on his stomach, fighting the sleep that's tugging at his satisfied eyes. They're filled with a tenderness that shines in the pale light of the moon. He sinks into the pillow and exhales when my fingers sweep over the lines of his shoulder blade. His eyes are on me, but his mind is elsewhere.

Sex exceeded my imagination and my wildest dreams. I knew he would be a passionate lover from the way he kisses. Each stroke of his tongue is a soul-searching exploration of the depths of my pleasure.

I unraveled under his quiet praise and the way he held my neck in place as he massaged my G-spot like they were long-lost friends. I wasn't prepared for the eye contact. It was intense, unwavering in its focus on me and my body's reactions to his thrusts.

"You're gorgeous, Puff." He reaches over to cup my face. I lean into his touch and revel in his nickname for me. "Are you sure it's okay if I call you that?"

"Yes." My smile is too big for my face.

"Good. Heather doesn't suit you."

That's because it's not my name.

I've tried and failed to reveal my identity. The timing was never right, with him popping in and out of Paris. I didn't expect our flirtatious meet-cute to go beyond a night.

Preston was supposed to be temporary, a memory I cataloged during my time in Paris. But he's more than that. My feelings are past the point of like, entering new territory, and I hope it isn't a one-way street.

He hasn't told me why he left London a week earlier than planned. His eyes were dark, hardened under the annoyance that crossed his face when he first walked in. I packed up the fashion magazines littered across the coffee table and stood to leave, but he dropped his briefcase, stormed into the living room, and enveloped me in a hug that stretched for minutes.

I thought he wanted space, but he wanted me.

"Do you want to talk about it?" I asked earlier tonight, but I didn't get a response.

Preston looks away with a strained sigh and stares at the headboard. We've yet to open the door to our full selves. Only windows we decorate with half-truths and glimpses into the lives we're shielding from each other. I don't think he's trying to be any more deceptive than I've been. He might know me as Heather, but the heart I'm opening to him is all Madison.

The sheets rustle when he turns on his side to face me. Moonlight drapes over the muscles I licked and down to the dark hair dusting his chest. My cheeks heat when I find his eyes on me after I peek at the pleasure trail of hair that leads to the power between his thighs.

His forearms aren't the only things with veins.

A smirk lifts his dimples. "Was tonight okay?"

"Tonight was amazing, but it would be better if you told me what's wrong."

He considers me, his eyes searching mine as he decides how much he wants to reveal. His shoulder wilts. "My father and I got into it," he says, running a hand through his thick hair. "I want to take our company in a new direction, but he's fighting me every step of the way. I refuse to become his carbon copy."

"So just be Preston."

His hands slip through my arms to pull me closer. He drapes my leg over his body, and I rest my chin on his chest. "I try every day, Puff." He kisses my forehead and shifts his eyes to me. They're softer, void of the baggage he left at the front door. "I can be Preston with you. It's a gift. *You're* a gift."

I wince with guilt. *You need to tell him.*

"Preston."

He sits up and kisses me with enough passion to make me dizzy. My nipples perk at the brush of his thumbs, freeing a moan at the slip of his tongue.

Preston takes my face in his hands. "I don't want to think about the man I have to be for other people. This is me—the real me. I know we don't have much time together, but I want you for however long you'll have me."

"Preston. I have to—"

"All I want is the real you, Puff. Not the you that you give to everyone else. Can you do that?" I pull away to object but fall short at his silent plea. "I just fired someone who only got close to me for personal gain. I can't take more deceit." His jaw tenses. "Please, Puff. Give me the real you."

He rises to his knees at my nod and seals his body to mine.

I want to tell him everything before we get too deep, but it's too late. There's no doubt in my mind I've fallen for him. Our lives are too different for anything to go beyond the time we have left. If I tell Preston I'm not Heather, it will crush him. Should he decide to toss me away like everyone else who tried to use him, I have no safety net out here. I only want him, but would he see it that way?

We only have six more months before I fly back to California. Until then, I'll give him what he wants.

I can give him me.

Chapter 27

Preston

Now

"I don't give a shit what you thought! I'm the CEO. I expect an update before the end of the week. Am I clear?"

The line goes quiet. I'm a patient man, but I won't repeat myself.

"Crystal clear, Mr. Donnelley," Simon quips through his veneers, no doubt mentally cursing me for the formal salutation I demand.

It's only a matter of time before he whines to my father. I give him a head start by slamming the headset into the base.

Prick.

Nonna would light me up with a wooden spoon if she heard me talk like that to an elder. Lionara Parisi is seventy-eight, but I still need to dodge the trajectory of her wrath. Then again, if she were here, she'd probably turn her spoon and sandal on Simon Nottidge for messing with her grandson.

It's rare for me to raise my voice, inside of the office or out. But my father does it all the time, and if his lackeys insist on testing me, consider class in session.

I'm no longer the scrawny kid who was forced to sit in the back of conference rooms before getting shipped off to boarding school. I grew into my gangly body, and now I fill out tailored suits and size thirteen shoes.

I tower over men like Simon who made me feel small growing up. It must be a mind fuck for the ones who are still around to call me boss. My edict is an iron fist when tried, and Simon will get a lesson he'll never forget.

The next phase of our sustainability initiative rolled out six months ago. A profitable portfolio of hotels and resorts satisfies shareholders, but I want to do more than line pockets. The Donnelley Brand underwent an overhaul in the last five years to be more environmentally conscious. We reduced our water and energy consumption with new systems. Reliance on single-use plastics is now a past practice, with alternatives in place sourced from companies that champion responsible disposal.

Investing in local economies through food procurement was an initiative implemented across all properties. General managers had a full year to work with their food and beverage managers and create a plan to source food from regional producers where possible. Only one was dumb enough to defy me and think he'd get away with it.

"Motherfucker," I mumble over the report KD provided me. Thousands of dollars wasted on flying in food that was available at nearby farms.

Simon Nottidge is an arrogant shit who's too mediocre to be anything other than ordinary. Placing him in charge of our New York hotel was an act of grace my father bestowed upon his longtime friend. Simon was fresh out of failing through an MBA bought and paid for by his family's legacy, and my father knew he would never reach the executive suite without his help.

Stephanie saunters through my open door with a tablet in hand. "I rearranged your schedule and set up a call with your brother first thing tomorrow," she says to the device in a tone more pleasant than my roar of a few seconds ago. Her eyes lift to the navy suit coat I tossed over the sofa hours ago, then to the papers scattered across my desk. "Can I help?"

"No, thank you. That will be all tonight." I peer down at the Manhattan report, my palms pressed into smooth wood.

A headache the size of a pain in my ass strums the vein protruding against my forehead. I ignore it and glance up through black-rimmed glasses at Stephanie, who's still in the same spot.

"Your feet stuck?" I eye the heels she walked in with that haven't taken her back through the door.

She became my executive assistant after Marie retired last year. Stephanie is savvier with technology and keeps pace with my demanding schedule, but she doesn't hold a candle to the woman who was around since I learned how to walk.

Marie told me stories about my mother and a different version of my father, one I've yet to meet. How she survived his wrath for so long is a testament to her pure heart. Marie stuck by my father after my mother's death, even when he hired a revolving door of second assistants to fuck. I'll never understand her loyalty to my family, but I'm happy she moved to Suffolk to be with her son and grandchildren.

I lift a brow at Stephanie, who seems determined to pluck the only nerve I have left today. She casts her mascara-lined grimace at me, and I punt it right back.

"You're in a mood." Her hand snaps to her slender hip in high-waist slacks.

"And you're observant. Please call Luther to escort you to the car park." With any luck, I'll make it home within the hour.

"Should I give Gisele a ring to schedule an appointment?" Whatever reaction Stephanie hopes to conjure doesn't breach my indifference. She has her suspicions, but she'll never know the true depths of how I relieve tension.

I'm in my office more than I'm at home, and I satisfy certain appetites with the utmost discretion. Unlike my father, the women who enter for pleasure aren't my subordinates. The few I have relations with are entrepreneurs and consultants who signed NDAs with the full expectation they'll leave thoroughly fucked.

Gisele is a corporate accountant, a divorcée in Chelsea with complex mocha curves and a high drive to match. Sex with her is the same as the others: transactional orgasms shared with consent. She is an amazing woman, but the object of my desire touched down in London hours ago.

"Not necessary," I say, to Stephanie's shock. "Enjoy your evening." My tone leaves no room for interpretation, and she finally accepts in a huff. Who I fuck doesn't concern her outside of checking my availability.

Madison is the first woman who's made me want more. Her body is a valley of peaks and soft lines, worth a lifetime of exploration, but her heart is the priceless treasure I want to savor and protect.

She was my anchor, soothing my darkest days with the pitch of her laugh and her smile. I didn't understand what it meant to find your soulmate in your twenties. As a grown man, I know what a gift it is. I have three months to prove that the second time around will be better than the first. Fate reunited us, and I refuse to let go.

I gave Madison her space today, outside of a few texts to make sure she's okay. I want her ready and rested.

Tomorrow, the chase begins.

Chapter 28

Madison

The walk to Preston's office felt like a mile even though only feet separate his sidewalk from mine. He probably owns it all, since his wealth climbs beyond the sculpted glass-and-steel structure that bears his name. The building spans eleven floors, eight fewer than the high-rise behind me, which he also owns, a continuity of simple lines and geometric forms.

The sun boomerangs between the mirroring structures and the steady traffic along the tree-lined street. Businesses are open at the early hour, the scent of fresh pastries drifting through the crisp air. It's a calm morning...except for my pounding heart stumbling to find its rhythm.

The revolving door might as well be a dark void ready to swallow me whole.

Seeing Preston shouldn't make me this nervous. Our casual texts are now a daily stream of random memes and facts. They remind me of a time when friendship was the core of our intimacy, when talking about nothing felt like everything.

"Just go through the door," I tell myself.

How foolish do I look staring up at a building?

I've seen Preston. I'm well acquainted with the rich musk of his cologne and the way his shoulder blades complement the hard shafts of his thighs.

His presence doesn't scare me. I survived his dimpled assault and the slow, steady grin he wields with ease. It's his intentions that give me pause.

"This is just a job," I whisper, eyes closed in a silent prayer.

Security is manageable through a stream of tailored fabric shuffling in every direction. An athletic man in all black approaches. He's handsome, with lean muscles, a high taper fro, and a dazzling display of white teeth.

"Ms. Monroe. I'm Dayo, Mr. Donnelley's head of security," he says in a deep baritone. "This way."

We bypass the central bank of elevators for a door with biometric access. It leads to another door inside a sleek concrete corridor with high walls and the illusion of natural light.

"Access to the private car park below is through here." He points to a door on the left and pulls out a key card from his pocket.

We stop in front of an elevator. Dayo swipes the card over a panel that turns green. "I'll have one of these to you before you leave. This way." He motions for me to enter when the doors open.

"How long have you worked for Preston?"

Dayo's lips part, spreading the sharp lines of his profile into a smirk. "We've been in business together since he took over the company eight years ago. He went to boarding school with my half brother, who lives in the States. This is my security firm."

"Nice." I nod.

I catch my reflection in the door. Dressing like Cher Horowitz wasn't intentional, but I went with it, feeling clueless.

Nerves crowd a sigh that slips out.

This is just another client. Nothing more, nothing less.

"You must be special."

"Excuse me?" I muffle a gasp as Dayo smiles down at me like he knows a secret.

His dark brown gaze sweeps over my black turtleneck and plaid high-waist skirt. It stalls on my thigh-high vegan suede boots.

"You're the first person to have a personal escort and access to the private lift."

"We have history," I say and face the doors, which are taking forever to open. How long until we reach the top?

The guttural chuckle at my side tempts a glare, but I roll my lips and keep my eyes ahead.

"Yeah, you special." The doors open. "Through there. See you soon, Ms. Monroe."

Polished stone the color of sand is my runway to what I'm assuming is Preston's office. The hallway is light with wood and marble wall panels. Glass doors line the right side. There's a gym, a sauna, and a full bathroom. The echo of my heels fades when I reach a weathered oak door. Next to it is a high-tech keypad.

Do I knock?

The door opens on its own, revealing a large room fit for a hotelier. The sun yawns through windows that are taller than the ones in my new bedroom and seeps over hardwood the same color as the door that magically opened. On the back wall is a gold shelving unit that extends to a black lacquered ceiling. In front of it is an oversized contemporary desk with enough space to seat eight. The black executive chair that faces a laptop and two screens is empty.

"Hey."

If Preston doesn't incite a heart attack from scaring me, his seductive stare will tempt me to check out what's behind the curtain.

Lord, the way this man wears a suit.

He's in the ink-blue one I found buried behind all the gray slacks and blazers in his closet. The merino wool outlines his shoulders, and a white dress shirt rests against the expanse of his chest. He's tie-free, the top two buttons undone below the strong column of the neck I sucked in a previous life.

I'm so mesmerized by the sensuous glide of his mouth that I miss whatever he asks.

"Sorry. What?"

His tongue dips between the seam of his lips. "You okay, Puff?"

Focus.

"Never better." I let out a breath to keep from inhaling his cologne. "Nice office." I peer over his shoulder to study a random photo and not his textured dark waves, which tempt my fingers to stroke the edges.

"Thank you. I wanted it to feel cozy since I spend most of my time here." There's no anchor to support the weight of his appraisal as it drags up the flare of my hips to the swell of my breasts. His exhale is a suppressed moan once he reaches my lips.

"You're breathtaking," he whispers.

My "Thank you" is thick and unsteady. I haven't been in his office for five minutes, and already I'm a pipe ready to burst.

Call him to come fix your plumbing.

Buying an adapter to accommodate English electrical outlets is at the top of my to-do list. The vibrators I packed are useless otherwise. If I'm not dating, I'll need more than my hands to get through these next three months.

"Hi," I say.

"Hi," he smirks.

"I, um—Thanks. For the penthouse and the clothes. It was thoughtful of you."

"You're welcome." He tips his head, a request for me to look at him and not the floor. His fingers squeeze around the door. They're the same fingers that held me in place every time he—

"Ready?" I pant.

His brow lifts. "Do I make you nervous, Puff?"

Damn these dimples.

"You wish." My silver hoops chime at the tilt of my chin. "Let's go spend your money."

I sashay out of his office to his laughter.

No jeans have ever tempted me to lick the seams before. But then there's the pair in front of me.

Preston's smile is bright and wide in the dressing room mirror. His phone has been ringing nonstop since we left his office through the secret entrance hours ago. He hasn't looked at it, outside of a couple of calls from his assistant. He's fully present, enjoying every outfit I curate for him.

Time sharpened the muscles of his cut frame. Every piece of clothing that touches his skin hangs like a masterpiece. His back is my favorite. I could spend the rest of the afternoon savoring the cotton that stretches and bends to his sculpted protruding lines.

He's thicker, more defined, but still the same Preston.

"These are comfortable," he says with a scratch to his goatee.

"You look good." I motion to the dark hair lining his chin. "Glad you kept it."

The light above the platform catches on his shadowed jaw as he examines it. "If you like it, I'll keep it. But this"—he peels off the taupe cable-knit sweater—"needs to go."

I avert my eyes from the muscles contracting in his lower abdomen. The happy trail that dips below his belt calls me out for being hot in the ass and unprofessional.

Preston hands me the discarded sweater. Our fingers graze, igniting a rush of heat that spreads to my toes. His breath fans over my cheek. "What else do you have for me, Puff?"

Clench and bear!

There's no point in denying gravity exists. I let physics do its job by lowering my gaze, which happens to collide with hard pecs. It's an Oscar-worthy performance of a woman unfazed by the sight of a muscled chest and the haunting gaze of its owner.

"One more thing." I shift into his personal space, so close now he could kiss my forehead. His inhale is sharp when I lean into the scent of his musk and lift the cardigan in my hand. "This has your name all over it. Preston. *Preston*."

My giggle morphs into a belly laugh at his disappointment.

"Funny," he deadpans and grabs his shirt off the velvet chair. "Tell you what. I'll take the last three jumpers you forced on me if you'll have dinner with me tomorrow."

How did shopping turn into a proposition for a date?

We've kept things friendly, outside of a few lingering glances and flirtatious quips. Spending time together shopping for clothes was surprisingly easy once the initial shock of being in the same space wore off. Time flew in three boutiques. Preston now has more un-collared shirts, jeans, and chinos to add to the sad cluster of casual clothes he exiled to the corner of his closet. Ironically, sneakers aren't scarce.

"What do you say, Ms. Monroe?" His eyes flicker from his cuff links to me. "You have to eat. Let me feed you."

"How do you know what I like?"

What the hell am I doing?

Preston shrugs into his blazer and leans forward to size me up. I'm in five-inch heels that are no match for the smile denting his cheeks above my hairline.

"I know what you like, Puff," he whispers with a wink. Then he leaves me in the dressing room with more thoughts than sweaters.

Chapter 29

Madison

Spending over a hundred dollars on two strips of bread and a tease of filling is criminal. No one should get away with pawning off "sandwiches" that would incite the Hunger Games, but that's what I get for running on mints for the better part of the day.

I pull another Tetris tile from the two-tier stand of white and gold cups with matching saucers.

"Why did you come here?" It's a question for myself and the crustless square of cucumber and cream cheese that's really more like a leftover.

There were better options for a late lunch, like one made in the top-of-the-line kitchen back at my place, but I didn't make groceries.

Not my place—Preston's penthouse.

I was up half the night, tossing and turning about seeing him for the first time since agreeing to our "arrangement." The past year flashed against the twinkling lights of Westminster through my bedroom window. It would be easy to blame my lack of sleep on jet lag, but that's a lie. Like these sandwiches.

Preston is applying pressure in all the right places, forcing me to contend with my old desires in a new form. For resentment and heartbreak to lose their grip and hold something different. Unexpected.

Parts of him are still the same—the pinch in his brow when he's deep in thought and the tease of his dimple when he's up to no good. That same determination from years ago is still there, along with the confidence that everything he pursues will fall into place.

I won't settle until I get what I can't live without.

"Well, hello."

"Bellamy," I say, caught with a mouthful of smoked salmon and lemon butter. One "sandwich" is not enough. "I didn't expect to see you so soon."

"I'm meeting someone. Here for tea?"

"Lunch," I say. More like crumbs, but whatever.

Her laugh is a polished snort suspended in disbelief. "Unless you plan on ordering another stand, you'll be here until dinner trying to get full." She winks and sets her red pocketbook on the table. Its scarlet hue matches her suit, one I included in the lookbook I sent after her wardrobe assessment. It's from one of last month's fashion shows, a striking contrast between her toasted ivory skin and the room's champagne walls draped in molding. The model who strutted in cursive wearing it commanded the runway, but not like Bellamy.

Everything about her screams, *Submit, or there will be blood.*

"Are you all moved in?" She unbuttons her blazer and slides into the chair across from me at the two-person table. Her legs kiss, teasing flared pants and a serious shoe game.

"For the most part. Still finding my way around. Hence the tea room." I chuckle and pick up another sandwich. "At least these fit in my purse so I can snack on them later."

My snort is an unrefined gargle when I see the disgust twisting into Bellamy's face. Mama raised me never to waste food.

"You're serious?" Her eyes survey the prism of pastels and bone-straight hair around the room.

Life is full of surprises, and Bellamy is one of them. She reached out after I sent her lookbook, and she was eager to collaborate. I wouldn't call us friends, but it's nice to know another face in London. Hers is often more of a scowl, but that's Bellamy. Bored, unbothered, and camera ready.

Ravenous is a topic we stuffed in the closet to collect dust. Aside from the NDA we signed, which threatens just about every legal action, I didn't feel I owed anyone an explanation for my grown-woman behavior. I'm not ashamed of getting licked to within an inch of my life in a semipublic space, but I don't need to relive the replay of Bellamy watching.

"Are you staying in Mayfair?" she asks while making a cup of tea.

"Westminster," I say. She doesn't reply. "What?"

"Nothing." She waves me off, but not in time to hide the flush inching up her neck. "New city, new flat. I take it you have prospects here?"

"A few meetings with fashion houses to discuss photo shoot collaborations, and an actress to style for a premiere."

It will be an adjustment to balance clients in other countries. I slowed down years ago after chasing the high of wanderlust and any opportunity to grow my brand. Now, I'm more intentional with the projects I take and who gets my time.

Like Preston.

"Something funny?"

"No," I say. "It's—nothing."

"That smile doesn't look like nothing." Bellamy leans forward. "Spill."

My skin heats at the face forming in my mind—the sharp planes of a firm jaw, the refined nose and very generous mouth.

"Aren't you meeting someone?"

"I'm always three steps ahead and twenty minutes early," Bellamy notes.

"I'm in London for work, not a chance at love," I say as a preface. My conviction is almost believable.

"But..." Bellamy prods.

"But." I force out a breath. "A client, an ex, is..."

"Is there a full sentence?"

"Impatient much?" I laugh. "Someone I was once close to recently hired me to be his stylist. He just crossed my mind." Like he always does these days.

Bellamy considers me, tapping a red nail against her cheek before she nods. Her low ponytail sways down her shoulder. "I'm here, if you ever want to talk about anything other than fabric and stitching."

"I'll keep that in mind."

Chapter 30

Preston

"Out! A fucking skid mark, you are."

William glances at the office door where I'm pointing and doubles over in laughter. Strands of sandy blond hair tip over his brow, and he swipes them away with his palm.

Is he crying?

He's been giving me shit since he found the bags of jumpers I bought while shopping with Madison this afternoon. I should've let Jesse drive it to my house, but I was in a rush to get back to the office. The hours I spent with Madison guarantee extra time spent behind my desk tonight, but it's worth it.

Having her this close again is a breath I can finally release. We're slowly falling back into old habits, and it feels fucking good. If spending time with her means stocking up on shirts I'll never wear, so be it.

"My sister-in-law's got you bonkers. You haven't heard a thing I've said, have you?"

"Done yet?" My patience is thinner than the fifteen minutes I have between meetings today. One more joke, and I'll toss him and his giggling ass out of my office.

William coughs to catch his breath. "I'm not used to seeing you infatuated with a woman."

"You were still away at university when we were together," I say.

I didn't *hide* Madison, per se, but I wanted her to myself. As the eldest Donnelley, my path was already mapped out. Finish my degrees. Learn the business from my father. Take over. What little freedoms I did have came with a fight, or at the expense of something that was just for me. With Madison, I got to be Preston. I hid my legacy from her to revel in the normalcy we created in my Paris penthouse. Away from any obligations outside of each other.

"You look good like this." William kicks his feet up on my desk but thinks twice after I toss my stapler at him. "A sap in love," he chuckles. "Can't wait to meet her."

"That makes two of us."

My father's voice cuts through the air like nails on a chalkboard. Stephanie scurries to close my office door behind him. She bows her head to avoid eye contact with the man who will no doubt fuck up my afternoon.

Unannounced visits are rare and never out of the kindness of my father's heart.

"What a woman she must be to keep you so distracted." He unbuttons his charcoal suit coat beneath an open peacoat and takes the seat across from William, whom he doesn't acknowledge. Typical. "Clothes shopping in the middle of the day," he chides. "I taught you better than to let pussy cloud your judgment."

"My judgment is clear, as are our profits," I counter and lean back in my chair. "The only pussy clouding my judgment is the general manager in New York. I need to fire him for incompetencies you excused for decades."

Watching Simon squirm during a recent video conference was worth having to count the droplets of sweat beading across his forehead. Resentment hardened the leathery skin around his eyes until fear creeped in when he realized my father won't be saving him from yet another fuckup.

The same panic cracks my father's confidence on the other side of my desk. Victor Donnelley's legacy and the allies he relied on to uphold it are becoming relics, left to perish by the son he tried to mold into his image.

"What you failed to teach me is a lesson you never learned," I say. "The love of someone you trust and cherish propels you to do better. To *be* better. All of this"—I motion to the office now bare of his influence—"will fade. I won't be a shell of a man once I step away, chasing after fleeting fucks and the ghost of the good ol' days. My greatest accomplishment will be the life I build with my lady and our home, one I won't avoid. How lonely it must be to not be able to afford what money could never buy."

At one point, my father was my idol. But I learned the true cost of what it takes to be him. It's a price I refuse to pay, which is why I'm holding onto Madison with my life. I lived a lifetime without her in an eternity of surface-level encounters.

My father clamps his jaw shut. His blue eyes lower with his voice. "Very well." He stands. "A word of advice: The love you put on a pedestal makes you weak. While you're chasing fairy tales, we're losing opportunities to expand. You still answer to the board." His gaze shifts to William for the first time since he stepped into my office. "Call your mother."

"You alright?" I ask once my father leaves.

Where my father pushes me to be his protégé, he ignores my brother. William gave up trying to please him years ago. It's one thing for a parent to raise you with high expectations. It's another to act like you doesn't exist.

"You don't need to protect me." His attempt at a laugh is shaky at best.

"Doesn't mean I don't care."

William is many things—an ass, a goof, and a flirt—but he's my brother. "You're better than him." The bass in my voice forces him to look up. "Always will be."

The corner of his mouth tips up. It's faint, but it's there. "Thanks." He stretches before hopping to his feet. "Let me get ready for my flight. See you soon."

Chapter 31
Madison

Dress comfortably.

Preston's text gave no other instructions about tonight. No hints. Nothing.

How on earth does he expect me to dress accordingly with no details? "Comfortably" could mean sneakers and jeans—not that I'd wear sneakers. My first steps were in heels, and my last will be too.

After pacing a hole the size of my frustration into my closet, I toss my hair into a high bun and pray I don't embarrass myself wherever we're going. I have a few meetings later this week, and I don't need to be on gossip sites looking a mess, especially next to a damn billionaire in someone's fancy restaurant.

I grab my oversized leopard clutch and matching heels on the way to the front door. I have one arm through my belted wool trench coat when the doorbell rings.

"Yeah, you special alright," Dayo says, wearing his signature black. "White toes too?" His slow whistle skates up the straps wrapped around my ankles to my vegan leather leggings. "You won't need that." He nods to my coat.

I frown. "Where are we going?" London isn't super cold this time of year, but I'll freeze in a silk cami.

"That's for me to know and you to find out." He winks, leaving me at my door as confused as I was when I opened it. "Leave the coat!"

Dayo is halfway down the hall once I reach him. It's dawned on me that we're headed to Preston's penthouse. My coat is still in his closet from the last time I was there. Maybe I can grab it before we head off to who knows where.

Dayo bypasses the elevators and rounds the corner like he's on a mission. It takes three steps to match his casual stride down the marble hall of mirrors. He stops in front of Preston's door and nods.

"I could've walked over myself," I say, somewhat out of breath from the jog.

"He asked me for the solid, and I'm not going far." Thick lips spread into a smile. "My place is downstairs. Go ahead and let your-self in. Enjoy your night."

He disappears into a private stairwell, leaving me for the second time tonight.

Preston was distant today. He texted me about tonight but was silent for most of the day. I took that to mean he was busy with some aspect of running a billion-dollar empire. Part of me expected him to cancel, not send his head of security to walk me to his place like I don't know the way.

I pull down the brass handle and trip over my own feet.

In the distance, beyond the open living room, is Preston. Is he wearing an apron?

He's bent over the oven, the fabric of his gray slacks stretching over an impressive ass. His light gray dress shirt is still tucked in, but his sleeves are rolled up to his elbows.

"You cooked?"

"Cook*ing*," he says over his shoulder. He pulls out a dish that has my stomach mimicking a dirt bike and places his oven mitts on the kitchen island. "Come here." The command is a low rumble over the sizzle of whatever is in the pans on the stove. "Leave the heels on."

My pussy pulses as he presses his flexed forearms to the island, which is illuminated in tea lights. Maybe it's safer to look a mess in somebody's fancy restaurant.

A tremor heats my thighs as I make my way to the man who's looking at me with raw possession. Alicia Keys's "Unthinkable" thickens the air with unspoken desire and conjures old goosebumps from a past life. They find their way back to my skin as I round the island and come face-to-chest with a tantalizing mix of musk and silent need.

Preston lifts my chin with a gentle finger. "Hi."

"Hi." *Breathe.* I collect my nerves and smile at the spread on the counter. "This looks incredible."

"It does." My eyes flutter at his focus on my profile and not the food.

I have self-control.

"Did you make all of this tonight?" I move to the other end of the island and stifle a giggle at the tiled lemon pattern that paints his chest. "Nice apron."

He looks down and shrugs. "It went with my shirt. Nonna packed a few in my bag when I saw her at Christmas. Wine?" He points to a bottle of red.

"Yes, please."

Uncorking a bottle shouldn't be sexy, but that's Preston. He maneuvers the metal corkscrew with ease and flexes those damn forearm muscles with those damn lickable veins. "I made the ricotta for the cassatelle yesterday. Everything else I squeezed in between the meetings I took from home."

"Remind me to kiss your grandmother," I say with eyes the size of my appetite.

"You can kiss me." His chuckle wafts in a trail of musk and spices as he makes his way to the cabinets. He grabs two plates, sets them on the marble counter, and sits beside me. The lights dim against the night sky from the large windows in the living room.

We say a quick prayer over the food and dig in.

Preston's mouth quirks at my moan that wraps around another bite. "Food is okay?"

"Amazing," I say to the golden crust of the eggplant Parmesan. "I had this in Florence a few years ago. It wasn't like this."

"Sicilian food has a different flavor palate. It reflects the region."

"I love it all. Do you normally cook like this?"

He shakes his head. "Most days I don't get home until late, but I try to cook on Sundays."

"What's so special about Sunday?"

An adorable smile provokes his dimples. "I call my nonna."

The answer shouldn't make me blush. Lots of people are close to their grandparents, but there's something about a man who adores his grandma the way he does.

"You're a good grandson."

His grin widens. "I try to be. Nonna is my heart. She doesn't like the hassle of video calls, so I don't see her every week. But we cook together if I'm not traveling."

As Preston explains, Lionara Parisi is a firecracker with a big heart and a tea towel she weaponizes when necessary. At seventy-eight, she's still active, even has a boyfriend he met over Christmas. He cringes bringing it up, but good for her enjoying her golden years to the fullest. From the photo on his phone, taken the last time they were together, she's a knockout. Rich mahogany skin wrapped in the second coming of Eartha Kitt. Preston absorbed many of her features, and his late grandfather's as well.

"Anyway." He shakes his head. "There are good Italian places nearby, but nothing beats homemade."

"Tell me about it," I say with a sigh. "Everybody and their mama has an étouffée."

"Mmm. I had shrimp étouffée in New Orleans last time I was there."

"You need to get out of the city and come over to Breaux Bridge. Mawmaw made the best crawfish étouffée and smothered okra," I say proudly.

"Oh yeah?"

"Chooo! The best, baby." I fork a piece of fish. "What?"

"Your accent. I like it, *baybee*," he mocks.

"I barely hear it anymore. Haven't lived at home since high school."

"Do you visit often?"

"Not like I should, but I also cook on the weekends. I'm making sauce piquant on Sunday. It'll taste different without my black pot, but I'll manage."

"What's in it?" Preston asks.

"Turkey neck, chicken wings, and sausage in my seasoning mix. Throw in your holy trinity—your bell pepper, onion, and celery—add stock, and scrape the bottom for flavor."

"You never cooked that for me."

"Maybe if you play your cards right, I'll fix you a plate." I wink at his frown.

"Don't be a tease," he smirks. "You never said how often you see your family."

I rub at the spot above my heart, the one that tightens whenever I talk about home. "I go back once a year, for the holidays, but I didn't make it last Christmas because of my travel schedule." Mama has threatened to get the switch if she doesn't see my face in person soon.

The only time my family left Louisiana was when I graduated Bodie. Heaven forbid I want to be on location, see a fashion show, or just exist on some island. I won't feel guilty for not falling into the time warp that's kept them in the same place for generations. I'm not ashamed of my childhood or them wanting to stay, but I wanted to expand my experiences.

"What about you?" I take a long sip of wine to change the subject. "Your English accent goes in and out. You were in boarding school, right?"

"In the States through what you consider middle and high school years. I lived in Connecticut and didn't come back until after college."

"Is that where you picked up your love for '90s R&B?" Total's "Kissin' You" bellows from a sound system.

The smile he gives me is as dangerous as it is seductive, his dimples on full blast. "Yes. Nothing else conveys that level of passion and longing."

"Don't forget heartbreak."

His gaze doesn't waver. "I haven't."

The heat creeps up, stoking a brush fire behind his eyes. I knew what I signed up for by agreeing to dinner, but I assumed we'd get to dessert before needing a fire extinguisher.

"What are you looking for in a partner? Tell me your ideals and nonnegotiables."

I huff. "Is this an interview?" We need more wine.

His thumb and forefinger stroke his lip, which is shadowed in neatly trimmed hair. "Consider it a tender offer."

"A tender what?"

"In loose business terms, a tender offer is a public bid to purchase shareholders' stock as a means of acquisition. The price is usually at a premium, to incentivize them to agree."

"Slow down—I don't speak Wall Street. You want to *buy* me?"

"Of course not." Preston scrapes a hand through his hair and looks away. "I'd never try to buy you, Puff. I want to *fight* for you during your three months here." His sigh is heavy as his eyes linger on my face. Searching. Pleading. "The ball is in your court."

The lump hardening my throat refuses to budge. "What are you saying, Preston?"

"I want your heart, baby."

Loving Preston was effortless the first time, but it came with a heartache that closed me off to trying to find it again. Years of meaningless sex and relationships I knew would never go anywhere became a security blanket.

The harder I try to ignore the truth, the more it persists. My pulse sprints at the possibility I thought was long dead. Here it is, staring me in the eyes. Preston has always been straightforward, and that's likely served him well in business. He sees what he wants and names it. Never one to beat around the bush, regardless of how it lands. Right now, he's quiet, resolute in his hooded stare and waiting for a response.

His thick hair, curling at the edges, gleams in the London night that settles over our dinner. There's no mistaking the power of his self-confidence. The handsome cords of his face are carved in quiet assurance.

A tender offer for my heart.

"We fell in love with pieces of each other," Preston says. "I want all of you. Give me the chance to pursue you beyond friendship. If you don't feel the same way in three months, you won't hear from me again."

Shock catapults into my lungs, taking the air with it. My eyes prick at the memories slicing me open, tiny paper cuts of our serendipity and its demise. I can't forget our last day together, but keepsakes from the good times are piling up.

They're here now. The way we fall into easy conversation and our bodies' reactions to each other. Him refilling my wineglass without my asking and me passing him the baking dish for the second helping he always gets.

The choreography of us is practiced, but the idea of an us again is terrifying.

If eyes are the window to the soul, Preston's are a lifeline, compelling me to peek behind the curtain. He's not staring with a haughty rebuke, numb to my cries for him to see the woman he fell in love with and not the opportunist he asserted I was. They're ablaze with sadness for what never was. What was smothered and never had a chance to grow.

He reaches for my hand. "We lost three months because of how things ended. I want them back. I want you back."

Chapter 32

Madison

"Take me off speaker before I embarrass us both. Matter of fact, let me call you back."

Kojo's tone is a ten-second warning. My phone rings with enough time for me to jump into a dressing room and answer his video call.

"Yes!" I whisper-yell in a dash to close the fabric barrier. This four-by-four space has a full-size mirror, navy carpeting, and zero privacy. There is a long gray curtain, but it won't block out our antics.

"You called me, Regine." His eyes bulge to tell me *duh*. He scoots off the bed, revealing a man in a durag lying facedown and knocked out. Onyx satin ripples above the nut-brown backside taking up the space behind my friend, who's ready to breathe fire down my neck.

"Football player" is all he says, unamused. His slippers pad across the hardwood to the kitchen, where he props the phone next to the coffee machine.

Morning sun from the Midtown skyline creates a kaleidoscope through the living room behind him. Kojo fiddles with a mug and leans back against the kitchen island. His arms fold across the olive floral silk robe that covers his lean frame. Only my friend coordinates a durag with his sleepwear.

"What is so important you woke me up at dawn?"

"It's ten a.m. over there."

He dismisses the obvious with a wave and yawns. "Anything before noon is early." His eyes narrow. "Where are you?"

"In a boutique, shopping for a client." My entire morning consisted of responding to emails before navigating from store to store across neighborhoods. I need a cigarette and a tray of pastries after dealing with London traffic.

Kojo's lips purse. "Okay, coin. Back to the mystery at hand. What did this man offer you? Aside from a homecooked meal."

"A tender offer," I say.

"A tender what?"

I chuckle. It's the same reaction I had. "It's some business term, when a person wants to submit a bid to buy shares or something."

"What kind of mess is that, Regine? Preston is fine, but his game is lacking." Kojo scoffs and rolls his neck.

I fold my bottom lip between my teeth to keep from laughing. Why am I cheesing in a boutique dressing room?

"Excuse me. What is *that*?" Kojo's head tilts, and he points at me like I have a stain in the middle of my lilac blouse. "Regine, did—" He's in front of the camera in half a second, his big eye staring down. "Did you finally give that man your panties?!"

"I—"

"My friend got that ding-a-ling!" he sings, doing a blasphemous holy ghost two-step.

"Kojo!" I seethe. This whole boutique will hear his "Hallelujah" if he doesn't close his big mouth. It takes two more pleas to get him to stop jumping up and down. "I didn't have sex."

That stops him mid-twerk.

"Then what am I shaking my ass for?"

I shouldn't laugh at how serious he turned after all that hollering, but I can't help it. "Preston wants to pursue me during my time here. He wants another chance at my heart."

I want you back.

We ended dinner soon after his offer, and I stayed up half the night running through a million questions.

Where would we be if we'd let time run out?

Would we have walked away regardless, or would we have held on until distance and life forced us apart?

"You are too beautiful and bright to be this damn dumb. Nope"—he snaps his fingers—"don't turn your lips up. For the past year, all I've heard is you whine and complain about ain't-shit men. You cut yourself off from dating. Now here comes Prince Charming, doing everything to show you the world, and you're calling me up to overanalyze. Get on that magic carpet and fly to your happily ever after!"

If I wasn't afraid of Kojo finding a way to teleport through the phone to pluck me in my forehead, I'd joke about him using Disney characters to read me to filth. He rarely yells or glowers the way he is now.

Our volume drops to a suffocating hush. He raises his brow, catching a golden ray of light over his hazelnut skin.

I'm in denial. He knows it, and so do I.

Preston never needed a tender offer to pursue me. He's been doing it since the morning he stood in front of my hotel room door. The three-hour ride to the airport. Wanting me here for three months, which I now realize is how long we would've had left in Paris if things hadn't gone to Hell. The candlelight dinner in his closet. The damn penthouse on the same floor.

"That man loves you, Regine," Kojo says, snatching me out of my thoughts. "The only thing you need to decide is if you love him enough to see where this goes. Second chances don't come around often. If you want him, go get him."

"When did you become a love doctor, Mr. Noncommitment?"

He scoffs. "Since the two women in my life want to act foolish about what's staring them in the face. Emma is no better with that man living in her house. All this denial is a promise for early wrinkles." He adjusts his robe and crosses himself.

Guilt prickles my skin in a rash of shame. Hearing Emma's name churns my stomach for the games I played with her friend. I hate mean girls, and I became the very thing I despised.

"I was thinking about reaching out to her when I'm in LA next month, to apologize." My photo shoot styling gig might be the perfect time to clear the air.

"Let it be for now," Kojo says in a tone that lets me know not to question him. His eyes narrow, but they lack contempt. "I already got chewed out. I think it's best for time to do its thing. You two will have to interact at some point. There's no need to force anything now."

"Okay."

"You just focus on Preston," he quips with a wink. "The one thing you can control is whether or not you talk yourself out of another chance with that fine man. Get out of your head and let him catch you. Acting like you won't like it. *Tuh!* Now get off my phone. I have a wide receiver in my bed, and I need to get into his end zone."

Kojo out sticks his tongue and ends the call. Guess we're done.

The only thing that's changed between Preston and me are the cards—now they're laid out on the table. I have the power to tell him to stop, and to say no.

Fifteen years was enough time to replay the death of our relationship. The places that needed fortifying. The truths we should've revealed.

Putting the past to rest isn't what scares me; it's the resurrection of what could be.

But how does he make you feel?

Like we might get it right this time.

Chapter 33

Madison

Fifteen Years Ago

"Where are we going?"

"Can you walk in those?" Preston's eyes drift to my platform loafers as they shuffle to keep up with his stride. "Want me to carry you?"

"Don't be silly," I huff, narrowly missing a crack in the pavement. "Where are we going?"

He brings our interlaced fingers to his lips. "Patience, Puff. We're almost there."

Preston called off his trip to London, and he's been full of surprises today. We ate breakfast in bed and made love on his balcony. It was the perfect lazy Friday afternoon. By three o'clock, we were out the door for the start of an adventure I'll never forget. So he says.

He warned me to wear flats, but it will be a cold day in Hell before I part with my heels. Thankfully, the weather is still relatively mild, and nothing's frozen over. I still wasn't prepared for the freaking Louvre. For two hours, a personal guide escorted us on a private tour through endless exhibits. Among pockets of crowds—and me in a pleated miniskirt and sweater—it was an intimate experience.

Preston has been more attentive, trading long hours at the office for time with me. Some days, we do McDonald's runs at his request. Others, we stay up late talking about who we would be if we weren't attached to our expectations, mine self-inflicted, and his courtesy of his family.

A romantic with a big heart.

He guides us to a man in a tux who's playing a violin next to the Pont des Arts. "Here." Preston's long coat is a shelter from the breeze off the Seine. "Better?" His breath fans across the pulse point in my neck, which he pecks, igniting a valley of butterflies. He buries his face against my throat, the warmth of his chest and the scent of his musk flooding my center.

Our bodies sway to the violinist in perfect step. Soon, the sun bows to dusk. Street lamps come to life, and the Louvre's pyramid illuminates the distance.

"This is beautiful." Aside from that, I'm speechless.

"I got you something," he murmurs into the curtain of my hair flowing freely toward the river.

His fingers tickle my side when he reaches into his coat pocket to fish out a gold padlock and key charm on a simple gold necklace. "Couples secure padlocks to the railing here to symbolize their love," he says, nodding to the hundreds of metal locks shimmering under the glowing tent of stars. "They write their names, lock it on the railing, and throw the key into the river." He shakes his head. "But we're not compromising the bridge's structure or fucking up the environment."

We chuckle.

"I got this necklace so you can have a piece of Paris. Something to remember us by."

Tears tremble on my eyelids, the distance a blur of embers in a violet sky. I never expected to fall in love. I fought against it at first, and I wish our circumstances were different. I wish this didn't involve deception, no matter how small or unintentional.

Would our dreams flow down the same path if distance and status didn't separate us?

Would Preston love all of me if he saw *all* of me?

His touch will fade.

So will his laugh.

But I'll have our memories, and I'll cherish them along with this locket.

Chapter 34
Madison

Present Day

I'm a liar with a to-go plate.

Every excuse I gave myself in the mirror stared back at me and said, *Try again*. The forty-eight minutes it took to hype myself up to come here was a fraction of the time I spent tossing outfits around my closet.

I'm dropping off food, not going to a job interview.

I all but skipped across the street like an extra in *The Wiz*. There's no reason I should be in Preston's office building, but I felt a neighborly urge to supply my friend with a lunch he never requested.

A liar with a to-go plate.

Denial is a strange place. I'm not a lifelong member, but I have a flash pass for all the main attractions. Dropping off food plates to "friends" isn't a habit of mine, but here we are.

Though "friend" is a title never meant for Preston. He's always been more, floating in the space between the man who checks off all my ideals and someone I could never have. The lines have blurred this time, and that has me acting out of character.

Like showing up to his job unannounced.

You've come this far.

I draw in a deep breath and step into the lobby. It's quiet for a Monday afternoon, which makes the marble pathway to the private corridor easier to navigate in plaid heels.

My heart drums in my chest, nervous that the security guard standing next to the stainless-steel turnstile will call me out for acting sprung. His lips thin, setting his wide chin into a tight line. I don't make eye contact as I press the key card Dayo gave me into the scanner and enter through the parting doors.

Suspicion is not a look I want to wear. The only bomb I'm carrying is the nerves that are about to explode out of my ass. It would make for a nasty cleanup in this black jumpsuit, but at least security wouldn't notice.

After a stare-off with the metal door, I tap my card to the pad, careful not to look over my shoulder at Bruce Banner in a navy suit. The weight of the closing barrier pushes me into the cement hall. It's so quiet you could hear a pin drop.

I know Dayo is somewhere in the command center laughing his head off. I haven't lived down the side-eye I got when I insisted Preston and I are friends.

Are you planning to stand here all day or bring him lunch?

I stare at the key card in my palm and the short distance between me and the elevator. Preston gave me access so I could come and go. It's not a big deal, except it is.

Everything will become real once I own up to what I won't admit: There's a force pulling me back to him. I dodge and fight, but its magnetism is impossible to overcome.

Yesterday gave me clarity. It was the only day Preston and I didn't communicate since his tender offer to earn back my heart. I missed speaking with him, missed our texts. He had to fly to Manchester unexpectedly yesterday morning and said he wouldn't be home until earlier today.

Waking up to "Good morning, Puff" had me kicking my slippers without an ounce of shame. When I'm caught up in the moment, I don't play out all the ways going there with him again will lead us back to the same fate. We have more experience under our belts now that we're older. We also live separate lives that don't revolve around each other, and on different continents.

I'd be a fool to assume a long-distance anything would work, especially with a billionaire whose schedule is booked a year in advance. But I'm here—with turkey neck, smothered okra, greens, and cornbread—willing myself not to overthink it and go with the flow.

I steady my to-go container and walk out of the elevator with my head and top knot high.

On instinct, my hand lifts to knock on his door, but then I remember the code for the keypad. A tiny light flashes green, and I step into his musk-filled suite wearing a smile that falls to the floor when my jaw does.

A woman with a Nia Long pixie cut and the features to match is squatting on his desk in red heels. Her chocolate brown eyes, which hold the thrill of arousal, hypnotize me in place. I don't realize she's completely naked underneath the fur coat she's wearing until she rolls her nipples between her fingers. She gasps and bounces harder on the surface-mounted dildo on wood coated in her cream.

"*Preston.*" Her tongue drags over her teeth, and the muscles in her flat stomach contract as she grinds her hips over the black silicone.

The dick alone is a sight to see. Judging by her short, toned legs, she's petite, but she's riding it like rent is due.

"Join me. I like to share," she pants, lifting one of her large breasts to her tongue.

Another moan snatches me out of my thoughts, hitting me with a swift uppercut. There is a woman in Preston's office riding a dildo on his fucking desk. The shock wanes, trading places with anger and humiliation. I let my guard down for him to hurt me again.

"Pass," I say in a clipped tone. It's hard to ignore her bouncing on a fake dick like a pogo stick at two in the afternoon, but I manage. I toss the food container onto the coffee table.

The main door of the office opens. Preston steps through with his brows raised to the ceiling. His mouth opens to speak to the woman summoning him with a red nail and a smirk. Then he sees me.

Turns out I'm not the liar; I am the idiot.

Hurt, confusion, and what looks like curiosity enforce my scowl. A boulder closes my throat, trapping the questions I don't want to ask.

Why is there a woman pleasuring herself on his desk?

Are there others?

Am I not enough?

"Madison." Preston's voice strains. He mirrors the step I take.

"Thought you might be hungry," I say to the container I left on the coffee table. "But I see you have company." My eyes dart to his desk ornament and return to the floor. "I shouldn't have come."

"Puff, wait." He trips over his feet to reach me. "Please." I tense at the hand around my arm, clutching me for dear life.

"Let me guess. It's not what I think. Who the hell are you?"

"The man who's trying to win you back, who'd never hurt you intentionally. I didn't ask her to come, and I don't know why she's here."

The huff I toss calls bullshit. "You expect me to believe that?" I yank my arm away and point to the woman on his desk who's too lost in an orgasm to be bothered with us. "She's still here."

"Gisele," Preston says without taking his eyes off me. "Did I invite you here?"

"No." The word rushes through a ragged breath. "It's been months. I wanted to surprise you."

"Get dressed and clean yourself up. You are not to step foot in my office again."

"Preston," she whines.

"Now." The word slides across his teeth like sandpaper. The warning is clear: Don't fuck around.

Gisele's sigh is her only rebuttal. Her heels scamper to the bathroom in the corner. The door closes, and Preston draws a breath, ready for damage control.

Who wouldn't feel outraged at walking into their lover's office only to find another woman? Preston's not my lover, but that won't stop me from telling him to go fuck himself with the dildo mounted on his desk.

His gaze roams the minefield of emotions on my face, searching for signs of recovery. Each breath presses my turtleneck into the jumpsuit that's welded to my curves. A blush sweeps across my cheeks like war paint. My lips purse, and I release a soft breath that surprises me.

Am I...turned on?

A single look is all it took for my mind to shift from never speaking to him again to letting my vagina take the mic on our behalf. I have more self-control than this, but the heifer ran out of the office with gasoline-soaked panties.

Blinks come in rapid succession as I fight to make sense of the battle to stay pissed at him and the desire that's flooding my veins. It's the same lightheadedness I had at Ravenous when I witnessed the scenes at play. That was my first time doing anything sexual with an audience, never mind with a stranger. He knew every pulse point. I wanted Preston then as much as I do now.

My skin prickles when he caresses my cheek. I shudder when he leans down to kiss the corner of my mouth. "I would never hurt you, and I apologize if you thought otherwise. Tell me what to do to make it better. I want to earn your trust."

The bathroom door opens, breaking our stare. I peel my eyes away to track Gisele's movement over his shoulder.

"Puff." The calm authority in his voice draws my focus back to him. "There is no one but you. Do you believe me?"

My throat wrestles a swallow, and my brows collapse. I nod.

"I need your words, baby," Preston says. "Do you believe me?"

"Yes" comes through a strained inhale. *What the hell?* From this close, getting high off his cologne is inevitable.

Hunger floods his eyes. Preston lifts me into his arms, and I delight in the soft arch of my back at his touch. I wrap my heels around his slacks as he guides us past a wide-eyed Gisele to his desk.

"Preston, what are you—" I yelp when his screens and laptop fall to the ground. My exhale trembles when my ass hits his desk. I try to look at Gisele, but he holds my chin to keep my eyes on him.

"She doesn't matter," he says, loud enough for her to hear. "Gisele never pops up unannounced. I don't know what inspired her visit, but I'll get to the bottom of it. After I take care of you."

My legs part on their own to make room for his thighs and the erection tenting his zipper. "I haven't fucked or even thought about another woman since you came back into my life. Do you believe me?"

"Yes," I whisper.

"Do you know how long I've waited for the chance to love you again?" He kisses the other corner of my mouth.

"No."

"Fifteen long fucking years."

My eyes spring open, flaring bright with the same longing. The invisible web between us tugs until it snaps. Preston's mouth swoops down to capture the moan dripping from my lips, which he licks with his tongue.

His fingers sear my flesh as he showers kisses down my mouth and to my jaw. I lift my chin to offer the smooth column of my neck, which he sucks. The pressure of my knees gripping his waist unlocks a growl. He grabs my ass and kneads the heat between my thighs.

My "Preston" is smothered by the slip of his tongue in my mouth. I gasp when he strips off his jacket and lowers his body over mine.

"Do you want her to go or watch?" He nips my chin and rocks into my pussy as it scents his office. "I can smell you, Puff." His tongue grazes my ear. "Choose."

The question hangs in the air as he kisses my brows. I lick my lips, unable to disguise my body's reaction. After a long breath, my mouth quivers when I say, "Watch."

That's the last word he hears before raw possession takes over.

Chapter 35

Preston

Three cups of coffee weren't enough to shake off the jet lag that's holding me hostage after this weekend's last-minute trip. I've been a functional zombie all day, smiling and nodding to keep up appearances. Operating on autopilot is a super power I wield when necessary, and it was essential after yesterday's four-hour round-trip flight.

I'm exhausted, but I'm wide awake now.

"Mmh." The turbulence of my thrust knocks the breath from Madison's lungs. A tremor touches her mouth as her jaw goes slack and her eyes widen at the force. Our eyes untangle, and mine settle on the spot where my thighs, wrapped in a marine blue suit, smack into the target between her legs.

She reaches for my belt, but I smack her hand away. "The first time you'll feel it is when I make love to you," I say. Her back arches off polished wood when my grip tightens. "Fuck, I want you, Puff." I swivel my hips into her spot. Her groan is so deep, I nearly come from the vibration.

Having her again sparks something feral inside me. I want to pleasure her, protect her, and cherish her for however long she'll let me.

The force of my body is a Mack truck, nudging the desk forward while teasing her walls. Every feeling I hold for her plays out on my face.

Adoration.

Reverence.

Hunger.

How the hell do I take off this jumpsuit without ripping it? Madison flips over to give me her back, and I pull the gold zipper down her spine. Her eyes lock on Gisele. I haven't seen her in months, which raises the question why she's in my office.

I was prepared to grovel and do whatever it takes to get Madison to trust me again. I still am, but the airiness of her inhale alerted me to a different need.

My Puff enjoys watching and being watched.

The symphony of her moans at my soft pecks to her back hardens my dick, which is fighting to break free. She meets Gisele's narrowed eyes head-on and pulls down her one-piece outfit to reveal a black strapless bra and thong.

Fuck, this woman.

Madison was never shy about her body. She loves every dip and curve—wide hips, thighs, and breasts that spill out of two hands. Her confidence is one of the things I love about her, and I'm here to be of service.

Her nipples pucker against the satin cups of her bra. I release it and cover her breasts with my hands.

"Let her see," she says, her chin tipped toward Gisele, who's too stunned to leave. Imagine that.

I spin Madison around to face me and bite my lower lip. "You're beautiful, Puff." I lower her to the desk and grunt at her exposed breasts. "I'm fucking these soon."

Her eyes roll to the back of her head at the first swipe of my tongue. I palm both of her titties together and draw the hardened peaks into my mouth. The long swipes and grazes of my teeth demand her euphoria.

Madison raises her hips for me to pull down the rest of her jumpsuit, and soon it pools at her feet. It's my mouth's cue to follow an invisible trail to the source that's leaking onto my desk.

"I can taste you from here," I murmur, settling into a squat and tossing her legs over my shoulders. "Don't run from me."

She braces but almost flies off the desk when I tug on the lace thong that's choking her plump pussy lips. The motion ignites a shockwave over the indent of her sensitive bud, which I suck into my mouth. I tease her with the friction of the black fabric and the heat of my breath.

"Preston!" she yelps when the thong rips in half before my mouth is back on her. I lap and swirl her engorged clit until her legs fall open and she digs her heels into my desk.

Slurps and pants echo off black walls as I feast on Madison, satisfying a fifteen-year hunger. She gasps at the building orgasm that threatens a foot cramp with how hard her toes are curling. When my fingers strum her G-spot, her voice hits a Whitney Houston note.

"Let it out, Puff," I say. She'd scoff if she weren't about to squirt in my mouth.

Movement near the office door has my eyes on Gisele. I slip three fingers inside Madison and glare. Gisele swallows and nods before closing the door behind her.

I shove Madison's legs farther apart and suck her with enough force to snatch her soul. She squirms, earning a chuckle and a pussy slap. "Quit running and let me taste you. You can take it, baby." I stand and flip us so my back is on the desk. My fingers dig into her round cheeks as I guide them to hover over my face.

A moan vibrates through my throat. Madison rolls her hips to draw more of herself into my mouth. The rhythm is a slow grind against the flick of my tongue. Pleasure shoots through the ceiling and into the clouds. Waves of ecstasy hold her hostage until she's bouncing on my face in a cry for release. Her orgasm is a downpour that flows through body rolls.

Madison tries to push off, but I hold her in place, French kissing pink lips to siphon the last of her juices. I finally come up for air with one last kiss to her inner thigh.

～ele～

"Are you okay?" My fingers, once glistening with Madison's essence, now rub slow circles into her back. She tenses at first but settles into the gentle rhythm, and her panic subsides.

I gave her a moment to reorient herself after I cleaned her up. She was stuck somewhere between satisfaction and fear, more shaken than she cared to admit.

It was only a matter of time before we talked about my kinks. I'd hoped to cook for her, to ease into what would be a complex discussion about curiosities and concerns. Instead, after Gisele's stunt, I had to move around my next two meetings. There's no way I'd let Madison leave after being blindsided—regardless of whether I demanded orgasms from her body or not.

"I can sit in my own chair," she sighs, but she drinks from the water cup I hold to her mouth. "I came here with a to-go container and somehow ended up on my back on the same desk where another woman was just balancing on a dildo with her vagina." She huffs and attempts to stand, but I quickly shut her down.

"I'd like to hold you a little longer, if that's alright."

My kiss on her forehead tempts her eyes shut. It's soft, a far cry from my grip to her neck while I ate with abandon. I shift her in my lap to make room for the blood rerouting to my dick. One arm snakes around her waist while the other grabs my fork for another bite of the food she brought.

Just like her pussy, it's delicious.

"Talk to me, Puff. I'll answer anything."

Her lips part to accept a forkful of greens. "Do all the women who come into your office get this level of aftercare?"

"No," I say to the crease burrowing between her brows. "I'm not an inconsiderate lover, but the few who come for sexual purposes know I'm not interested in anything beyond physical gratification."

Madison scoffs and anchors her arms across her jumpsuit. "Except for your tender offers, right?"

"*Offer*," I correct, tilting her jaw so I can soften it with a kiss. "Look at me, Puff." The laugh that tumbles out of me earns me a fist to the thigh. I didn't mean to do it, but the wrinkle in her nose and the stubborn pout in her lips are adorable.

"There's only one woman I want." I nudge her neck with my nose, lowering the titanium wall she erected in the last half hour. It's not by much, but I'll take the win.

Her head rolls in my direction, a shadow of annoyance turning her hazel eyes into slits. "Do you expect me to believe that someone who has women coming to his office for dick appointments is suddenly ready to settle down?"

"I hope you'll believe that a man who first tasted the love of his life fifteen years ago has been failing to fill the void of her absence ever since."

My words suspend in the air with her delicate gasp. Madison is the first woman I fell in love with, and she'll be the last.

Her gaze softens, searching for signs that my confession is a lie. A lifetime cut too short reflects in our eyes. Of two people who once avoided love finding it in each other.

"You can't mean that," she whispers.

"I do, Puff."

The graceful lines of her throat force a swallow. Madison resets. Anger is no longer a guard—fear is.

"How did that start?" she asks, unable to meet my eyes, which are still locked on her. "The women coming to your office."

"Encounters outside of work come with certain expectations I won't meet. Dinner means romance, and staying the night runs the risk of someone snooping or telling the tabloids where I live."

"Makes sense, I guess."

"What else can I answer? I was serious about earning your trust."

Madison chews her lower lip. "You asked me if I wanted Gisele to go or watch. How did you know I would say watch?"

I trace a path from the nape of her neck to the curves of her ass. She melts under my touch, and the sweet scent of magnolia takes residence in my office.

"Truth?"

She nods, her eyes imploring me to explain the part of her kept dormant and now unlocked.

"Your eyes." She shudders as my fingertips brush across her neck. "The breath you held." The back of my hand caresses the arch of her sacral region. "The flush heating your skin." My grip tightens at her uneven breath. "Your pupils are dilating right now. I figured you'd say yes because I think you're an exhibitionist."

"A what?" A bitter edge creeps through her desire.

"Someone who gets pleasure from being watched," I say with a kiss to the shell of her ear. "Do you remember how wet you were with her eyes on your magnificent body? Did you like it, Puff?"

"Yes," she says without hesitation.

"You know what else? I think you're a voyeur like me."

Madison's inquisitiveness at seeing Gisele mount herself onto a dildo was undeniable. She was angry—understandably so—at the idea of me pursuing her while playing with others. She still enjoyed the show, the same way she enjoyed watching the scenes at Ravenous.

"Does she do that every time she visits?"

"It's not uncommon," I admit. "She works a high-stress corporate job and comes to me for release. I swear to you, I haven't called Gisele or anyone else since you came back into my life. I don't *need* any theatrics. It's entertaining, but it's not a requirement. I like to watch, and I participate sometimes, when I feel like it."

"What about when we were in Paris?"

I shake my head. "I didn't unlock this part of me until years later. Work left little room for anything else. Over time, the few women who held my interest signed NDAs and agreed to keep our relations private. They come and go, like Gisele, who I met two years ago. We only see each other twice a quarter, and only in my office."

"And Stephanie?" Madison's eyes flick to mine.

"Never. Unlike my father, I don't screw my assistants. She manages my schedule, but that's all. My office is soundproof, and I only allotted thirty minutes for those meetings in the past. Gisele wasn't on my calendar today. I never approved the request, and I'll have words with Stephanie."

Madison exhales and relaxes in my arms. The fact she's still letting me hold her is a good sign. I kiss her cheek as she settles against my chest.

"This is a lot to take in, Preston," she says with a shadow of alarm. "I have no claim to you, regardless of how I feel."

"You have my heart, Puff. Always have."

"If we're going to give us another try, I have to be the only one. Gisele might share, but I'll be damned."

I chuckle and pull her closer. "You are and will always be enough. I'm open to exploring kinks with you, but I don't need them. The entirety of you fulfills me."

The air shifts to allow breathing room for the idea of an us to take root. I'll do whatever it takes to make Madison realize she's safe loving me again. I wait for her mind to decongest of the doubts and fears still clinging to her.

After a few seconds of silence, Madison whispers, "I have a confession. Today wasn't the first time I've done something like that in front of someone. There was a place...with a man. I wanted him to be you."

"Did you now?"

Her lip quivers at the swipe of my thumb. "Yes."

"I have a confession of my own. I invited you and your friend to Ravenous that night." The name startles her gasp and activates my smirk. "I created it, as a safe place to indulge in fantasies without compromising your identity."

Shock chases the words back into Madison's throat. Her eyes widen as she stares, speechless.

"You were there?"

I nod.

"It was you, wasn't it?"

"Yes, Puff. It was me."

Chapter 36

Madison

Vintage never misses.

I reach for my wineglass with the goofiest grin. Photos from today's fitting look back at me from the mood board on the wall. Weeks of planning, sourcing, and groveling are worth every swatch and sample flooding my living room.

The red carpet isn't ready for what I'm bringing.

A top fashion house cleared my client to wear its vintage black blazer to a premiere this Saturday. No one has seen it since it turned heads on the runway forty years ago. Every major outlet will cover it and Noura Sky under flashing lights in two days.

The single-breasted crepe blazer is an experience in person, but it dazzles on camera. Intricate pearls trace a woven gold pattern across the black fabric, with velvet tapering down the center that leads to a hand-stitched design. It's long, and Noura will wear it with a pair of custom stilettos to match. She'll show it off on the red carpet for interviews before a planned costume change we spent half the day perfecting. One does not sit on their ass in archival fashion with such detailing.

I envisioned Noura's look the second her team reached out. The Tunisian actress is a rising star, and this will put her on every radar ahead of her breakout role.

Styling red-carpet fashion is a responsibility I don't take lightly. It's storytelling through silhouettes and cuts. Every texture and material is a visual timestamp that cements a piece of its own history. Countless hours go into perfecting an ensemble behind the scenes, and they're far from glamorous.

I worked my ass off to get where I am. Attending A-list events. Luxury accommodations. Nothing came easy, which makes every best-dressed list an award.

My phone buzzes.

Jewel

Meeting friends for dinner. Okay if I crash at your place?

Yes of course. Are you alright? Do you need anything?

Jewel

Only for you to stop worrying.

You're grown, I know. Promise me you'll call if you do. No arrests. Love you.

Jewel

Love you too auntie. Enjoy your time in London.

That I can do.

"Cheers." I lift my wineglass to the board and make a mental note about Noura's second outfit. It's an emerald-green velvet suit with black lapels.

Nights like this are my favorite. A chance to shut out the world with takeout Chinese and insulate myself in fabrics. Styling is a formula of complexities I solve through garments and accessories. I know what to expect and how to adapt. It's different from the uncertainty gnawing at me since I left Preston's office on Monday.

Inching closer to forty comes with a rhythm of routine and affirmations sharpened over time. I like what I like, and I understand my body's needs. Changing course when I've lived on cruise control for years is a whiplash I'm still recovering from.

Memories of Ravenous and Preston's office slam into me like a highway collision whenever I allow myself permission to feel freely.

I don't recognize the woman staring back at me when I look in the mirror. She's still me—a jambalaya of thickened hips and curves with hair streaked from the Louisiana sun—but she's different. Evolving.

Something inside of me was set free when Preston told me he was, in fact, the masked stranger at Ravenous. I expected anger to surface but only felt relief knowing my first public experience was with him. I wanted him to be behind the mask, and now, he's encouraging me to take mine off.

It took everything I had not to laugh in his face when he used the terms "exhibitionist" and "voyeur" to describe me. *Me.* It's taboo, a dirty label, like a cheap knock-off you wouldn't get caught wearing.

I never considered myself someone with a kink, but the more I dig, the more I find pieces of me that were here all along.

Naming what gives me pleasure removes the shackles of shame. My kinks don't define me. They're parts that make me whole.

Preston has been supportive from afar. He left the country on a business trip days ago but answers questions I'd once have never dared to ask. He put me in touch with the Ravenous consultant, who oversees programming. They're a pleasure educator and help create safe spaces for kink exploration.

The curiosities entice me, but I'm afraid of falling back into old habits with newfound pleasure. I want more, but I'm nervous to step so far into this world that I lose the rest of myself.

The doorbell rings.

Unless a million dollars is on the other side, nothing good comes at nine o'clock at night.

I navigate around open boxes and Chinese food containers. I'm a mess in a flannel two-piece set and a messy bun with markers sticking out. I open the door and blink twice. An older man with woolly, chalk-colored hair smiles. He's wearing an executive coat and holding a silver-domed dish. "Madison?"

"Yes."

"I'm Gene, one of the pastry chefs in the restaurant below. Pleasure to meet you."

"Nice to meet you. I didn't order anything."

His handlebar mustache shifts. "Mr. Donnelley requested these for you." He slides the plated dome into my hands. "There's a card inside. Have a lovely evening."

"Thank you."

Um, what?

I resecure the deadbolt and head to the kitchen, where the island shines under overhead accent lights. There's an assortment of French pastries beneath the dome.

Profiteroles.

Pain au chocolat.

Éclairs.

Chouquettes.

My favorites are all here.

On the plate is a folded manila card. I smile at the familiar handwriting.

Puff,

I imagine you're in the kitchen, troubling your lip with those colored markers in your hair. I remember the days when you'd isolate yourself before a big exam. In the spirit of tradition, here are a few of your favorite midnight snacks.

I'm sorry to miss your event, but I know you'll shine bright like always.

Miss you terribly.

Love,

P

"He remembered," I whisper.

To say I'd transform into a gremlin before midterms is putting it nicely. I was antisocial and very cranky. Preston found a way to love me and always used my infatuation with pastries to lure me out for a forehead kiss. He gave me my space but always reminded me he would be with me every step of the way.

My ringing phone has me shuffling to the couch with a switch in my step. I answer without peeking at the screen or telling my grin to have a seat.

"Hey, you," I coo, unable to control myself.

"Hello to you too," Bellamy says with an evident smirk on the other end.

"Sorry," I sigh and settle into gray cushions. "I thought you were someone else."

"The ex for a client, perhaps?"

I smile and glance at the curated dessert tray. "Something like that. Did you need something?"

"Suggestions on an outfit for an unexpected benefit tomorrow," she says. "I do apologize for the hour. But since you're up"—her voice shifts—"I want recommendations *and* details about what has you grinning."

I bite my lip and head back to the dome for a snack. "How long do you have?"

Chapter 37

Madison

"Put those heels to work, Regine."

I hop over a small puddle and pull my vintage faux fur midi coat to my chest. My best friend, who's leading us to God knows where, tightens his grip on my hand as we rush with no destination in sight.

"If you tell me where we're going, I could get us there faster," I say, sidestepping another puddle. "Why are we on the Upper East Side, anyway? There are martinis and empanadas closer to my apartment."

"Hush."

I'm complaining with good reason. One, there is no justifiable excuse to go this far for food. What isn't around the corner is a click away on an app. Two, the clouds only broke ten minutes ago, which means the puddles I'm dodging can show up their sisters if it rains again. We have no umbrellas nor any critical need to be outside. That brings me to point three: We keep birthdays casual.

Takeout.

Toes in a foot spa.

The Real Housewives of Potomac.

Sometimes if Kojo doesn't complain about watching his acquaintances act a mess, we throw in *Real Housewives of Atlanta*. The point is, we have a tradition of keeping our birthdays in the house where they belong. With all the ripping and running around we do for our careers, recharging is necessary.

Kojo flies to me when I'm in New York, and I fly to him when he's in Atlanta. I came home days after Noura's premiere, an event that landed my client's name on the lips of every reporter who attended. With Preston still away for work, I didn't want to spend my birthday alone. So, I'm home for a week, and I'll ring in another year closer to forty with my best friend.

"Here we go," Kojo says. His pace quickens down 106th Street, my hand still in his like we're late. *What* we're late for has yet to reveal itself.

"Let's go see Central Park."

And this is where I leave him.

When my heels reroute in the other direction, the crystal fringe on my dress whips across my legs like a hair toss. I did not leave the heat I pay for and the cake on my counter to play tourist.

"Nope, we're almost there." The newsboy cap covering Kojo's fade tips toward the end of the street. A lamppost awaits, cloaking a broken sidewalk in shadows.

"Where is *there*?" He erases the step back I take with his wingtip boots, and his peacoat invades my personal space. I'm spun by the shoulder, and we're off once again on our adventure, which might end in a felony.

"Live a little, Regine. It's a celebration!" His grin widens at my scowl. "Don't act like we didn't have fun tonight. You only turn thirty-eight once."

"And I prefer to do it without getting run over by a cyclist," I grumble.

Today wasn't a bust. After breakfast and a rainy day of movies, Kojo told me to dig deep in my closet for something vintage. He took me to a bar on the Upper East Side because of its *Madison* Avenue location, which was about as believable as his smirk. There were drinks and off-key singing, both of which we could have found in my neighborhood.

In his *Newsies* outfit, Kojo is a complete Broadway musical, which is another surprise tonight. I've never seen him dressed so proper. He's wearing a cable-knit sweater with a dress shirt *and* tie underneath, and corduroy pants. His dreads are in a bun under his cap.

He's either teaching law somewhere or trotting off to the English countryside.

Cars slow, illuminating the crosswalk. The heat of the engines rises in the headlights as we cross over to Fifth Avenue and follow a path of large stone tiles into Central Park.

LED candles in white paper bags light the pathway to a manicured landscape surrounding a fountain. Across from it is one of those igloo structures made for outdoor dining. Light from the nearby high-rises catches in the night sky.

Incredible.

"What is this?" My inhale becomes a gulp of air when Preston steps out of the dome. His smile reaches me from the feet between us and the soft music that filters in from somewhere beyond the foliage.

"In case it wasn't clear, Regine, that man loves you," Kojo says from my side. I hear him, but I can't take my eyes off said man, who's making his way to me.

Musk with a hint of nutmeg embraces my senses with the gentleness of a forehead kiss. In a long black coat and pants, Preston is a model of sex and seduction. A matching beanie covers his hair, and framing his face is a trimmed goatee.

The urge to run to him careens over the realization he's here in New York.

"What are you—"

"Hi, Puff." The huskiness in his tone pours warmth into my veins when his bear hug clasps my body to his. A jolt surges from my neck to my toes at his minty breath skating across my face.

Kojo always says, *If he wanted to, he would*. Actions speak louder than words, and Preston's being here speaks volumes. If he's in the air, he texts. Away on a business trip, he calls. We haven't put a label on what we are, but him making time for me means more than he'll ever know.

"You're here." I reach to kiss him, unable to help myself.

"I am, baby."

He kisses me and extends a hand to Kojo. "It's nice to meet you. Thank you for stalling."

Kojo tips his cap and shows every damn tooth in his mouth. "Anything for this one. So, you're Preston." He steps back to scan him from head to toe. "I get it."

"Is this why you're dressed like that?" I snicker.

"I had my source of inspiration." Kojo rolls his eyes. "Enjoy your evening, love. I'll check in tomorrow." He pulls me in for a hug and kisses my cheek. "Let him in, Madison. You deserve it."

"Thank you." My voice carries in a whisper.

"Take care of her, Fancy Brit," Kojo coos. "You two are adorable! *Puff*," he mocks with Idris Elba finesse. "I can't!" He disappears behind hedges that gently blow in the cool breeze.

That's my friend. Forever over-the-top.

"He's really something." Preston's chuckle is low, amused without judgment.

"The best."

His laughter fades into the soft caress of his gaze, like he's seeing me for the first time. He cups my face. "Can I kiss you?"

"You already did," I smirk.

Preston lifts my chin and brings his mouth to mine. Our lips brush in one peck that becomes another.

The taste of us is a free fall of emotions. There are no words, only a vow to live in the now we sear with a slow kiss.

We break apart at some point, our breaths a tiny cloud of heat in the air.

"Dinner is ready," he says.

"Refill?"

"Yes, please." I lean over the table with my flute, which Preston fills with champagne. "This"—I marvel at the wooden stands that hold a buffet of classic comfort food—"is amazing." I always wanted to dine in a heated igloo, but I've never had time because of all the winter fashion events. He went all out and made it unforgettable.

Throw blankets are tossed over accent chairs to create a cozy vibe. Pulled pork sliders, cheeseburgers, and fish and chips are our feast. They're bite-size for our dinner for two. It's a small miracle I still have room to breathe in the pear-colored dress that clings to my silhouette. Dessert is questionable...unless a pastry somehow manifests on the table.

"It took a few favors, but it helps that my mother was a member of the conservancy," he admits. "She spent a lot of time here."

"Oh."

"My father said he spent what felt like hours convincing her to leave the gardens. They were her favorite place, a break from keeping up with a CEO's schedule. I come here when I'm in New York and need that stillness, or to feel close to her."

His eyes wander to the distance beyond the transparent window panels, searching for the apparition of a mother he lost hours after she pushed him into the world.

Losing a parent so young is a different type of suffering. I miss Mawmaw, her deep belly laughter, Sunday meals, and swearing every June bug to Hell. I have decades of memories I can call on when her physical absence picks at my grief. It's a scab that will never fully heal.

Preston mourns a woman he never met, the blanket of a mother's adoration he'll never experience.

"Thank you for sharing her favorite place with me. She would be proud of you," I say to the sadness finding residence in his expression. "Your kindness and your heart are a reflection of her love."

"Thank you, Puff." His shoulders ease, his gaze flitting between me and a place beyond my bare shoulder.

I automatically swipe at an out-of-place hair. It's a pointless gesture, because the moisture in the air is forcing the ends I spent hours straightening to bend back to their natural curl pattern.

"What?" I frown under his appraisal.

"I want to show you your gift." He stands to put on his coat, then pulls my chair out.

My eyes narrow. "This was gift enough," I say to his chest as he secures my coat around my shoulders. "Where are we going?"

I'm guided by the hand for the second time tonight. Unlike Kojo's little scavenger hunt, we don't go far.

Preston takes us to a bench on the other side of the fountain. High-rise buildings freckled in lights wedge us between the Upper East and West Sides under a few stars and the moon behind the clouds.

"Remember when you told me the Pont des Arts was your most memorable date?" His eyes shift to mine.

I nod.

Our video call during his recent trip to Manchester turned into a night of twenty questions. From his suite and my kitchen, we rediscovered old truths and learned new details about the people we've become.

"It was a night I'll never forget," I say about our date at the Louvre fifteen years ago that ended with a slow dance next to the famous bridge. My fingers hover over the padlock necklace hanging under the halter neckline of my dress. It felt right to wear it close to my heart tonight.

"Central Park has thousands of benches with engraved love notes. I purchased one in memory of my mother, in the Conservatory Garden she loved." His thumb grazes a silver plaque. "*Gioia ru me core* ," he reads. "It's Sicilian for 'joy of my heart.'"

Tears form in my eyes at the longing and affection wrapped in the declaration. "Beautiful."

Preston offers a sad smile and reaches for my hand. We walk to the next bench, feet away, which has a silver plaque just like the one we left. He shifts me to his chest, his arms a wool-lined shield from the chill in the air. "This is a place of peace for me. A reminder of love lost but contained in eternity. That's what you are to me, Puff. My peace. My heart. My future."

I draw a sharp breath when he turns us toward the engraving.

Madison

Ti amerò fino al giorno dopo per sempre.

Preston

"This one is in Italian. It means, 'I will love you until the day after forever,'" he whispers against my ear.

Every tear I've held back finds its way down my cheeks. I cry for the time we lost. But it's right here, next to the love he memorialized for all to see. The dawn of a smile finds the strength to grow.

Love isn't always lost.

Sometimes it circles back. Louder. Bolder.

My "Thank you" is smothered by Preston's mouth on mine. His hands slip up my arms, pulling me into the rapid thud of his beating heart.

What lies ahead remains unknown. Tonight, I want to focus on the present moment and the gift that's been mine all along.

His heart.

Chapter 38

Preston

Neon signs bathe our town car in a glow. The seven-teen-minute ride to Madison's flat is a silent countdown. Her head is on my shoulder, our fingers threaded together on my knee.

My life until this point has been an autopilot blur. I've existed, but now I feel myself coming back to the real me, and it's because of her. I expect at any moment to wake up from a dream without the fresh scent of magnolia or her textured curls brushing over my cheek.

I type out a message to Dayo, pocket my phone, and take Madison's hand once we arrive. The security we had at the park will disperse for the evening.

Madison guides us by the front desk attendant with a smile. We step into the lift and float up floors to the twelfth. Our destination is at the end of a long, carpeted corridor with black doors. Whoever the designer was spared no ceiling lights. They're illuminated bread-crumbs, leading us to the place we'll share our first night together.

"Home sweet home." She unlocks the deadbolt. Another lock unfastens to reveal an open floor plan with a backdrop of windows.

"It's no Westminster penthouse, but it has a view." There's no animosity in her tone, only pride for the space she calls her own.

"It's nice, Puff." I nod to the Hudson River. Moonlight floats across the dark surface and catches on adjacent high-rises.

It's a beautiful view, but it's not the one that interests me.

Madison reaches for me at the same time I move toward her. Our mouths collide in a slow, drugging kiss of tongue and desire. I swallow her gasp at my hand on her neck, holding her in place. A smile spreads across the pillow of her lips at my groan when she sucks my tongue, moving back and forth with enough force to make me come.

She yanks at the lapels of my overcoat, which I push over my biceps. My suit coat is next to fall to the ground. I work on my tie while her fingers fly over the buttons of my shirt. Our kiss breaks so she can take in my chest and the trail of hair that extends below my belt. Her tug on the leather forces my bare chest against her breasts, which are cased in a dress I'm seconds from ripping off with my teeth.

She unbuttons my trousers, pulls down the zip, and grips her target now growing against my leg.

"Madison," I grunt when my trousers and briefs follow her to the floor. "Baby, it's your birthday. Let me take care of you."

"You do take care of me," she says with lust and affection reflecting in her eyes. My ass clenches at the first swipe of my tip. *Shit.* "It's my birthday." She kisses the precum. "Show me what you got, Thumper."

I narrow my eyes at the nickname but lose focus when she thrusts me deeper into her mouth. The trousers around my ankles lock me in place for her thick lips to massage the pillar of flesh she strokes with the curve of her mouth. "*Fuck,* Puff."

Once Madison's mind is set, there's no stopping her. Not that I'm complaining. We're tenacious in the same way. If she wants to suck the skin off my penis, I won't argue with her.

I gather her hair into my fist and pump into her with slow and measured strokes. Madison needs no guidance on bringing me to my knees. She proves it with the flick of her tongue under my head, which she rolls over until she reaches my spot.

"Damn it...*shit.*" My right foot taps the hardwood in rapid succession like the *Bambi* character she nicknamed me after. At her moan, I widen my stance and thrust into her relaxed throat. I change speed to savor the drag of her flattened tongue. "Eyes up. Suck me harder."

Madison whimpers at my grip on her hair. It's tight but not tight enough to hurt her. She confirms her comfort with a hum that shoots straight through my nuts. The gargles and saliva dripping down her stretched mouth nearly send me through the ceiling with curled toes.

"Just like that, Puff," I grunt.

My dick thickens as her moans mix with a gag. Her throat eases to grant space for my head to tap the back. A hand wraps around my shaft. Madison's pace quickens, her head bobbing, her nails digging into my ass as I get lost in loud slurps and the heaven of her mouth.

"Puff. I'm about to come." It's the only warning I can muster through clenched teeth.

Blood pounds in my ears, and my foot is about to stomp a hole through the floor. I brace a hand on the wall and come down her throat.

My breaths are erratic, my chest heaving at the tremors of the aftershock. Madison swallows eagerly, like she's working for extra credit. Her hazel eyes lift under long, hooded lashes.

I don't know what kind of witchcraft she practices, but I need her ring size now.

"Up," I instruct, staring at her in awe and confusion while shaking the feeling back into my legs. I kick out of my shoes and trousers. Her eyes crinkle with a knowing smirk until I toss her over my shoulder.

"Preston!" Her giggle wanes into a moan as I slap her ass.

Who's laughing now?

I swipe a plate that holds a single-tier chocolate cake from the kitchen counter. Dark ganache drips from the top to the base, with various truffles along the edge.

"What are you doing?"

"Bedroom" is all I say. She points to a room on the right.

The lights are off, but night glitters through the windows to unveil a monochrome room painted a dark color. Gray maybe? It resembles my office but has a ceiling light bathed in crystals above the bed.

I set Madison on her feet and place the cake on the mirrored bedside table next to the window.

Her dress winks in the moonlight, dancing across the curves of her smooth, pecan skin.

"Do you mind?"

The silk in her voice reawakens my dick, which is still bobbing free. She gives me her back and drapes her curls over her shoulder to expose the zip of her dress.

I unfasten the clasp and dust open-mouthed kisses down to the small of her back. The edge of a black lace thong peeks out from the curve of her ass, and I lick it. It's impossible not to stroke my dick, now pointing at the ceiling.

"Thank you," she says over her shoulder. The edge of her mouth lifts at my fist over my length. I could stay on my knees for the rest of the night but rise to my full height. The straps of her dress cascade down the soft lines of her body and catch on her nipples. Her breath quivers when I tug on the engorged tips.

"Mmh," she murmurs, head against my chest. Her hand reaches for my hair, which she crinkles in her grasp.

The dress snags over her wide hips before it pools on the floor.

"Preston," she pants. "Yes."

My mouth latches on to the hollow of her neck as my hand strokes and twists her left nipple. My other hand slides down her rib cage to the soft flesh of her belly. Another moan crackles in the air when I change nipples and glide over the seat of her black thong, which is now saturated in her essence.

"Don't hold your breath, Puff." I lick her whimper and glide two fingers up her slit in a long stroke. Her legs part, summoning me to caress the slick heat between her thighs. I curve my hand to add pressure to the subtle ridges of her G-spot.

"*Preston*." Madison writhes against me, hips rolling and back arched. She bends into my palm, which is pressed against the valley of her heaving breasts, and comes in a long, satisfied moan.

"Your climax is my favorite sound." She screams at my smack to her pussy. My dick swells at her throaty groan. "Do you hear how wet you are? Dripping all over this fucking floor." I give her another smack.

"Preston." She stumbles forward at the threat of another orgasm.

"What you running for?" I keep her in place with my hand wrapped around her throat. "Take what I give you, baby."

Madison's panting wanes when she resettles against my chest—right where she belongs. Her breath hitches at the sudden loss of my fingers inside her.

"Taste yourself." I feed her two fingers coated in her juices, pumping them in and out of her mouth. "I wanted to give you dessert first, but I want mine now."

I press the softest kiss to her cheek and pull out my fingers, circling her nipples with her saliva. The hard peaks glisten in her fluids, drawing my mouth to lap and suck. I use my teeth to nick the sensitive skin and send her into overdrive.

"Oh, my—" Madison's head falls back. She gasps for a breath she releases to the ceiling.

"Do you trust me?" I press her breasts together and run my tongue from one nipple to the other.

"Yes," she says. Black lashes fan over her skin now beaded with sweat. She whimpers at a tug.

"Press your titties on the window."

Hazel eyes fly open and catch flecks of gray in the pale light. Madison swallows hard, her gaze darting from me to the outside world beyond panes of glass.

She moves around me with the grace of a model in heels. It takes four steps for her to reach the glass. Her fisted hands unfurl, and she presses her palms into the Manhattan view.

"It's cold." There's a shiver in her voice, one I'll warm soon enough. "Are you coming?"

Our eyes lock over her shoulder. "Enjoying the view," I admit. Her body is a work of art. The delicate curve of her ass leads to flared hips and dimples in the small of her back.

I take my place behind her and kneel. With our height difference, I'm at eye level with the round globes that have been teasing me all night. I bite a cheek and suck it with a loud pop.

"Lift for me." She raises a sparkly heel to the footstool next to the window. "Look at this pussy." Her mewl at a long swipe of my tongue excites my dick.

Everything about Madison is infectious, but I spread her cheeks and devour her pussy like a starved man.

"*Shit*," she mumbles, her face pressed against the side of the glass.

I swirl my tongue into the juices dripping from her lips. She jumps at the lick to her asshole.

"Preston." Her legs shake. "I—oh."

I push her thighs apart and suck harder, nose to ass. She groans and rolls her hips into my face. "Fuck yes, Puff. Throw it back."

And that she does.

Her body heat paints a fog on the glass. "I think someone is watching," she moans.

Sure enough, a light is on in an adjacent building. It's not close to make out the figure facing us, but someone is there.

"Want to stop?" I ask.

She bites her lip, a rush of pleasure filling her cheeks. "No." Her tiny smile rivals the fire in her eyes.

"Very well." With one final lick, I stand and thrust three fingers into her warm channel, which is clenched in a viselike grip. I pull them out to smack her lips. "My Puff is an exhibitionist, and she likes spankings," I say to her moans. "Come again so you can take this dick."

Madison's breath becomes erratic as it mixes with her gasps. I reposition my grip to slide in and out of her sex with more speed. My hand is a cup against her swollen G-spot, rubbing circles. She latches on to my forearm and pushes harder. The force of her fucking my hand stiffens her body on a scream.

"Hah! I'm coming!"

Slurps quicken until I pull out as a gush of liquid squirts onto the glass and the floor.

"Holy"—she gulps for air—"shit."

I scoop her into my arms and lay her in the center of the bed. She curls her legs into the air and pushes her hands against her mound, straining her breasts between her arms. She's in complete bliss, head back, mouth open, eyes closed.

Magnificent.

"Are you okay, baby?" I keep my tone light so as not to disturb her postcoital high from the nipple stimulation and squirting. The exhibitionism was a bonus.

Madison's teeth scrape her bottom lip. Her eyes dance over my face. "Can I have one more birthday present?"

"Anything."

"You." She nods to my dick, which is basking in her approval.

"Are you sure?"

Her heels spread to reveal her bare, swollen pussy. "Please," she whispers. "Have you been with anyone else?"

"Of course not, Puff." I frown. "I've had zero sexual interactions since I saw you in January. I promise I haven't touched Gisele, or any other woman."

"I know…" She looks away, her brows creased in deep thought. "Is it wrong that I don't want anything between us? I'm on the pill, and we have our STI panels from…" She glances at me with a shy smile.

"Ravenous," I finish for her.

"Yeah."

Using condoms is a longstanding practice for me, even at Ravenous. But I want Madison in every way possible. Just me and her for the rest of our lives.

The bed dips under my weight as I crawl between her legs. I stop to savor the air scented with her essence and press a kiss to her inner thigh. Not feasting on this pussy every waking moment will be one of my greatest challenges.

Madison reaches for me and seals our mouths. The kiss is gentle, unrushed. I curl an arm around her hip to pull her closer. Our tongues dance, making space for us to sink deeper.

I get lost in memories that now thread into the present. How did I get so lucky to have her twice in the same lifetime?

I kiss the tip of her chin, and we groan as my head breaches her entrance. Her gasp lodges in her throat before it explodes through the curves of her lips. A crease between her delicate brows forms at the tug and pull of pleasure swaying with pain.

"Okay?" I ask.

"Never better," she huffs through a moan.

I mirror her grin and push into the friction of her tight walls, which stretch to let me in. Our exhales tangle with every inch until I'm fully seated. My thumb glides over the soft line of her cheek. I seal my mouth to hers and hold the soft dip of her hip to pull out and thrust deeper.

Just me and her. For the rest of our lives.

Chapter 39

Madison

Can aspirin relieve a headache in your vagina?

Preston was always a passionate lover, but the way he left me tired, speechless, and contemplating the meaning of life is wild.

His tongue expelled me of all reminders of mediocre lovers who've licked my pussy with little energy and zero enthusiasm. Forget anything with a hand. Half of them fingered like they were digging for spare change in the cracks of a couch.

Preston did more than please me last night—he revived my mind, body, and soul.

It was perfect. The dinner. The bench next to his mother's with that inscription.

I will love you until the day after forever.

Soft snores gently lift the muscles in his back. Half of his body is above my duvet, concealing the ass that pistoned into me and the long, toned legs that slammed into the backs of my thighs when he took me from behind.

When we were in Paris, waking up next to him was my favorite part of the day. I'd watch him sleep on the days when early meetings and constant travel didn't take him away. In sleep, his usual sharp and confident profile was at peace. Sometimes, I'd catch his dimples when he smiled at whatever had his mind at ease. They're here now.

His lashes curl over his eyes, which are creased with crow's feet. The first hints of silver lightly dust his tousled strands on the pillow that cushions half of his face.

No one has ever gone to such lengths to earn me. I can lay our past to rest where it belongs. I want to accept his tender offer with no reservations.

But there is one reservation....and I can't shake it.

Somewhere in the back of my mind is a voice warning me that what's too good to be true often is.

"The purpose of sleeping in is to sleep," Preston mumbles. He pops an eye open and grabs my arm. "Come here." I leave my side for his chest when he rolls over and nestles me into the crook of his arm. "What are you up to?"

"Thinking," I say.

"About?"

"This. Us."

His lips tip into a grin. Why does he have to be so fine this early? "I see," he says, stroking his goatee, which I might've sucked on more than once last night. "Ready to accept my tender offer?" He casts me a glance with hooded eyes.

"I didn't say that." I giggle at the grumble that rattles his broad chest. "I'm not trying to be difficult. There's just a lot to consider."

"Like?"

"Like you being a busy CEO, for starters. If you're not in meetings twenty-four seven, you're traveling."

Preston kisses the headscarf I had the sense to put on after our shower earlier this morning. "I will always make time for you, Puff. Delegation is a value among my team. I can't guarantee there won't be moments of busyness—or the need to travel—but I'll always check in and ensure you're comfortable. You are my top priority."

Good answer.

"Just like that?" My brows narrow.

"I know the boss pretty well." He winks and pulls my thigh across his waist. "What else?"

"There's the obvious location issue. Your life is in London; mine is here."

"True," he nods. "We still have time to figure that out. I won't go longer than a week apart, though."

"So, what—I pack my things and move across the pond?"

"If that's what you want."

"And wait for you to get home?" *Tuh*. "What about my life and my career?" London treats me well, but that doesn't mean I'll become his shadow.

He sits up against my upholstered gunmetal headboard and takes me with him. "I respect you tremendously, Puff. Your business included. My company's headquarters and board are in London. If you want to stay in New York, I'll move, but I'll need to travel two, maybe three times a month to check in." His fingers curve under my chin. When I meet his eyes, there's a soft assurance in them. "My being a hotelier does not mean you have to give up your dreams for me. My brother can run the London office if necessary. KD, our

CFO, is in Paris. Me in New York could work. I want you to be comfortable and feel like you have a voice, because you do.”

“You have an answer for everything, don’t you?”

“For you, always.”

The breath I release is sharp. “Thank you,” I say. My voice lacks its usual guardedness. “The women in my family are all strong, but they sacrificed their desires to support their spouses’ dreams. I want a family of my own, but not at the expense of putting my goals on the back burner.”

“We’re partners, Puff. Equals. I admire your work ethic and the space you create for yourself in the fashion industry. You’re smart, beautiful, and exceptionally talented. I’d be a fool not to support you the way your man should.”

“So you’re my man now?” My mouth quirks up. “That’s news to me.”

He shrugs. “Been waiting for you to catch up. I know what I want. We can go at your pace, but you’re it for me, baby.”

I squeal when he pounces on me. There’s no point crawling away with his grip on my ankle. The burn in my cheeks from laughing fatigues my muscles to mush. They match my legs, which he used as bendy straws all night. Preston smacks my ass and drags me back across a bed of rumpled sheets.

My vagina pulsates at his face between my cheeks. He takes a long sniff and groans. “If you don’t get this pussy out of my face, I’m sucking on it until you soak the sheets again. Ass too.”

"You are so nasty," I laugh and flip onto my back. He finds a home between my thighs and kisses my lips—the ones on my face. "I don't recall you being a super freak in Paris."

"Says the woman who sprayed the floor and window in front of an audience last night." The smile hovering above my face fades. "Are you sure you're okay?"

"Yes, for the third time." I smirk and drag a hand up the muscles flexing in his arm. "I don't want to put on a show every day, but I enjoyed the rush."

I was so high on pleasure last night that it took me a minute to register we had company. The face was a mystery of dark lines and shadows, but the burly outline of a figure was undeniable. We were far enough away to keep some privacy, which turned me on even more. The thrill of being on full display was an indescribable power. Me commanding attention while Preston worshipped me on his knees with his tongue...

Phew!

"I want to do it again at some point," I say. "At Ravenous."

Preston's stare raises the hairs on my arms. My heart jolts, and my lips part to suck in the air that's now thickened under his gaze. Fine and intense mix through angled brows, perky lips, and a sharp jawline.

"That can be arranged," he says, his voice a steady timbre. "We only host a handful of events a year, so as not to compete with the established clubs."

"Is that what you want, a full-time club?"

He shakes his bedhead. "No. The allure of Ravenous is its limited access. Pop-ups on our properties here and there."

"Okay."

"Ask what you're thinking." His fingers brush over my bottom lip, which is caught between my teeth.

"I like having an outlet to explore my…kinks. Will you be at every event?"

"Not every. I went to Vail because it was our first one in the States."

It's still wild to think a pop-up play space was right under my nose at the singles' retreat. Not that I would've been shaking my titties for all to see. Kink exploration is a new territory I'm settling into.

More like diving into spread-eagle, but okay.

"I can send William and KD from now on, if you want," he adds. "Because of the different laws, our London pop-up will be the only one with intercourse." He leans onto his forearm to graze the side of my face with his knuckles. "I've done a lot over the years, Puff. I enjoy Ravenous, but it's not a requirement for my pleasure. If you want to play in public, we'll go. If not, I don't need to be there, outside of checking logistics occasionally." His lips brush mine. "I have everything I need right here."

I welcome him and the slide of his tongue. Crushed to his chest, the weight of his body is a blanket. His dick prods at my entrance, exploring its developing slickness.

"Okay," I murmur.

Preston kisses my lips again. "What else did you want to do? I'm yours for the day and at your service."

"At my service, huh? I know somewhere you failed to perform."

His frown meets my grin as I nod to the untouched birthday cake on my nightstand.

———ele———

Knowing how to ride a horse comes in handy when you're straddling a man with a third leg.

The burn in my thighs spread over smooth, prominent quads extinguishes at Preston's mouth on my nipple.

"Fuck me, Puff," he grits out in a strained voice. His arms surround my waist like vines, his legs in a sprawl to match my pace.

I grin when his right foot twitches. Someone is happy.

"You good, Thumper?" My breathy laugh becomes a yelp at his nip to my collarbone.

We've been at it for...I lost track, but I imagine it's almost noon. I have cake crumbs in my ass, icing smeared over my breasts and booty, and not a single care for the mess we're making in my bed.

Preston reaches for what's left of my chocolate ganache cake and pulls off a piece. Neither of us thought to grab a fork before playing with our body parts.

Baked goodness breaches my mouth at the press of his fingers. Preston pulls my mouth to his by the back of my neck, and we trade cake with our tongues. His hands slide down my waist to hold me in place as I grind harder over his length.

With the way he's hitting my vital organs, it's a miracle I can chew and ride dick at the same time.

The wave of another orgasm rises to a crescendo that turns into an icy bucket of water when my bedroom door opens and Jewel waltzes in with a smile.

"I got her right here. Oh my fuck!"

"What are you doing?!" I try and fail at pulling up the sheets. Whatever's not on the floor is under the weight of the man whose penis is still inside of me.

"*Ki moun nonm-çála?*" a voice asks from the phone.

Whatever color is left in my face fades alongside my dignity.

My mother is on a video call with Jewel, asking about the man in my bed. He's hard and very much naked.

Jewel snaps out of the shock that naturally comes with catching your aunt in the act. "*Mo chagrin, auntie!*" Her natural curls spiral over her face as she drops her gaze. "I had an exam yesterday, and I forgot to call. I got my Mawmaw on the phone—"

"Still naked, Jewel," I hiss.

"Yup! Um." She thumbs to the living room. "Going."

"Oh, my word." I groan into my hands. "*Bon fèt*, Madison."

"She wants to see him!" Jewel yells from my living room.

Of course she does.

"My mother would like to meet you. How are you still hard?"

The dick brushing my uterus twitches, and Preston levels me with a stare. "I'm still inside you, Puff. Ask me that question again."

The cake smeared across his mouth would be funny if my family didn't have a front-row seat to us fucking.

Six minutes and the fastest duck bath of my life later, we're on my sofa, facing off with Babet Monroe. Eyes the shade of coffee dart between me and Preston, who's wearing his suit from last night. A curved brow lifts but dissolves into a poker face of rich cheekbones, full lips, and espresso skin smoothed in shea butter.

"Who are ya people?" she directs at Preston.

He clears his throat with a glance my way and the nerves of a high school boyfriend caught sneaking out the window. "Hello, ma'am. I'm Preston Donnelley. My people"—he blinks, unsure how to answer—"are from Italy and England. Sicily, specifically."

"*Ki çé tô louvraj*?"

"She wants to know what you do for work," I tell him. My mama speaks English just fine but will toss in Creole simply because she can.

"I own a hotel brand, ma'am."

My mother's stare could bend metal. Her mask is in place, but I catch the intrigue. "England and Italy," she repeats. "What else is in ya?"

A dimple appears at the edge of his smile. "My grandmother is Black Sicilian," Preston says in complete adoration for the woman who influenced his life. "My mother was too."

"Was?"

"She died after childbirth," he clarifies.

Mama's frown softens. She stares at Preston, her eyes misting at the thought of a child losing their parent on their birthday. We never navigated that form of grief together. But his birthday is a few months away, and I plan to be there for him however he needs.

My hand twines with his, and he sets them on his thigh.

"I'm very sorry, *cher*," she says.

"Thank you, ma'am." His tone dulls but remains steady.

Mama shifts her attention to me. "How long this been going on, Maddie? Jewel got me on the video to see my daughter smeared in cake and fornication."

"Mama."

"Nah, child. Don't 'mama' me. Let me find out you got a whole man under our noses this entire time." She takes in Preston, who looks ready for a photo shoot with his semi-tamed hair and dreamy eyes. "Her daddy is off messing with a boat, so I'll ask on his behalf. What are your intentions with my child?"

"Mama," I plead.

"Hush. You're thirty-eight now, but you're still my baby."

"If I'm fortunate, Madison will be my wife," Preston says like he's telling her the weather. "I love and have loved her in the fifteen years that separated us."

Her crown of coiled black hair swivels in my direction. My sigh is silent, to ward off a virtual pop in the mouth. "Madison Désirée Monroe!" my mama snaps. "I could've had more grandbabies by now? Whatcha waiting for?"

I cut my eyes at Preston, who's grinning from ear to ear at his new accomplice. "Mama, we have to go. I love you."

"Love you too, *cher*. I expect you home this summer. Bring my son."

Preston waves. "Goodbye, Mrs. Monroe."

"Call me mama, *baybee*," she all but coos at the man who was licking icing out of my ass twenty minutes ago. Then she hangs up.

"I think she likes me," he says.

"She likes the idea of her almost forty-year-old daughter married and pregnant." I roll my eyes as he shifts closer to kiss my cheek. "Think you have a new friend?"

He grins. "I hope."

"Good luck getting through that one." I nod to Jewel, who's glowering at her tablet with a rage that grew from a simmer to a boil in a matter of minutes. "Jewel eats the rich for sport. Especially billionaires."

"This you?" She flips the screen to reveal an article about Preston's net worth. The proof is in Times New Roman, not that he can hide his wealth in this age of information and internet detectives. Thirty seconds is all it took for the switch to flip and Preston to calculate the drop from the living room window.

"Um." He clears his throat.

"It wasn't a question," Jewel declares. "Come on, and bring your wallet."

I pat his leg and leave him in the lion's den known as my niece's lair.

"You too, auntie!" she calls from the front door. "We're going to Brooklyn."

Chapter 40

Preston

"Can I take this off? I promise to keep my eyes shut."

"That smirk says otherwise." I kiss Madison's lips and pat her leg, which is draped in some silky fabric I want to peel back like curtains. (I already did in the bathroom on the plane, but that's beside the point.) "Five more minutes."

"*Preston*." All the blood in my body rushes to my other head at her soft groan.

"Do that again."

Her laugh gets caught in a snort. "You are so nasty!"

I pull her to me and run my nose up her neck. "Patience, baby."

Jewel would kick my ass if she found out I used the private jet. To her surprise, William and I fly commercially with light security for most business trips. My ass still hasn't healed since she handed it to me last week. Madison's niece has a future as a lawyer or professor the way she schooled me without missing a talking point or taking a breath.

On the subway, I sat through question after question about my character, my carbon emissions, and how the ultrawealthy are an existential threat to the planet. There was no arguing with her. Not that I got the chance.

Dayo had a time catching up but managed to follow us to Jewel's university in Brooklyn. The time I spent with Madison and her niece was priceless, aside from my accountant calling to ask if I got robbed.

Our tour of Jewel's dorm ended with her using my money to buy groceries for every student she found. Under no circumstances did she give me a pass. It doesn't matter who I am to her aunt or the sustainability initiatives I enforce in my company. Billionaires create an imbalance of power by hoarding resources—even those born into wealth who have the best intentions.

"Ethical billionaire" is an oxymoron. A title we use to pat ourselves on the back while benefitting from exploitation, whether it's caused by our hands or not.

I sweat more through Jewel's cross-examination than I do when facing my own board. I'm not naïve enough to think I completely won her over, but I did get her "blessing" for this trip.

Tonight is a surprise. There was no way to get Madison through airport security without her seeing or hearing our destination.

I want our first time back in Paris together to be special.

She's patiently awaited the big reveal since our flight from New York and the forty minutes we've spent in the car since. Joe's "If I Was Your Man" drifts through the back seat of our town car. A smile lifts Madison's lips at the carefully curated playlist. I love R&B, but I'm masking any signs we're in France.

"Is all of this necessary? I promise being with you is gift enough."

I lift her hand from my thigh to my mouth. "It's not enough and never will be. I want a redo of our firsts, and I want all of your lasts."

"Thank you in advance, for everything." She smiles.

My time in New York was for Puff. I refused to spend another week apart and flew back for her birthday. I took a small detour to fire Simon in person, but Madison had my attention.

I peck her forehead. "You're welcome, baby. Hope you like your surprise."

"As long as my mother isn't on a device." She chuckles at my groan.

Nothing about meeting her family while balls deep inside of her is funny. I was mortified and held her tighter like we weren't naked and covered in cake. If only my arms were long enough to shield all that ass covered in icing handprints.

Sticky situations have occurred before, but none that involved meeting someone's mother.

Babet Monroe was not pleased to see her daughter in her birthday suit. Nonna sniped me with her stare countless times when I messed up. Black women aren't monoliths, but their ability to put you in your place with a single look is universal.

The moonlight cascades over stone facades. It travels down the satin fabric teasing Madison's eyes, to her nose and the space between her neck and the top of her cleavage. The trees lining the avenue wave shadows across her face as the car stops.

I nod at the driver, who hands me noise-canceling headphones.

"I'm covering your ears so you don't hear anything," I say, carefully navigating around the bun on her head. "Let me know if the music is too loud."

I load the playlist on my phone, press play, and call Madison's name. When she doesn't answer, I get out of the car and tip the driver, who's removing our luggage from the boot. Madison shivers when I open her door. With my hand in hers and her trust that I got us, she steps onto the cobblestone street and follows me inside.

The ride in the lift gives me time to take in the bottom lip she's worrying between her teeth. Coming back to the penthouse with her feels like home. I haven't crossed the threshold in fifteen years, avoiding the hole in my heart after losing her.

Mirrored doors part to unlock a capsule of memories. I take her hand and guide us through the place we once shared. Vases of pink and white peonies fill the living area, with the ambient light of the sconces warring with the moon shining through the windows.

I take our coats, unpair the Bluetooth, and remove the headphones. Faith Evans's "I Love You" hums from my phone as I remove the blindfold.

It takes a second for Madison's eyes to adjust to the light. Her brows dip, and her gaze drifts to the sofa where we spent many nights drinking wine and listening to music. It lifts to the dining room table I chased her around before the first time we made love and glides over to the balcony with a view of the Eiffel Tower.

"Welcome back," I whisper.

Tears roll down her cheeks. I kiss them away. Sobs fade into moans through the night as the echoes of our past blend with our future.

"You are divine. And this dress." I pull apart Madison's faux fur coat and groan. "Let's go home." I nuzzle her neck.

"I want to meet your brother."

"He'll be there tomorrow."

To the driver's credit, he keeps his eyes straight ahead. There's no partition to separate the sounds of our kisses and my hands traveling over her vegan bodycon dress.

I'm insatiable, as if I wasn't driving into her guts on the balcony just this morning.

Work called me into the Paris office this afternoon. I didn't want to leave, but I have an avalanche of work waiting for me once I'm back for good. I needed the break and savored the time away, reconnecting in the place where Madison and I first fell in love. Stocked tea and fresh pastries from the corner bakery she loved were waiting on the kitchen counter when she woke up.

My tongue savors the taste of her mouth as I angle her head against the headrest. The exploration ignites shockwaves through my body, hardening the imprint against my thigh.

"Baby," Madison moans at the pressure of my hand on her jaw and the graze of my tongue dipping between her lips.

"I missed you, Puff," I mumble.

We stop in front of the hotel where we're having dinner. My hand never leaves the small of Madison's back as I navigate through the foyer to the lifts. The restaurant is on the top floor, overlooking the surrounding district.

A woman in a black and white suit greets me by name and guides us through square tables with rose-pink tablecloths. The dining room is a quaint space surrounded by aged brick, high chandeliers, and gold antique molding. On the other side of a set of double doors is a private salon with windows that rise to the ceiling.

William makes a beeline across weathered wood floors when he sees Puff. He's so excited to finally meet her that he lifts her before I can give a proper introduction.

"I've been waiting for this day," he says, trapping Madison in a bear hug.

"Easy," I chide.

"My apologies." William's wink says otherwise. He sets her down with another hug. "Thank you for bringing him back to life," he murmurs and pecks her cheek. "Come. I want to hear all about you."

William grabs Madison's hand and guides her to the table. His suit is a subtle contrast to his blue eyes, which are crinkling at the corners like it's Christmas morning.

He slides out an upholstered chair for her and whistles. "You, Maddie, are wearing that dress."

"And you'll wear a neck brace if you keep it up." She snorts as I drop into the seat next to her in a huff.

"It's all good. Right, Maddie? We're practically family the way you got this one whistling love songs around the office." William leans closer to pretend he's telling her a secret. "Right after his holiday in the States, he had every picture of you he could find— Chill, bruv, I was only taking the piss!"

Madison is in tears, head back and laughing as I chase my dick of a brother around the table, who's cackling louder than her. I grab him by the tie and ruffle his sandy blonde hair with a smirk. My eyes don't leave hers when I slap him on the back, harder than necessary, and wink.

"Not ashamed to admit I'm a man in love," I say. "You don't need all the details about how I was before you put me out of my misery."

"I kinda do," she giggles.

"I like you, Maddie," William says across the table.

The wait staff filters in and out between our appetizer, soup, and discussion about Madison growing up in Louisiana. We're still waiting for the main course when the salon door opens.

"There you are. Didn't think you'd make it." I wipe my mouth with a napkin and secure the button on my black suit coat on my way to greet KD, who doesn't return my smile.

We missed each other in the office this afternoon. Between her holiday and our travel schedules, I haven't seen much of her this month. Something is different, but I'm not sure what.

"Hey," she says in a flat tone between our kisses to the cheek. Her eyes slide over my shoulder before returning to mine.

"You okay?" I frown.

"Never better." She straightens in her suit and heels that put her around my height. "It's good to see you." The first genuine statement of the night.

I've known KD long enough to know when I shouldn't prod. Feelings aren't an area where we confide in each other, but when shit gets real, we'll stand in each other's corners.

"There's someone I want you to meet." I pull her toward the table, wearing a wild grin and ignoring William's smirk.

Aside from Nonna, he and KD are the people closest to me. They're my family, my inner circle. I want Puff to get to know them.

"KD," I say, "this is Madison." The smile stretching across my cheeks falters. "Puff?" Her skin is flushed, and her eyes are wide.

"This is *your* Madison? Small world."

I look between them. "You two know each other?"

"Yes," KD says, matter-of-fact. "Madison was kind enough to do a wardrobe assessment while she was in London last month. I hired her as my stylist." Her eyes roam over Puff from head to toe with newfound enthusiasm. "I see why you fancy her, Pres. She's exquisite."

"KD," Madison repeats with a pinched brow.

"It's a nickname only close friends call me," she tosses on her way to William.

Something about their exchange doesn't sit right. Two people who have a decent business relationship aren't usually so cold with each other. KD keeps throwing glances at Madison, who looks like she's seen a nightmare in human form.

I wrap my arms around Puff and kiss her lips. "Hey. You okay?"

She blinks out of whatever fog has her in a hold. "Bellamy never told me you two were acquainted."

"KD is my CFO, and an old friend. We've known each other since we were kids. Did something happen?" I look to KD, who's still engrossed in conversation with my brother.

KD is always cautious of new people—not that we have many entering our circle. Unlike William, she takes time to thaw. "Warm" and "bubbly" aren't words I'd use to describe her.

Madison crosses her leg, baring a thigh in black panty hose I want to tear, and settles a napkin across her lap. KD takes the seat to my right, which leaves William across the table with two extra chairs.

I lean over and whisper, "Are you sure you're okay, Puff?"

"We'll talk about it later," she mumbles before turning back to the table. "I didn't realize we'd have more company tonight." Her voice is clipped as she smooths the nonexistent wrinkles in her dress.

"What—"

"We always go out for dinner after our executive meeting," KD offers. "It's been our tradition for years."

"Well, in the spirit of tradition, can we get the fuck on with the night? I'm starving," William deadpans. KD brushes him off with the flick of a wrist.

"You'd have to actually attend more than one of these dinners before you complain about them," she volleys.

"I'm here now, aren't I?" William points a roll at KD and takes a hard bite.

"A miracle, that is." I chuckle at their bickering, thankful for its lifting the tension. My hand finds Puff's thigh under the table and squeezes. "It's always me and KD whenever you're MIA."

"Which is all the time," she adds with a polished laugh.

William rolls his eyes and scoffs. "You'll have to excuse her, Maddie. She swears she's family."

"Don't be foolish, Will." She turns to Puff with a smile creeping above her water glass. "I am part of this family, and I'm not going anywhere."

Chapter 41

Madison

Fifteen Years Ago

A dim flame flickers on a narrow wick. The scent of vanilla lingers before I blow out the lone taper candle with a heavy sigh. Light clings to the small feast on the table, reminiscent of my childhood. It was full of good butter and hours spent next to the stove.

Roasted turkey.

Rice dressing.

Greens.

Ms. Odilia's coveted deviled eggs.

A taste of home for Thanksgiving. It's not a holiday they celebrate here in Paris, but Preston vowed to spend the day with me. At least, that was the plan before a last-minute work trip called him back to London.

Under normal circumstances, such an abrupt pivot wouldn't bother me. I don't question my place in his life because he goes out of his way to show me I'm a priority.

But I'm not sure where I fit now.

He's quieter, more reserved.

I've become an afterthought. These days, he only remembers to tell me he'll be away once he reaches his destination.

The silence is a cold reminder that, beyond the walls of this penthouse, we live worlds apart. In a few months, I'll go back to a life of cramped dorm-room living and humid summers on the bayou.

I hope we can squeeze in more time until we revert to the people we were before that fated day in the museum. Time is running out, and I fear this is the beginning of our end.

Chapter 42

Madison

Present Day

I never read *The Art of War*. I don't fully grasp the philosophies of battle. But I did watch *The Karate Kid* growing up, and striking first without mercy is what I intend to do.

My snake print heels glide across hardwood in a calculated march to the executive suite. At dinner last night, Bellamy batted her lashes and laughed down memory lane with Preston and William like I wasn't there. Her attempts to talk around me were as petty as her inching closer to brush his shoulder and tell jokes that would get her booed off a stage.

Preston and I got into it on the ride back to the penthouse. He still thinks Bellamy choosing me as her stylist is a coincidence. I can't prove it, but I know calculated when I see it.

The fact that she went to such lengths to cozy up to me is disgusting and trifling. It's not a coincidence she booked a consultation and pretended to be friendly to get updates about Preston. I never told her his name—not that I needed to with the games she was playing.

Now it makes sense why she was glaring at me at Ravenous. I didn't know I was with Preston, but she did.

Research into prospective clients only goes so far. There are no social security numbers or tax returns. Bellamy was vague about her "financial consultant" work, which I now know is her role as CFO. Preston's company website doesn't post headshots, not that I would've thought to look. And besides, she admitted to using her first and middle name.

Like I said, calculated.

Desperation and merlot were both plentiful last night. Bellamy couldn't contain her jealousy whenever Preston held my hand or kissed me. It's clear they're close, and it's clearer she wants to break free from the friend zone he keeps her in.

The perk of being a recovering mean girl is the ability to spot ulterior motives. Game recognizes game, and I'll dance in the gutter with the best of them.

Make no mistake, Preston *is* mine. His heart, his moans, and that dick. We might not have a title, but I'll be damned if Ms. Prim and Proper Pantsuit thinks she'll play in my face.

The Donnelley Brand's Paris office has Bellamy's name all over it. The gaudy chandeliers and ornate gold molding scream, *Look at me!* Who the hell needs cherub wall sculptures lurking in the corner?

"May I help you?"

Next to a black fireplace is a gilded desk where a woman sits wearing a collared dress and a deep scowl. Beady black eyes slide up my sheer black panty hose to the high-waist shorts peeking out from underneath my blazer.

She can wield her Viola Swamp nose, daggered brows, and pointed chin at someone else. My outfit is an office edit inspired by the runway. I look damn good.

"I'm here to see Mr. Donnelley. I have an appointment." Squeezing myself into Preston's schedule today took a special conjuring of patience.

She reaches for her phone. "I'll need to clear it with Ms. Kidwell."

"I have an appointment."

"And I need to clear it with Ms. Kidwell," she grits through veneers and flips her black hair over her shoulder. There's something she mumbles in French about Americans being rude.

The nerve.

"That won't be necessary. I'm—"

"Madison."

Bellamy saunters over to Cruella's desk and smirks at the older woman. With a streak of gray and red lips, she's still watching me like I pissed her off for breathing. It wouldn't surprise me if she skins Dalmatian puppies for fun.

"I'll take care of her, Rosalind," Bellamy says, her eyes trained on me. "This way."

She leads us down a hallway with more obnoxious chandeliers. Black and white photos of Donnelley properties framed in gold line a wall across from a bank of windows.

We reach a white door with a gold plaque bearing Bellamy's name. She motions for me to enter.

"Have a seat." She shuts the door and nods to the cream chair across from her glass desk. Wall molding extends from the floor to the ceiling with matching panels. Unlike the rest of the building, it's cozy, homey, with beige drapes and furnishings.

"I'll stand. Where is Preston?"

"Busy working." Bellamy leans against her desk and crosses her bare legs at the ankles. The mini skirt hugging her narrow waist flashes slim thighs. "How can I help you?"

"You can't." I cut my eyes at her with a fake smile she returns.

Bellamy lifts one shoulder, picking an imaginary piece of lint from the houndstooth blouse molded to her breasts. A nipple will pop out if she breathes the wrong way.

"Like I said, Madison. Preston is busy."

"I'll wait. Like *I* said, I have an appointment."

Her grin spreads. "About that." She pushes off the desk and takes slow steps into my personal space. I'm not violent by nature, but I feel the temptation to let my hands go. "I took the liberty of removing you from his schedule." *What?* "He has a lot on his plate here in Paris. The call he's on now will last for most of the afternoon. Then we have a dinner reservation with a client. But I'll tell him you stopped by."

It occurs to me that Bellamy has never seen Preston in love. She's been a mainstay, which explains why she's so protective over him.

That, and she's a bitch.

"You're stunning. More beautiful than anyone I've seen him with." My frown curls the corners of Bellamy's mouth upward. "Enjoy him while it lasts. They never do."

"Mmm." I nod. "Tell me something. Does it get cold lurking in the shadows, waiting for him to see you? I was that delusional once.

While we're sharing advice, here's a tip: Fall in love with someone who will actually love you back."

All pleasantries fade. The anger she suppressed now flushes her ivory complexion. Her chin sets in a stubborn line, and her high cheekbones go hollow on a deep exhale.

This is who I wanted to see.

Preston and William don't pick up on the games she plays, but I do, and now she's showed her hand. I believe Bellamy cares for Preston. I also believe she thinks he'll wake up one day and realize he wasted years not choosing her.

He made his choice; she's looking at it.

Not that he's ever mentioned her outside of a professional setting. This little display is a last stand out of fear.

"You'll never be what he needs." Venom drips from her blood red lips.

"And you're pitiful for pretending to be someone you're not," I snap.

"I took a page from your book," she scowls. "Aren't you the same person who lied about who she was so she could take another student's place because she was too poor to afford it on her own? You don't belong with him, or with us. Consider this payback for the hurt you caused him."

"You don't know what the hell you're talking about!"

"Don't I?" Bellamy steps closer. "Who do you think was there for him and will be once this ends?"

My stomach curdles at the implication of them together, but I keep my chin and my top knot firm.

"I'll let you get back to work," I say. "I'll see him when he comes home, *to me*."

"Don't wait up," Bellamy counters, envy smoothing her tone. "I look forward to us spending more time together. Me and Preston's friendship is as old as you are, and it isn't going anywhere."

Bitch.

———

"Mr. Donnelley is unavailable. Would you like to leave a message?"

Answer your damn phone.

"No, thank you. That won't be necessary," I say to a woman who isn't Cruella. "When do you expect him back?"

"He left with Ms. Kidwell. Have a good evening."

The last message I sent Preston never reached him. It was an "oversight," along with the bad habit he's developed of leaving his phone on airplane mode.

I don't want to call him a liar, but somebody is full of shit.

Since we came to Paris, Preston has been inaccessible. He's out of bed at an ungodly hour and tiptoes in closer to midnight. The conversations we do have between his meetings are brief. So are the texts he sends asking about my day and apologizing for his absence.

I'm not a clinger who needs proof of life at the top of every hour, but I won't tolerate disrespect or be played a fool for the sake of love. For me, trust is given until it's revoked. Preston says he's underwater with work, and I'll believe him until proven otherwise.

But I won't pretend his early mornings and late nights with Bellamy don't sting. It's only been a few days since our showdown in her office, which left me in the dark and on read. She's probably off somewhere gloating in designer heels.

The sigh I release buckles my lungs. The heaviness is a blip under the weight of an empty penthouse that's become a storage locker of past love and current frustration. I rub my palms over my eyes, exhausted from mentally scrolling through scenarios that end in a broken heart or with Preston's body at the bottom of the Seine.

Bellamy has been a part of his life since they were kids—thirty-eight years, she so graciously reminded me. That's a lifetime. With their work dynamic, it's sensible for a CEO to spend time with the CFO.

Maybe they left the office to meet another business partner for dinner. Maybe there's a work event Preston failed to mention.

I'm always three steps ahead.

"We are not this girl," I tell myself on my way to the kitchen for a glass of wine and an eclair.

I'm a lover, not a fighter with a mean cut-off game. At least, I was before Preston. No man would have me worrying a hole into an antique rug at seven p.m. on a Saturday.

Preston has worked late before, but not like this. It's never been this hard to reach him.

I never wanted to be the person waiting by the phone like I have for the last few days. Yet, here I am, with no plans or business of my own that's worth trading in my loungewear.

These feelings—fear sloshing with anger—are why I'm not in a rush to commit my heart to the potential of being broken again.

With another exhale, I grab the ingredients for my pity party of one and go into Preston's home office to play *The Oregon Trail*. Alone.

Chapter 43
Preston

"Sorry to cut this short. Do you have what you need?"

"It's good insight our coalition can use," Jewel says in a blur of curls under a beanie. Glass buildings flash in the background. "I'm on my way to a rally but can share out."

"Please don't get arrested." Madison will eviscerate my balls more than she already has if that happens.

Jewel snorts and glances at the camera. "Like I told auntie, I'm grown. I have class in two hours anyway. You just worry about not showing your ass again."

Since the unfortunate encounter Jewel has yet to let me live down, we've developed an unlikely alliance that's slowly becoming a friendship.

I pay for it, through regular investments in coalitions, mutual aid, and direct services that help people on the ground. I wouldn't expect anything less from this wide-eyed climate activist.

This is our second week of one-to-ones, as Jewel calls them. I pick her brain on climate initiatives and answer questions about billionaires to sharpen her strategies against oligarchs in the fossil fuel industry.

We're in agreement that grassroots leaders from frontline communities should be at the center of the climate movement. My role is that of silent accomplice, funding coalitions with solutions to address the climate crisis. Jewel is educating me on the importance of direct investment in the most impacted communities and the harm of the nonprofit industrial complex. Many well-intentioned organizations take space and resources away from frontline leaders and allow foundation support to dictate decision-making, not the people with lived experience.

Our check-ins, while brief, have been eye-opening. It's one of the few meetings I look forward to on a calendar that's become too crowded for me to think, let alone breathe.

"Same time next week?" Jewel navigates through signs about funding climate resilience.

"That should work, but I'll let you know," I say.

"Okay, Richie Rich. See you around."

"How many votes have we secured?"

"Not enough to neutralize your father," KD says from behind her computer. Her eyes soften in apology. "At best, three. My father and brother won't veer from Victor."

"What about the trust instrument?"

I sigh at her headshake. "The trust your grandfather set up overseas doesn't grant beneficiaries automatic access to all administrative information," she says. "You must request it directly from the trustee or seek court action, which doesn't guarantee disclosure."

"Fucking hell." I pinch the bridge of my nose and close my eyes to ward off another headache. We've been at this for hours.

Outside of calling my cousin Sal to stop my father's heart, any attempt to end my father's stronghold on the company is a hopeless pursuit. My grandfather ensured that, shifting Donnelley Brand assets into an irrevocable trust. He was so focused on maintaining the grip on his legacy that once he retired, he never cared about the implications of a sole custodian overseeing the billions in our family chest.

Company shares.

Every piece of real estate we own.

Bonds.

Brokerage accounts.

As successor trustee, my father manages it all. William and I are beneficiaries of the trust but have no control over it. Our father keeps us in the dark and only provides minimal documentation when I threaten legal action. Even then, I'd have to fly out to Anguilla with time I don't have to get a court to rule in my favor.

Between the sustainability audit on our properties and a deep dive into our finances, I don't know up from down anymore. Only one person is enjoying trips to the Caribbean, and I'll be damned if he pulls off what I think he's trying to.

"Maybe there's a way to work with Victor. A resort in Anguilla is a lucrative investment." If it wasn't for KD living a life of compromise to appease her father, I'd wonder if she were working for mine. The only reason he wants a property there is to move our headquarters.

It's criminal how simple it is to stash wealth by parking it offshore in jurisdictions with lower tax rates—or none at all—except it isn't.

"I will not help my father shift our profits to dodge fucking taxes. Is that the kind of man you think I am?"

It's a serious question, because I don't know who I'm looking at. KD has been one of my closest friends since our nannies set up playdates when we were younger. We both want to do more than our fathers did and use what we have to leave the world better than we found it. Or so I thought.

Her shoulder lifts in a resigned shrug. "All I'm saying is, choose your battles carefully, Preston. Why make an enemy who will stop your projects every step of the way? Tax havens aren't illegal—"

"They're immoral." My tone leaves no room for discussion. An estimated half-trillion in corporate tax revenue is lost every year. Funding for public services gone so the super-rich can line their pockets. Many of these tax havens lack the proper transparency and financial reporting, exacerbating economic inequities to the detriment of everyday people who are left footing the bill.

KD's sigh comes with a look that says she doesn't give a shit regardless. Her office chair creaks when she moves from behind her desk to sit on its glass surface. She shifts her weight and crosses her legs, inching the slit of her black pencil skirt further up her thigh. Her palms rest behind her to prop herself up, and her breasts are crushed to the deep V of her silk shirt.

"I'm sorry," she says to a spot on my tie. Chestnut eyes take a slow drag up my suit. "We've been at this for a week straight. Why don't we take a break?"

Her expectant look is one I know well. Months ago, I'd have lost myself in her soft flesh. Hope sparks desire in her gaze, parting her long, toned legs.

My cue to leave.

"Where are you going?" She frowns when I pull my coat over my suit.

"Home to Madison."

"Madison."

"Yes, my lady," I reiterate. The few hours I get to spend with her before I'm back out the door aren't enough. I check my phone and curse—it's in airplane mode again. Odd.

Thinking of you, Puff. Can't wait to see you.

"So that's it?" I glance up from the emails and messages flooding my screen to KD's glower. Her arms are crossed over her chest.

"That's what?" My brows dip at her question and the flare in her tone. "We've been here for hours. I'm going home."

"Home," she scoffs, trying on the word before she spits it back out.

"Yes, home," I repeat.

"And our arrangement?"

"KD," I call for my lifelong friend. "We spoke about this; we knew what it was. Casual. Nonexclusive. No feelings."

"Except your feelings *are* involved with someone else." She wipes away a stray tear.

"Madison is the love of my life. I lost her once, and I'll never put myself in a position to lose her again," I say. "You need to respect her and our relationship."

"You can't trust her," she states, matter-of-fact. "She lied to you once. She already broke your heart."

"And that gives you the right to act like a child?"

"I was protecting my friend."

"You were protecting dick you no longer have access to," I say. "Don't bullshit me with your fake concern. A friend would have spoken to me about her fears. Not do what you did."

I didn't want to believe that KD, of all people, would go so low as to hire Madison to play games. It's out of character, but so is her crying. She's never reacted this way before.

"I care for you. We've been like family, but I will not tolerate any disrespect to Madison. She's not going anywhere, and if problems persist, we'll need to discuss your time here at the Donnelley Brand."

"Preston." KD trembles. Her shoulders slump, and her hands fall to her lap. "How could you say that to me?"

"I'm not trying to hurt you," I say, my tone soft. "But if you put me in a position to choose, you won't like the outcome. It's her, every time."

Had I known KD would develop feelings, I would've cut off our casual arrangement before it started. William always joked she was in love with me. I never believed him because of our mutual aversion to romantic commitments, something we once shared.

It would sting to lose her as a friend and CFO, but I meant what I said.

"I'm heading out," I say, two steps closer to her office door.

"Stay," she pleads.

"I'm serious, Bellamy." I slice open a new wound using her name. "Will this be a problem?"

"Of course not." Her expression is a mask of stone. "We're professionals. We have a business to run. I just don't want to see you hurt again."

"My relationship is for me to worry about. Understood?" I've never meddled in who KD was or wasn't fucking. I didn't care one way or the other and assumed the feeling was mutual.

She nods. "Understood. We still have a lot to cover." Gold bracelets chime with a flick of her hand. "Why don't we order in and give it two more hours?"

"Thirty minutes. I need to make a call." I'll take Madison out tomorrow and try to fix the strain taking root in us.

I'm halfway to the door when KD calls my name.

"Yeah?"

"Be careful," she says. "Some women don't appreciate feeling strung along."

Chapter 44

Madison

Liquid courage does wonders when you have nothing to lose.

Emma cuts her eyes at me for the fourth time tonight. The warning in her grimace deepens when I grab my clutch and my French 75 and move to sit next to her. We were only three seats apart, but it was close enough for the ire in her moss-green sneer to burn my exposed shoulder. It stings, but if I only get one chance to address the elephant tap-dancing in the room, I'm taking it.

My "Hi" mimics the Joker when he was pretending to be a nurse after blowing up Harvey Dent's fiancée. How no one knew it was him in *The Dark Knight*, with that hideous wig and face full of white makeup, is as ridiculous as I look now. I glance at Emma, whose brows are about to touch her top lip, and slide onto the barstool beside her. My bodycon dress hugs my knees, and it takes a second to get the memo that we're sitting before I can breathe.

I want to compliment her strapless floral number, but I can't gauge if her scowl will come with a drink in my face or a slap. Not that I'd blame her. I'd hate myself too if I were the monster she thinks I am.

"Are you going to eye-fuck the side of my face all night, or do you have something intelligent to say?"

Okay then.

My nails drum over the champagne flute I'm looking into like a crystal ball. Worst-case scenario, Emma causes a scene that lands me in the hospital and both of us on the news. Or maybe she ignores me. She owes me nothing after the way I've treated Justice.

I drain my glass. Liquid courage. "Can we please talk?"

Emma is so silent I peek to see if she heard me.

It's confirmed with a glare she tosses back with her martini. "Let me save you the trouble: 'I'm sorry, I made a mistake.'"

My snort at her nasal taunt catches us both off guard. I don't mean to laugh—it's a dig at my expense—but hours of cocktails and loneliness will make you a glutton for punishment.

At the after-party for the photo shoot I styled, Emma was a cameo I didn't expect. A handful of crew and models stayed behind to celebrate haute looks in high fashion.

It was clear Emma knew Jonathan, the photographer who brilliantly captured styles I curated, by their hugs and air kisses. She floated through our section of the bar with her mahogany hair and a smile that faltered when she thought no one was looking.

Who or what was the reason behind her blank stares into the distance remained a mystery. Keeping my mask in check has been a battle since I left Paris.

Preston hasn't stopped calling or texting since. It took him a day to pull his head out of his ass from whatever had his attention for a week straight.

Her.

I gotta admit, Bellamy schooled me in our silent game of chess, tipping the board in her favor. Preston was nonexistent, tucked away in her office and wherever else they conducted "business." With William back in London, I conjured images of every position Preston had Bellamy between their late nights and private meetings.

Spread over her desk.

Against the window.

Facedown in a pile of documents saturated with their sweat.

Alone in a penthouse day after day, I couldn't stop the thoughts or the silence. So I left.

Had Preston held a conversation long enough, he'd have known about the job that had me on a red-eye to Los Angeles. The pay is great, and the shots will be in a major fashion magazine for all to see.

Why stay frustrated at home when you can be frustrated cashing a check and enjoying a Friday night with champagne?

The party ended some time ago, leaving me and Emma as the last two seated at the bar. It's fairly empty, the remnants of cocktail glasses left on the honey-wood counter. A large mirror between top-shelf bottles reflects low-hung chandeliers and the worst attempt at an awkward conversation.

"You're still a bitch," Emma says.

I choke on champagne that threatens to shoot through my nose. "I'm a good person once you get to know me!"

"You mean once you get past your thirsty ways of running after married men?" A brow lifts. "You're lucky you didn't catch a beatdown."

I open my mouth to defend myself but think twice. Emma makes it sound like I set world records chasing down unavailable men. I am guilty of flirting with Terrence while he was with Justice, but I never *ran* after him until I saw him at the singles' retreat. It wasn't a run, anyway. More like a slow strut with confidence that evaporated after he sprinted toward Justice. Twice.

The gut-punch of embarrassment faded, but not the guilt of my actions. "You're right," I say to Emma, who's daring me to lie. I don't scare easily, but now I flinch. "You don't fight, do you?"

"Do I look like I'd chance ruining this dress over you?"

It looks vintage, so no.

I nod at the bartender, who's eyeing my drink for a refill. He offers a sympathetic smile. His salt-and-pepper hair contrasts with the blue-gray stare he snaps at Emma, warning her to be nicer.

If he only knew.

"I appreciate your willingness to sit with me."

"Like I had a choice."

Right, because I came over to her.

"I really was a bitch," I admit through a breath.

"Was?"

I deserve that. Back to my glass my eyes go. "I can't apologize enough for my behavior at the singles' retreat. Before." The loose waves reaching past my shoulders fan at my headshake. "I was in a bad place and wanted... There's no excuse for how I treated Justice. I never expected Terrence to leave her."

"You're not that delusional." Emma's gaze roves over me. "Maybe you are."

I was.

Envy weaved itself with entitlement. I never crossed lines I couldn't come back from, but I left a path of destruction because of my selfishness.

Emma is talking, but the chaos of my thoughts is louder. Is this how Bellamy feels about Preston, so fed up with the world around her that she latches on to affection at any cost? It's funny how you don't focus on the casualties you create until you become a target.

The tears I hold back weigh heavy. "Trust me when I say I feel awful. I've done a lot of soul-searching since the retreat. Work I should've done years ago. I'm not a person who plots and schemes to take people down."

No matter how I justify the actions I knew needled under Justice's skin, I bear the scarlet letter. Change can't afford the past, but I don't want my poor judgment to define who I am. Emma is close with Kojo, which means the likelihood of us together beyond random after-parties is up there. I'm not delusional enough to expect a friendship, but I hope we can be cordial.

By some small miracle, Emma and I navigate the minefield of my past actions and regret. I'm a drink away from calling it a night and heading to my hotel room upstairs, but I can't shake the feeling that's been troubling me since I got the courage to come over.

"Are you okay?" I gauge her reaction to my inquiry. "You don't owe me anything—least of all an explanation—but I recognize it. The mask to make everything look like it's fine when it's not." My grip constricts around my glass. "I wore it for many years. Still do."

Preston is slipping away, the same way he did in Paris. I can feel it, and I'm not ready for the wave of heartbreak to return. I barely survived it the first time.

"When is feeling ignored enough?" Emma's voice is faint, but the heartbreak is clear. Her arresting features—a blend of high-arched brows, smooth cheekbones, and pursed, full lips—loosen the facade held up by her willpower.

"Let me know once you find out," I mumble.

Preston is probably off to another three-hour meeting. Busyness comes with the CEO territory, but it doesn't give him the right to invest in pursuing me only to snatch the effort away once he hooks me.

"You know what? Fuck this." The rise in Emma's tone startles me while earning the bartender's frown. "I don't want to feel this anymore," she says, pointing to her heart. "No more!" I jump again.

"No more tears!" is a charge she releases into air thick with unspoken grief and the classical music that cascades from a hidden speaker system.

Her frustration—from love, loss, and possible lies—activates my voice, and I scream, "No more!" It earns another curious glance from the bartender, but ask me if I care.

"He left me for another work emergency, like I'm luggage he can put down and pick up whenever he wants," I say. "I'm sick of it."

I'm sorry, Puff.

I'll be done soon.

Just a few more hours.

Every feeling I repressed to be the understanding partner slams into me. "If he wanted me, he would come and get me, but I'm not waiting around to find out."

I'm ranting to Emma like I pay her an hourly rate and call her "doctor." It fades with a double take at a person who's staring at her back. His approach swallows the distance in long strides. My mouth dries, but I manage to whisper his name.

"Miles."

They were both at the singles' retreat with their respective best friends, which I assume explains whatever this is. Terrence's best friend and Trevante Rhodes's long-lost twin is here, and he only has eyes for Emma.

From what I remember, he's as enthusiastic about commitment as Emma, who avoids relationships at all costs. It's still weird to me that she and Justice, who are polar opposites, are so close, but I've seen stranger things.

Like Miles pining for Emma in the middle of a bar.

Why on earth is he here? Did they...*no.*

He clears all suspicion about his intentions with his chocolate stare that hasn't moved from its target. His shadow stretches over her tighter than the tee that's straining to accommodate the thick arms folded over his broad chest.

Emma repeats "Miles" to make sense of it but freezes at his "Kitten" in rich baritone. Her lips part, and her eyes go wide before narrowing to face him.

A brief staredown ensues, but Emma incinerates it when she tells him to "Save it."

What requires saving is an answer I'd like to know. She and Miles are a pairing I never would've guessed. She asks me if I'm good on my own. I am, but I would rather stay to see how this plays out.

"Did you two—"

"Not your business," she reminds me with the same clarity in her tone she used to call me a bitch. "You and I aren't there yet, but this was nice."

"It was," I say to Emma, who is already on her way to the door. "See you around, Miles."

My eyes slide from his small afro to his beard. Those weren't at the singles' retreat.

I snatch my ringing phone off the bar, scowling like Emma at the name on my screen.

"What excuse is there today, Preston?" I storm off without a goodbye for Terrence's best friend or a hello for the man who's two-stepping on my last nerve.

"Puff, I'm sorry. I didn't mean to be so distant."

Damn him and his seductive voice!

"I'll make it—"

"You'll always make it up to me," I gripe. I follow it up with a laugh, not giving the slightest damn who hears me. Nothing about this is funny except for the apology stuck on repeat.

"You changed."

"Puff."

"Don't 'Puff' me!"

The marble floor of the lobby absorbs the blow of my heels on their short path to the elevators. Somewhere between the bar and the foyer, my strut went from Olivia Pope to Annalise Keating real fast. The day is finally catching up with me.

It's then I notice my missing clutch with the key card to my room. *Great.* I stomp my ass back to the bar, fried from the photo shoot and this conversation.

"Leave something?" The question comes from the phone I peel away from my ear. I didn't drink *that* much damn champagne, not enough to bend the laws of physics.

Preston is here.

With my black clutch and a smile, he says, "Hello, Puff."

Chapter 45

Madison

Only a man who ignored me for over a week would cross an ocean to play in my face.

My grip on my phone is the only reason Preston isn't modeling an imprint of it on his forehead. His audacity is tempting me to test my luck with an assault charge.

The nerve of him to stand here *and* smell good.

Preston's smile falls, taking the dimples I love with it. He's smart enough to know I wouldn't welcome him with open arms and an invitation to fuck me through a headboard.

I snatch my clutch from his hand and sneak another glance at the frown knitting his thick brows, the teeth sinking into soft lips. The goatee that prickles my thigh.

Another second, and I'll ride him first and ask questions later.

Reroute.

I stab the elevator button and say a quick prayer of thanks when the doors open immediately. Nine more floors until a warm shower and a soft bed soothe my resentment for the night.

"I'm sorry, baby," Preston says to my back. The buttery murmur coaxes the hairs on my neck to stand at attention. He steps into the elevator and stuffs his hands into his jeans with a sigh. "You didn't answer any of my calls or texts. What did you expect me to do?"

I shrug. "Not ignore me in the first place."

Is it a petty response? Of course.

Do I care? Absolutely not.

The elevator music is no match for my heartbeat, which is pounding under Preston's stare. He's silent, his head tilted to track my every move. Anyone who faces off with him in the boardroom must have a superpower. He swapped out his suit for a cable-knit sweater pushed up to his forearms and relaxed-fit jeans over toffee brown high-top sneakers.

It's his eyes that have me sucking in a gasp. The haunting cognac gaze is daring me to keep it up.

So I do.

Liquid courage.

"Are you sleeping with her?" If he is, he can keep his tender offer and whatever feelings he has for Bellamy.

The look he aims my way traps me in a silent eternity. "How could you ask me that? I love you, Madison. I want only you, and I'm not pursuing or sleeping with anyone else—KD included." Hurt laces his voice, as if I offended him. Maybe I did, but what am I supposed to think when Bellamy has gone out of her way to stake her claim?

"How do you not see it? She's in love with you, Preston."

"I've never felt the same way."

"But that doesn't stop someone from loving you!" I toss up my hands. *Duh!* "It takes a special kind of pressed to seek me out. Did she tell you she saw us at Ravenous? *Watched* us?"

That gets his attention. "What?" He frowns.

"She also canceled some time I booked on your calendar in Paris."

Confusion swims through the haze of emotions contorting his face. He runs a hand over his goatee and shakes his head. "I—she's never acted like this."

"Because no one ever made her feel threatened. Don't you think it's weird that your phone magically put itself in airplane mode when you were in the office? You've seen Bellamy as a friend and colleague, but not for who she is: a woman in love." I hesitate to ask what I already know. "Have you slept with her in the past?"

His "yes" is low, filled with regret and fear.

I knew it.

The elevator opens to my floor, granting me a pathway of aqua carpeting for the somber walk to my hotel room. Part of my leaving Paris was to ensure I had the strength to do it should I ever need to leave Preston for good. I've starred in enough mess, and I won't play myself entertaining some *Dawson's Creek* situation between childhood friends.

Joey ended up with Pacey. And after how many seasons of heart-break?

Exactly.

"We had an arrangement, to make ourselves available if we were in the same city. It didn't happen every time, but I won't lie and tell you it was infrequent."

That explains Bellamy's willingness to run behind him. The heat from Preston's desire causes fourth-degree burns. Aside from loving with all the space in his heart, he's a giver—his tongue being a primary vessel of choice.

"Please don't shut me out, Puff," he says against my hotel room door, desperation choking his voice. "In all my years knowing KD, she's never acted out or been jealous. Work is our only relationship. I spoke to her, and I'll enforce stronger boundaries. We won't communicate unless it's absolutely necessary. Tell me what you need to feel okay."

For you to toss her into exile.

The sensor submits to my key card. I step behind the door, unsure what to do or how to feel. That last part is a lie. I feel angry, sad, and scared. We both have pasts, and we both have to interact with people who know us intimately. The only difference is that his is present, not in history where it belongs. A coworker he relies on to close deals.

"Do you have any idea how it felt to stay up night after night waiting for you? Wondering why it was so easy for you to ignore me when you were with her?" I draw in a heavy breath. "I already put myself into some half-assed love triangle once, and I won't do it again. You and Bellamy have decades of history that predates me."

"Fuck history," Preston spits. "You have my heart. You're the only woman I ever loved, the only woman I'll spend the rest of my life loving. KD is a confidant in business, but us knowing each other since we were kids doesn't give her—or anyone else—the right to disrespect you."

"Except she already did, and she'll do it again!"

"Please trust me, Puff. KD knows this is the first and last time she'll cross a line. Nothing will happen between us."

"You can't promise that." My voice cracks. "I know what it's like to hold onto something that isn't yours."

Preston lifts my chin. "I know what I'm fighting for, baby. Please trust me. I don't want to lose us."

"I've played second for too long. I'm tired of being an option," I whisper.

"You're my choice. The only one," he says, sealing his promise with a kiss that knocks the air from my lungs. Then the door clicks shut, and I'm hoisted into his arms. The slide of his tongue against mine ignites a groan that swirls freely to the pit of my stomach.

"I love you" is his chant as Preston moves us to the bed. We shed our clothes, his name an incantation for the magic his tongue stirs between my thighs. Skin to skin, I come undone at the suction of his mouth.

"Tell me when to stop, Puff." Preston's mouth travels up my ribs, outlining the tips of my breasts with each lick.

"I want you," I moan at his fingers fondling my G-spot. I meet him thrust for thrust and explode from the orgasm, curling my pedicure into the fitted sheet.

Preston lifts his head to search my eyes. "Are you sure?" At my nod, he lines himself up with my entrance and pushes into me. The slow burn of his tip steals my breath. "Stay with me, Puff," he whispers.

I whimper as his hips roll into my center. Images of Preston with Bellamy overwhelm me. Their moans mixed with pleasure, her smirk spread into a smile.

Riding him.

Tasting him.

Savoring intimacy now reserved for me.

"Stay with me, Puff. Please." Preston thrusts deeper, pinning my knee to his side. Tears form as I watch his hooded gaze trace over my face. "It's me and you, baby."

"Me and you," I repeat. My voice is raw in a fight to cling to this moment. To us. "I love you."

"I've always loved you, Puff."

Chapter 46

Preston

"Have you considered staying out here for the summer?"

"You planning on keeping my auntie across the pond?"

I grin. "Is that a serious question?"

Jewel and I have kept every one of our check-ins since the day we met. Our video calls are a highlight, outside of spending time with her aunt, who she assumes is heading back to New York. Having Jewel here would be a win-win. She mentioned London-based groups who advocate against environmental racism and the impacts of climate change on low-income communities.

"Sure you don't want to reconsider? I know a guy with free housing..."

"*I know a guy.* Don't try too hard to sound like us," she jabs with a snort.

"I spent many years at boarding school outside New York. I don't try, I am," I wink.

Jewel sits up from what has to be the largest bean bag I've ever seen. "Did you go to school over here because of your mama?"

And to get away from my father.

I nod and clear my throat. "My mother died after childbirth during one of my father's work trips. Environmental conservation was her passion. I picked it up and donate to the same charities. But I want to do more."

"Great-Mawmaw lived in St. James Parish—part of what we call 'Cancer Alley'—until she moved in with us because of respiratory issues," Jewel explains about the former matriarch of her family. "I loved every minute growing up with her as a kid, and I assumed she moved because she wanted to be closer. Not because of cancer."

She wipes away a tear. "Many people are living out death sentences in frontline communities because of fossil fuel plants stationed near neighborhoods that look like us. Regulation is a joke, which is why it's no surprise Louisiana is one of the top carbon-producing states. This is why I fight, Preston. Because billionaires inflict harm. They donate to charities and pat themselves on the back with one hand and receive tax breaks in the other. We've normalized their existence at the expense of ours."

Hearing Jewel weaponize her pain for the greater good stirs at my chest. She's among countless young activists, unashamed and unafraid to challenge the status quo.

I'm not directly responsible for her great-grandmother's death, but I benefit from the same systems as the people who are.

"You once asked me what more you can do," she says, the window of vulnerability now shut behind stoic eyes underneath a hoodie of curls. "Your efforts are commendable, but you understand billionaires and equity can't coexist."

"I do."

A slight smile peeks out. "My answer to you would be to take yourself out of the equation. The fewer billionaires this world has, the better off we'll be."

My sigh carries through the corner office I inherited from my father. Financial stability isn't in question, ultra-wealth is.

"Anything else?" My question earns a chuckle. Jewel knows, as I do, that untethering myself from my legacy won't happen overnight.

"Yeah, Richie Rich." She smiles. "Keep loving my auntie the way you are."

"I intend to."

For the rest of my life.

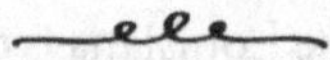

"I told you to take them off."

Madison squirms in my lap, inviting my dick to prod the cotton material that separates us. I groan and cup her breasts over her shirt when she rolls her hips. "Don't play with me, Puff." I nip her neck.

The look she aims over her shoulder is all I need to lift her, unzip my trousers, and sit her on the rod she wants to tease so badly. Granted, I did pull her into my lap to share the lunch we ordered, but I was the perfect gentleman. Until she bounced on me reaching for the soy sauce as if she didn't know what she was doing.

"Coat my dick, baby. Fuck." My fingers dig into the skirt bunched at her hips.

This woman must have cowboys in her lineage the way she rides me with precision. She tosses back a smirk, lifts up, and swirls her hips over my tip in slow circles to tease an orgasm. Her pelvis rolls, and she bounces her ass.

"Hey, Thumper," she says, her hands spread on my knees, her grin flooded with pleasure.

"Shut up," I pant as she laughs at my leg shaking uncontrollably.

"You can take it," she teases.

"So can you."

Madison's gasp is an aphrodisiac. I want to hear it every day. Her hands fly to my desk when I stand up. The motion leaves her cheek firmly pressed into polished wood, just the way I like it. I wrap my hand around the back of her neck to hold her in place.

"I told you not to play with me." I kick her stilettos apart and smile at her whimper. The smack to her round ass echoes across the office.

It's another rainy day in London. Perfect for fucking between meetings.

We've been inseparable since I flew to Los Angeles over a month ago. I was serious when I told Madison I love her and will do whatever it takes for this to work. Delegating tasks I should've taken off my plate years ago and removing myself from meetings that could've been emails created more space to pursue the woman whose pussy is seconds away from putting me in a coma.

KD took leave when we returned to London. She's been quieter than usual, only sending word about her departure through her assistant. I care for her, but I won't allow Madison to feel like she's in competition for my heart or my loyalty. She has both. I was serious when I told KD the games have to stop. If they don't, she's out—friend or not.

My release comes in grunts. Madison grins through a breathless sigh, the evidence of our arousal coating her thighs.

I spin her around, and her ass hits the desk. "Paint your name on my pussy," I whisper into her ear.

Black heels anchor her to the edge of my desk. With her eyes on me, the tops of her fingers trace her swollen lips. They spread through our cum and trail up to her clit. Her breath snags, the hazel in her eyes darkening.

The sight of her and the promise of another orgasm soaking her hand and spelling her name reanimates my dick. She makes it to "S" before I'm back inside her.

We can't keep our hands off each other—here in London, in New York while Puff handled her business, and in Austin where we met up with Kojo. Imagine our surprise when we ran into Justice at a café. Our Texas reunion allowed Madison the chance to apologize for whatever harm she caused.

Life is perfect.

My office resets to paperwork on my desk and the lukewarm food we moved to the coffee table near the sofa. Our clothes are back in place, with only a few wrinkles to hint at our activities.

"Mr. Donnelley, I have Ms. Kidwell," Stephanie announces through the intercom.

Madison's hand falters, but she eats a bite of sashimi with a tightened grip on her chopstick. "I'm okay," she says, too far from my desk to reach. I move toward her, but she shoos me away. "Handle your business."

I nod and hit the button to respond to Stephanie. "Send her through." I pick up the receiver but am met with a dial tone. Did she hang up?

The main door to my office opens. KD struts past Madison without a glance. My brows pinch at why she's in front of my desk and not on the other end of the phone line.

"I'm in the middle of lunch with my lady," I say with what little courtesy I can muster at her dropping by unannounced, "and you're on leave for a few more weeks."

"That's why I'm here." She lifts her chin. "What I have to say can't wait."

Is she quitting? Losing her as CFO would sting, but it might be for the best.

"Go on." I motion to the floor and lean back in my chair.

KD tucks her hands into her suit coat pockets. Her top peeks out from behind lapels and high-waist ankle trousers. Her mouth twists at the fact I haven't told Madison to leave. Call me an asshole, but I don't want her feeling like another woman can run her out.

Seconds pass until KD sighs. "I guess you can stay for this," she says to Madison, her glare trained on me. "I'm pregnant."

Chapter 47

Madison

I laughed. A deep belly howl clogged the office silence and commanded space. I couldn't stop my laughter or its tears at Bellamy's desperate attempt to hook Preston.

I'm not ashamed to admit I peed a little, because how are those two words *not* funny?

I'm pregnant.

I thought Maury Povich would waltz out to say, "You are *not* the father!" A pregnancy reveal the day before UK Mother's Day is nasty work, but I give Bellamy credit. I would never fake one.

The laughter burning my lungs mutated into a knot in my throat when I saw Preston's pained expression.

I stopped laughing immediately.

Bellamy is pregnant with his baby.

My stomach lurches in demand of another dry heave into the toilet. I'm very much without child, but I get sick thinking about the bond Preston and Bellamy will share. One that prompted him to use condoms with me so as not to further complicate a complicated situation.

A baby.

Baby.

We've only made love twice in the two weeks since Bellamy waltzed into his office. Every attempt is an awkward placement of limbs with no eye contact. Our intimacy is gone, and I don't know how to get it back.

I reach for toilet paper, wipe the saliva from my mouth, and stand. All it took was a few days in Paris. A detour from Preston and Bellamy's casual arrangement. The fact that a child is the byproduct of his desire for her makes me question if the feelings he held for his longtime friend were nonexistent when he started pursuing me.

It was easy for Terrence to fade to black. We only see each other in passing, and we certainly weren't fucking. Preston swears he hasn't thought about Bellamy sexually since I came back into his life. Sleeping with a close friend isn't a practice of mine. I don't know what is and isn't possible when it comes to matters of the heart.

It raised questions that had me looking at him differently.

Does his mind focus on business when he's with her, or the memories of their pleasure?

Will her changing body excite new curiosities as she carries their child in her womb?

Will his undying love for his heir shift his feelings for the mother of his child—a lifelong friend he's known longer than me?

What I do know is Bellamy is now seventeen weeks. She wasn't showing the day of her reveal, but now she has a fuller, rounder stomach. One she rubs every chance she gets.

She confirmed her pregnancy at around eleven weeks, when Preston worked long days and nights by her side in Paris. It turns out her leave was to process the pregnancy, as well as Preston and I together.

Cold water pierces my skin, an attempt to wake me up from this nightmare. Flashbacks of Preston passing off a candlelit dinner as a styling consultation pull me through a forest of suits surrounded in musk in the walk-in closet. The bistro table and chairs are now anchored to a past that no longer aligns with our future.

That I moved into Preston's penthouse last month is another change. It was pointless to stay down the hall in mine. If he wasn't in my bed, I was in his. He joked how living together was a sign I'd accept his tender offer, and he pulled out all the stops to get me to agree. Homemade dinners he cooked in nothing but an apron. Endless foot massages. Waking up to his head between my legs.

Now he walks on eggshells, terrified I'll leave and too guilt-ridden to face me. What time we do spend together is not the same.

I clamp my lips to hold in a sob as I stare at the section of his closet that's just for me. I'm trying my best to be okay. I tell myself tomorrow will hurt less, that I can be supportive and not feel like my world is being ripped apart.

Preston having a child on the way is no different than if his baby was already in his life. It happened before we got together. That doesn't erase the lingering feelings, the waiting for the chance to ask what if.

What if he wants to give a relationship with Bellamy a try for the sake of the baby?

What if decades of friendship blossom into the love he's been waiting for?

A loose cream turtleneck sweater flies off the hanger at my tug. I toss on ripped jeans and grab a pair of oxfords.

I need to get out of here.

Raindrops splatter the pavement under gray skies. The sun has yet to peek out, not that it would brighten my day.

The blisters streaked across my feet from hours of walking have numbed to a dull ache. There is no destination in mind, only distance from the home I haven't left in weeks.

A gust of wind flips my umbrella inside out. I take cover under an awning and bend the panel back into its proper form. My hair is a different story. Persistent rain coiled the edges into a mane of frizz. It's tied up in a messy bun, emphasis on the mess.

Joyful laughter shifts my attention from the umbrella that's about to meet the fate of a trash can to Bellamy. Her grin tints her rose-colored cheeks and crinkles the eyes she lifts to Preston, who's staring down at her with a faint smile that slowly becomes more pronounced. They linger for a moment on the edge of the sidewalk. Her hand is on his, holding the bump of their baby.

I never expected Preston to despise his child—who would want a man who does?—but witnessing his happiness up close while I live with his agony at home twists the knife deeper into my heart. I haven't seen him smile in weeks, but here he is, offering it freely to a woman he claims he doesn't love.

Sensing eyes on him, he looks up. The smile drops into a frown. He says something to Bellamy, who nods and takes their umbrella. There's no gloat or smirk. If anything, she looks remorseful.

"Puff."

"Hey," I say, tipping my umbrella back to accommodate our height difference. "I was just out."

His brow lifts. "In the rain?"

"When is it not raining here?" My attempt at a smile is too much to bear.

"I tried calling earlier. KD had a doctor's appointment. It was my first time seeing the baby." Sadness tugs at his words, and he clears his throat. "It's a girl."

My chest squeezes under an invisible weight. I draw in a deep breath but can't steady myself to ignore the ache that's eating me alive. I gulp and pray that the tears lining my vision don't fall.

I don't want to break in front of her.

"I-I'm sorry," I stammer.

The reality of what their baby means hurtles through my rib cage. Them shopping for the nursery. Preston holding Bellamy's hand and kissing her forehead during birth. Celebrating milestones together as a family.

Preston reaches for me, enveloping me inside the warmth of his jacket. He kisses my forehead and tightens his grip. "Please don't cry, Puff." His voice is a low rumble. "I love you so much, and I'm sorry—for all of this. I want to be a good father, but I don't want to lose you."

"I know. But watching you two together makes me feel like the mistress."

He pulls away to hold me in a stare. "You're the woman I love. I want a future together."

I press a kiss to his lips and step away. "It hurts too much to think about what that looks like. There's a lot for you to focus on right now." I raise a hand and take another step back when he moves forward. "Please."

His jaw clenches, but he nods.

"You should get her out of the rain." I nod at Bellamy. She's shifting from foot to foot, looking between us. "Her health is important."

"Madison," he says.

"I'll be fine. I have to go."

If my oxford shoes do one good thing today, it's turn me in the other direction and force me to walk away. Eyes narrow at me, the woman with no jacket and a fuzzy bun who's crying like she just left a funeral. I reach into my clutch and pull out my phone. Tammi picks up on the third ring.

"Tam."

"Maddie, what's wrong? Did someone die!?"

"I—I don't think I can do this anymore." Pain explodes, shooting shrapnel through my heart and into my voice.

By some miracle, I make it back to the penthouse. My eyes are puffy and my nose is like a faucet, but I'm here. Tammi listens to the emotional monologue of my life.

"Come home, Maddie," she says.

I nod like she can see me and stuff the clothes I brought from New York into my suitcase. "There's a nonstop flight leaving in a few hours." I give Tammi the information.

Once I'm packed, I roll my suitcases out of the bedroom and stop into Preston's home office for a pen and paper. A photo of us sits in a silver frame next to his desk. He took a candid shot the morning after our first night together. I'm grinning up at him from under the covers. My hair is wild, matching his expression of untamed adoration.

Inside the desk drawer is a legal pad. I grab a pen but stop when I see the sonogram. It's a copy, but it shows the baby's profile. A tiny head, a little nose, and the outline of a mouth. The bundle of joy that will change his life forever.

Tears come in another wave, one that forces me to grip the desk.

"This is my karma," I choke out through a low, tortured sob. "It's what I get."

My cries drown out Tammi calling my name until she screams it to get my attention.

"Enough of that," she snaps. "You are a good person who made a shitty judgment call in the past. We've all been the villain in someone else's story, but it's up to us to change. You did, and you apologized. I won't pretend this situation isn't messy, but give yourself some grace."

"She won't let go," I whisper to my phone. "I know Bellamy—I've been like her. She'll latch onto him with this baby and make my life hell in the process."

"So leave this Jerry Springer situation. You have a right to protect your heart and mental health while Preston figures things out. Staying cooped up in that penthouse with no support will make you sick. Come home."

I write a note and reserve a car through a rideshare app. Dayo is in the hallway when I open the front door.

"I hope you don't mind, but I followed you back to make sure you were okay." The sad smile he offers wobbles my chin. "Allow me." He reaches for my luggage.

"You're not here to stop me?"

"He better not!" Tammi shouts through the phone.

"Damn, I'm not," he chuckles, flashing perfect white teeth.

Tammi stays on the phone as I make my way down to the car. She hangs up once I confirm my ride has arrived and Dayo won't kidnap me.

He holds the back door open but hesitates. "It's not my business or my place to say, but Preston regrets hurting you. I hope you two can make it through this. He's never been happier, and I assume you haven't, either."

I nod and offer a hug that he accepts. "Goodbye, Dayo."

The car pulls off the curb and into the dreary day. I make it through customs and the eight-hour flight without crying.

When I reach New York, I break down at Tammi and Kojo waiting for me with dumplings and open arms.

"We got you," Kojo says with a kiss to my cheek. The promise is similar to the one he made the first time we met. The night Preston broke my heart and never looked back.

Chapter 48
Preston

Fifteen Years Ago

Scotch burns my throat on a hard swallow. I nod to the wait staff and return the glass empty.

Like me.

My father greets a diplomat with a firm handshake and a grin he lets fall when he inches closer to me. "Take care of it here," he mutters. "She is not to step inside." Steel-blue eyes slide to my profile when I don't answer. "Do you need me to handle your mistake?"

"I got it," I snap, not sparing him a look.

With a crisp nod, he steps off to the side for a conversation with a small group in matching dinner jackets.

A procession of dresses and formal evening suits flows up the red staircase rolled out for tonight's opera. I stand anchored at the top. My hands are clasped in front of me as I search for the face I wanted to wake up next to for as long as life allowed.

That changed tonight.

The woman who pretends to be Heather's steps are cautious, her soft pink dress hovering inches from the ground. Our eyes connect, and the curves of her mouth bloom into a smile.

This was our night, our chance to step out hand-in-hand in front of the world. But she ruined it with her deceit.

"Hey." She reaches for a kiss but pauses when I don't move. "What's wrong?"

Tension curls my neck to crane down at the liar who expertly opened my heart and home. She's breathtaking in the dress I paid for, along with hours of hair and makeup.

"Preston." Her tone is cautious, hesitant. She's looking at me like she can't decipher my expression.

"You are a disappointment." My voice cuts through the silence between me and the last person on earth I'd expect to hurt me.

How she can stand here and pretend to look offended is a masterclass of deception.

She clutches the glittery corset bodice that matches her manicure. "You can't mean that," she whispers.

"Can't I?"

"W-what's gotten into you?"

"I hate liars, no matter how pretty they come."

The trap of her own lie constricts her throat. She closes her eyes and swallows. "I planned to tell you."

"When?" I step closer. "On the plane home after you used me? Once I spent a small fortune feeding and housing you? Fucking you?" She winces. "I begged you for something real, and you proved to be an opportunist."

My father kept me after a meeting to reveal that the woman I let into my life and home is nothing but a liar. A broke university student. I didn't want to believe it, but the proof he had was damning.

The real Heather Franklin has blonde hair and brown eyes. Her body is far from the palette of curves I've worshipped the last six months. Her smile can't wake the sun or make the hardest days easier to survive. My father refuses to show me who this imposter really is, but he doesn't miss a beat in reminding me how I put our family business in danger.

I still don't know how she knew I'd be at the art museum where we met. The Talented Mr. Ripley horror stories of people in our networks being scammed—or worse—are warning enough to sever ties with a parasite before it's too late.

I let my guard down, only for her to trample over my trust and heart pretending to be someone else.

"Preston, I swear, everything I told you about me is true."

"Except your real identity. You weaseled your way into a study abroad program like you weaseled your way into my life. Was I a mark, someone who could cover your expenses?"

"What? No." Her voice raises, but she catches herself. "I am sorry I lied. I do love you. What I feel is real."

"And what I feel is betrayal," I toss, no longer giving a damn who hears. "Do you know how many people slither up to me and my family under false pretenses?" I cut my eyes to my father. It hurts to look at her. "I loved you, Puff." My voice trips over a crack. "I can't see beyond the lies."

"Please don't do this. My real name is M—"

"You have until the end of the month to get out of my penthouse. The only reason you aren't sleeping on the street tonight is because I know the real you is poor. Security will make regular check-ins to ensure you don't vandalize or steal anything. I suggest you move up whatever return flight you have. You're no longer welcome here."

"Preston."

"I leave for London tonight for good. In case it's not clear, you no longer exist to me, Heather. You never existed at all."

"Preston!"

"Security!" Three men in matching suits and earpieces appear at my side. "She doesn't belong here," I say to Puff's tearstained face. "Show her out, and make sure she doesn't come back."

"We'll file a formal complaint with the authorities if she does." My father steps forward.

Her breath hitches, and she stumbles at the escort guiding her off the premises by the arm. Gala attendees stop and stare at the crying woman. What a fucking spectacle.

I tell myself not to look one last time. My heart splinters when I do.

I wanted her to be different.

A firm hand lands on my shoulder. "Come on, son," my father says. "Let her go and move on. She showed you who she is."

He guides me up the grand staircase, but not before I glance back at Puff rushing out the door. Thick cinnamon hair sways across her back, and it takes everything I have not to chase her.

"Son."

I let her go.

Chapter 49

Madison

Present Day

My thumb grazes over the message. Preston texted it today and has every day since I left London. Eleven messages with the same eight letters clawing deep at the hole where my heart used to be.

"Talk to him," Kojo says from the corner of his studio between a tower of boxes piled to the ceiling.

I let out a long, audible breath and concentrate on the runway layout taped to the wall. "We should tweak the sequence and put Jordan before Andrew."

"Regine."

"Use this patch on the satin cape." I point to the high-waist tuxedo suit on one of the mannequins. "People will go wild over the collar."

"Enough." I'm now shoulder-to-chest with Kojo. He cups my face and angles my chin so I'm looking him in the eyes. The frown creasing his brow wrinkles the lines in his forehead below a bun of dreads.

"I'm okay." A bland half smile is all I have the strength for.

"You're not, and that's okay."

"I'm fine, Kojo," I huff. "This will look good under the lighting we chose."

"You're not okay, Regine."

"Someone has to pack up the rest of your studio while you're in Paris for the show." Leave it to Kojo to plan a move to Austin while finalizing the runway show for his Rustin collection, "Utopian Promise."

"I don't give a shit about my show! You've been a zombie, working yourself to the point of exhaustion. You can't block out what happened."

"I'm not. There's a job to do. I'm doing it." I brush past Kojo with a choked laugh and head to the conference table that's draped in fabric samples.

I'm never one to hate good fashion, but the cream crocheted short set and brown sandals in pursuit annoy me to no end. Kojo's spring-summer collection is the only subject up for discussion.

"You know good and damn well that's not what I meant," he snaps, hands on his hips and neck ready to hula-hoop. "You have to let it out, Maddie."

"I don't want to feel anymore! Is that what you want to hear? That I stay up all night questioning if I made the right decision?"

Leaving London wasn't a choice I made lightly. Preston was blindsided by the baby news and barely kept it together, especially with the CEO demands pulling him in every direction. I wanted to be there for him, and I was, until I was the one alone. Early conference calls turned into meetings that bled into the night. Bellamy's position as CFO has her by his side around the clock.

Between his constant work and Bellamy's pregnancy, there wasn't a chance to figure us out. There are too many moving parts, and that creates uncertainty. The last thing I wanted was to add another puzzle for Preston to solve.

I love him, but I have to take care of me too.

"I tried so *hard* to be supportive." I gulp at the sting of tears. The ache in my throat twists the last shreds of my control. "It hurts to breathe, Ko. I miss him every day. But I lost the strength to stay."

I've cried myself to sleep every night. It hasn't soothed the bitter taste of jealousy stirring inside me that another woman—a childhood friend he regards as family—is carrying his child. They were intimate weeks before he found his way to my hotel room door. It's not a stretch to picture them figuring out a relationship beyond co-parenting, especially if I'm not in the picture.

I want to be stronger, to pretend their connection and new life bond aren't eating me from the inside. But they are.

The high-pitched voice breaking through a strangled cry startles me. I don't recognize it's coming from me until Kojo wraps his arms around my shaking body.

With Jewel back in Louisiana for the summer, New York felt too small. My apartment still bears Preston's scent. My favorite dumpling place became our spot. My mental health needed a change of scenery, so I packed a bag and joined Kojo here in Atlanta before he flies to Paris for his fashion show, a city with bad memories that stack higher than the Eiffel Tower. I'm on my way to Miami and wherever else work takes me.

Kojo drops his chin onto the top of my head and sighs. "Regardless of what happens, you'll be okay. You haven't said anything since Tammi and I came to New York. I love having you here with me, Regine, but don't keep this in. Always set your truth free. No one expects you to have it together. This situation is messy."

"Very." I blow out a breath.

"Damn near Tubi level." He kisses the top of my head. "But you'll be okay."

"I'll be okay," I repeat.

He squeezes me tighter. "Do you feel better?"

I nod. "Thank you for being there for me."

"Always," Kojo says. "Let's get you cleaned up. Can't have you snotting like Viola Davis in *Fences*. You'll scare the models."

"Shut up!" A laugh sneaks out.

"Ah, look at that." He points at my smile. "The first one in weeks. Let me go grab the lunch menus."

The chords to The Spinners' "I'll Be Around" fill the tiny studio space. Light from the windows pierces through tiny particles speckling across exposed brick and found tables. I glance at my phone.

Always set your truth free.

I miss you too.

Chapter 50
Preston

"I'm sorry. She's not in at the moment. Would you like to add a message to the six others you left?"

William pats my shoulder. "That won't be necessary, thank you. Come on." He pivots me to face the doors. "Let's go. You tried."

I cut my eyes over my shoulder at the front desk attendant. The least he could do is deliver my messages. And maybe polish his balding head.

The bins lining the pavement smell like stale beer and chips from a nearby bar. New York gets muggy in the summer, and the first day of the season is no exception.

"Any luck?" Dayo lowers his head at my pointed stare.

"Pres. It's time to go—at least for now," William says from behind me. He lets out a dejected sigh at my headshake. "Okay."

Dayo opens the back of our town car for William and I to toss in our suit coats. He closes the door, and I begin my nightly walk around Madison's neighborhood with a concerned little brother and a bodyguard in tow.

We've been in the city for two days after stops in Atlanta and Miami. All it took was a response to my text, and I was on the first plane out to Madison. I'm following her around, forsaking business obligations for the chance to talk to her in person. To prove I won't stop fighting for us.

On the outside, I manage the appearance of keeping it together. On the inside, I'm a fucking wreck. I can barely sleep without her next to me. I even moved to my other home in Knightsbridge after she left. Nothing is the same without her.

I tried to hold on as long as I could.

Please don't be mad at me.

I recite the words from the note she left on the kitchen counter next to her key. It's become my chant, a reminder of the void in my life and my heart out of reach.

The last time I saw Madison was when I bumped into her after KD's appointment a month ago. I felt the baby kick for the first time on the sidewalk, which caught me by surprise. I didn't spot Madison, who was only feet away from us, and I won't forget the look on her face when I did.

Shame tightened my lungs at the tears she forced away until the pain became unbearable. Our conversations up until then were minimal—not from a lack of trying. Neither of us knew how to navigate my new normal. We were still dealing with whiplash from the news.

I struggled to look Madison in the eye knowing it's my fault, never mind make love to her. I never wanted to tie myself to KD like this, but wanting and having aren't the same. I still struggle with that weekend. The condom broke, but KD is on birth control.

Still, no matter how we got here, I vow to be a better father than the one I had.

KD moved back to London to be closer and now works with me out of the main office. She wasn't happy when I rushed her home after her appointment, but I saw Madison's eyes. I was losing her. A fact that was confirmed when I arrived home to an empty house less than an hour later.

"Eat." William thrusts a barbecue lamb skewer in my face. He passes two others to Dayo, who devours everything but the wooden sticks. "Damn, Deep Throat."

"Fuck off," Dayo chides, tossing his rubbish into the bin. "I'm grabbing halal." He heads across the street to a corner spot we discovered during my daily walks.

I pop over from our office for lunch and after dinner in hopes of seeing Puff. Texting is the extent of our communication. She's not ready for a call yet, but I'll take whatever I get.

Madison

> You have a child to worry about, and I don't want to get in the middle of any mess.

I reread one of her recent texts and sigh. She has every right to feel the way she does, which is part of the reason I gave her space after she left. How could I beg her to stay when I was struggling to come to grips with the fact that I'm going to be someone's father?

It wasn't fair to Madison, but I refuse to let her think I stopped loving her—or that me and KD will rekindle something that was never there. Our interactions are solely baby-related now. William takes meetings with her unless it's imperative I'm there. He and Dayo are the only ones who know about the baby. Outside of Puff, who I plan to win back.

"How long are we in New York?" William gnaws on his skewer like our father didn't shell out hundreds of thousands on etiquette lessons.

"At least a week," I say.

"Jewel did you a favor disclosing her aunt's location. How much did that bribe cost?"

"A month's worth of groceries for struggling neighbors in her parish back home, funding for political education about climate change, and bail fund investments for mothers and caregivers."

If it weren't for the trust Jewel and I established, she would've told me to fuck off a long time ago. Madison didn't tell her niece about the baby, but Jewel knew to give me a hard time.

William whistles. "Whatever it takes."

I nod.

Dayo returns with some chicken over rice, which he shovels into his mouth. Then we do our laps until it's time to go back to the office.

The sun is lower, no longer strangling us with its heat, but it's still boiling. William and I model sweat marks on our shirts rolled up to our elbows. Dayo is breathing easy in a light polo and shorts with trainers.

I sigh at another unsuccessful attempt but welcome the blast of cold air once we reach our Donnelley property. The Upper East Side location is a beaux-arts building with ornamental windows and a grand staircase.

"Good evening," Sadie, our new general manager, greets. She hands me a thick manila envelope. "This came for you."

"Thank you," I say.

Dayo heads to the security room, and William and I take the lift to our tenth floor offices.

"You know you have to let go at some point, right?" I meet William's frown with one of my own and open the envelope. He runs a hand through his blond hair, which remains unbothered by the humidity.

"I love Madison for you, but you can't keep chasing her. You got a baby on the way no one knows about and our father on your heels trying to deprioritize damn near every initiative you have in place. Bow out, bruv."

My eyes snap from the document in my hand to my brother. "What did you say?"

"Bow out. All of this isn't the answer."

"Take myself out of the equation." I repeat Jewel's words as I zero in on a highlighted clause.

"Exactly." William's relief comes through ragged breaths. He's been more than my brother these last few weeks. He's been my best friend, a surprising voice of reason who kept me fed and out of jail.

My steps slow off the lift, until I'm laughing for the first time in over a month. The answer to ending my father's reign has been here all along. "You're a genius," I say.

"Obviously." William pauses. "Want to clue me in?"

His face twists at my grin. "I'm calling an emergency board meeting. I quit."

Chapter 51

Preston

"Will someone explain why my time is being wasted on a Saturday?" My father looks between me and William. The lines on his forehead deepen with a scowl. "The next board meeting isn't for another week."

A haze of curious glances and confused stares hangs over the conference room. In front of every seat is a ring binder of documents. William and I spent two days pulling them with our legal team in anticipation of today's meeting.

"Let's get straight to it," I say from the window, thumbing the smooth edges of the padlock and key charm in my pocket.

The afternoon sun streaks the pavement that will be empty of foot traffic until Monday. Shops are closed, with only a breeze tickling ball-shaped flowers in full bloom on the tree line below. There are no tumbleweeds blowing through the street to commemorate this noontime showdown, but both of my barrels are locked and loaded.

"The Donnelley Brand is heading in a new direction," I say with smug delight. "Effective immediately, I resign from my position as CEO." A hush muffles the air I inhale with a deep breath.

"What is the meaning behind this, son?" Crawford is a man of few words, but he's always kind to me. As the eldest board member, he was present when my grandfather led, as he was with my father.

I meet the concern settling in his gray eyes with a smile. "I want more for the Donnelley Brand," I explain. "We have a social responsibility we haven't taken seriously, but that will change very soon." I walk to the conference table but don't sit down. My father smirks from the head at the other end, his steadfast arrogance stitched into his three-piece suit. "I was prepared to draw up a tender offer in order to acquire the company, but I think I'll take it instead."

My father's chuckle is a cynical rumble. "And how do you expect to do that?" he asks with deceptive calm. "What few victories you've gained, I let you have. Need I remind you who the largest shareholder at this table is?"

Clouds bend to cast a darkness over his fair skin and salt-and-pepper hair. It settles into the sharp edges of his jaw, betraying his frustration. Victor Donnelley would disown me before ever handing over the keys to the kingdom.

Too bad he has no choice.

"If you open your binders to section 1-A, a copy of the company's trust instrument is available to view," I say about the guiding document that defines the terms and conditions of our company trust. "I've asked Mr. Wilson, our lead solicitor who verified these documents, to be present. Mr. Wilson, would you mind summarizing the highlighted clause?"

Henry secures his glasses and narrows his bushy brows. They're the same khaki color as his unkempt hair. Add a lab coat, and you'd think he went back to the future.

He clears his throat. "The trust the Donnelley Brand currently resides in names the first grandson of Alexander Donnelley to become its protector. The title is not applicable if he serves as an employee of the company."

"And what are the vested powers of a protector should he no longer work for the Donnelley Brand?" I bite my lip to stifle a grin at my father, whose mouth chews around a frown.

"The trust instrument affords the protector the right to appoint and remove trustees, change beneficiary interests, and amend the trust," Henry explains to the blank faces in the room—all except my predecessor, who barely contains his glower. My brother, on the other hand, is the poster child of peace. William brought a snack tray of fruits and cheeses for today's showdown.

"Thank you, Mr. Wilson." I nod to Henry and cut my eyes at the room. "As I said, the company is heading in a new direction. A trust resettlement will occur, transferring all Donnelley Brand and related assets from the Anguilla trust into a new one here in London. The days of not paying our share in taxes are over." I look to my father. "So is your rule as trustee."

My grandfather was a vindictive bastard. But he never intended for his own son to operate with full control of the company, which is why he instilled a protector clause. He assumed my relationship with my father would be contentious like theirs was. My father knew about the clause, and he encouraged me to be acting CEO so he could keep his hold over the company as the sole trustee with controlling interest.

"In your binders is an outline for the future of the Donnelley Brand," I continue. "We will become a benefit corporation, transferring our company's ownership into a purpose trust to guarantee our profits fight environmental racism and climate change. The new trust will retain one hundred percent of the company's voting stock and the right to determine the new board composition and charter changes to reflect our new mission. I will help guide the new trust, and William will take over as interim CEO until there's an official vote. All nonvoting stock will go to a community-based collective with the necessary (c)(4) designation to take political action."

Take yourself out of the equation.

Jewel's ability to reimagine the world challenged me to think outside the box I restricted myself in. It was inevitable that I'd break my family's trust and relinquish power. With William's support, we'll ensure a lifetime of sustainable efforts while shifting our profits to support the greater good. Harboring wealth ends with us.

Hugh Kidwell jumps up from his seat and slams a meaty fist on the table. "This is bullshit! We all hold voting stock. You can't strong-arm us into becoming fucking tree huggers! I vote no."

"Your vote no longer matters," I snap. "Mr. Wilson?"

"Section 2-c in your binders is a copy of the articles of association," Henry says, pushing his thick glasses up the bridge of his wide nose. "There is a provision to force a sale of shares from minority shareholders. Section 3-d outlines the shareholder agreement, including a clause for the company to buy back minority shareholders' shares. Mr. Donnelley legally operates within his right, as he now oversees the trust and fifty-eight percent of its voting stock."

The articles of association and shareholders' agreement were a bonus. Alexander Donnelley refused to relinquish power to outsiders without safeguards I'll use to my benefit.

"It's about time this company headed in a new direction," Crawford counters. "James, Thomas, and I accept the buyback terms listed in the shareholder agreement. With our total eighteen percent of voting shares returning to the company, I believe you exceed the seventy-five percent threshold for a voluntary liquidation." He winks. "Good luck, son."

The three men gather their binders. They shake my hand and William's before leaving the conference room. With access to their shares, I can transfer the company's assets into our new venture without any remaining minority shareholders receiving shares in the new company. Hugh can kick and scream all he wants, but his days of influencing the Donnelley Brand from under my father's shadow are over.

"Elliot, why are you still here? Kissing Victor's ass no longer secures you a seat at this table." William picks up his empty tray and scoffs at the sweat accumulating on Elliot's balding, mole-covered head. He goes pale and doesn't blink until William returns to his seat and snaps his fingers inches from his face. It's enough for him and his murky brown suit to jolt out the door.

Hugh motions to my father. "What can we do, Victor? This won't hold in court."

"I assure you, Alexander Donnelley outlined his wishes to the letter in the trust instrument," our solicitor says from the other end of the table while gathering his papers. "I assisted in the trust's creation, and I can guarantee that the guiding document is iron-clad. A written notice of Victor's termination as trustee has already been filed, as have the legal documents for the trust resettlement. I scheduled a call with Preston and William to review the details on Monday. Gentlemen, it's always a pleasure. Enjoy the rest of your afternoon."

Hugh's rambling is the soundtrack to the war of remaining glares. He's pacing back and forth like he had a claim to my family's empire.

Michael assesses me from under an inquisitive brow, curious how I snatched control from my father's fingers—something he's yet to do with Hugh. William is on the phone behind my former desk, his Italian slip-on shoes propped up on the polished surface. He's an annoying shit at times, but he is the only person I trust not to lead this company with greed. William always supported my sustainability efforts, and he believes in centering local economies. That's why he developed the relationships to do so while reducing our carbon footprint. This new vision will require him to travel more as CEO, but he'll tackle it happily. William always loved being on the go, while I prefer to stay in one place.

There's only one place I'd rather be, and I'm on the first flight out after Monday's meeting.

Every day without Puff feels like eternal damnation. Everything is falling into place, but it means nothing if I can't have her.

"How did you do it? The trust instrument isn't public knowledge." My father buttons his gray suit coat on his way over to me. "I made sure of it once you assumed CEO."

"He had a damn good CFO," KD says from the door. "It took some work, but I pulled everything we needed."

"Bellamy Evangeline, are you—"

"Pregnant," she supplies to her wide-eyed father, running a hand over the bump that's protruding from her wrap dress. He stumbles to his chair for support. "Over five months now."

KD has the pregnancy glow. She's filling out more, her once slender shape giving way to new curves. The joy of expecting is in every smile she offers, which happens more and more often these days.

If Hugh Kidwell was at risk of a stroke before, one is imminent now. He'll pop a blood vessel if his eyes grow any bigger. His gaze shifts from KD's face to her belly before he stands and trips over himself in a rush to his daughter. He falters at her raised hand.

The frown currently wobbling her chin has me out of my chair, inspecting her for any signs of discomfort.

"What's wrong? Is it the baby?" I haven't stopped pursuing Madison, but I still check in with KD to ensure our daughter is okay.

"I don't deserve you, Preston." She wipes away a tear and sighs. "Have you looked at your email?"

My brows pinch. "No. I had my phone on silent for this meeting. You're scaring me, KD," I say to her pained stare and restless fingers rubbing her wrists. "What's wrong?"

"I'd certainly like to know," Hugh puffs. "You got my daughter pregnant *and* stole the company? You are a bastard, Preston."

"No, he's not!" KD's bark hits her father like a jab. "Preston has always cared for me. Treated me as his equal. He fought for me to have a seat on the board, and you took it away from me because I wasn't Michael, your precious son. You never call or visit, so don't pretend you're the doting father you think you are."

Hugh shrinks half a size when he winces. There's nothing he can say to erase decades of him devaluing his daughter.

"Hey." I reach for her. "What's going on?"

Her eyes brim with tears. "I wanted this," she says, her voice choked. "Us. The chance to make you happy."

"Bellamy," I sigh.

"I know," she nods and wipes her cheek. "I'm not her and never will be. Your actions are loud and clear. The way you pursue her. You love Madison."

"I'll be here to raise our child. You know that, right?"

She forces a smile. "I do. Preston, you're a good man, but this isn't your baby."

Black walls close in as the foundation beneath my shoes threatens to crumble. The beginning drums of a migraine pound behind my temples, a steady beat to drown out the room. Hands are flailing, and mouths are moving. I don't hear anything until my brother's piercing scream.

"You let him believe he got you pregnant as a way to keep him?" Michael grabs William's shoulder and shakes his head. William would never hurt KD, but he isn't chambering the anger rising in his voice. "Do you have any idea what you put him through? We treated you like family when yours thought you were shit! Back up, Michael!" He pushes at her brother. "I'd never lay a hand on a woman, but I will knock a bitch out today."

I close my eyes to ease the ache in my ribs and keep the room from spinning. William and Michael's argument fades under the betrayal of one of the closest people to me. It's a knife I never saw coming, a blade puncturing remnants of the care and trust I had for someone intent on upending the life I'm fighting to live with Madison.

Fatherhood is a life sentence I once feared, but thinking about it recently brought me joy. I didn't know how or if Madison would choose to tether herself to the complicated web KD and I spun, but I was determined to love my child fiercely. A child that isn't fucking mine.

"Preston, wait," KD pleads when I pull away. "I swear I did not trick you. When I found out I was pregnant, I knew it was a sign that we were meant to be a real family. I love you. You were my first, and I hoped—" A sob racks her chest. "Everything is ruined!"

"You kept this pregnancy a secret for months. *Months*," I seethe. "The games with Madison weren't enough? You had to almost pin a baby on me? Do you have any idea the harm you caused? I cared for you, as a friend and a partner in this business."

"Preston."

"Goodbye, Bellamy." My vision tunnels on the door. I have to get the hell out of here.

Something told me to push for a paternity test. But I was so caught up in trying to seize the reins of this company, I never stopped to question Bellamy.

Too many men shrug their children off and leave them for mothers to raise alone. I never wanted a child with Bellamy, but the seed I thought was mine would never want for anything, in this life or the next.

"It was a mistake!"

I keep walking.

"I heard you talking to William about Madison after you returned from holiday and realized she's the one. I was jealous. I didn't mean to sleep with him!"

What in the entire fuck?

I can't look at Bellamy, but I glare at my brother.

"I *never* touched her, bruv," he asserts with his hands in the air. "I swear to you, Pres. It wasn't me."

"Well, who the hell is the father of your child?" Hugh scolds.

Bellamy's sidelong glance is all I need. "Fucking hell," I say. "My *father*."

The least he could do is look remorseful that he has a child on the way outside of his marriage. But he seems bored, as if the revelation that he's having a baby with his best friend's daughter, who's half his age, is an inconvenience.

"I was lonely on the Malaysia trip," Bellamy reveals. "You broke my heart, and he was there. It just...happened."

William leaps for our father, but Michael pulls him back. "You son of a bitch! Have you no fucking decency?! What about my mother?!" He squirms in Michael's grasp, testing the strength of the buttons ready to pop from straining over his chest. His face is beet red, and his eyes demand blood.

"Had I known a one-time fuck turned into a pregnancy, I would've told her to abort it." My father's nonchalance earns him my fist to his face. He stumbles when my knuckles connect with the soft tissue of his nose and pulls a hankie from his suit coat. I hope it's broken.

"You disgust me!" I spit. "Whenever I think you can't stoop lower, you prove me wrong. It's always about you, no matter who you hurt." I shake my head. "How could my mother ever love someone like you?"

Hurt flashes in his eyes. "Leave her out of this." His voice is a low gravel.

I huff. "You always do."

"I loved your mother!" My father bangs his fist to his chest in a roar. "I haven't lived since Antonia took her last breath in the hospital on the day you were born. You think you know loss? Your grandfather threatened to disown me and strip away my inheritance if I married your mother. The only reason he gave a shit about you was because you came out shades lighter and he could use you to hate me.

"I coped with Antonia's death by pretending it didn't matter that I never got the chance to say goodbye. Life took from me, so I returned the favor. Preston, hate me all you want, but you were conceived in love. Not a day goes by that I don't think about your mother, wishing I knew how to let her go. If you learn anything from me, don't let love consume you like I did. You'll never recover when it's snatched from you."

I've never seen my father get emotional, much less cry. He wipes the only tear he lets fall and heads for the door. "You are my constant reminder she's gone," he says over his shoulder with sad eyes. "Antonia would be proud of the work you're doing. I'm sorry I was a disappointment, son."

Hugh chases after him without a care for his daughter, who's sobbing.

"I'm sorry," Bellamy sniffles.

"Do your baby a favor and take care of yourself. It's time for you to leave." Any attempt to make sense of the fact that the child I thought was mine is actually my sister will cause an ulcer. KD and my father will need to work out their dynamic. I want no part of it.

"I expect your letter of resignation on my desk Monday," William says with a power I no longer possess.

Michael hugs his sister, who cries into his suit as they leave.

"I never understood why he hated me until now." William's eyes are still on the door our father stormed out of, the shock petrifying him in place.

"He doesn't hate you. He hates himself," I say. William looks up. "I'm sorry you've been a casualty of his regret. You're my best friend, Will, and a better man than he'll ever be."

Our father was hard on me, but he ignored William's existence.

"Yeah, bruv. I hear you." He nods and stuffs his hands into his pocket. "Thank you for always caring." He huffs. "Sad as it sounds, you were the only father figure I had."

I pull him into a hug. "I love you, Will."

"Love you too, Pres."

"Fuck," I sigh. "The end of an era and the start of an eighteen-year *Jerry Springer* episode. You think he still remembers how to change nappies?"

William snorts on his way to the liquor cabinet, where he pulls out two crystal tumblers. "Let's hope they ship our sister off to boarding school, for her sake." His smile fades. "This will crush my mother. She begged him for another child for years."

"Briar deserves better. She should leave him."

He nods. "Maybe this will do it."

We clink glasses in the middle of the room that's no longer my office. Books I never read rest on shelves between heirlooms and art passed from one Donnelley to the next.

"You ready to say goodbye?" William asks before a sip of scotch. My "Yes" is instant and earns me a sidelong glance.

The last sixty hours have been a scramble to prepare for today and line up William's COO replacement. Hadiza accepted the position, and she starts next week. As vice president of hotel operations, she's been his right hand with guest experiences and management.

"Work had its moments, but we did good here. Now it's yours," I say.

William never expressed a desire to run the Donnelley Brand. My father always intended to pass it on to me. It's time for my brother to step out of the shadows.

"It's *our* time. This was always our legacy. You made sure of that when you brought me on as COO," William says. "I'd like for you to be part of the new board, as chairperson—votes pending, of course. You're the reason this company is headed where it is. Let's rebuild it together."

Rich amber singes my throat on a swallow. "I'll consider it if that's the direction the board wants to head. You'll always have my support."

"Good. I fucking hate doing interviews. I won't cry if you're still the face of all this."

"You're not passing off your responsibilities to me," I tease. "I'm not the CEO anymore, and I'm taking back my time." I set the tumbler on the bar and grab my jacket. Not wearing a suit every day will take practice.

Good thing you went shopping months ago.

A smile dents my cheeks when I think of the heart-shaped lips and smooth pecan skin I haven't tasted in over a month. I miss Madison. The way her lashes sweep across her cheekbones lifted in a laugh too big for her face, how her body so peacefully melts into mine while she sleeps.

My life is in transition, but I haven't lost sight of the most important piece.

"Tell my sister-in-law I said hi," William laughs. "Come on, I'll buy you a pint as a going away gift."

Chapter 52

Madison

"Touch that billfold, and you'll hold your paintbrush in your mouth for the rest of your days." I reach for the black pleather booklet and pull the check to me. My glower remains on my brown-eyed companion, who lifts a brow and the corner of his lips like I won't stab his hand with my fork.

Our server waltzes to our table and takes my card, giggling under the lust-drunk spell of hooded eyes and a square jaw swimming in a goatee. "I'll be right back, you two."

The assumption I'm on a dinner date threatens my chicken and waffles to make a second appearance. I can't go out with Joseph without someone thinking we're together. It's gross.

Joseph Catlett's Nawlins charm plays across his vowels and the honey tips of his coiled hair with a fade he keeps as clean as the white tee that's become his daily costume. He finally grew into his broad nose, and his once-twiggy body now carries muscles.

He's handsome, but he's also my first cousin.

The man of the evening lifts his hands and tosses his napkin on the table. "You got it."

"Just remember me when they hang your paintings in museums. I expect a VIP ticket." I smile. "I'm proud of you, Seph."

"Appreciate you, Maddie."

My cousin is a man of few words, but he translates empty canvases into love letters. He's a phenomenal painter whose work is in galleries in DC, where he lives, Miami, his hometown New Orleans, and now Harlem. It's been months since we've seen each other, which makes tonight my treat.

We're in a cocktail bar, catching each other up on life, our careers, and our nonexistent relationships. He's three years post-divorce, and I'm—

I don't know what I am.

Confused.

Frustrated.

Mourning?

With all my recent styling gigs, the days are longer, but not long enough to reach the depths of the void of not having Preston in my life.

"You should call him." Joseph's voice lulls me out of the regret that's holding me hostage. It's the same command Kojo declared. Joseph's small smile is the one he'd offer when I scraped my knees trying to follow him and his friends around the ward on my bike. Joseph is five years older and more like a big brother than a cousin.

"Did you forget the part where he's having a child with another woman?"

"A woman he keeps leaving to chase *you* around, Maddie. How many cities did Preston magically appear in?"

I look away. "Two. Atlanta and Miami." I've been waiting for him to pop out of the bushes here in New York, but it hasn't happened.

"He needs to focus on his daughter," I defend.

"And he will," Joseph says. "From what you've told me, he doesn't seem like the kind of man to abandon his responsibilities. His daughter won't stop him from proving the place you hold in his life. Call him."

"I'm afraid, Seph. I get hurt every time I allow myself to get close."

He reaches across the small table and takes my hand. "If you give up now, you'll regret it for the rest of your life. Don't be like me. Love hard and don't let go."

Joseph is Uncle Remy's son. They both translate their emotions into art—painting for Seph and jazz for mama's brother. Seph doesn't talk much about his divorce from Morgan, but he doesn't have to. The pain of losing her is a reality he carries daily co-parenting their son, Duke. It's been three years, and the longing hasn't faded from his art. I catch him staring off into the distance to relive memories of happier times with her.

Neither of them has moved on. One day, I hope they'll find their way back to each other.

"You should take your own advice," I say. "I know you love her."

"Never stopped." A heaviness tightens his chest and rests in his sigh. The lump he tries to swallow lingers in his throat. "Too much time has passed us by. We can't regain what we lost. For now, I live in the joy of raising our son."

"Duke is the best," I say.

Joseph returns my smile. "That he is."

Nightfall comes for dusk on a balmy breeze. Today's humidity didn't wring my curls, which are resting in a high bun. Summers in New York are nothing to play with.

I peek at my phone before tucking it into my purse. I texted Preston earlier today, then I took Joseph's advice and worked up the courage to dial the number I memorized by heart. He hasn't responded. Not that I'd expect him to, given the day.

Today is his birthday and the anniversary of his mother's death.

My platform heels balance on wide stone pavers as I make my way over to the fountain with lily pads. The garden looks different, dressed in layers of tulips blooming around manicured hedges. I set the bouquet of white lilies on the bench Preston engraved for his mother and brush pollen from the weathered wood.

"For you," I say to the silver inscription winking in the streetlight.

It felt right to come here tonight. I wanted to be close to Preston and feel him here with the love he declared for all to see. It's a place I frequent when our distance weighs heavy. I love him, and I'm struggling with how to live without him.

I reach for the cupcake in a cardboard to-go box. It's French vanilla with buttercream frosting. "Happy birthday, baby," I whisper. "Make a wish wherever you are."

"It already came true," a deep timbre murmurs behind me.

A soft gasp escapes me, and a quiver surges through my veins, which slice open under his gaze blurred with tears. He's kept his distance whenever we were in the same city, but he's here now. My heart skips, pushing one foot in front of the other until I'm running.

I wrap my hands around his neck, careful not to smear icing across the nape. "I missed you," I weep, inhaling the scent of his musk. My lashes dampen at his chin on my head and his grip tightening around my waist.

Preston's hands explore the hollow of my back until they lift to wipe away my tears. He cups my face in awe before the smooth surface of his lips meets mine. Our tongues brush, igniting a fire no distance nor person could extinguish.

He slips his hands up my arms to bring me closer. "I can't live without you, Puff." His lips tremble through another kiss.

"I'm sorry for leaving. I couldn't—"

"Never apologize for taking care of yourself. I understood. It hurt, but I understood." Preston's eyes shift from me to his mother's bench.

"I wanted to honor her today."

"Thank you. This is the first birthday I don't feel hollow inside." His words are a broken whisper. "God, I missed you."

The kisses he presses to my face are an elixir on my skin, smoothing fresh wounds with assurances we'll be okay. We have to be, because life won't allow us to be apart. No matter the years or miles, we always find our way back to each other. Standing here in his arms, I wouldn't have it any other way.

"There's something I need to tell you."

"So help me if there's *another* woman having your baby, Preston," I grit.

"The baby isn't mine," he says.

"Which one?"

His brows knit. "There was only one, and she's not mine."

"What?" My head draws back, and my mouth opens.

"It's my father's." I blink as my brain stumbles to catch up. Did he just say his daddy? "I found out a few days ago. I wanted to tell you in person, but first I had to wrap up a transfer for William to become interim CEO."

"Bellamy is having your sister?" I ask, to make sure I heard correctly. "And she tried to pin the baby on you?"

Preston shakes his head. "According to her, no. She heard me talking about you after the retreat and found comfort in my father." He grimaces.

"William's mother—"

"Is seeking a divorce," he says. "Her solicitors already received an anonymous tip that should help with the prenup."

"Bellamy is having your daddy's baby?" I repeat, at a loss to form new words.

Kojo clocked it. This is a Tubi movie.

"Please tell me the paternity test doubles as a letter of resignation." I know my limits, and being the bigger person past a certain point is not one of them. Little Miss Tried It can take her womb and her handbags and go.

"Did you not hear me say that William is interim CEO?" Preston's eyes light with a twinkle of mischief, as if unemployment doesn't bother him. Maybe it doesn't. He does have access to billions, after all.

"I want you, Madison. A fresh start with just the two of us."

"I'd like that." I smile. "How do you feel about stepping down?"

"Like I can breathe." He kisses my lips. "Now that I have full control over my family trust, I can make the changes I want from anywhere in the world." He laughs when my brows hike up to my forehead. "A lot happened this past week. I found a clause in the trust when I was here—"

"You were in New York?"

His smile dissolves. "For days," he emphasizes to prove his point. "I stopped by your flat and left messages with the grumpy front-desk attendant with the combover."

"Gerald never gave them to me. But he mentioned a possible stalker who kept coming to the building. Almost called the police."

Preston huffs. "Prick. I may have stopped by a few times." His grin spreads at my smile. "Two or three times a day, when I walked your neighborhood with William and Dayo."

"You didn't."

"And did." I snort at his animated attempt to mock Kojo. He interlaces our fingers, all signs of laughter erased from his face. "I'll always come for you, Puff. I love you."

"I love you too." Our kiss lingers until I remember the cupcake softening in my hand. "This is for you. I don't have a candle, but you should make a wish."

Cognac eyes slide over me with a softness he pairs with a forehead kiss. "I told you, it already came true. I have everything I need."

"Almost," I say to the frown lines on his forehead. "I accept your tender offer." My squeal at my heels leaving the ground scares the birds out of the trees.

Preston picks me up like I'm weightless and crushes me into his polo shirt. I wrap my legs around the waist of his jeans and settle in the adoration of his gaze.

"Do you mean it?"

"*Ti amerò fino al giorno dopo per sempre,*" I repeat after weeks of practice when missing him became too much.

His grin is wild and free. "I will love you until the day after forever."

Epilogue

Madison

Three Years Later

"**D**ear God, this is divine." Justice takes another bite of gelato and tips her face to the cloudless sky. She draws in a deep breath and grins, her black natural curls pineappled on top of her head.

She's in pure bliss, and she's only called her and Terrence's mothers, who are watching their kids, twice since we started our walking tour. It's their first trip out of the country without Edie and Gracie, their three-year-old twins, or Mattan, who's a little over six months.

I was pregnant with Alessandro at the same time she was carrying her son. Our little guy is almost a year old, and he's a ball of energy. He's having the time of his life in Breaux Bridge with his grandparents and cousins. For the record, I've required proof of life every hour.

"This was a good call," Justice says to the cone of caramel, raspberry, and vanilla gelato she's about to French-kiss. A blueberry cheesecake macaroon is the crown jewel, and she devours it with a shimmy.

I lick the salted caramel that's pooling at the top of my waffle cone, grateful that my aviator sunglasses and the maze of nineteenth century buildings provide some shelter from the sun. "Is there anything else you wanted to see?"

"Oh, I think we're good for today," she laughs. "Em and Kojo are on their way. Thank you for abandoning your heels. I had fun."

"Only for you, but let's not make a habit out of it," I chuckle. My platform slip-on oxfords style well with my marigold spaghetti-strap summer dress, and they didn't decimate my feet after three hours of walking.

We lost Emma and Kojo half an hour into the day. They headed off to the Passage du Havre to shop, then detoured to a spa. Jay and I sampled food and wine in Montmartre, which turned into lunch and a stroll to Moulin Rouge.

Everyone—Terrence and Miles included—is in Paris to celebrate Justice and T's sixteenth wedding anniversary. Preston and I didn't have to travel far, as we made the City of Love our permanent home two years ago.

The four-bedroom single-family house we bought in the sixteenth arrondissement, with a garden and a private alley, was only one of life's changes. Justice is now a close friend. Emma too, believe it or not.

Therapy equipped me with the tools to heal myself and the relationships in need of repair. Reconciliation was not without honest conversations, acknowledgment, apology, and forgiveness. What took the deepest work was freeing myself of the things that no longer served me.

Fear.

Guilt.

Resentment.

All of it had to go so I could receive this version of my life, a version I never knew was possible. It's soul work in constant progress.

"I'm glad we spent the day together," Justice says, her face spread into a smile.

"Me too." I pull her into a side hug, careful to not get what's left of my cone on her two-piece jumpsuit. "Blush is your color."

She twirls her Tinker Bell shape and lifts a tennis shoe. "I have a damn good stylist."

"That you do."

"You're in Brazil next month?"

I nod. "For Noura's premiere in São Paulo."

"You two are *the* Hollywood duo."

Every collaboration with Noura Sky has turned to gold. She's a sweetheart and now my priority client, booking films and guest appearances left and right. Outside of Justice and my work with Kojo, which is now an advisory role, I only keep a handful of clients now, and most of them are celebrities.

With all the best-dressed lists Noura is on, the demand for my services has been nonstop. But I won't compromise my life at home trying to be everything to everybody.

Preston and I slowed down our travel schedules to be present with each other and Alessandro. We still see the world, but we don't let it rule our lives.

"Jewel will be down there," I add, "learning about climate initiatives and how to safeguard the rights of Indigenous people."

Justice whistles. "I'm scared of your niece. She's a force."

"That she is. A year left in law school and already orchestrating lawsuits," I laugh. The baby whose dirty diapers I once changed is now changing the world. "Parishes across Louisiana are suing oil companies, to hold them accountable for decades of damages. My grandmother's old parish is taking legal action for the polluting plants being disproportionately placed in Black neighborhoods."

Jewel is our pride and joy. Spending the summer in Breaux Bridge inspired her to go straight to law school after graduating from Brooklyn University. Our family will have its first attorney, who will no doubt fight in the streets and inside courtrooms for climate justice.

The whine of an engine cracks through the air. A scooter pulls up next to the curb, kicking up gravel. Emma hops off with a dismount that would score ten out of ten for not flashing all of Paris. The driver's tongue plummets to the ground and unfurls like a red carpet for her deep V-neckline halter minidress.

"Thank you," Emma says to the man who's still glitching. She leaves him with his drool and steps over the curb in single-strap stilettos the same chartreuse as her backless dress that's causing heart attacks.

The color is gorgeous on her amber skin. With her mahogany hair in an updo, Em looks like a model on a magazine cover.

"Why are you on somebody's scooter?" Justice asks.

The answer speeds down the street with cocoa-buttered legs kicked in the air. Kojo lets out a *Whoo!* and jumps off the scooter once it comes to a stop. He passes his helmet to a brunette man with a wink and seasons his sashay for his audience of one.

"He's cute, right?" Kojo fans his fingers over his shoulder. "Is the Moms Gone Wild walking tour over?"

"You missed gelato." I stick my tongue out at his pout. "Where are your bags?"

"Being delivered to the hotel," Emma says.

Justice's face scrunches. "I can't believe you sat on that seat with that hemline. Miles would flip."

"Blame this one." Emma thumbs at Kojo. "He had the bright idea of asking for a ride. Trust me when I say I don't want or need to hear Miles's mouth."

"But you will."

Manicured hedges rattle next to a private home. Miles appears, scaling over a wrought iron fence. His white sneakers hit the pavement first, flexing the muscles stretching his white shorts and the gray button down rolled up to his elbows.

"So we're riding around Paris with strangers and pussy out?" Miles approaches his wife.

Emma's moss-green eyes stretch two sizes. "How did you get into someone's yard?"

He shrugs. "They weren't home, and I didn't feel like walking this long-ass block to get to you. I cut off the security cameras. We're straight."

"Where is Terrence?" Justice frowns at the hedges.

"He's bringing our rental car around. Back to the matter at hand, Mrs. Walker," he says to Emma, who's now half a foot below his eyeline. "You trying to see me on *Locked Up Abroad*? You and our pussy better not play with me. Aye, my guy. Lemme smell the back of your shirt real quick."

Miles inches closer to the man on the scooter. Whatever trance he was in dissolves. The scooter roars to life, and he defies speed limits in order to escape Miles's hulking frame.

Kojo shakes his head and laughs. "Here they go." He retreats back to the scooter with the handsome brunette, who's oddly relaxed and unbothered by the drama. "I'll see y'all tonight for dinner…if I'm not tied up."

"You're foul as hell, Ko. I thought we were friends." Miles points a finger at him.

"You know I'd never put Emmy in harm's way!" Kojo yells over the scooter's engine. "We were only on for three blocks. Love you, Trevante! Bye!"

The scooter speeds off, with Kojo's legs back in the air. Justice is on her phone, calling "the Gigis" about her kids. Miles and Emma went from arguing to tonguing each other down in the middle of the sidewalk.

This part of the ninth arrondissement isn't super touristy—not that it would stop Miles from cupping Emma's ass or her from pulling down his neck to reach his lips.

"I promise I covered my pussy with my purse." She lifts the square accessory, which is no bigger than a slice of bread.

Miles pecks her lips and groans at her hands inside his back pockets. "Good girl, kitten." He smacks her ass. "I'm always coming behind you. Have me out here looking like Liam Neeson in *Taken*."

Emma smirks. "No more hacking on this trip." She nips at his lip, and he dips his tongue back into her mouth.

Time for me to go.

"See you later, Em," I laugh. She can't hear me with all the moaning and rubbing.

Justice scoffs and slips her phone into her clutch. "Newlyweds," she giggles. We link arms and head in the opposite direction.

Miles and Em said "I do" last year. It was a beautiful wedding in Malibu, overlooking the vineyards. Perfect for the two people who swore off commitment.

Preston and I exchanged vows on his nonna's property in Sicily two years ago. He proposed a couple months after his birthday, when I moved to London. We're at the end of the newlywed stage, but you'd never know it.

A compact SUV rolls up. Inside is a very stuffed-in Terence, who looks three sizes too big for the toy vehicle. He squeezes out wearing a white tee, gray shorts, and a grin for his wife.

Justice doesn't have a chance to say hello before he's on her. Mouths part, and their hands find a home on each other's bodies.

"Newlyweds, huh?" I chuckle at the moan that slips out of Justice.

"Sorry." She wipes her lip with a shy smile and eyes for only her husband.

Terrence runs a hand through the black curls Justice agitated. "Hey, Madison."

"Hey."

It was awkward at first, joining this friend group. But, like me and Preston, life had a way of pushing us together.

Preston hired Justice at the Donnelley Brand after the firm she started won a national award for the marketing campaign for Terrence's state-of-the-art training facility. Jay went on to earn two others, and their working relationship took off. She and I had many heart-to-hearts, with Terrence and Preston developing their own friendship. T's exclusive training program is a hit in Donnelley hotels, which gives us an excuse to fly to Austin every year.

Emma took longer to crack. Kojo gave us space during our initial collaboration with his Rustin brand. Justice and I are closer, but me and Em have a bond that includes swapping clothes and shoes.

Everyone now lives in Austin. The pressure is heavy for us to follow suit, but Preston and I love Paris. It's magic when we all come together. Tammi even gets in on the action from time to time. Her and Smokey are coming to Paris for Christmas this year—five kids and all.

"Do you want us to drop you off before we head to the hotel?" Justice thumbs to the rental with a nonexistent back seat.

"No thanks," I say. "I think I'm gonna walk around for a bit."

Terrence's brows narrow. "You sure?"

"Positive." I smile when his worry lines match his wife's. When I don't have security with me, I share my location with Preston and

Dayo as a precaution. "I haven't been over here in a minute. You two get out and enjoy your child-free anniversary."

"I did want to take you to the Eiffel Tower." Terrence stares down lovingly at Justice, who melts.

"Let's do it."

They kiss again before they're off.

I smile at the day and make my way over to Rue Chaptal. Sunlight catches on the limestone facade of a building, illuminating Juliette balconies.

Summertime in Paris is my favorite. The weather is warm, and the city comes alive with festivals and outdoor movie screenings.

My phone chimes in my purse.

Dominique

Someone is sleepy again.

"Aww." I melt at the photo of Alessandro knocked out in my sister's arms, mashed red beans and rice in his tiny fist.

He's the perfect mix of me and Preston, with my heart-shaped lips and perky nose and Preston's long lashes and dimples. His mess of thick curls has the same auburn streaks mine did growing up in the Louisiana sun.

My baby is tired.

Good morning over there. I see y'all got him eating good. Thanks for the pic. Love you.

Dominique

Love you too.

My relationship with my sister wasn't easy to navigate, but we made it to our place of healing. Both of us had to let go of years of assumptions and guilt to get to where we are now. Preston and I visit Breaux Bridge every summer. It's the only time of year Jewel can get back and we can all be together.

We've settled into new family traditions while honoring the former practices that made us who we are.

Life with my in-laws is a different story.

Briar cleaned house—literally. She took most of Victor's money from his personal trust and what little was left from the Donnelley Brand once Preston cut him off. News of Victor Donnelley fathering a child outside of his marriage—with his former friend's daughter, no less—eclipsed the royal family coverage in the tabloids. Part of me felt bad for Bellamy, who left London to flee the paparazzi and have her baby in peace. She moved up north, to York, where she raises a now three-year-old Daisy alone.

Preston and William have seen their sister a handful of times. We all tried to visit once, after Alessandro was born, but Bellamy isn't ready. The father of her child only sends checks, and there's still hurt she's working through.

I had to let go of mine to move on. I didn't want to carry it, and I chose to fill my life with things that bring me joy.

William is still William. He's come into his own as CEO, and he's spearheading changes that force the hospitality industry to take notice. Preston is an ambassador for the Donnelley Brand. Their profits now funnel into communities most impacted by environmental racism and climate change.

Through direct support and legislative victories, the community-based collective is doing amazing work. Jewel still taps in as a thought partner, and she'll support as legal counsel once she passes the bar. As for the Donnelley family's billions, Preston and Will are on track to deplete the chest, outside of ongoing revenue for the collective to use at its discretion. The brothers created a foundation to give away all the money in their individual trusts over the course of their lifetime. They'll still live comfortably and have a modest inheritance for their children, but they're resetting the scales for better equity.

We see Will at least twice a month. If we're not hopping over to London, he's in our refrigerator and the guest bedroom he claimed as his own. Ravenous is still very much alive and thriving. The Donnelley Brand's Paris hotel now has pop-ups, and we indulge from time to time.

If Kojo only knew how wild this mom gets.

A breeze catches in an alley, fluttering leaves creating a canopy from the sun. My oxfords crunch on the aged pathway that leads up to a familiar property, a cream building with sage shutters. They're the same color as ours at home, as a symbol of the place where we met.

I haven't been back to this museum since I was twenty-something and scrambling for an affordable place to eat. Little did that Madison know the wonders that were written in the stars for her. There was heartbreak and drama—lots of it—but so much love.

"Like what you see?" I smile at the voice speaking French behind me. It still makes my pulse race.

My eyes shift away from the old building to a sharp jawline with a trimmed goatee, thick brows, and teasing dimples. Warm honey skin peeks out of a white polo tucked into navy chinos.

"Maybe." I force my cheeks down to feign indifference.

Preston lifts a brow, and I snort.

"Do you like what you see?" The question I volley back is in French, and it earns me a nod.

"Very much so," he says, his rich timbre licking my ear. "Have dinner with me. Tonight."

I smirk and turn away. "I'm a happily married woman."

"I don't think he'll mind."

"Is that right?" I laugh at his nod.

He bites his lip and steps closer. His gaze is a slow drag up my hips to my nipples, which are now hard beneath cotton fabric. I scream internally, trying to hold it together as he swipes his tongue across his teeth.

"I don't dine with strangers," I whimper, the last of my restraint to not maul this man.

Preston looks better than the day we first met eighteen years ago. He's slowly becoming a silver fox, hard in all the right places.

I let my eyes drop to the bulge tenting his pants.

"You'll get that tonight. After I feed you," he says. His fingers wrap around my waist, his voice a low rumble. "I checked your location and saw you were here." He smiles. "It's fitting for today."

"What's today?"

"The day we met. Here." His eyes lift to the museum behind me, a house preserving romance and the start of what would become our love story. Life has a way of always rerouting us to where we need to be.

"Have dinner with me," he says again.

"You're still a stranger," I tease while running my fingers through his hair.

"We should fix that." He kisses my lips. "Preston."

The opportunity for a do-over doesn't come around often. When it does, seize it with your whole heart.

Some love stories deserve a second chance.

I look him in the eyes and smile at forever.

"Madison."

THE END

Acknowledgments

Well, folks. We've come to the end of the ride. It's time to put away the Chance at Love Series, at least for now.

Will we revisit it in the future? Perhaps.

I see glimpses of Zo's story as a widower who finds love again. I also see Reina and her soccer player love before they got engaged and how Terrence's younger sister secretly falls in love with one of his business partners. I want to write more outside of this series before I spin the block.

So, for now, we'll let Preston and Madison close us out.

While writing *The Seven Month Itch* (back in 2021), I vividly saw Madison and Preston's story. Their mentioned time in Paris and running into Justice at the coffee shop—not to mention being at Emma and Miles's wedding!—left me intrigued. I wanted to know more and had to mentally file away their love story until the time was right.

Readers didn't care for Madison (understandably so) and wanted the next book after *The Seven Month Itch* to focus on Miles and Emma. *Miles Apart* had me struggling! I couldn't see the story clearly and stalled with *Ella Gets the D* as a standalone to buy me time.

Through it all, Madison and Preston were patiently waiting in the wings.

Tender Offer is, without a doubt, one of my favorite books I've written. I've had fun writing them all—except when I was late on a *Miles Apart* deadline because of serious writer's block and almost threw the manuscript into traffic—but I enjoyed this journey. I tasted the meals they shared, smiled at them finding their way back to each other (and their non-date), and waved goodbye to the characters from the series who came together to be part of Preston and Madison's happily ever after.

To date, Preston gives Miles a run for his money as my favorite cinnamon roll I've written. (I love Julian, but I'm not trying to fight his fan club.) I don't know much about the small piece of Sicilian heritage that's part of my family quilt, but I wanted it represented. While we won't see Preston again (at least, I don't think), be on the lookout for Nonna and his cousin (hey, Sal!) in a standalone mafia rom-com on the way.

As for Madison, she's a reminder that second chances extend beyond romantic partners. Many of us, myself included, have played a villain in someone else's story. (I never went after a married man or anything like that, but you get what I'm saying!)

It was easy to make Madison how she was in *The Seven Month Itch*. There was no background or context to what informed her decisions. We saw a glimpse of her character arc in *Miles Apart*, and I hope readers see her differently in *Tender Offer*.

Forgiveness, grace, and healing are tenets throughout this book and my work in policy advocacy outside my identity as a romance author. We see these themes manifest in different ways, and I hope they strike a chord.

Goodness, this is getting long!

In closing (lol), thank you for coming on this ride with me. From *The Seven Month Itch* to *Miles Apart* and now *Tender Offer*, your support keeps me going.

None of this would be possible without a strong support system. To my cinnamon roll husband, your words of encouragement breathe life. Thank you is too small for all you do.

I'm forever grateful to my family, friends, and readers who've become friends and for your support. The street team for this book was extra special. I can't thank you all enough! And a special thanks to those rocking with me who are part of the "I Hate Madison Club" (*coughs, Nika and Brittany, coughs*). Bless y'all for not liking her but giving her a chance because of me, lmao.

That's it for now. We're switching gears to rugby romance. *One Knight's Stand*, the first book in the Buffalo Steel Series, releases 12.18.25!

The Chance at Love Series is the first I've written. This isn't a goodbye, but a so long for now.

Want more of Madison and Preston? *Subscribe to my newsletter to receive the welcome email with the links to my deleted scenes!*
https://tanvierwrites.substack.com/

Patreon subscribers will get an <u>exclusive bonus chapter</u> of Madison and Preston back in Ravenous. (Spoiler: It's STEAMY.)
Join here:
www.patreon.com/c/tanvierwrites

Curious how Emma and Miles got together?
KEEP READING for the first chapter of *Miles Apart*, book two in the Chance at Love Series!

Miles Apart
Chapter 1

Emma

"Do you have to go?"

I glance up at doe eyes in the mirror and bite back a smile. West waits for me to change my mind, and for a brief moment I allow myself to entertain the thought that he wants me to stay for more than my body.

He's cute—adorable, even—but he has much to learn.

My attention falls back to the concealer in my hand. It will be a miracle if I don't walk out looking like a yellow highlighter. This lighting is awful, even for a standard hotel room decorated in three shades of beige. I drop makeup into my overnight bag and adjust the strapless sweater dangling off my shoulder. "I had a good time last night," I say.

Gracious tongue.

Steady strokes.

Four out of five stars.

West sits up in bed with a grin too big for a woman about to leave him. The tartan duvet pools at his waist, showcasing an array of lean muscles engraved into tanned ivory skin.

"So let's do it again," he begs, his lower lip dipping into a pout. There's a lightness in his tone, one mixed with confidence and the hope that his ability to please is enough to keep me here. Firm hands tatted at the forearms push the rest of the decorative pillows to the floor. West leans against the wooden headboard and spreads his legs to stroke his length over the sheets.

Tempting.

Men in their twenties are wild cards. Most fuck with the intensity of a jackrabbit, which is why I keep them at bay. Not this one. West was a pleasant surprise who didn't let direction hurt his ego. Guys my age could learn from him. Even at twenty-nine, five years younger than me, he took the time to discover what pleased me instead of what got him off.

West and I met at the kickoff mixer for the weeklong singles' retreat. I'm not here for the hope of a happily ever after. I'm here for dick and to pull my best friend out of the fortress of her home back in Austin. She's on her way to divorce, but that doesn't mean life is over.

Justice's night ended exactly as expected. She took one look at people on the prowl for love and lust before she headed up to our suite and spent the night with room service.

I had other plans.

West caught my eye behind the bar across the crowded room. It didn't take long for our stares to linger before I sat on the stool in front of him. We exchanged names while he made my martini. His forearms flexed under the rolled sleeves of his white button-down. The lust in his eyes reflected in mine as our fingers touched on the stem of my glass. We went up to his room after midnight with the promise of orgasms.

A delicious welcome to Vail, Colorado, after a full day of traveling.

Hooded blue eyes pierce mine in a silent plea for me to stay. One night is all I'll give.

There are the Joan Claytons of the world—women like Justice who color-code their linens and believe in soulmates. I never felt an itch to attach forever to a partner. I'm with the Toni Childs of the world—those who try you on for size before swapping you out with their outfits. Relationships slow you down and expose you to wounds. She tried the "I do," and look what happened. I've seen a loveless marriage up close. Now, I'm witnessing the aftermath of a broken love story with my best friend.

I'll pass.

The hiss of the zipper on my thigh-high boot breaks our stare. West moves to pull me down when I saunter over to the bed, but he isn't quick enough. I meant what I said. Last night was enjoyable, but this eagerness for me to stay is why I don't make a habit of sleeping over.

I saw.

I conquered.

I came—more than once.

"Now, West." I straddle him for no other reason than to be a tease. "You were good." My lips press to the shell of his ear. "Let's see what this week holds. I know where to find you." I ruffle the dirty blonde waves I gripped when he explored the depths between my thighs, grab my overnight bag, and make my exit without a last glance.

West is a fuck boy in its purest form. He reeks of it, much like his Old Spice deodorant. His boy-next-door good looks and pickup lines might leave others pressed, but not me. I'm not a woman to look for more out of a one-night stand. We take what we need and move on. No idling. No waiting by the phone. No pouting of any kind—a lesson for West to learn fast.

The best way to teach is by example, right?

The front door closes behind me with a soft click. I didn't expect to sleep with someone this early into the retreat, but what can I say? West is good with his hands, behind the bar and in bed. He had the stamina to match my pace, but when I'm done, I'm done.

I like sex—love it, crave it—and enjoy the act with whatever flavor I want to taste for the night. Sleepovers are usually off the table unless I want seconds. I did with West, but now we can move on.

My phone pings with a text that pulls a smile at the *Sister, Sister* melody. No matter the years that pass—twenty, in our case—my best friend always checks in to make sure I'm okay. I don't tolerate many people in my life, but Justice will never not be my person.

Justice

Hey, about to order room service for breakfast. Want anything?

A room service attendant smiles at my nod and stops in front of a door across the hall. The scent of eggs and French toast wafts from plates on the cart. Breakfast does sound good.

I shift my overnight bag on my shoulder to type out a message to Justice I'll be up to our suite soon. Unlike the standard rooms, ours has two bedrooms, one on each side of the wide living space. There's a fireplace and jacuzzi on the balcony with views of the surrounding valley. It's rich in luxury and knotted wood flooring.

Hey, hon.

Another message appears once I hit send, stuttering my silent walk over plush carpeting to the elevator. My jaw tightens at the name on the screen, one that paints my cheeks the same color as my manicure.

Carter Davis.

Carter

You can't ignore me forever.

The hell I can't.

Doesn't he have more important matters? A press conference? The rider that guarantees my father's favorite almond brand will be at his next event? Annoying Senator Douglass's daughter is not on his congressional to-do list, I'm sure.

I flip back to the text with Justice in a huff. The problem with a twenty-year friendship is that will see right through any attempt to act normal, and she will push for answers. It's in her nature to care, the same way it is to hug for no damn reason. I'll handle Carter myself. This week is about Justice, not me. She went through too much for me to pile on my mess.

In less than twenty-four hours, we discovered the estranged husband she left seven months ago is at this retreat, which I picked for our annual girls' trip. She needed time away from drowning herself in work as a distraction from her separation, to meet new people and decide if divorce is what she really wants. Clearly, her ex is wasting no time getting back in the game.

Our trip comes with a week's worth of activities I'd choose a colonoscopy over doing, but if snowmobiling and horseback riding put a smile on Jay's face, I'll grit my teeth. I slipped in a spa day and a whiskey tasting to lower her guard. Speed dating and the private date that comes with it will be a tough sell, but Justice will survive.

Carter

Call me. You have ten minutes.

This asshole.

I close my eyes and draw a deep breath. *Why do you fight us?* Carter's words in my father's study last Thanksgiving play on a loop. The way he whispered them while my mother argued with the kitchen staff about cranberry sauce in the hall still makes me shiver. How his hand crept up my arm to trace his thumb against my throat. He's always been an arrogant prick, but he never touched me. Not like that.

I don't mind a man who takes charge, but I prefer him not to have an affiliation with my family. My mother's constant reminders that I'm not living up to our family legacy and am wasting away my "childbearing years" are bad enough. They're the reason I keep myself on the opposite side of the country, with good weather, a lucrative fashion career, and access to all the dick I want without shame or judgment.

Juliette Douglass would pick out my wedding china tomorrow if Carter was serious about pursuing a relationship. He comes from money, is a loyal lapdog to my father, and is the only one in her eyes who could tame me out of my "wild ways."

My defiance is a declaration of the love I have for myself and the life I create for me. I adore my body, feel empowered by the autonomy to share it, and have no desire to be a mother. It doesn't make me less than or undesirable.

The elevator doors open to an empty car of mirrored walls. My fingers hover above the button to my floor. I can't see Justice right now. She's no stranger to Carter or my family drama, but, given her Terrence sighting, she needs her own space to process without distractions.

Worked up an appetite last night the menu won't satisfy. See you at lunch.

Let Justice think I'm still in someone's bed.
Now to deal with Carter.

—*—

"Emma." My name is a taunt on his lips.

"What do you want, Carter?" My sigh travels between time zones and the thin fibers of my patience. This is fucking up my post-coital high.

"Did you lose your manners in the mountains?"

My eyes roll at his chuckle. I don't need to close them to picture Carter seated in his leather office chair and bespoke suit. His ego matches his six-foot stature. It's big enough to fill Congress and this restaurant.

I signal to the bartender for another Bellini. I'm at the end of the bar tucked between foliage and a wall of mirrors, the perfect spot to people watch and eat breakfast. If only I hadn't lost my appetite because of this call and the person on the other end.

Carter is attractive, but I can't stand him. My regard for him shifted over the years he's worked for my father. No amount of fine can fix that awful of a heart.

"Does my father need something?" I push out the question to rush Carter off the phone.

"I need you," he says, his husky tone licking my ear. "John has a fundraiser this weekend in Denver. His only daughter should make an appearance."

"Is Blair not available to play poster child?" My cousin is everything the good senator wants in a daughter: obedient, vanilla. Throw in a ride on the private jet, and she'll do a special cheer.

There's a pause before Carter lowers his deep voice. "She's not you."

Silence dances between us with the intensity of a livewire, one I've reinforced since I met Carter when he interned for my father during his sophomore year of college. He ignored my high school crush until I graduated from Bodie University. I was no longer the same girl who made every excuse to stop by my father's office, knowing one of Virginia's senators was too busy to see his daughter. I became a woman who grew into her own, wanting more and no longer willing to chase after anyone in order to be seen.

It pissed off my family that I chose a lesser-known institution in California over my father's Ivy League alma mater. They couldn't control my desire to attend the same school as Justice, nor my decision to put the middle of the country between us. No matter their efforts, the money they threw at me to come back home to the DMV, nor the threats to take away the trust fund I never used, I held my own—unbought or sold.

Carter took notice of my rebellion, and so began the decade-plus game of cat and mouse. I became the unattainable trophy to acquire, driven by lust and his desire to please my father. Carter evolved into another desperate-for-power suit on Capitol Hill. He's remained on my Do Not Fuck list, which is a testament to my willpower.

Low-cut fade.

Caramel skin.

Blue-green eyes.

Carter is Jesse Williams, a self-absorbed version doused in fine.

I love dick, but not everyone gets admission into this pussy.

"You are John's daughter," Carter declares as if I'm the one who needs the reminder. "You can afford a few hours to support the campaign."

"I'm here to enjoy a trip with my best friend, not bend over backward for donors to make my father look good."

"Saturday night. We'll charter a plane to pick you up and take you back. As for how far you can bend"—Carter's voice drops—"we'll test your limits later."

"I told you, I have plans." I clear my throat after a long swallow. My boots rub to keep my knees from parting. The change in altitude is messing with my head because my Do Not Fuck list might make a liar out of me if he keeps this up. I'm strong, but shit, I'm human too.

"Cancel them."

"Not happening."

Growing up, Justice and her family welcomed me with open arms. I was the kid of an influential politician with access to privilege but without the one thing money can't buy. Some fancy jet and a twenty-thousand-a-plate fundraiser aren't enough to ditch my friend. Nothing is.

"Is that an invitation to come get you?"

I hang up without a second thought. It's too early for all that. The devil is a lie, as Justice's mother says.

"Someone's testy," a familiar voice says from behind, raising every hair on my neck.

Miles steps next to me, and I ask God what I did to deserve not one but two men tempting me to pose for a mugshot. "How in the hell are you here?"

"You want my flight number?" Miles rolls his thick lips between his teeth. I follow the wet path of his tongue and scoff at the grin forming.

My now-room-temperature parfait streaks my bowl as I take in the ripped figure in my private corner, the one with a smirk on his goatee-framed mouth and a gaze up to no good.

Of course, he came.

Miles is a threat in ways Carter will never be. I'll dodge the latter without issue if I limit my trips home to Alexandria, Virginia, which

I do. Miles is a different story. If Justice and I are a package deal, so are Terrence and Miles. They've been friends since they were damn near babies, and that pushes us together for obvious reasons. Our paths don't always cross, but when they do, it's this mix of sexual tension and contempt.

I've sidestepped Miles, those thick arms, and rich chocolate skin, for over a decade. We've been doing this dance since college, when Justice and Terrence started dating. He tosses a dig my way, and I toss it right back. The problem is, we both love sex, which isn't an issue until you almost do it during a trip to your respective best friends' house. We shouldn't have come that close, which is why I've kept my distance and double-check before visiting to make sure he's not there.

Test-driving the best friend of my best friend's husband is out of the question. Miles hits too close to home, even if a juicy ass and solid chest deserve a look under the hood.

Miles assesses me from the corner of his eye before turning his full gaze on me. The soft arch in his brow lifts, and a smile ghosts his lips to show white teeth. He folds his arms crowded in thick muscles over his chest, pulling the black tee and outlining every muscle in his torso.

I tear my eyes away to look at anything other than the amusement flickering in his, and my gaze lands on the gray beanie covering the fade he keeps fresh.

Fuck him.

We cannot.

"It's nice to see you, Em."

"Wish I could say the same."

"Is that how you feel after the last time we were together? What was it, two years ago?" His expression darkens, daring me to pretend the night in question didn't sear itself into my mind.

Memories filter back to the long walk to my guest room, fresh from a cold shower to keep my vagina in check. I passed Miles's room as he came out in sweats, headed to the bathroom that I left to soap down every hard muscle on his body and what lies between his legs, which left an imprint against the gray cotton.

We stood inches apart, no best friends around to force us to retreat to our corners. We argued as we always do. The source of our ire that evening? Movie trivia. But at that moment, I couldn't stop my eyes from raking over the shirtless torso before me. It was at the perfect height with our size difference.

"Ready for a taste?" Miles teased. His words were playful but his tone was sharp. Hungry. The man matches energy, and his stare told me to run.

I locked my bedroom door behind me to keep from sleepwalking and sucking the skin off his dick. By morning, Miles left. Something about a work trip. I stopped visiting Austin at the same time he did since that night. The energy between us threatened to crush my lungs, and a bitch enjoys breathing.

Carter is a lot to handle at times, but Miles is a different force.

I unclench my hands and steady my glower. "Do us both a favor. Keep yourself and Terrence far away from me and Justice, or there will be hell to pay."

If a single look could kill, Justice would choose my tombstone instead of an omelet from a room service menu.

Miles's stare coasts down my neck to where my heart is drumming inside my chest. He considers me, the light from the bistro chandelier catching in his diamond stud. The cloud lifts from his eyes, and he winks. "Put your claws away, kitten. Junior must not have satisfied you if you're still this wound up. Is he up yet for round two?"

"I am not wound up," I say too quickly. "And stop watching me, stalker."

Miles must've been at last night's kickoff mixer. I saw Terrence, who made a beeline for Justice after a man in an Al Bundy outfit hit on her. Miles was nowhere to be found. But he clearly saw me. He always does.

His shoulder lifts to shrug off the accusation. "You're hard to miss." He nods to my phone on the counter. "When you're ready for a grown man to take care of you, come find me." Miles leaves with a casual strut, too unbothered to rush, and an ass that would make Calvin Klein billions.

The bartender returns with a folded paper bag he places next to my bowl. "Would you like another to-go box?" He motions to the untouched berries and granola sliding through low-fat Greek yogurt.

"Yes, thanks." I frown at the bag. "Is this for someone else?"

"The gentleman settled your bill and asked us to rush an order." He checks the taped receipt. "Pancake and eggs from our children's menu. For Junior?"

TENDER OFFER

A smile breaks.
Let the games begin.

© Frenchy Press LLC

Tanvier Peart is a future bestselling romance author with a healthy obsession for snacks and happily ever afters. She is a good girl with kinks who spends her days working on policy and enjoys the wild life of being a wife and soccer mom. By night, she writes and reads romance books with steamy scenes. When she's not lost in the land of smut, Tanvier enjoys long walks down snack aisles and the chorus of grunts at the gym.

Want to stay up to date on all of Tanvier's bookish news? Sign up for
her newsletter:

https://tanvierwrites.substack.com/

Connect with Tanvier online:

@tanvierwrites

(Instagram, TikTok, Threads, Facebook)

www.ingramcontent.com/pod-product-compliance
Lightning Source LLC
Chambersburg PA
CBHW011314310726
48973CB00011B/2924